Counting the Flames

BOOK ONE

HALCIE DAWN

CARE ANNOUNCEMENT

Halcie Dawn's novels contain serious and complex content.

For a full list of Trigger Warnings and/or Content Warnings,
please visit https://www.halciedawn.com/my-books

**Please note: *Counting the Flames: The Flames Duet Book One* contains images
of violence, including descriptions of a mass casualty incident.

For Pops and Mimi

Thank you for raising an amazing son and daughter.
For gifting me with a loving, supportive, funny, sexy,
and honorable husband. He's my miracle.
And for blessing me with the kindest and
most loving sister-in-law.
We miss you, and we love you.

And

For everyone who needs their numbers

It's okay to need them. It's okay to say them.
And just so you know... My number is five, too. Said
backward.
At a very fast pace.

Author's Note

Counting the Flames is Book One in *The Flames Duet*.
This is <u>not</u> a standalone novel
and should immediately be followed by...
Dancing on the Ashes: The Flames Duet Book Two
Available Now

The Hill Family Universe

The Flames Duet is a standalone duet in a larger, interconnected parent series of duets and novels—*The Hill Family Universe*. While *The Flames Duet* can be enjoyed by itself, the reader will experience a more immersive and pleasurable reading journey if *The Reality Duet* (*Escaping Our Reality* & *Finding Our Reality*) and *The Skeptic's Duet* (*The Skeptic's Playbook* & *The Believer's Game*) are read first. *The Flames Duet* <u>will</u> contain spoilers about your favorite Hill Family characters and events from *The Reality Duet* and *The Skeptic's Duet*.

The Hill Family Universe

The Hill Family Universe is a large, interconnected parent series of duets and novels. While each duet—or singular novel, when applicable—can be enjoyed by itself, the reader will experience a more immersive and pleasurable reading journey if the suggested reading order is followed. Reading the duets out of order <u>will</u> result in spoilers about your favorite Hill Family characters and their defining life events.

Suggested Reading Order
The Reality Duet

Escaping Our Reality: The Reality Duet Book One
Finding Our Reality: The Reality Duet Book Two

The Skeptic's Duet

The Skeptic's Playbook: The Skeptic's Duet Book One
The Believer's Game: The Skeptic's Duet Book Two

The Flames Duet

Counting the Flames: The Flames Duet Book One
Dancing on the Ashes: The Flames Duet Book Two

Hey, Y'all

Counting the Flames: The Flames Duet Book One

For my spice lovers…
Hang in there with me, y'all! I promise it's coming.
And better yet, I promise it's good. Hella good.
Just wait until Book Two.
Read Book One, and then settle in with a cold glass of sweet tea for
Dancing on the Ashes.

For my eagle eyes…

Yes, I know Chapter 36 says 'Sea' instead of 'C'.
It's intentional. Trust me…you'll soon see why.

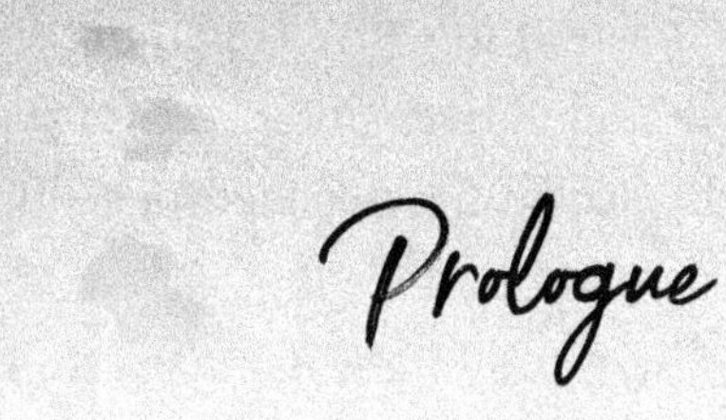

Prologue

Ridge

Present Day

"I can't believe you're getting married."

My brother's voice echoes through the speakers of my truck. There's an underlying shock to his tone that reminds me of when we were kids.

I can't believe you got the last piece of cake.

I can't believe you won at checkers.

I can't believe you got a date with her.

Chuckling, I make a left turn, heading toward one place I never thought I'd go. "Don't act so surprised, dipshit."

Cullen snorts in the phone, and I can hear the telltale sound of him stacking cases of beer in the cooler at the bar. "You know that's not what I mean. I'm just saying I never thought you'd..." He sheepishly trails off.

But that doesn't matter. I know exactly what he wants to say.

I never thought you'd marry someone like her.

Like Kimber.

And if I'm being completely honest, neither did I. If you'd asked me ten years ago to describe the woman I wanted to spend the rest of my life with, she definitely wouldn't sound anything like Kimber-Shay Willis. But times change. And so did I.

Especially after everything that happened within just the last two-and-a-half years.

Someone was finally arrested for the disappearance and murder of one of my closest childhood friends. I considered Carrie my family. Of course, she wasn't *actually* my cousin, but I still called her that. Still loved her like that. Then, my best friend was wrongly accused of a crime he didn't commit. Accused of using his power, influence, and money to hurt someone. It nearly cost him everything—the love of his life, the family he was meant to have. Finally, and thankfully, Holt's name was cleared. Unfortunately, that's when something even worse happened. Holt and Merit's son, my godson, was kidnapped. That was only one month ago.

Holt did what he had to do, and Daire is home. He's safe and sound and perfect. He's only three-and-a-half months old so he'll never remember what happened to him, thankfully. But we'll remember. Forever. And that's not just because Holt's broken arm is still in a cast and Merit's face is still healing from surgery.

Cullen clears his throat, trying to backtrack. "I just mean, I never thought it would happen this quick."

He's right. In the big scheme of things, it did happen quickly. Kimber and I only started dating over the summer. I think everyone was shocked when I proposed on New Year's Eve. Well, everyone except for Kimber. She basically set the stage for it. I wanted it to be a private moment, something between just the two of us. She wanted it to be at the stroke of midnight in front of half the town at the annual New Year's Eve party thrown at her family's flagship luxury car dealership.

So, I know it's quick. I'm not stupid.

But I want a family. I'm not getting any younger, and I want a life with someone.

I wanna grow old with someone.

Make babies with someone.

"I know it seems rushed. But it just feels right, you know?" My reply is strong and firm, giving no indication of the small little tendril of fear that slowly creeps up on me from time to time, making me question whether or not I'm doing the right thing.

It's just nerves. Everybody goes through that, right?

Marriage is a big deal. A really big deal. The biggest.

And not every couple out there can have the unwavering and epic kind of love that I've grown accustomed to seeing. My parents? Holt and Merit? My other friends, Crutch and Ella?

Well, they're the exception and not the norm.

And I'm fine just being in the norm. Give me boring conversations, squabbles about who's doing which chores, and weekly family trips to Costco. I'm cool with that. Because I've already had epic once before. And it didn't end the way I wanted it to. It *couldn't* end the way I wanted it to. Why? Because it wasn't the right thing to do.

Hell, I bet ninety percent of the marriages in the world are filled with perfectly normal, non-epic love.

Fine. By. Me.

Cullen sighs. "As long as you're happy. That's all that matters." Shuffling the phone, he puts me on hold while he signs for a liquor delivery. "Sorry about that. So, what are you up to?"

I work my neck back and forth, stretching my muscles. The movement has my bandage snagging against my shirt. I take a peek down at my chest, making sure there's no breakthrough blood soaking through the fabric. "Headed to meet the wedding planner."

"That's right." His laugh vibrates in my ears. "Kimber was very proud of the fact that she got an appointment with Wexler Events on such short notice. She wouldn't stop talking about it."

Tell me about it. Wexler Events is one of the top five premiere event planning companies in the Southeast, and Kimber refuses to meet with anyone else. Of course, I'm hoping they'll cut us a little break on the pricing because of Dad and Cullen. Together, they run the best catering company in the entire state, *The Elegant Taste.* Dad cooks, and Cullen has the vision. He's wanting to grow the company and make his mark on it. Just the same way he did with the bar, *The Last Call.*

In fact, C could have planned the whole wedding for us, but Kimber wants the status that comes with being a client of Wexler Events. Fucking status. Like I'm gonna get some kind of red-carpet treatment if I flash a wedding program with Margo's portrait on it. Nope. Cost of the power bill will still be the same. Wait at the doctor's office will still be the same. Fight during rush hour traffic will still be the same.

"Well, I doubt you're meeting with Margo Wexler herself. Last I heard, she's working an event in Atlanta for a movie studio. Are you meeting with one of the other planners?" he asks.

"Yeah, Amy. Amy Smith."

"Oh, shit. I heard she was back. I haven't seen her yet, though."

"Back? Back from where?"

"She left town a few years ago. Something about taking care of sick family. But she's really good. The best, actually. She only worked for Wexler for about a year and a half before she left. I was kind of surprised to hear that Margo hired her back. You know that woman's bat-shit crazy and holds a grudge like a kid with a stolen pony."

He's right. Margo is crazy. Both he and Dad hate working with her. Fortunately, most of the time, she only works personally on the bigger jobs out of town and uses the planners on her staff for the local events. "You worked with her before? This Amy girl?"

"Yeah, several times. She started as an assistant but was quickly promoted to a planner. She was the lead on several big parties and weddings that we catered. Before she left town, that is."

"Well, let's hope she's ready for Kimber," I deadpan.

Trust me, I know that sounds bad. But Kimber likes things...a certain way. She can be a little hard to take in the beginning. She's a completely different person once you get to know her, though. Well, not *completely*, but she will be once she adjusts to the love that I can give her. And the love that my family can give her. She just didn't have the kind of family life that I did growing up. I mean, shit, she even calls her dad by his first name. She just needs love and support. And as my wife, she'll never receive anything less.

Because I only plan on doing this once.

Marriage means forever in my book. Come hell or high water.

Cullen hums through a long moan. "Mmm, I don't know about that."

"Don't know about what?"

"If Amy can handle Kimber. Amy, well, she…she's different," he answers slowly, concentrating on his words.

"What's that mean?" I pull into a parking spot in front of Wexler Events. Looking around for Kimber's Mercedes, I'm not surprised when I don't see it. She's late for everything.

"I don't know. It's hard to describe." He smacks his lips, "But hey, I haven't seen her in years. She's probably different from how she used to be. Who isn't, right?" He pauses for just a split second before he changes his tone. I can literally hear him smiling through the phone. "But there is one thing I hope hasn't changed…"

I know where this is going. It probably has something to do with big boobs or a tight ass. "Oh, yeah?" I draw out my syllables, playing naïve to my baby brother's teenage-like hormones.

"Her looks. She's fucking hot. Like, steaming hot."

I can't help but laugh. Cullen may sound like a pig, but he's a really good guy. Sweet and charming and goofy and protective. And he may fool a lot of people, but he can't fool me. He can't fool anyone in our family. He wants to settle down just as badly as I do.

"Well, that's good to know." I lean my head back on the headrest and close my eyes, allowing the mid-January sun to soak into my skin and heat me from the inside out. Playing into his hand, I lace my voice with sarcasm. "Too bad for Amy this stud is already taken."

Nearly Ten Years Earlier

Chapter 1

Ridge

I'm bored.

I immediately regret the thought as soon as my brain thinks it. It's the rule we all abide by: never take boredom for granted. Boredom means people are safe. Boredom means they aren't having their lives upended by a raging fire, a horrific car accident, or an unspeakable tragedy.

A fireman's motto… boredom is great. Bring on the boredom.

Let me work out. Let me clean the rig. Let me run drills. Let me cook some food. Let me teach a class of first graders how to *stop, drop, and roll.* Let me be bored forever.

But…

But the other motto we have, the one that we never talk about, the one that would make us complete assholes if we were to say it out loud, is… let me see some action tonight.

Give me a purpose. Let me help someone. Let me provide support. When people are in their lowest and darkest moment, allow me to save them.

Of course, we can't say it because that would mean we *want* something bad to happen. But that's not the case. We don't *want* bad stuff to happen; we know it's *gonna* happen. No matter what, something bad is always gonna happen. So, what do we really want?

We want it to happen when we're on duty. We're trained for it. We're ready to make a difference. We're ready to put our lives on the line for you.

And God above, I love it. Every single minute.

I walk back and forth across the front courtyard enjoying the breeze and the smell of the ocean air as it floats inland from a couple of miles away. Lifting my head, I study the sky. I can't really see the stars. The small shopping complex and movie theater across the parking lot steal the opportunity from me. But that's all right; it's cloudy tonight anyway. I even felt raindrops during the call we had earlier. But alas, nothing happened. A few sprinkles hit my shoulders, and then it stopped.

I think back to the vacationing grandfather, now sitting in the small hospital emergency room having his finger stitched up. Knives and oyster shells don't mix.

We're a lucky town, really. Don't get me wrong, I've had my fair share of horrible calls in the three years I've been here, but for the most part, we're fairly tame. We don't see the action that the other beach vacation cities do. Nestled on the central west coast of Florida, White Sky isn't far enough up the Panhandle to get the wet and wild college spring-breakers. And we're not far enough down south to entertain the rich and famous northern snowbirds. Plus, our town is somewhat rural. This shopping complex and movie theater is as crazy as it gets. There are no clubs. No modern-age martini bars. No strip joints. We're the perfect place for families. And that's exactly what we get.

How'd I get here? To this calm, cozy, safe, little beach town? To this twenty-first century, secluded oasis? Recruitment from Alabama Fire College. Most of my class wanted to run off to the big cities, where the starting pay for a firefighter is much higher. Me? I've never been much of a city guy. What I wanted was more training. More ways to save lives. White Sky agreed to sponsor my attendance to paramedic training if I signed a four-year contract. I just hit year number three. Last week in fact, on my twenty-second birthday.

And that's actually my position, currently, on this tour. Paramedic.

Ridge Conway, Firefighter Paramedic.

Even if a fire breaks out right now, paramedic duties are my first priority. Once that's done, I can work the line. Which do I like better? That's like asking my mom to choose who she loves more—me or my brother, Cullen.

Well, maybe that's a bad example.

Mom will always love me more. I mean, c'mon, I am the woman's firstborn.

We only have one main station in White Sky. We have an engine company and a truck company with five guys in each company each shift. Three rotating shifts. And of course, those of us with our paramedic license also have to work the ambulance during tour. We work 24 on/48 off. Which gives me plenty of down time at the public beach, which just happens to be across the street from my apartment. I even bartend part time at the beachside bar.

Although we're a small department, we're still bigger than a lot of those in rural America. If something big breaks out, we can always call on the volunteer departments scattered throughout the county. And Tallahassee is only an hour away. Last year, a structure fire broke out in a three-story condo complex that was being remodeled. It was a beast. Tallahassee companies worked that stretch with us.

I scuff the ground with my boot and turn to head inside when my eardrum pierces with the blare of the familiar alarm, instantly igniting my love-hate relationship with the inanimate object and what it stands for. The dispatcher's voice muffles over the station's speakers.

The fire alarms have been pulled at the movie theater.

I spin around, looking at the theater in the distance, searching for any signs of flame or smoke.

Nothing.

I see a couple of people milling around on the sidewalk, but as of yet, there's no huge crowd streaming out the front doors.

Where is everyone?

The theater's only got three screens, but still, it should be crowded. It's a Friday night in April; it's not like the ocean water is steamy and hot, packed with people taking a night swim. What else is everyone gonna do? Especially the kids too young to hit up one of the few haggard, old beach bars in town? I guess there's always mini golf. But last time I went there with a date, both the windmill and the clown's face were broken. In fact, on the eighteenth hole, we had to shoot our ball into the clown's left nostril—where someone had made a hole with a hammer—to return the ball because his mouth wouldn't open.

So, all that to say, the sidewalk in front of the theater should be packed with people.

And it's not.

But I get it. Some dumbass kids probably pulled the alarm as a joke. It happens all the time. Everywhere. Offices. Apartment buildings. Stores. Schools. That's why no one is ever in a hurry to leave. They stand around looking at each other, wondering if they can just ignore the alarm and stay put.

No.

No, you cannot.

For future reference, run.

Excuse me, I mean, you should walk in an orderly and expedient manner to your nearest exit.

Shaking my head in disbelief at both the dumbass kids who pulled the alarm and the dumbass patrons who don't run—I mean, walk—I race into the bay, slide into my turnout gear, and jump into the ambulance. As per the usual, I'm waiting on McDonald to finish. "C'mon, McDonald! You're killing me! I could've run across the parking lot, bought a tub of popcorn, and watched *Titanic* by now."

He finally climbs in, shooting me a bird in the process. Laughing, I pull out, following behind the engine and the truck. We turn on the lights and give a small sample of the siren. It's not like we need to knock traffic out of the way. We're literally two-hundred yards from the scene. Parking, we climb out, and I immediately toss my jump bag over my shoulder, waiting for instruction.

Technically, we're not required to dress in full turnout gear when working the ambulance, but I prefer to be prepared for anything and everything. Life can change on a dime, and emergency calls are no exception. And my goal is to make sure everyone involved gets to spend their tomorrow in a grocery store and not a morgue. So, if dressing in my gear saves me thirty seconds of execution time in the middle of a call, then I'm all damn for it.

Shelly, one of the theater managers, is talking to the Chief. You can tell she's nervous, waving her hands in all directions. She's actually friends with the Chief's daughter, so it's pretty funny to hear her call Chief Latner 'Mr. Dave'.

"I don't know what's going on, Mr. Dave. I didn't see any smoke or smell anything. And there's supposed to be a failsafe that when the alarm goes off, the movies stop playing. But I don't think that happened. Even from the box office, I still heard them going. They were so loud. Maybe Landon set the volume wrong tonight." She pops a shoulder in the air, trying to shrug through her jitters. "I can go in with you and clear the auditoriums."

"No, hon. That's what we're here for. I don't need you going back in there in case something is wrong."

About that time, the front doors open and a group of about ten middle school-aged kids come meandering out, lazily flopping left and right like they don't have a care in the world. "Hey, guys, hurry up!" I scream at them, urging them to pick up the pace and put a safe distance between them and the theater.

"I can't believe our movie stopped. It was at the good part too," a girl with braces complains.

A tall lanky boy with a horrendously bad haircut pushes his glasses up on his nose. "Yeah, someone probably pulled the alarm on purpose. Just like at school. And I spent my allowance on this movie because I like the video game so much."

One of the other department guys, Hartselle, ushers the kids away and tells them to stand at the far end of the parking lot. "This will take a while," he says. "Y'all should probably call your parents to come get you."

I glance up at the marquee. Only three movies are playing. One is an animated movie based on a popular video game. And the other two are action movies. Just the kind I love. Fast-moving with violence, shooting, and explosions. Of course, I hate spending money on movie tickets, though. I'm happy to wait a year if it means I can just pay the rental price or stream it for free.

I'm about to pipe up and let Shelly know the failsafe worked—at least for the kids' movie—when Chief blurts out his instructions. "Alright guys, we're gonna divide and conquer." He splits us into three teams. A group entering the front, a group entering the west side, and a group entering the east side. The two sets of side doors auto-lock, preventing entry from the outside. They are used as exit-only doors and stay locked to keep people from sneaking in and watching movies for free. Chief heads to the west to open that set of doors, and Shelly comes with my group to the east to open that set. I'm paired with Hartselle and Battles. Which is fine by me, they are both good guys.

Hell, everyone in our department is a good guy.

They're lugging all of their equipment and air tanks, but still able to jog at a fast pace, keeping up with me. Once we make it to the side of the building, Shelly's hands are shaking too badly for her to open the doors. Smiling, I hold out my hand. "Shell, let me get it, okay?"

She looks at me with big doe eyes, innocent and sweet. She's actually a year older than me, but she seems so much younger. She asked me out when I first moved to town. I wasn't attracted to her, so I went on the obligatory first date so she wouldn't be embarrassed, and then afterward played the friend card. But it all worked out for the best. She's actually engaged now. Todd? Mike? Why can't I remember his name right now? Anyway, he's a chill dude, works on one of the offshore commercial fishing boats.

She nods, handing me the key. After unlocking them, I pull the metal double-doors, propping the left one open with my foot, and nodding for Battles to grab the handle on the right-side door. I glance down the long corridor, squinting my eyes and studying everything in my field of vision. I can actually see all the way to the other side. I watch as that door opens and Chief looks around, taking in the same sights as me.

No smoke. No flames. Just the flashing light of the fire alarms painting the ceiling. And the loud-as-fuck chirp that follows every ten seconds.

A small part of your brain never gets used to that sound. It's louder than loud. It's all-consuming. Shaving away slivers of your brain cells, slice by slice, like a cheese grater.

From the corner of my eye, I watch as a couple of police cars pull into the parking lot. Sending Shelly on her way to deal with the police, I step in, walking with a slow yet determined purpose, paying close attention to everything in my line of sight. I've been in this theater dozens of times; I know the layout like the back of my own hand. Halfway down the corridor, the hallway opens up, and the movie theater lobby and concession counter will be on the left side. The third group of guys will be meeting us there since they're coming in the front doors. Once we determine the common areas are clear, we can start searching the movie auditoriums and other rooms that are lined on the right side—bathrooms, janitor closets, food pantries, a party room.

I'm about ten feet inside when I hear it.

Gunshots. And it sure as shit doesn't sound like it's coming from a movie screen.

And it's followed by muffled screaming.

"What the hell?" Hartselle ponders in a state of perplexity.

Both him and Battles are behind me. I turn sideways, wanting to see if their overactive minds are processing information the same as mine.

"Shit. Is that—" And I never get to hear the last words from Battles.

Because he explodes. Right in front of my eyes.

Chapter 2

Orah

I'm bent over Tabby, shielding her body with mine. I wrap my left arm around her head, huddling her close to me, shrouding our faces with a curtain of my blood-soaked hair. Afraid to move my right hand, even just a little, I press against her lower abdomen in a futile effort to stop her bleeding. It's not working. The paper towels are soaked. We're both semi-propped up against the wall. I wonder if I should lie her down? Is that what I should do? But what if she chokes on blood or something?

Adrenaline drugs me, making me hyper and sluggish, all at the same time.

The smell of iron tickles my nose, making me want to throw up. I gulp down a mouthful of bile, wincing as the sting slithers down my throat and fires behind my breastbone.

But a nauseous stomach is the least of my worries.

Because I thought the gunfire was done.

I was wrong.

Not only did it start up again, but now things are exploding. The walls in the large storage room vibrate, rattling my teeth. My ears ring, humming with the reverberating sound of the two large blasts.

The room may be soundproof, but nothing can protect you from a noise like that.

I squeeze my eyes shut. I close them so tightly spots of purple and red and yellow dance behind my eyelids.

Please stop. Please stop. Please stop.

My wordless pleas fall on deaf ears. Because nothing stops the destruction. It just keeps coming.

Is it coming for me?

Again.

Screams. Gunshots. Running.

Tabby's hot breath grazes against my neck. Her head lobs to the side. She's passed out again. She's in and out of consciousness. I have no idea if that's a good thing or a bad thing.

Bad because it means she's hurt. She's losing blood.

Good because she's not having to think about this. Not having to worry. Not having to pray that we make it out alive.

One. Two. Three. Four. Five.

Five seconds and no gunshots.

What does that mean? How many people are hurt? Hurt like Tabby. How many people are dead?

All of a sudden, the door flies open. My head jerks up, prepared to see one of the shooters again. Prepared to come face to face with my destiny of dying. I did it once and avoided it. I don't know if I can do it again. Not in a closet, with nowhere to run.

It takes several beats for my eyes to adjust. My body recognizes what it sees before my mind does. Relief cools the acid churning in my stomach, chilling it like a cold winter's rain.

It's not a shooter. It's not a bad guy.

It's a fireman.

And the fireman is here to save me.

Chapter 3

Ridge

I toss the jump bag from my shoulder, untangling it from my body. Thumbing the volume on my radio, I turn it down, deafening the screams and yells and orders of everyone clattering across the channels. My heartbeat thunders in my brain, pounding against my temples like a drum. Wildly glancing to my left and right, I attempt to digest my options—a small desk cluttered with paperwork and a laptop, or a large metal shelf. It's tall. Six shelves high, stacked and stocked with cleaning supplies. Quickly settling on it and deciding not to waste valuable time with taking everything off the shelves, I squat in front of it and try to pick the whole thing up, eager to barricade the door as quickly as possible.

With everything on it, it's easily three-hundred pounds. And cumbersome. A gallon jug of glass cleaner wobbles and hits me in the head, clattering to the floor. "Motherfucker."

I can't do this without adjusting my grip. Worst case, I'll have to slide it across the floor. At least everything is carpeted. There shouldn't be any loud scraping noise drawing attention to my location.

"I can help."

The whisper scares the shit out of me, and I jump a mile. My hand immediately curls into a fist, ready to pound any threat.

I might lose. But I'm not going down without a fight.

I blink. Once. Twice. Three times.

Except this isn't a threat.

It's a woman. Well, maybe she's a girl. It's hard to tell because of all the blood. Her body is wrapped around another, playing guardian to the unconscious redhead with a face full of freckles.

My body freezes. I stop breathing. My mind goes blank.

What the hell am I supposed to do?

I'm… empty.

Barren. Void.

Bare. Deserted.

I can't even remember my own name.

Who am I? What am I doing here?

"I can help you," she offers again. "And then you can help me. We can save each other."

Her eyes widen, waiting for me to respond. Even across the room I can see the color. Gray. Brilliant gray eyes. Like swirling storm clouds on a blazing hot summer day.

She's scared. That's plain to see. But she's not crying.

She's brave. So fucking brave.

Every memory I've ever had comes racing back into my brain. Every moment of training. Every piece of knowledge. I know exactly what I need to do. I know exactly who I am. I know exactly what I committed to all those years ago. What I commit to every single time I put on my uniform.

I need to save her. Save her and her friend or die trying.

There's another spurt of gunfire in the distance, knocking urgency into my actions. Turning back to the shelf, I settle on the best place to grab it. Taking a deep breath, I squat and lift the whole thing in one swift movement. A few rolls of toilet paper drop to the ground, but everything else stays put. I move it quickly and efficiently, blocking the door. Knowing that I now have two other lives depending on me, I debate stacking the desk with it. But I have to play the odds. Not only do I need to protect us from the threats lurking outside of this room, but there may come a time when this room could be our tomb if we don't have a route for a quick escape.

I shrug off my turnout coat, grab my discarded jump bag, and race over to the girls. I need to triage the situation. I better start with the one who can talk.

"Where are you hurt?"

Her eyes dart to the shelf. "I didn't help you."

Her voice sounds shaky. Disjointed. She's probably going into shock.

My hand reaches out, cradling the side of her face. Her jet-black hair looks wet. But it's not. It's soaked in blood. The metallic smell of iron is overpowering, replacing the smell of gunpowder and burnt flesh in my nostrils. There's a scrape across the top of her forehead, but other than that her face looks perfect. Angelic and flawless. Her cheeks and nose are pink, tinged with sunburn. Her white sleeveless shirt is missing a few buttons at the top, and the blood has soaked through, staining her simple white bra with crimson. Her bright yellow shorts are splattered with blood and...soda?

"Where are you hurt?" I repeat, mimicking the whisper she's been using. It's clear to see the walls are soundproofed—the thick concrete blocks are lined with dense fabric panels—but we still have to be cautious. At least, the fire alarm chirping stopped a minute ago. My brain already feels like fucking mush, and I don't think I could function with the obnoxious noise still humming through the dense walls, no matter how muffled it might be.

Her eyes lock with mine. Taking a deep and staggered breath, it catches in her chest. Her emotions strangle her. Her lip quivers.

"Shhh. We're gonna make it through this. But I need you to be strong." I graze my thumb back and forth across her cheekbone. "Remember, we're gonna save each other."

Her eyes flutter closed, fanning her black eyelashes like a sleeping porcelain doll. Licking her lips, she nods, finishing the deep breath that was paralyzed in her lungs. "Okay." When her eyes open, she's back.

My brave girl is back.

"I'm not hurt." She nods down at her blood-soaked shirt. "It's not mine. It's hers."

I glance up and down her body. "You sure?"

As soon as she nods again, giving me confirmation, I shift my focus, knowing that she may be okay, but her friend is far from it. My brave girl has been doing the best she can to stifle the blood pouring from the girl's lower abdomen, but she's fighting a losing battle. The pile of paper towels she's been using has basically disintegrated into a bloody sludge.

"She's been shot?" I ask.

"There's three holes. Two in front, right here." She wiggles her nose as her hand presses into the bloody quicksand of flesh and paper towels. "And one in her back. I guess she got shot three times." My brave girl's voice wobbles, but she keeps her composure.

Three holes. Maybe one is a through-and-through. Opening my bag, I immediately start gathering my supplies. I can see the unsteady rise and fall of her chest. "How long has she been out?"

"It comes and goes. She keeps passing out and then waking up. That's a good thing, right? I mean, that's normal?"

Ignoring that question, I immediately glove up. "I need to take a look at it."

Her hand doesn't move. Not a single millimeter.

I stare deeply into her stormy eyes. "What's your name?" My question is more of an edict, not leaving room for debate.

"Orah."

"Orah," I repeat, savoring the sound on my tongue. "I'm Ridge." I nod at the freckled redhead. "Who's this?"

"Tabby. Her name is Tabby. She's my best friend."

"You've done a really good job of helping your friend. You've kept her alive. But I'm here now. I've been trained for this. You have to let me take a look at it." I lay my hand on top of hers. "But I'll need your help. Can you help me?"

Studying my eyes, she swallows and gifts me with a nearly imperceivable head bob, before moving her hand away from Tabby's lower stomach. Ever so slowly. Blood oozes, drenching Tabby's already-soaked clothes. Grabbing the shears, I cut through her shirt and shorts, making room for me to see the damage. Sure enough, there's two entry wounds, basically side by side in the middle of her lower abdomen, right above the line of her panties. Grabbing her shoulders, I roll her, trying to assess her back. "Pull her shirt off, Orah."

Double and triple checking her back, I see only one exit wound, on her lower left side, about two inches from the beads of her spine.

"We need to lie her down. Flat. I need room to work," I say, bracing her neck, trying to stabilize it.

Orah stops breathing when there's another volley of gunfire outside the room. For a moment, we both freeze, eyeing the barely visible door behind the huge shelf, wondering if someone's about to come in. I count to five. When nothing happens, I turn my focus back to Tabby. I work quickly, giving soft and commanding orders to Orah when I need her help.

Obviously, I'm confined on what I can do in the middle of a storage room.

In the middle of Hell.

Slowing the bleeding as much as possible with QuikClot gauze, I pack her wounds, establish an IV, and push antibiotics and pain meds. They're definitely not the same ones a doctor would choose in a hospital setting, but I'm working with limited supplies here. Orah hooks the IV on a nail protruding from the wall. A nail that held a monthly calendar with ocean views. This week is circled in red with the words '*Eric's Vacation*' written on it.

Whoever the hell Eric is, he's one lucky bastard.

Tabby's pulse is thready, and her breathing is shallow. I've tried to rouse her several times with a sternum rub. Knowing my strength, I know it should be painful for her. Besides a soft flitter of her eyelids, nothing happens.

I have no idea what internal injuries she's dealing with. But she needs a hospital. And more experience than what I can offer. And she needs it now.

Once we've done the best we can, I make my way over to the door, bending my head and quietly listening for any activity on the other side. It's been a while since we heard any gunshots. Or explosions. Or screams. I'm not able to hear anyone speaking at a regular tone, so I honestly have no idea what's going on out there.

Flicking the volume up to a soft murmur on my radio, I click to speak, overriding the hectic commotion of everyone chattering.

"This is Conway." I decide there's no need to be formal. I've just seen half my brothers-in-arms murdered. I'm over rank and formality. "What the fuck is happening out there? Someone, give me something."

"Ridge?"

Hearing Chief Latner's voice is like a soothing balm, calming a fear that I thought would never be tamed. I thought he was gone. As soon as the explosive—which I'm assuming was an IED—detonated, killing Battles and slamming my body into the wall like a ragdoll, I yelled down the corridor, hollering for everyone to retreat. I couldn't even hear my own shout; the ringing in my ears was all-encompassing. I just know I tried to scream as loud as my body would allow. Smoke and ash filled the hallway, and I couldn't see who made it out before the subsequent explosions started killing again.

I couldn't function.

Everything was too wild.

Too devastating.

It was like the spawn of Satan was traveling through my heart, ripping any happiness I'd ever felt directly from my soul.

My brain didn't even have time to process what I was seeing when the gunshots started again.

I saw Hartselle fall to the ground, watching half his skull splatter across a life-size cardboard cutout of a unicorn, advertising an upcoming children's movie, instantly knowing he had been shot and was dead. And instantly knowing the only reason I *wasn't* was because I was crumpled against the floor, still reeling from the blast.

Shuffling to my hands and knees, I crawled forward, immediately forcing my body to stand and find shelter. I needed to get to safety and regroup. Even though my thoughts were cloudy, I knew I couldn't go back the way I came. I couldn't try to race out the door. It was pretty obvious that the corridor was rigged, ready to decimate first responders.

"Ridge? Are you still there?"

"Yeah. I'm here. Battles and Hartselle... they... they didn't make it."

There's a long pause while he digests that information. I'm sure he already had a feeling, but now, I've confirmed his fears.

"Who else?" I ask. "Who else is gone?"

"Don't worry about that now, son. Where are you?"

"In a storage room. Some kind of janitor's closet, maybe. We have it barricaded."

"We?" the Chief questions.

I glance over at Orah and Tabby. "I've got two victims with me. Females. One has multiple GSWs."

"Multiple? Is she stable?"

Orah watches me, her eyes intently tracing my movements. Spinning around, I lower my voice even more, "It's not good, Chief. She's critical." Looking down at the thick and flamboyant burgundy carpet, I'm mesmerized by the swirls of red and orange. It reminds me of a casino I went to in Biloxi.

It's then I see the carpet is drenched with spots of blood.

And it's everywhere.

"We need to get these girls out of here, Chief." I take a deep breath, trying to wrangle my nerves. "Before I lose them too."

Chapter 4

Orah

He's worried Tabby's going to die.

He lowered his voice, but I still heard him.

He's trying to be calm. He's trying to protect us. Protect me.

But apparently other people he knows died. Other firefighters? And he's scared for us. He'd never admit it. He'd never show it. But I can *feel* it.

I can feel what he's feeling.

The muscles in his back clench. Lifting his hand, he reaches around and massages his shoulder blade. Somehow, Tabby's blood even got on the back of his gray T-shirt. It soaked through, covering the emblems. The 'sky' part of White Sky is covered in reddish-black. And the once-white pelican is no longer white. Ridge pulls his hand back around to his face and studies the half-dried liquid rust covering his already stained hands. I can *feel* his frown.

Ridge.

My mind speaks his name. Even through the chaos, the syllable tinkles against my eardrums, soft and airy, like windchimes against a light breeze in the middle of spring. Sunshine and flowers and hummingbirds.

But I'm not sure if I'll ever get to see those things again.

I close my eyes and try to picture a hummingbird. But I can't even remember what they look like. Are they big or small? Slow or fast?

Doesn't my grandmother put hummingbird feeders in her backyard?

Why can't I remember what they look like?

Try as I might, my brain is blank. Except for him.

He doesn't even have to turn around; I already have him memorized.

Committed to memory as the last person I may ever see.

His dark brown hair, styled short, is thick and wavy. His strong, angular jaw is decorated with facial scruff. He even has stubble above his lip. I wonder if it would tickle or scratch if I were to kiss him.

I mean, when he kisses a *girl*, I wonder if it tickles or scratches *her*.

I take that back. I'm not thinking about that kind of stuff.

Not now. Not again.

His dark brown eyes are outlined in a light brown-yellow color. They immediately make me think about the Tiger's Eye stone I bought at the history museum on our fourth-grade field trip.

And he's tall. Way taller than Dad and Boaz. And they're both six feet.

I can't help but wonder how old he is. What made him want to become a firefighter?

Does he have a family?

And if he dies saving us, will he regret it? Will he regret opening this storage closet door?

"What's being done? When can I get them out of here?" He's still talking to the man over his radio.

"We have no idea what else has been rigged to explode, Ridge. We can't send anyone in until we know that. It's all booby-trapped. But everyone in a hundred-mile radius is on their way. SWAT is coming from Tallahassee. As soon as they're here, we'll breach."

"How the hell do you plan on doing that?"

There's a stifled rumble on the other end. "We'll figure something out. We're getting you and everyone else out of there alive."

Ridge looks over his shoulder at me, motioning for me to give the IV bag a little squeeze, just like he showed me. "Is there a fatality count?"

"Nothing firm. We have no idea how many have been hurt in the auditoriums." He shouts an order to some people in the background, and Ridge immediately jerks, turning the volume down a little more on his radio. "Sharpshooter's ready. As soon as SWAT is here, they're taking him out. One way or another."

I should say something.

"Ridge..."

He takes several steps toward us, ready to check on Tabby, thinking I'm calling him because of her.

"There's more than one," I lament in grief and disgust.

His chapped lips part. "What?"

"There's more than one. There's two." I look down at my best friend. Ridge covered her body with his fireman's jacket, giving her a little bit of modesty. "We were chased by two of them." I blink, thinking about the possibilities and probabilities. "I guess there could be more, but there's at least two."

Swearing under his breath, he walks over to the far corner of the room and quietly speaks back and forth on the radio. This time, I can't hear what's being said. Eventually, he stops talking and does something to the device. I'm not sure if he mutes it or turns it off completely.

As soon as he does that, there's another burst of gunfire.

Pop. Pop. Pop. Pop. Pop.

It's so much louder than the times before. Like it's right outside the door.

Grabbing a large wooden broom, Ridge stomps on the end of it, breaking the bristles away, leaving a jagged spear-looking weapon. I can't help but cringe. The breaking wood was noisy.

What if *they* heard us?

Ridge looks over at me, putting his finger to his lips, telling me to be quiet.

He takes a couple of steps toward the door, ready to defend us. Ready to fight.

Fortunately, nothing happens. I silently count to one hundred, praying for stillness with each and every number.

I don't think I've ever been so relieved.

Laying the makeshift spear next to me, Ridge grabs the end of the large desk and slides it across the carpet, placing it between the door and me and Tabby. Sitting on the floor, he rests his back against it, taking Tabby's vitals and checking her bandages.

Now, the bad guys have to go through a door, a shelf, a desk, and...Ridge...before getting to me and Tabby.

He furrows his brow and gives Tabby another shot of something from his bag. Deciding that's the best he can do for right now, his head drops back. Closing his eyes, he sighs, giving himself a moment to think. But it's only for a second. Just a quick reprieve. And then, his eyes pop open, and he gifts me with a small smile.

I like the way his lips look. A soft pink against his tanned skin.

Even chapped, I like the way they look.

"So, Orah's a really unique name. I like it. Is it a family name?" His query seems so normal, so benign. A complete contradiction to our predicament.

Instead of responding, I change the subject, asking the question that's physically hurting me. The question that's burning a hole in my stomach, burning me even more than the acid swirling around my insides like water in a sink drain. "Will SWAT get here in time? What if *they* come for us before then?"

He gawks at me, wondering how much of the truth he should tell me. I'm about to beg him not to lie when he interrupts my thoughts.

"I'll answer your question, and then you'll answer mine, okay? That's the deal. And you have my word, I won't lie to you. I won't sugarcoat it." He drags his hand down his face, scratching his growing beard. "After everything you've been through tonight, I think you can handle the truth."

He lifts an eyebrow, waiting for me to respond. So, I give him a simple nod.

"Yeah, I'm worried about SWAT not getting here in time. They've gotta get here and then come up with some sort of plan to breach. They can't just bust in guns-blazing. We have no idea where the IEDs are planted and what will trigger them. Are they on a timer? Tied to a cell device? I have no idea." He cocks his leg and braces his forearm on his knee. "But I can promise you that I will do everything in my power to keep these guys away from you. I'm not going to let them hurt you. I'll do whatever I have to do."

The power and truth of his vow take my breath away. I just met him. And he's willing to die for me.

When I don't say anything, he taps my shoe with his. "Go. Your turn."

"My name is Zipporah. It's not a family name. My parents just liked it."

"Zipporah? Like Moses's wife? From the Bible?"

I smile, splitting my own dry lips. "You know about her?"

He cocks his head, looking at me like I'm crazy. "I live in the South. I went to Vacation Bible School every single summer. I know who Zipporah is." His face softens. "She saved Moses's life."

"Moses saved her first, remember? She was at the well with her sisters when Moses protected them from shepherds trying to chase them away. He saved her first." I blink, mesmerized by the softening of his features as he listens to me. "And then, she saved him later."

Ridge sits in silence for a few seconds, studying me. "What's your middle name?"

"I don't have a middle name. Zipporah is complicated enough." His laugh catches me by surprise and makes my fear disappear. It's only for a split second, but it's a split second that I'll cling to for the rest of my life. "And my older brother is named Boaz."

"Ahhh. Boaz, son of Salmon and Rahab. He was the family redeemer for Ruth." He cocks his head to the side and taps his finger in the air as he spouts the lineage. "Boaz, Obed, Jesse, and then King David."

I can't help but smile. "Someone *did* go to Bible School."

"Told ya," Ridge banters, giving me a sly wink, before leaning forward and checking Tabby's pulse again.

My legs are starting to fall asleep, so I reposition my body. Suddenly, a sharp and vicious pain pierces my chest. It's like someone's stabbing me with an ice pick. I wince, crinkling my eyelids into a tight line. Fortunately, the pain subsides just as quickly as it started.

Ridge mutters something to himself, pressing his fingertips into Tabby's soft skin as he eyes his watch. His movements are precise and flawless. He's smooth. Fluid. Made for this. Under less stressful circumstances, I would be content to sit and watch him for hours. But the low rumble of noise coming from somewhere in the building reminds me that I'm very much in the middle of a stressful situation.

The freakin' epitome of it.

Hearing the same thing as me, he glances back toward the door. Discreetly wrapping his hand around the handle of the broomstick, he turns back to me, trying to appear unfazed by the sounds. "So, you live here?"

I shake my head.

"You don't live here?"

I pin him with a glower. "It's my turn to ask the question."

His perfect mouth crooks into a soft, one-sided smile. He bobs his head in my direction, giving me permission.

I look over at Tabby—my bloodied, naked, broken, unconscious best friend. I lay my hand on her ankle. Her sneakers are still tied. For some reason, I find that strange. "Is she dying?"

When he doesn't reply, my heart beats faster. My fear escalates. I'm scared to look at him, but I know I have to. There really isn't any choice, is there? He's intently studying me, scalding me with his Tiger Eyes. "You said you wouldn't lie." My whisper breaks. Even my words are afraid. "I can feel what you feel."

His lips crack open, and his breath fills the distance between us. "I don't know."

I blink rapidly, willing my unshed tears to stay in place. "Ridge?"

"I'm serious. I don't know. There's only so much I can tell with the equipment I have here. Her lungs sound clear. Her pupils are normal and reactive. But I'm not happy with her blood pressure or her pulse. I have no idea what kind of internal damage she has. It's obviously very extensive. She's in trouble. She needs more than I can give her."

"She's more than my best friend. She's like my sister." I shake my head back and forth, trying to contemplate a life without her, and it's just not possible. There's so much I want to tell him. About how Tabby and I met. About how she refused to tell our gym teacher that I'm the one who really cut through the badminton net with a pair of scissors and not her. She got three days of in-school suspension for that.

And, more importantly, how she's always liked me for me.

But I can't. Not now. If I start talking like that, it'll sound like a goodbye. And this isn't goodbye.

It can't be.

So instead, I deflect. "We don't live here. We're on vacation. It's Spring Break."

Once again, he sits for a minute, not saying anything. Eventually, he scrubs his hand down his face. I like it when he does that. He always taps his finger against his chin when he's finished. "Well, this is a pretty shitty vacation, huh?"

Before I can even stop it, a giggle escapes. "Yeah, I guess it is."

"Spring Break from where?"

"We're from South Carolina. A small town about forty-five minutes outside of Columbia."

"Spring Break from what? College? High school?"

I feel myself blushing. For some reason, it feels weird telling him my age. I don't want him to think I'm nothing but a child. I want him to know I can handle myself. That I can help him. That I can do whatever he needs me to do to make sure we get out of this situation.

But there's no point in lying. He's not lying to me.

"High school. It's our junior year."

"You're sixteen?" The ultimate professional, Ridge hides his surprise very well. I've gotta give him credit.

"Seventeen. I'll be eighteen next week. I'm the oldest in my class." I cringe as soon as I blab the last part. It makes me sound like a petty little kid.

He sighs. "I can't believe you're having to go through this. I'm so fucking sorry, Orah. I'd take it all away if I could."

And I believe him. Every single word.

My breath catches in my lungs, sending an electric shock of pain racing down my sternum, into my stomach, and all the way to my feet. When it hits my left foot, the pain pulses, reminding me of my sprained ankle and the crappy turn of events that led to us being trapped in this small room.

I'm watching my best friend die, and it's all my fault.

Without me, maybe she could've made it out.

Absentmindedly, I rub the swollen skin. It's like it's doubled in size over the last few minutes. But it really doesn't hurt. Not like my chest. I think the stress is finally getting to me, and maybe, I'm about to have a panic attack. My brain feels foggy and hot.

When Ridge wraps his hand around my ankle, I'm knocked from my daydream. Like someone pushed me out of a crowded elevator at the very last second, right before the doors closed shut.

"You told me you weren't hurt?" he protests with urgency and concern.

His eyes lift, and for a beat, we stare at one another, absorbing the moment. We're so close, I can see the small spattering of sun freckles across the bridge of his nose. His dark brown facial hair is dotted here and there with black stubble. There's a small mole on the right side of his neck. And I can see the thick and banded cord of his muscular shoulder barely peeking out from the collar of his shirt. And those muscles are smeared with blood.

Just like me.

Just like everything around me. Smeared. Tainted. With my best friend's blood.

But what's more important than all those physical characteristics I see is *the kindred spirit I feel*. And because of that, I don't have to answer him.

We both know the truth.

A sprained ankle is nothing.

I didn't lie.

I'm not hurt.

I'm not like Tabby.

He swallows and nods. Just once. Letting me know he understands. Rummaging around on the floor for his discarded medical supplies, he grabs an ACE bandage and taps the heel of my platform wedge. "Not the most practical shoes."

"Yeah."

He frowns, thinking. "We may have to run. I can wrap it with your shoe on or off. Off is better of course, but there's all sorts of shit out there. Glass and shrapnel and..." He trails off and quietly clears his throat. "Well, stuff you don't need to step on." He doesn't wait for me to voice an opinion. "It's settled, we're wrapping it with your shoe on."

I can't wait to get out of these damn shoes. They feel like a coffin.

Glancing around our temporary living quarters and makeshift hospital, I see some plastic bins stacked in the far corner. Some of them toppled over when Ridge moved the desk. It looks like they are filled with promotional goodies, and if I'm not mistaken, I see some house slippers. Like the kind my granny wears with her pajamas.

"Are those shoes?" I say, pointing in their direction.

Grabbing his spear and giving one quick listen to the door as he passes by, Ridge scoops up three plastic baggies and rushes back to my side, kneeling in front of me. Ripping one open, his eyebrow lifts in question as he studies the woman's fuzzy white slipper. It's decorated with a screen print image of a hot, young actor. A guy who played the heartthrob in last summer's epic teenage romance. He played a time-traveling pirate whose mother was a siren, and he was the only hope of saving the entire world from an apocalyptic series of hurricanes and typhoons. Well, him and his love-at-first-sight mermaid.

Ridge flips them over and over in his hands. "There's no size. It just says small."

I look at the petite house shoe and shake my head. "I can't do a small."

He holds it up next to my swollen foot and smirks when he sees the size difference. Tossing it to the side, he rips open the next package, grinning triumphantly. "Large."

He spends the next few minutes wrapping my foot. And I chastise myself the entire time. Not only because I'm ashamed by the flood of unfamiliar desire and tingles that travel across my body with his touch; but also, because I find myself worrying about whether or not I shaved recently.

And what kind of friend does that?

Worries about whether or not her leg is silky smooth for the hot firefighter while her best friend is fighting for her life...

"There we go." Treating me like Cinderella, Ridge slides the slippers on my feet. His blood-stained fingers leave streaks of pink across the white fur.

And now they're marred.

Just like me.

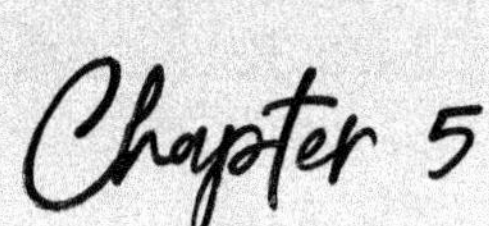

Ridge

She wiggles her feet back and forth, looking at the stupid-ass slippers, and wincing when her ankle gives her a tinge of pain. "Thank you, Ridge." Her whisper is scratchy and hoarse. And when she looks at me with innocence and gratitude etched across her beautiful face, I nearly come unglued.

Pushing off from the floor, I quietly pace back and forth.

This is bullshit. Complete and total bullshit.

She's just a kid. They both are.

They came here for a fun, little vacation, and this happened. They don't deserve this. No one does.

"I never saw this movie."

Her comment catches me off guard, and I stop mid-step.

"I've never really liked romance movies. I've always liked action movies. You know…" She slows. She's thinking the exact same thing I was earlier.

Just the kind I love. Fast-moving, violence, shooting, explosions.

A single tear slides down her rosy cheek, and she quickly looks the other way. Disguising her actions, she wipes her face and then squeezes Tabby's IV bag.

So. Fucking. Brave.

Looking at my watch, I see it's almost time to check in with the Chief. Since I can't really have my radio on, for fear of drawing attention to us, we decided intermittent check-ins was the best course of action while waiting on SWAT. And the bomb squad. And whoever-the-hell-else can play a part in the damn cavalry. "Listen, I'm gonna check the radio again, okay?"

Her eyes widen, and she looks past our arbitrary *Home Alone* hazards and stares at the door. "They won't hear?"

"I'll keep it quiet. Just like before."

"I know. I trust you."

Every word she utters makes me feel like I'm being gutted by a fishing knife. Because she's treating me like a hero, like someone who saved her.

And what if I can't save her?

What if there are no heroes in this story?

Grabbing the broomstick spear, I lean close to the door, straining to listen. I don't hear anything. And that could be really good or really bad. Walking to the far corner, I flick my radio to the secure channel, thumbing it to the lowest possible volume.

"Chief?"

"Ridge? Shit, son, it's good to hear your voice."

"Yeah, you too. Please give me some good news."

"SWAT's twenty minutes out. Bomb squad's right behind them. A breach plan is already in motion. Assuming SWAT agrees, it shouldn't be long after they get here that something happens. We've already got some things in the works."

"What things?"

He pauses, giving me only silence.

"Chief, I've got a girl dying in here. Either you tell me what the hell is going on or I'm tossing her over my shoulder and running out of here. Guns and bombs be damned."

"The skylights."

I blink. Did I hear him right?

"You're coming through the freakin' roof?"

"There's a twenty-by-twenty skylight right in the middle, where the auditorium hallways meet with the lobby. We've already got guys up there. They've been watching with cameras. The offenders have been walking around some, but just in that small section, and only every so often. It stands to reason they don't have that area rigged for explosives. Our guess is, they kept that part and the auditoriums bang-free."

"If y'all have been seeing them, then fucking take them out. You said you have a sharpshooter. Tell the bastard to shoot."

"It's not that easy, son. They haven't had a clear enough shot to get it done quickly. The skylight isn't only hurricane proof; it's bulletproof. They would have to shoot multiple times to get through, and by then those fuckers would know we're coming in. If they decided to pop every explosive they have in the building, the whole thing could come down. We have to wait until we know what we're dealing with."

I turn around to check on the girls, hoping Orah can't hear me. But I'm not that lucky. Her face tells me she's hanging on every word.

"So," the Chief continues, "we have to wait until the masses are here. It'll be one giant, coordinated breach, which includes sending down bomb-sniffing dogs in the first wave."

"So, everybody's jumping through the ceiling? Like *Mission Impossible* or some shit? With fucking flying dogs in harnesses, pretending they're Tom Cruise."

Fuck all these movie references playing in my head. I hope I never see another movie as long as I live.

I guess I shouldn't think like that. Technically, I may not live too much longer.

He chuckles, trying to make light of the situation. "I thought you liked action movies."

"Yeah, not anymore."

"Ridge? I wanna talk." Orah's plea garners my attention, slamming into my brain with rapid speed. Her request is barely audible, but I hear it nonetheless. Like my eardrums were made to absorb her vocals—no matter the place, no matter the distance, no matter the decibel.

My brow furrows. "What?"

"I wanna talk to him."

"To my Chief?"

She nods.

"Orah, this really isn't the—"

"Please."

Her gray eyes captivate me, making my soul ache. How can I deny her?

The simple answer is...I can't.

I can't deny her.

I'm not that strong.

"Chief, hold on a second." I stride across the room, kneeling in front of her. Despite my better judgment, I do it before I can change my mind. "I have someone who wants to say something." I keep the button pressed, not giving Chief a chance to question what's about to happen. Leaning close to her body, I angle my shoulder underneath her mouth. "Whisper," I prompt, gently reminding her.

"Hi." She looks into my eyes, silently asking if she should keep going. When I nod, she gives me a soft smile. "My name is Orah. Orah Smith. I'm here with my best friend, Tabby. Tabitha Morrison."

I finally release, giving the Chief a chance to respond. It's painfully obvious that he's completely shocked that I'm letting a civilian use my radio. It's a total breach of protocol. "Ummm. Hi, honey. I'm Chief Latner. Are you okay? Is the firefighter still there?"

"I'm here, Chief," I interrupt. "She just wants a minute, okay?" I shift my focus back to Orah, giving her permission to continue.

"Are my friend's parents there? Tabby's parents? Their names are Emmett and Laurie. Emmett and Laurie Morrison. He's really tall and skinny with red hair. And she's got brown hair. She was wearing a pink sundress tonight." Orah sighs, shaking her head. "Well, anyway, can you tell them that Tabby's hurt? Ridge is taking really good care of her, but she's hurt. Bad." She looks over at her friend, studying her shallow breathing. "But tell them that she's not alone. That she'll never be alone. I'll never leave her. No matter what happens."

The Chief's voice crackles through. "Well, we have everything blocked off so the public can't get close, but I'll send someone to find them, okay? I'll let them know that you're with her. Is that what you want, sweetheart?"

Tears well in her eyes. "Yes. And if I don't make it out of here, I need you to tell my parents that I love them. Their names are John and Ann. Tell them I love them and my greatest gift in life is having them as parents. And... tell them I'm sorry."

My chest clenches, and my stomach grows queasy.

The Chief's voice rustles through our cocooned bodies, giving us comfort and sorrow at the same time. I mean, there's just something about a man using his '*dad*' voice. No matter how old you are, it makes you feel like a kid again. Suddenly, you're transported back in time; it's like you're a ten-year-old, crying over the devastation of your wrecked bike and skinned knees. But... Dad can make it better. "Honey, you have nothing to be sorry for. We're gonna get you out of there. Just hang tight. Hang tight and listen to whatever the firefighter says, okay?"

I click the button, but Orah just waves me away, mumbling under her breath. "I have everything to be sorry for."

I reach out, ready to grab her chin, ready to chastise her for thinking any of this is her fault; but alas, the Chief summons me.

"Ridge?"

Quickly standing, I walk away from her and back to my corner.

"I'm gonna respect your decision about what just happened. Mainly because I don't have the heart to fucking rip you a new one right now."

I bypass him and his scolding. "It's been too long. I need to get off the radio. When do I need to check in again?"

"Twenty."

"10-4."

I take another break to listen at the door, finally settling back across from Orah when I don't hear anything. But my hackles are instantly raised because it looks like she's grimaced in pain. And she's holding her upper stomach, under her right breast. "Orah, are you—"

Relaxing her face and shifting her position, she hits me with a question, interrupting me. "How old are you?"

I ignore her. "Are you okay? Why are you holding your stomach?"

"It's time for my question. Not yours."

I scoot forward and press my fingers to her neck. Her pulse hammers powerfully, beating against my fingertips like a drum. Her heart rate is definitely elevated, but shit, so is mine. "My question trumps yours. Are you okay? Why were you holding your stomach?" My other hand skirts across her chest, lowering beneath her breast.

A small, breathless giggle flutters between us, and she gently pushes my wandering hand away. Her touch makes my skin feel funny.

Electric.

"A girl can't have heartburn after eating movie theater popcorn and candy?"

"Heartburn?"

"Ridge, I'm fine. I promise. It's just the stress of everything." Her eyes dart back and forth across my face. "How old are you?"

My brow furrows, but I keep my fingers in place, making sure I don't feel any threadiness in her pulse. Reluctantly satisfied, I sigh and sit back, hiding my own grimace when my back grazes against the desk. Fuck, that's starting to hurt. "How old do you think I am?"

She bites on her bottom lip. I can't help but notice it's even more dry and cracked than a few minutes ago. I bet she's thirsty. "You have a man's body. Not a boy's body." Her remark surprises me. I'm pretty sure my mouth drops open. "But your eyes are young. They're so dark, but then you have that light brown circle around them. It makes me think of Tiger's Eye. You know, the gemstone?" She shrugs off her rambling, "Anyway, I'd guess twenty-four."

It takes me a minute to recover. I feel like I'm being pulled down in a sinkhole, being swallowed alive by the earth around me. I clear my throat, reminding myself how to talk. "Twenty-two. I just had a birthday last week."

For a nanosecond, the worry in her own eyes disappears, and she gifts me with a brilliant smile. "Happy Birthday, Ridge."

Chapter 6

Orah

Twenty-two.

Four years and two weeks older than me.

And look at him.

He's saving lives. He has a job. He's a professional. He... he's... such an adult.

He makes everything I've ever done seem insignificant. Childish. Foolish. Stupid. Especially what I did tonight.

Just thinking about my life makes me want to scream.

And the sad part is, I may never get a chance to correct it. I may never get a chance to be a better person. I may never get a chance to do things differently.

Because I may die.

We all may die.

And for the first time in my life, I can honestly say the '*we*' part scares me more than the '*me*' part. I mean, just look at the two of them. Tabby and Ridge. They're amazing. How is this world supposed to keep turning without them?

I really don't know how I feel about dying. Maybe the scariest part is knowing that if I die tonight, I'm not leaving a very good legacy in my wake. I haven't really been a good person.

I've been a popular person.

And with that comes bitchiness, indifference, and superiority. The thought of being judged on my previous actions makes me break out in a cold sweat.

I didn't change. Because I thought there was time.

I'm young.

There's always more time. Right?

Shame creeps over me, covering my anxiety like a cloak.

If Ridge could see the real me, would he even want to save me? Probably not.

"Where are you?" His graveled timbre slowly lures me to the surface.

"What?"

"Where are you? Because you're not here. You're thinking about something."

I struggle to swallow. It feels like my throat is lined with cotton blankets and hot sauce. I shake my head. "It's nothing."

He frowns. I watch in fascination as his hand reaches out and intertwines with mine. Even through the dried and caked blood, I can feel his calluses. "It's obviously something." His eyes follow mine. He stares at our hands, not even blinking. His thumb traces my pale pink nail polish. "I can feel what you feel." He tosses back to me the exact same words I said to him.

And it takes my breath away. Like a sucker punch to the lungs.

A tear slides down my face, and I quickly wipe it away. Who knows what my face looks like. It's probably covered in blood and dirt. I thought I felt a cut on my forehead earlier, but I'm not sure.

A momentary calm falls over me. It's like my burning nerve-endings are being extinguished, if only for a minute. "And what do I feel?"

His jaw twitches. "You want more time."

My heart collapses in my chest, suffocating me from the inside out. And this time, it really does hurt. A pain that's almost unbearable. I want to grab my side. Something hurts, and I need to press on it to make it stop. But I'm too scared to move. I don't want to let go of his hand.

His free arm reaches up and grabs the back of my neck, bending me closer to him. So close our foreheads touch. So close his hot breath skirts across my cheek. So close I can feel his heartbeat in my own body. "You're gonna have all the time in the world. No one's getting to you. I'm not letting anyone near you. Do you hear me, Orah? You're gonna have every second for the rest of forever. I'll make sure of it."

My mouth opens. My brain searches for the word thank you, but never finds it.

Because my best friend starts coughing up blood.

Everything's been moving in slow motion again. Well, slow and fast all at the same time. Like I'm hyped up on speed, the world around me flipping in frozen snapshots at a supersonic rate; yet I'm trapped in quicksand, unable to move my body, using all my strength just to blink, just to breathe, just to live.

I do everything Ridge tells me to do.

New bandages. New QuikClot. Scooping my finger in her mouth to clear out blood and mucus.

And in between it all, his expert hands do what they're meant to do. It's like he should be a doctor. I find it really hard to believe he actually fights fires too.

A couple of times, Tabby tries to talk. Ridge tells me to keep her quiet and calm so I bend close and whisper in her ear. I think, like me, he's afraid that all of the extra noise will attract unwanted attention. And with Ridge occupied with Tabby, it's not exactly like I can defend us with the broomstick spear.

I'm on the Homecoming Court, not the wrestling team.

After what feels like forever, things finally seem stable with Tabby again. Well, as stable as it's gonna get is what Ridge says.

Looking at his watch, he curses. "I'm late. I've gotta turn the radio back on, okay?"

I nod.

Standing and stretching his back, a drop of Tabby's blood falls from his forearm. It plops onto her makeshift blanket—his fireman's jacket. Soaking into the thick yellow fabric, it instantly makes a new brown stain.

This time, he doesn't bother going to the far corner. He turns on the radio and starts talking right in front of me. I listen eagerly, soaking in the details of what will either be my rescue or my demise.

SWAT is here. The bomb squad is here. Something or somebody called breach experts are here. Dogs are here. And they're all making their way to the roof. And us? Well, we're the sitting ducks. Waiting to either fly...or get shot.

Or explode.

Anything is possible.

I've never been a control freak. I've never felt the need to have everything planned. But now? Now, I have this deep, intense yearning to know it all. Every single detail. These guys—these demons—took away the control I didn't even know I wanted. And now, I want to take it all back.

Ridge is about to answer a question the Chief asked when his head cocks to the side and he stops breathing. My body instantly reacts to his, like we are tethered together by an invisible chain. The hairs on my arm stand straight, and my ears start to ring because I'm straining so hard to listen.

"Chief," Ridge faintly croaks, "I'm turning it off. They're coming. Get us the fuck out of here. Now." Without waiting for a reply, he thumbs the radio off. Stooping to grab the broomstick, he puts his finger to his lips, once again hushing me, even though I'm already silent.

The muscles in his shoulders bunch, his jaw tenses, and his eyes bounce around the room, scanning for anything else that may be better suited for fighting. Not finding anything, his grip on the makeshift spear tightens, turning his knuckles white. Tiptoeing around the desk and sneaking to the door, he scowls, not happy with the fact that the shelving unit doesn't sit flush with the door. There's still a little room. A little room for that door to open. A little room for something bad to happen. Not to mention, there's no inside lock.

I know. I looked for it earlier tonight.

When I was using this room for things I wish I could forget.

For things that happened a lifetime ago.

Because for me, a lot of shit has changed in two hours.

We both hear the muffled voice at the same time. Distorted, but turning clearer with every step the bad guy takes. Every step that's bringing him closer to us.

"Little pig, little pig, let me in." Five seconds pass. I know. Because I count. "Little pig, little pig, let me in."

One. Two. Thre—

"I know some of y'all are hiding. There's no need to be scared." He cackles with a sadistic laugh. "We've waited long enough. We're bored. It's time to play." Despite the soundproofing, I can hear him tapping something against the wall as he walks down the hallway. "And trust me, you'd much rather me find you than Devin. Devin's not in a very good mood right now."

Pop. Pop. Pop. Pop. Pop.

The gunshots are so rapid I can't even count them. They're so loud they nearly drown out the screams of the people they're tearing through.

Nearly.

But not quite.

Tears spill down my face, burning my chapped skin. I cover my mouth with my hand, begging my sobs to stay buried. My heart thunders, fast and violently, like it's about to explode right out of my chest. Nausea drenches my stomach like a monsoon, and I taste the metallic tinge of blood on my tongue.

Ridge looks over at me. It's just a quick second. A moment frozen in time where I can feel his unspoken words of encouragement. *We've got this.* His eyes burn into mine, giving me strength and courage where I have none. He thinks I'm brave. I can feel it. But he's wrong. Any bravery I have is because of him. His fearlessness is soaking into my pores, dripping into my spirit.

And then... our moment is ruined.

Ruined because the doorknob starts to turn.

The soft sound of the door creaking open bursts my eardrums, violently ripping the tender skin, making me wanna cover my ears just to shelter my brain from the reverberating echo. It opens just a couple of inches and when it hits the edge of the shelf, the guy on the other side curses. I wonder which one it is. The guy with the blond hair? Or the guy with black hair? The one who shot my best friend? Or the one who stood next to him and laughed?

I watch in wide-eyed horror as the barrel of a long black gun slides through the small slit of the door and into the room. It happens so slowly. Millimeter by millimeter. Creep. Creep. Creep. And it's pointing right in my direction.

After that, everything happens fast.

It happens in flashes. Blink after blink after blink.

In film class last year, we watched a Charlie Chaplin movie from 1914. You know, an old, silent movie that flickers on the screen. I'm reminded of that. The events play before me, bursting like fireworks, flickering bright and then fading.

Flicker. Fade.

Flicker. Fade.

Ridge drops the broomstick, grabs the gun, and pulls it as far into the room as he can. And in the process, the bad man's hands slip from the trigger and slide through the open crack of the door. The gun must be tied to him or something because it doesn't fall to the ground. Instead, it swings back to him like it's dangling from a necklace. Using all of his force, Ridge shoulders the door closed. The sound of bones crunching churns my stomach.

If there is one bone that isn't broken in this murderer's hands, it will be a miracle.

And this boy doesn't deserve miracles.

Blood instantly pours from his skin, soaking into the orange and red carpet. He wails, screeching like an owl, and drags his mangled hands back to the other side. "Aghhh!!"

He's screaming. Just the way he made Tabby scream. Just the way he made me scream. And who knows how many others.

But his scream is cut short.

Well, not exactly cut short, more like drowned out. Dwarfed. Overshadowed. Completely fucking dominated.

Ridge is already reacting, flying into action before my brain even has time to process what my ears are hearing. Slamming the door shut, he races back across the room, moving faster than I've ever seen anyone move. Leaping in the air, he slides across the desk, barely letting his feet touch the ground before he's grabbing me and folding me across Tabby's broken body.

And then, he covers us with his own. Spreading his arms, his giant stature cocoons us. He's determined to keep us safe.

He's ready to die. For us. For me.

He's given in to it. Resigned to it. Accepted it as fate.

There's a cacophony of havoc. The explosion has too many noises. Each sound competes against the other, vying for the top spot. Shattering glass, splintering wood, rapid gunfire, violent yelling, scattered running. And what even sounds like concert pyrotechnics.

I close my eyes, squeezing so hard I see the spots again. I count them as they float from one side of my closed eyelids to the other.

One. Two. Three. Four. Five.

One. Two. Three. Four. Five.

The pain in my upper stomach and chest has become almost debilitating. I draw short, quick breaths through my lungs, trying to make it easier to breathe. Even my blood-soaked clothes feel wetter, clinging to me, rubbing me raw. My body shakes, shivering in a state of constant hypothermia.

Ridge's lips graze the top of my ear. "Shhh. I'm here, Orah. I won't leave you. I need you. We need each other. We can save each other."

Outside these four walls, there's hate and anger and despair. But here, inside these four walls—between the three of us—there's nothing but love. Love and peace and compassion. And if these are my last seconds on this earth, I can't think of two other people I'd rather be with.

My best friend.

And the love of my life.

Because whether I live for sixty more seconds or sixty more years, I know I'll never love another man the way I love this firefighter named Ridge.

Chapter 7

Ridge

When it finally stops, I almost can't believe it. It felt like it would never end. The breach and ensuing fight sounded like a damn hurricane. Walls shook. The cleaning supplies on the shelf rattled. I watched as Tabby's eyes fluttered open, widened in horror, and then collapsed closed again. I held Orah's trembling body underneath mine, rubbed my hands across the chill bumps covering her arms, and whispered words of encouragement to her. I'm not even sure what I said. I was too busy praying for her safety to really focus on the words tumbling, unfiltered, from my mouth.

Besides, it was so loud, she probably didn't hear me anyway.

When things finally quiet down, I hear muffled commands being shouted. It's pretty easy to decipher that the cops have control of the building now. I hold my breath and listen, trying to grasp the instructions being ordered outside of our sanctuary. I can't make out exactly what they're saying, but I do hear a dog barking.

I guess, depending on how he's trained, that could either be a good thing or a bad thing.

Leaning back, I stare at Orah. She's folded over Tabby, frozen in the position I threw her in. Her face is turned to the side, and she's completely motionless, not even blinking. Her remarkable gray eyes are haunted. Disjointed. Unfeeling. She's not crying, but I can tell she was. Dried tears cling to her sun-tinged face. The scratch on her forehead must've gotten scratched again because there's a small bead of blood collecting in the already scabbing skin.

It's plain to see that whatever childlike innocence she had before this night is gone.

Lying on this floor, with her legs tangled with mine, and her hands wrapped around the shoulders of her dying best friend, is a *woman*. A beautiful woman hardened by the reality of life.

So scared and yet so brave.

Two things I can only imagine she'll be for the rest of her life.

Two things that will forever be competing to rule her mind. Rule her body. Rule her soul.

Two things that are so different yet so intertwined.

One thing that will constantly try to rip the *sanity* from her world, and the one thing she'll need above all else to fight the *insanity*.

And I can't help but wonder which one will win.

Fear or bravery?

My fingers reach out, gently pushing a tangle of raven hair away from her face. It's sticky and stiff from congealed blood. Despite that, I catch a small whiff of coconut, and I can't help but smile.

In times like this, you have to be grateful for the simple things. I guess for me, that's the smell of coconut shampoo.

"Orah? Sweetheart, it's over. I hear the police. They're coming to get us."

She doesn't even flinch.

I cup her cheek, gently grazing my thumb back and forth across her soft skin. My hands are filthy, covered in dirt and blood. The grime mixes with the moisture still hiding from her tears. I draw a line down the side of her jaw, watching in awe as the red-brown concoction marks her.

I can't help but think I'm marking her as mine.

Suddenly, her eyes shift, locking with my own.

Was she right? Can she feel what I feel?

Eventually, she blinks, wrenching me from my reverie.

I instantly chastise myself. Fucking get it together, Ridge. She's a patient. A patient you're responsible for. Two lives are depending on you right now, and you're just lying here like you have all the time in the world.

Clearing my throat, I push up from the floor. "The police are here. They're coming to get us," I repeat. I glance at Tabby's IV bag. It's nearly empty. This help needs to freakin' hurry. "I'm gonna clear everything from the door. Once they sweep the hallways, we need to get her out of here as quickly as possible."

"What if he's still there? On the other side of the door? Just waiting to come in?" she asks.

"He's not."

"And if he is?"

"I'll take care of it." I'll stab the bastard with the broom if there's even a hint of life in his worthless-as-shit body.

I make quick work of pushing the desk back to the other side of the room and moving the shelf out of the way. Picking up the spear, I slowly open the door, positioning myself between any possible danger and the girls. I'm not really sensing any peril, so I'm doing it more so Orah won't see what's on the other side. Because I do have a feeling that whatever's there is not gonna be pretty.

And it's not.

Lying just inches from me is a kid. But this one is dead. I say kid because he looks like a child playing dress up. Playing army men. Or cops and robbers. In all honesty, he's probably older than me. He's got two bullet holes in his face. One in his jaw, exposing his bloated tongue and broken teeth. And one right through his left eye socket. Blood is everywhere. It's hard to see what other damage might be there because he's wearing all black and decked out in tactical gear, including a bulletproof vest and stocks of ammunition. He's got handguns strapped to both thighs. Still wrapped around his neck, nestled beside his body, is a large automatic rifle. His hand is still on the trigger. His hands are bloodied and bruised—red and black and blue. I even see a bone sticking out of the skin. It's obvious my door trick did some damage. But it wasn't enough to stop his intent to destroy us. If the police hadn't come when they did, we could all be dead.

All three of us.

And the thought of Orah and Tabby dying makes me physically ill.

"Drop it! Don't fucking move!"

"Hands in the air!"

"Freeze!"

The swarm of SWAT and other members of law enforcement, yelling commands in my vicinity, scare the shit out of me. Quickly dropping the weaponized broom, my hands fly in the air. "Firefighter! I'm a friendly!"

They take a few seconds to size me up, and then the guy leading the pack slowly lowers his weapon and motions for the others to do the same. They're dressed like something out of the movies, right down to the helmets strapped with cameras.

"Firefighter?" he asks.

I nod, suddenly realizing how dry my throat is. "Ridge Conway. White Sky Fire Department."

"Ridge Conway," he repeats. "You got two civilians in that room with you?"

"Affirmative. One is critical. Multiple gunshots. She needs air evac. Now."

"And the other?"

"Just shock and a twisted ankle." I think back to Orah holding her stomach. "But she needs immediate medical attention too. There may be something I can't see."

Turning, he shouts a new set of orders to those around him. Finally lowering my hands, I take a small step forward and look out into the corridor. It's hard to process everything with the flurry of activity going on. There has to be fifty officers, plus a few K-9s, slowly and methodically searching every inch of the open areas. Turning my head right and left, these images are the things nightmares are made of. They will haunt me until I take my last breath. Blood and bodies and smoke and destruction. And not even all the bodies are whole. And what makes it even worse is seeing Hartselle and what's left of Battles lying limply down the left hallway.

My eyes blur, and I break out in a cold sweat. I have to grab the doorframe to keep from going down. I take a few beats to center myself. I've got to find a way to get Orah out of here without her seeing all this carnage. She's seen enough. More than enough. Looking behind me, I check on her. She's sitting up now with her back against the wall. But she doesn't look good. All the color has drained from her face. Her lips are slightly parted, and her breathing looks rapid and shallow.

"Ora—"

The SWAT officer interrupts me. "We've already found six more explosives in the lobby," he says with a point behind him. "Bomb squad is working on containment for the area, blast barriers and such. Because we can't wait hours to clear this building. We've got people bleeding out as we speak. So far, the dogs aren't picking up anything else down this way," he nods to the hallway that I crawled down. The hallway where my brothers died. "We're doing one more sweep before we move everybody out that way." I watch as four dogs sniff the walls and bodies and movie cutouts. "Your Chief already told us you had a critical patient. We've got dozens of paramedics just waiting for the word to get in. We have no idea how many injured we are dealing with. We've got at least forty ambulances already outside. One air evac is here. It's been designated for your patient. Others are in route from all over the state. Not to mention Georgia and Alabama."

"Is the other one dead? The other shooter?" I ask.

His lips thin into a hard line, and he looks down at the body sprawled on the floor between us. "They've both been neutralized." Clicking his fingers, he orders someone to shift the body away from the front of the supply room entryway, reminding them not to disturb anything on his person because it's evidence.

"The movie auditoriums?"

"We're clearing you and all the other survivors and wounded from the common areas first. Then, we'll start on the auditoriums. We've had some communication back and forth, though. They're yelling, telling us about some of the injured. Two of the auditoriums are chained shut, padlocked. Looks like they were trying to chain the other one, but stopped for some reason."

"Why the hell were they locking people in?"

"We don't know the whole story yet, but we found some cannisters of cyanide gas in the HVAC room and the projection room."

Holy. Shit.

"Clear! Sweep's clear!" One of the dog handlers screams from the end of the hallway.

The SWAT officer circles his finger in the air. "Let 'em in." It's obvious he's giving permission for the other paramedics to enter. Paramedics and firefighters just like me. Turning back to me, he lifts an eyebrow, "Giddyup, Ridge Conway. Time to save some lives." Pulling away, he screams for half his team to block entry to the unsafe areas, and he moves down the hall to work on clearing another zone.

When the doors open and I see stretcher after stretcher race into the theater, it feels like the sun coming out after a tornado. "I need one here!" I holler, waving my arm back and forth. Running into the room, I tear my jacket from Tabby's body. There's more blood on it than I remember. On the side *not* covering Tabby's injuries.

Was there this much blood on the outside of my turnout coat before?

Maybe my memories are already starting to fog.

Undoing her IV hookup from the empty bag, I glance at Orah. Her eyes dart excitedly around the room, like a frightened puppy looking for someplace to hide. "Don't worry, Orah. There's about to be a lot of activity going on, but you're used to it. Remember? You helped me. We've got to get Tabby in the helicopter as soon as possible. And then we'll leave, okay? We're walking out of here together.

You and me." I speak low and calm, hoping to temper whatever anxiety is coursing through her right now.

The next five minutes are perfected chaos—taking Tabby's vitals, hooking up a new IV bag, dosing her with meds, and repacking her soaked and war-torn wounds. When she's ready for transport, one of the medics, a woman with curly brown hair in her mid- to late-fifties, gently pushes me away. "We've got it from here, Smokey," she verifies, using a common firefighter's nickname. "You did good."

Battling the urge to go with them, I stand in the doorway, watching as they sprint from the room, hurrying to the waiting chopper.

This is it. We made it. We survived.

Tabby's not out of the woods, though. Her wounds are serious. More than serious. We've just got to pray that she keeps on surviving.

Now, it's time for me to get Orah to safety. And then? Then, I'll come back in and help whoever else may need help. Why? Because it's what I do. It's who I am.

Give me a new jump bag and I'll be back in the fight.

From the corner of my eye, I see Orah stand. Using the wall for support, she slinks up, crawling one hand at a time. Shit. I bet her ankle hurts. I may need to carry her.

As soon as Tabby disappears through the outside doors, I turn back to Orah. "Orah, don't walk on your—"

I thought the worst was over. I thought the end was in sight. I thought maybe, just maybe, one day my life could be somewhat normal again. A normal day at work. A normal day at the beach. A normal day watching my best friend play football.

And now I know, there's a chance that nothing in my life will ever be normal again.

Because if something happens to Zipporah Smith, I lose all chance of having a regular, ordinary future.

If she isn't in this world, then I shouldn't be here either.

I watch in complete panic as fresh, wet crimson blood soaks through her bra and shirt, quickly creeping down the front, drenching the white. Before now, she was half red/half white. Now? Now, she's all red. Blood red. And it drips onto her yellow shorts, making the splatter that was there look insignificant. She reaches for me. But I'm too far away. "Ridge..."

And with that, her eyes roll back in her head and she collapses.

Chapter 8

Ridge

Fear. This is the definition of true fear.

I'm not sure I've ever felt it before.

Not during the tornado from when I was in high school. Definitely not with any fire that I've walked into. And not even tonight, when Battles exploded or Hartselle was shot.

But now? Watching My Brave Girl collapse in a pile of her own blood?

I'm. Fucking. Terrified.

Hauling her lifeless body into my arms, I sprint from the room and down the mangled hallway. People are watching. People are yelling for me to stop. People are jumping the hell out of my way. But none of them matter.

Only Orah.

I burst through the metal double doors, instantly assaulted by the swarm of lights and by the sounds and smells of the outdoors. Red, white, and blue lights swirl and flash, reminding me of the nightclub some of Holt's teammates drug us to when he turned twenty-one. The blades of the air ambulance beat in the distance, whooshing through my brain like a blender. And the smell... the ocean salt I love so much mixed with death and desperation.

Call it luck or fate, all I know is the first person I see is McDonald, racing toward the doors with a pristine stretcher and a jump bag bursting at the seams with supplies, and I couldn't be happier. "McDonald!"

His eyes widen and his step flounders, if only for a second. "Ridge?"

Grabbing the gurney, I yank it from his hands, bringing it closer to my body. Gently laying Orah down, I immediately start shouting for supplies and barking orders.

McDonald's not my inferior; he's my equal. My co-worker. He's not supposed to take direct orders from me. But I guess something about the look on my face tells him that I'm taking the lead, and he better buckle-the-fuck-up because I need some help. Slapping the jump bag on the stretcher between Orah's legs, he immediately starts pulling out everything we may need.

I don't even wait on the shears; I rip the remaining buttons right off Orah's top and fling it open. There's so much blood. And I can't see where it's coming from. Not even bothering with gloves, I push my hands around on her stomach, tearing the button from her shorts and forcing them lower on her hips so I can palpitate her lower abdomen and pelvic region. I don't feel any rigidity or wounds. Following behind me, McDonald cuts the middle wire of her bra and peels it back, exposing Orah's breasts.

"Clean her up! I can't see anything!" I scream.

I confiscate the stethoscope from his neck, and I'm devastated when I hear her racing heart and diminished breath sounds on her right side. "Pneumothorax. Her right lung is collapsing."

I'm vaguely aware of others around me, others helping and doing their jobs. Someone grabs her left arm and is attempting to start an IV. Someone else is taking her pulse ox. Yet another person is shearing her bundled shorts and makes a quick comment about Orah menstruating. McDonald is doing the best he can to clean the congealed and pooled blood from her torso so we can see what we're dealing with. What he wipes away doesn't get replaced. It doesn't even look like she's bleeding anymore. I don't understand it. My eyes and hands travel her body, feeling her breasts, counting her ribs, pressing her stomach. Where the hell is she wounded?

"I don't see it. Where is it?" McDonald keeps cleaning, thinking something will magically appear. He even looks inside her belly button with a flashlight.

And I remember back to our room. I remember her holding her upper right stomach and claiming the pain was nothing more than acid reflux. Cupping her right breast in my hand, I lift it.

And there it is.

A small bullet wound tucked neatly into the firm skin where the base of her breast meets with her torso. The part normally covered by the underwire of her bra.

"Shit…" McDonald mumbles under his breath.

Fumbling for the half of her bra just flopping off to the side, I drag my finger across the underwire. Sure enough, there's a section marred and jumbled, with the wire poking out. Like someone hit it with a hammer and then cut it with a wire cutter.

"Give me more light!"

Someone shines a light on the wound, and we can see it's blocked with a huge clot. That must've been why she wasn't bleeding in the room. Her body had naturally clotted the wound. Then, when she finally stood up, the clot broke, sending the blood pouring out of My Brave Girl.

And it's pretty clear to see, this little bullet has done some serious damage.

"Give me the decompression needle!" I'm raging through the words even though McDonald is already handing me what I need. "Pack her wound," I tell him. We never know when the clot will break again.

Someone next to me tells me they've already pushed drugs in her. Even though she's passed out, the last thing we need is for her to wake up screaming when I do the decompression to release the air trapped in her pleural cavity. The air that's slowly squeezing the life from her lung and suffocating her. And without giving myself too much time to dwell on it, I find the second intercostal space and stab her chest wall with the needle.

We spend the next few minutes stabilizing her. When it's as good as it's gonna get, I start running with the stretcher to where I saw the helicopter. But...I don't see it anymore.

"Ridge! Stop!"

I'm blindsided when Chief Latner slams his hands into my chest, nearly making me stumble. I'm quite a bit taller than him so he flicks my chin with his finger, forcing me to look down. "Son, I've been calling your name. I need you to focus."

What the hell does he think I've been doing?

I've been focused on keeping Orah alive.

"You've done what you can. You need to let them take over," he says.

I ignore him. "She needs air evac. Where is it?"

"It already left with her friend." He points to the distant blinking light in the sky. "We're waiting on the others."

"Waiting?! What the hell does that mean? When will they be here?"

"ETA ten minutes."

Ten minutes. Has he lost his ever-loving mind. "Are you shitting me? Ten minutes here. Five minutes load time. And then a twenty-minute flight to the trauma center in Tallahassee." I toss my hands in the air, shaking with anger. "She may not have that long."

"Ridge, they're coming as quick as they can. We called in every available one. We've got a ton of critical injuries. Even Tallahassee can't take them all. We've got all trauma centers within two-hundred-and-fifty miles on alert."

Chief is trying to give me words of wisdom. He's trying to make me see reason.

But you can't make me see reason where there is none.

This shouldn't have happened to her to begin with. On top of that, I should have caught that she was wounded. I'm a trained professional, for fuck's sake. And now, you're telling me she may die because we are waiting on a helicopter.

Not. Happening.

Spinning the gurney, I immediately start racing to a waiting ambulance, forcing everyone else to sprint to keep up with me.

"What are you doing?" Chief screams.

"I'm driving her. I can beat that. I can beat thirty-five minutes."

"It's an hour drive. Best you can do in an ambulance is probably forty-five. Wait on the chopper, son."

"Chief, I can do this!"

"No! You're too invested. You're acting erratic. You're going into shock. If you think I'm letting you behind a wheel, you're out of your mind."

My heart feels like it's being crushed. Just like Orah's lung.

McDonald comes to my rescue. "I can do it, Chief. This time of night? Not to mention the state troopers have traffic blocked. I can make it in thirty. But we need to go right now."

Chief Latner glances back and forth between the two of us, gauging how far he wants to take the argument, trying to wage what may be the best outcome for Orah. He sighs. "Fine. But you," he points at me, "stay here."

Over. My. Dead. Body.

I shake my head. "I told her I wouldn't leave her. We need each other."

One of the other paramedics holding her IV bag interrupts. I don't even know his name, but I know he works for a city about forty-five minutes south of White Sky. "I'll ride in back with him. But we need to go. Now, Chief."

Finally acquiescing, the Chief moves out of the way. I holler to no one in particular, "Load the fucking sled! Hurry!" I'm hooking Orah up to the monitors, when he bangs on the window, sending us on our way.

Bending next to her ear, my oath crawls from my scratchy and raw throat, begging to be heard. It's a promise stitched into the fabric of my very being. "You saved me. Now, let me save you."

Chapter 9

Ridge

The nurse arches an eyebrow. "I already told you no. Nothing I'm saying should come as a surprise. You know the HIPPA laws."

Screw HIPPA.

"I just need to know if she's okay." I shake my head, forcing myself to make a correction. "I just need to know if *they're* okay." I scrub my hand down my face. "I don't think you understand."

She sighs, frowning in a moment of empathy. "Look, I was working the Trauma Team shift in the ER on Friday night. I was here when you brought her in. I *do* understand." She looks around at the other nurses and doctors and assistants roaming the ICU floor. "We all understand."

"Then you know what I'm going through. I just need to know her prognosis." I lean across the counter, licking my lips and flexing my bicep. I'm not sure if this will work; with my luck, this nurse is married. Or has a boyfriend. Or has a girlfriend. "In fact, if you just happen to pull up her chart on the computer screen and you just happen to take a bathroom break, I'll completely understand." I give her a wink.

Yep.

Definitely not working.

"Listen, Casanova," she drawls, with a scowl filled with disdain instead of sarcasm, "I'm not some foolish little girl. This is my job. A job I happen to love and don't take lightly." She points to my badge, labeling me as a firefighter and paramedic, "That badge may have gotten you access to this restricted floor, but it doesn't give you the right to think you can do whatever you want. I'm gonna say this one last time, and I'm gonna say it slow so you can really comprehend it... you cannot have any information on patients without the approval of their families." She sits back and folds her arms across her chest. "Now, are you gonna leave? Or do I have to call security?"

Leave.

That's what I did, and I'll never forgive myself for it.

McDonald was right. He made it in thirty minutes. In fact, I'm pretty sure he missed his calling as a NASCAR driver. The Trauma Team was waiting on us in the ambulance bay. It was all hectic and chaotic, controlled and streamlined. A mad dash, synchronized in perfect choreography. Just like we all train for. If this woman was there, I should be falling on my hands and knees and thanking her, not giving her a hard time. But the truth is, I can't tell you if she was there Friday night or not. Because I was solely focused on Orah.

I was out of my mind with worry.

And when they wheeled her behind closed doors, wheeled her where I wasn't allowed to go? It nearly broke me. Emotions and adrenaline and intensity crushed down on me like a five-ton brick. I wasn't even sure if I could put one foot in front of the other. Bracing my arms against the wall, I buried my head. I'm not a crier, but shit if the tears didn't start to come.

And then, Chief radioed. He needed us back.

There were others who needed help. Others who were hurting. And so, I had to leave.

It's my job.

But Friday night was the first time I ever wanted to quit. Because I didn't want to help anyone else. I only wanted to help her. I wanted to hold her hand and touch her face. I wanted to beg her not to leave this world. Because I'd only scratched the surface of Orah

Smith. And I knew my life wouldn't be complete until I learned every little thing about her.

I promised her I wouldn't leave. And I did.

I left her. And I'll never forgive myself.

Standing up straight, I give a simple nod to the nurse. "Thank you. Thank you for everything you did for her. And for everyone else. I hope you never have to go through another night like Friday night."

Her lip quivers, making me feel like an even bigger shithead. "You too, Firefighter."

Shoving my hands in my pockets, I start toward the elevator. I'm passing by a small family room when a man and woman walk out, carrying some bottles of water and granola bars. He's shorter than me, about six-foot or so, with brown hair and a short beard speckled with gray. She's got short black hair and is wearing a gray sweatshirt with the outline of the state of South Carolina on it. A yellow flower is drawn in the middle of it.

When she looks at me, I see it.

They're not exactly the same color. I mean, no one could have eyes the same color as Orah's. They're one of a kind. But this woman's eyes are very similar. Bright and gray and...brave.

My footing slows. "Uhh..." I'm not exactly sure how to proceed. But I don't have to worry about it. Because she does it for me.

She gasps. Blinking, she looks me over. Once. Twice. Three times. Besides the badge clipped to the pocket of my shorts, there's nothing indicating me as a man of any position or authority. I'm wearing an old ratty T-shirt, a ballcap, and tennis shoes.

"Ridge?" She takes a step in my direction. Her hand reaches out. It instantly reminds me of Orah. Reaching for me.

And me. Failing her.

"Are you Ridge?" she asks again.

I nod, embarrassed by the tremble in my voice. "Yes, ma'am."

Dropping the granola bars to the floor, she launches into my arms, laughing and crying. "Oh my! You look just like she said. I can't believe you're here."

Her hug is tight and fierce. It's the same kind of hug my mom had for me when I finally made it home to my apartment late Saturday afternoon.

Her tears soak my shirt. Closing my eyes, I hold her close, relishing the connection to Orah. No matter how small.

Eventually, she pulls away, wiping her eyes. Glancing at the man, whom I can only assume is Orah's dad, she smiles and points at me. "It's *him*. It's Ridge."

A loving smile engulfs his face. "I gathered that, hon." Shifting the water bottles, he holds out his hand, introducing himself. "I'm Orah's father, John Smith."

"Sir, I can't tell you what a pleasure it is to meet you."

Men.

We're a funny breed.

We try to be strong. I do it. My brother does it. My own father does it. But sometimes? Sometimes, something just crushes you. The weight of knowing what could have been pulls you into the sea and tries to drown you. It becomes unbearable.

It happened to me Friday night—when they wheeled her away from me, when they wouldn't let me see her.

And now, it's happening to John. Unable to hold his emotion any longer, he pulls me into his own embrace, coughing and choking on his tears. "Thank you. Thank you for saving my little girl."

And we stand like that. Letting those words seep into existence.

Eventually, he gives my shoulder one last squeeze. "Thank you for saving *both* of the girls."

One of the water bottles slips from his grasp, and I instantly react, catching it before it hits the ground. Ann's laugh is soft and subtle. "She said your reflexes were fast."

She.

"Orah? Is she okay? And what about Tabby?" I look over in the direction of the nurses' station. "I asked, but of course, they couldn't tell me anything."

Ann frowns. "Oh no, I'm sorry. That didn't even cross my mind. It's really good that they're so private here. Everyone's been calling. News stations, politicians, people we've never even heard of. But it's completely fine for you to know. I'll make sure I add you to the list or whatever. You know? The list to get information about her status."

"So..." I trail off. I don't want to be rude, but I'm dying a slow damn death in my ignorance.

John sighs. "It'll be a long recovery, for both of them, but they're gonna be okay. I mean, the doctors want to keep them here for at least another week or two before we travel home. And there's always the risk of infection or bleeding. Or another lung collapse for Orah, but...all in all, they should be okay."

"The bullet? I mean, it was just one shot, right?"

His face fogs, like he's thinking of a distant memory. "Apparently, she fell. They both did. She was on all fours trying to get up when she was shot. That's why it was such a weird angle. It nicked her rib, ruptured her diaphragm, and caused the collapsed lung. It lodged in the soft tissue." He shakes his head back and forth. "It should've caused more damage. They have no idea why it didn't. Why it didn't rip through her body with more force. They said it had to have been traveling at only a fraction of the speed. The only thing they can think of is that the gun malfunctioned."

Ann sniffles. "They said it should have been a kill shot."

Fuck. Me.

My chest tightens. Anger blazes deep in my soul, burning bright like a road flare on a dark night. I want to bring those two assholes back to life so I can fucking kill them myself. With my bare hands.

Taking a deep breath, I try to center myself. Dragging my hand down my face, I tap my chin. One. Two.

"Can I see her? Would that be too much to ask?"

"Of course not. She'd love to see you." She puffs her lips in a frown. "But she's sleeping right now." A slow grin creeps along her face, erasing the sadness. "Would you like to see Tabby? She's awake."

"Absolutely."

Meeting Tabby's parents is just as touching and raw as it was with Orah's parents. I can't help but think back to Orah's description of them. And Emmett Morrison is in fact tall and skinny with red hair. After the introductions are done, my attention falls to the girl I've never even seen fully conscious.

Her parents shuffle around the hospital bed, motioning for me to sit next to Tabby. Orah's parents, John and Ann, quietly excuse themselves.

A bright smile falls across her face. "You must be the hero," she teases.

Sitting down next to her, I squint my eyes, pretending to think about who she is. "You look different with your eyes open, but I'm guessing, you must be the best friend."

She giggles, scrunching her nose. Her arms reach out, searching for a hug. I quickly lean forward so she doesn't have to stretch too much. I don't have the rundown of her injuries, but the last thing I want is for her to bend in an odd way and hurt herself.

People in the hospital always smell the same. Like dried blood, rubbing alcohol, disinfectant, linen starch, and morning breath.

Tabby must be thinking the same thing as me because she fusses, "Sorry, I know I'm stinky. Four more days and I should be able to shower."

I chuckle. "I've smelled stinkier." I stare at her, soaking in her youth. She looks so much younger than I remember Orah looking.

Maybe I'm just remembering everything wrong.

"Well," I say, "I guess I should properly introduce myself. I'm Ridge Conway."

"And I'm Tabitha Morrison. You can call me Tabby, of course." She cocks her head to the side. "You know, you're even better looking than she said."

Laurie Morrison gasps. Turning pink, she shakes her head in disbelief. "Tabby..."

"What, Mom? It's true." She turns back to me. "I knew you had to be good-looking because Orah avoided answering the question. Normally, she has to talk about how hot the guy is. Like over and over and over. But you? When I asked her, she just said you were handsome, and then she changed the subject."

"Sorry, Ridge," Emmett adds. "Tabby's never been a shy one."

"That's quite alright, sir. I definitely have some of those in my family."

Tabby settles her head back down on her pillow. "Sorry. I guess that wasn't very tactful. It's just...I'm seeing you for the first time, you know? It's like everyone's read this book, and now I finally get to read it too. I'm just excited."

"So, you don't remember anything?"

"From the storage room? No. Orah said I was awake for several minutes before I passed out. But I don't remember that. I don't even remember getting shot. The last thing I remember is Orah and me in the restroom. We had gone to the concession stand to buy a drink because she said her stomach hurt, and then we went to the bathroom. I think I remember hearing the fire alarm, but I'm not sure."

I glance over at Emmett and Laurie. "Do the doctors..."

"Think she'll remember?" Emmett asks, finishing my thought. "They aren't sure. They said there's a good chance that some of the memories may come back to her. Or they may not. It might be her brain's way of protecting her from the trauma."

"I don't wanna remember," Tabby rants pointedly and without any indecision whatsoever. She nods down to her stomach, hidden by the bedding. "Trust me, I have enough to remember from that night."

"How are you? Is everything okay?"

Her face falls and tears well in her eyes. "I was shot twice. The bullets did a lot of damage."

She gulps loudly, trying to swallow her sadness. Laurie gently strokes her shoulder, taking over the conversation for her daughter, fighting the burden for her child. "The damage was extensive.

The bullet that went through her body, tore her large intestine. They were able to repair it and clean the surrounding areas. Of course, she'll be on extremely high doses of antibiotics for the foreseeable future to prevent any possible infection from forming. The other bullet—the one that didn't come out—lodged into the tissue surrounding her uterus. There was damage to basically all of her reproductive organs." Laurie coughs, choking on her own sob. "They had to do a full hysterectomy."

Holy. Fuck.

I gather Tabby's hand between mine. Her fingers are slender and child-like against my own.

What in the world am I supposed to say? How do you comfort someone after something like that?

Tabby's just a girl. This reality is hard enough on her right now. But what's gonna happen ten years from now? When she's a grown woman? When she's married and in love and she and her husband are supposed to be deciding if they want to have a family or not? Don't get me wrong, I know there's plenty of ways to have a family—to have kids—but to have one of your choices completely ripped away from you?

Ripped away from you so fucking violently?

By absolutely no choice of your own?

That isn't something that any woman deserves.

"Tabby, I'm so sorry."

"I know. Me too." She wipes the snot from her face with her free hand. "It's not even really sank in yet, you know?" She takes a tissue from her dad and does a better job at wiping. "The doctors say I'll need to go to therapy. To talk about my feelings and everything. And plans for the future." She rolls her eyes. "I'm not sure how I feel about having to keep talking about it. I mean, I don't really want anyone to know." She looks over at me and blinks. "Of course, it's okay for you to know. I mean, you saw where I was shot. You kept my insides inside of me. You had to know something was going on *down there.*"

"Sweetheart, I knew you were injured badly. But without imaging, I had no idea what kind of internal injuries you were dealing with. My goal was just to keep you alive." My heartbeat feels low and thick and cold. Like it's trying to beat after being buried under ten feet of snow. "I wish I could've done more. I would do anything, give anything, to have saved you from this." I clear my throat, trying not to get emotional again.

She squeezes my hand. "You did save me, Hero. You saved me *and* my best friend."

"I... I just did my job." But for some strange reason, that sentence that I'm so used to saying, sounds inadequate. It sounds fake and hollow. Because this? What we went through? It was so much more than just my job.

Wasn't it?

"Well, I'm pretty sure I can say thank you on behalf of my entire high school." She shifts in bed and winces when a pain shoots through her body. Quickly recovering, she adds, "I mean, she is the most popular girl in school. A total bitch. But a popular bitch."

"Tabby!" Laurie's jaw drops, and she immediately scolds her daughter. "How can you say that?!"

Tabby just rolls her eyes. "Relax, Mom. Orah knows I say that. It's no secret." She looks back at me, pinning me with her gaze. "But I love her. I know the *real* her. And she has the best heart of anyone I've ever met. It's just sometimes hard to see." She sighs, "She's the best friend that anyone could ever ask for."

Nothing that Tabby is lobbing my way comes as a shock. The volley of information doesn't surprise me. There's no fly ball hitting me in the face.

Because as much as I hate to admit it, I stalked Orah's social media.

After taking a forty-five-minute shower on Saturday night, where I washed off the blood and body parts, and after hugging my parents and brother for the five-thousandth time, I found myself staring at the ceiling, watching the ceiling fan spin around and around. I debated going back out into the living room and talking to them, but I couldn't drum up the energy for any more conversation. Of course, I felt terrible that my parents were sleeping on the pull-out sofa and Cullen was sleeping in the recliner. I begged my parents to take my bed, but they refused, knowing I needed the rest. What could we do? It's the hazards of having a one-bedroom apartment.

As soon as news of the shooting broke, they jumped in the car and headed down here, without even packing anything. Their only concern was me. And that thought alone makes me the luckiest damn guy on the planet. It was pure luck that C had come home for the weekend from college; from what I gather, even my dad was too upset to drive, and my baby brother had to do most of it while my parents worried and sobbed. And of course, there was the one-thousand phone calls and texts I had from everyone else. Holt. His parents, Ray and Teresa. His sister, Raylee. His cousin, who-I-basically-consider-my-cousin, Ella. Hell, even Detective Marcum called to check on me. He's the police officer assigned to the disappearance of Ella's sister, Carrie. It's been nearly six years, and we still know nothing. But we all became close during the investigation, and his concern for me is touching.

Frustrated with my alert exhaustion, I kicked off the covers and grabbed my phone. Knowing I shouldn't do what I was about to do, I typed her name in my search bar and held my breath.

And there she was.

My Brave Girl.

Smiling, laughing, posing.

And there's no denying what Tabby just said.

Orah is popular.

And... kinda bitchy.

In every post, she was perfectly made-up. I mean, it's like she's an influencer or whatever-the-hell they call those people. Flawless makeup. Perfect hair. Obligatory girl-pose with her hand on her hip and her boobs and butt poked out. Clothes just sexy enough to garner attention, but not too sexy that her parents would keep her locked in her bedroom. And the captions? Holy crap, the captions made her seem so shallow and self-centered.

Pep rallies. Homecoming. Going for a walk. Bonfires. Working out. Prom. Doing homework. Parties. Even buying gas.

Every post made a huge—and I do mean absolutely huge—ordeal out of everyday, ordinary things. I mean, does the world really need to know that she had one dress for the Homecoming Court presentation and a completely different dress for the dance? Are the masses really that concerned about the fifty-five different flavored syrups she puts in her frozen coffee order? Are her followers so desperate for entertainment that they need to know if Orah uses leaded or unleaded gasoline?

Nothing about the girl on the Internet reminded me of My Brave Girl.

Sure, the raven-black hair was the same. The storm-cloud gray eyes still grabbed my attention. Her rosy cheeks and sun freckles were the same.

Listen, I'm not blind. I know Orah is extremely attractive.

I know that.

But these pictures and posts and reels all seemed so fake. So... unlike her.

And the worst part? The worst part was that her identity and what happened to her was already public knowledge.

We've got really stiff laws in this state surrounding the privacy of crime victims, especially when those victims are minors. The news can't report their names or show their faces. They can't even hint at any identifying information. But none of that really matters in today's world. Nothing is private, and everyone finds out about it.

That's why I don't even have Facebook or Instagram or TikTok or Snapchat or anything like that anymore. With the NFL Draft coming up, everyone was trying to get to Holt through me. So, I deleted every app. Which makes the fact that I was social media creeping on Orah via my little brother's accounts all the more pathetic.

But just like me, other pathetic souls were trolling for information on the gorgeous girl involved in the mass shooting. Sure, there were messages filled with condolences and encouragement and prayer, but there was also the other stuff. The stuff that wasn't so nice. And of course, those assholes had to tag her and post right on her timeline. Front and center.

Only evil people face this kind of punishment. She must have done something to deserve it.

I heard she pushed her best friend in front of her to protect herself. Now, her best friend is dead.

Damn, this girl is FINE! Is she dead? That sucks.

I heard her face got shot off. Serves her right after stealing my boyfriend so she could have the hottest guy in school as her date to Homecoming. Of course, she dumped him right after the dance.

She's definitely not nice. Can't say I didn't see this coming.

I'd eat chocolate sauce off those tits for days.

What was she doing down there anyway? I heard she drove down to Florida to buy some drugs.

She's a total cocktease. She probably teased the wrong cock.

I don't know her, but she's sexy-as-fuck in these pictures.

I could definitely nurse her back to health. I like me a nice, young girl.

Karma. Karma. Karma. That's all I'm gonna say.

Well, hello, beautiful. Fuck me. As soon as you're better, of course.

I heard she was a part of it. A part of the killing. I heard she shot people. Just wait for more news to come out. I'm pretty sure she's a killer.

After the last comment, I had to close it. I couldn't stand to look at it anymore. And when I checked again on Sunday afternoon, her accounts had been deleted. All of them.

"Did you hear me? Ridge?" Tabby's question pulls me out of my spiraling thought.

"Oh, I'm sorry. What did you say?"

"I asked if you're doing okay?" She waits a second, continuing when I don't immediately reply. "They won't let Orah walk yet, but they let me. When I went to see her, she told me that you went through a lot. I asked what, but she wouldn't tell me. She just said that your heart was broken." Her whisper is strained, like she's not sure if she should keep talking. "She said she could feel it."

The truth of that statement doesn't even sink in. It's too powerful. Too raw. Too filled with honesty.

Because how *do* I feel? How *am* I doing?

Fuck, if I know.

All I know is that I feel like my heart is turning into ash and scattering away with my every exhale, with each minute I don't get to see My Brave Girl.

"Knock. Knock." Ann peeks around the corner, smiling. "She's awake. And she's asking for you."

Chapter 10

Orah

I'm thankful I got the ICU Beauty Treatment today. Sponge bath, no-rinse shampoo cap, and more importantly, teeth brushing.

Normally, I would be repulsed by those simple things. I'd be upset that my hair and makeup and clothes weren't perfect.

So angry that I'd probably refuse visitors.

Even *him*.

But I don't feel that way today.

In fact, I haven't felt the same since that first shot rang out.

And if I'm telling the complete truth, I haven't felt the same since I followed Levi out of that storage room twenty minutes before that first shot.

The shot that shattered my world. When all we wanted was to turn and run.

I look down at my hands, making sure my IV isn't tangled around my arms. All the blood has been washed away, cleaned by the nurses and doctors and even my mom. I can't help but find it funny that my pink nail polish still looks the same. Through it all, it stayed. Not even a chip.

I can feel him before I see him. His essence floats through the air, shifting the molecules, making room for not only his physical presence, but his spiritual one too. Taking as deep of a breath as I can, I grimace through the pain and wait…

One. Two. Three. Four. Five.

Dad steps into the room. "Hon? You ready?"

Yes. No.

And there *he* is.

The second he crosses the threshold, a calm rushes through my body, overpowering my nerves. Silencing the noise. Strangling it. Tossing it into the dungeon and locking the door.

I remember everything from that night.

Every fucking detail.

It's in my brain, twenty-four-seven. I can't unsee it, and I can't unfeel it. But having him here makes it all better.

He looks different without his firefighter clothes on. Like a normal guy at the beach. Well, not a normal guy. Ridge could never look *'normal'*. His thick, dark brown hair is hidden underneath his ballcap. His facial hair is a little scruffier than I remember. I guess he hasn't shaved in a few days. He's getting close to having a short beard. I like that. Both Dad and Boaz have beards. A pale green T-shirt, advertising a beachside bar, drapes over his muscular frame, drawing attention to his broad chest.

There's no denying he's a man.

He stops in front of my hospital bed and stares at me, soaking me in. Neither of us says anything. For whatever reason, I guess that makes my parents uncomfortable. Like they think we're afraid to talk because they're here, watching us. That's not the case. We're just…connecting. Casting the invisible line between us. Relishing in the fact that we're both still living and breathing.

Together.

Apart.

Wrapping her hand around Dad's arm, Momma tugs him toward the door. "We'll just give y'all a few minutes. We'll go for a quick walk and get some fresh air. Okay, honey?"

I don't answer her.

Why? Because I need to talk to Ridge first. But I don't know how to start. There's too much to say.

A whole lifetime of things to say. To disclose. To reveal.

Slowly, he walks closer to my bed, eventually settling into the chair on my left side. Sighing, he drags his hand down his face and taps his chin.

It's then I see it. A blood stain on the top of his shoulder, soiling the green fabric of his shirt. I don't remember him bleeding in the supply room. How could I have missed that? "You didn't tell me you were hurt." My voice is still scratchy from the intubation.

I instantly reach for him, but his reflexes are too fast. His fingers wrap around mine, stopping their wandering journey. "You didn't tell *me* you were hurt," he frets, echoing me. He impatiently works to clear his throat of the intense sentiment that's choking him.

I look at our hands. For some reason, it strikes me as one of the most beautiful things I've ever seen. His rough-hewn, calloused hand wrapped around mine. It's even more beautiful now than it was on Friday night. I notice several small cuts and abrasions on his skin. My thumb finds a healing red scratch and traces it.

"Orah." He softly demands an answer.

My eyes dart up, finding his. "I didn't know. I promise."

He sighs, gently shaking his head. "But I should have known."

It's plain to see he blames himself. I have no idea how he could blame himself for any of this. I'm the one responsible. I'm the one who put me and Tabby in this hospital. I'm the one who put that blood on his shoulder.

Visions of me crawling across the floor come to mind. Tugging and pulling and pleading with Tabby to move. Scrambling to get to my feet so I could run and failing because my ankle wouldn't cooperate. It's a nightmare I'll never be able to forget, never be able to escape.

"Ridge, I was shot and didn't even realize it. There's no way you could've known. Absolutely no way."

His eyes darken, clouding with thought. "But I knew something was hurting you. I could see you were in pain." He takes a deep breath, free and unencumbered, with complete ease. It makes me jealous for when I'll be able to do the same thing again. "I'm trained for this. I didn't do what I should've done with you. No matter what you said, I should've given you an exam. Checked you out." His hand tightens around mine. "I'm so sorry. Please forgive me?"

I can't even speak.

He's a man.

A grown man.

Kind and smart and accomplished.

And he's asking for the forgiveness of a child.

Because that's what I am.

A stupid and spoiled little brat. An imbecile who had no idea that every single decision has a consequence, albeit good or bad.

And if he ever finds out what really happened? Well, he'll hate me. Just like I hate myself.

"There's nothing to forgive. Please," I tug his hand closer to my body, emphasizing my speech, "please never apologize to me again."

"Only if you promise to do the same."

I blink, waiting for him to smile or laugh—because surely, his comment is a joke or something—but the serious expression etched across his face doesn't falter. "What?" I ask.

He clears his throat. "I'm not sure why you blame yourself for this, but you do. For some reason, you wanna apologize to me. I have no idea why. But it's ridiculous, and it has to stop. I don't want your apology, either. Nothing about this is your fault. Nothing."

If he only knew.

True, those boys—those little shits—aren't my fault. I don't know them. And I don't know what made them do what they did. I couldn't have stopped them from their intent to cause destruction and mayhem. But I could've stopped them from hurting Tabby. From hurting me. I'm the one who made us go to the movies. I put us there. And then I'm the one who told them no. And in doing so, got us shot.

He accepts my silence as agreement to his plan for neither of us to say we're sorry.

Smirking, he lazily wobbles his head from side to side, trying to lighten the mood. "So, no apologies. Ever? What if... I say French fries are the most disgusting food known to mankind and start a campaign to have them outlawed?"

My laugh hurts. But it also feels so damn good. "Then, I may reconsider my position on apologies. Most definitely."

He flashes his perfect smile, with his sparkling white teeth and his bitable lips.

Look at him. He's... I mean, well, I feel like Ridge is *everything*.

How am I ever supposed to live without him now?

Anxiety fires in my stomach, making me queasy. Today was the first day they let me have solid food, and the pitiful little biscuit and powdered eggs from this morning aren't doing much in the way of helping. I know I shouldn't ask what I'm about to ask. But I do anyway. "So, does this mean we're going to keep talking?"

The good humor falls from his face. Looking down at our intertwined hands, he clears his throat and pulls away, clamping his own hands together like he's ashamed. Like we were just doing something wrong.

It's devastating.

And deep down, in that second, I know that my feelings for him will never bring me anything but pain.

He stumbles over his words, his tongue clumsy in his mouth. "Wha–what do you mean?"

"I thought you didn't wanna see me. Or talk to me. I thought I may never see you again."

His brow furrows. "Why on earth would you think that?"

I shrug my left shoulder. "It's Wednesday." I look down at the uncomfortably starched hospital blankets and count the lines of blue-striped trim.

One. Two. Three. Four. Five.

When I glance up, he's looking at me, trying to read me with his piercing brown eyes. He gives me a quick nod, knowing there's more to my statement than just me confirming the day of the week.

"I woke up on Sunday. They kept me sedated until then. I know what we went through was terrifying and horrible. In some ways, it doesn't even seem real. It seems like I watched it all happen from outside of my body, you know?" He nods again, giving me the strength to continue. "But when I woke up, I was so alert. It's like I'd been asleep for years, and then all of a sudden, I wasn't tired anymore. And waking up with that tube coming out of my mouth? Not being able to talk or take a breath when I wanted?" My vision blurs. I quickly wipe my eyes, refusing to let any tears stream down my face. "That was so damn scary. A machine was breathing for me, Ridge. An actual machine. It was only a few seconds before my parents and the doctors started talking to me, before they started telling me what all was going on. But for those few seconds? I was scared to death. And the only person I wanted to fight that fear with was you."

His lips crack open.

"I asked about you." I chastise myself, wondering if I shouldn't be admitting such things. Helping me and Tabby on Friday night was a part of his job. I have no right to expect anything more from him. "I asked if you were okay. But nobody knew. I begged my parents to find out. Someone from the governor's office eventually told them you were safe. Safe and sound."

One. Two. Three. Four. Five.

"So, I waited. Waited for you to call or come see me. Which I know sounds completely stupid. For one, I don't even have a phone right now. I have no idea how you would've even called me. And two, I know your obligation to me stopped the minute you dropped me off at the hospital doors. And I should respect that. I know I should. But... I..." Emotion obstructs my battered throat, making it impossible to swallow. "I'm just really glad you're here."

He sucks in a harsh breath, the cryptic noise catching me off guard. And when he exhales, the regret in the air is palpable. The soft murmur of a curse is barely audible. "Orah, I'm so sorry. I did call. Fifteen times. But they wouldn't give me any information on you because of the privacy laws. I wanted to come see you and Tabby sooner, but I couldn't. We were all on-duty until late Saturday after-noon. I didn't even fall asleep until early Sunday morning. I wanted to come up here first thing on Monday, but I was in mandatory de-briefs all day Monday and Tuesday. Today's the first day they've left me alone."

"They?"

He scrubs his hand down his face, yet again, and taps his chin. Twice. I think he always does it twice. "Everyone. Fire department, sheriff's department, FBI, DEA, Homeland Security, State Bureau of Investigation. Hell, I've even had to meet with the governor and people from the White House."

I'm so damn pathetic. And stupid.

Of course, he had to do all of that. I've refused to watch any of the news coverage about it, but I know it's there. And I know it's the only thing anyone is talking about.

"Oh, Ridge, I'm so sorry. I can't believe I've been so selfish. Please forgi—"

He immediately cuts me off with a gentle tone and a soft, jesting smile. "So much for neither one of us ever apologizing, huh?"

I snort, which then makes me yawn. "Yeah, we're a real pair."

His hand creeps across the bed. My heart flutters waiting for him to wrap his fingers around mine again. But that doesn't happen. He stops about an inch away. "Yeah, I guess so."

"You called fifteen times?" My question is distorted by yet an-other yawn. Unfortunately, all of the medication keeps me drowsy.

He cocks an eyebrow. "Did I say fifteen times?"

"You said fifteen times."

"Well, let's just say it was so many times that I started trying to disguise my voice. And if you're very lucky, Orah Smith, one day I may let you hear my drunk pirate imitation."

I smile, fighting my heavy eyelids. Each blink weighs a thousand pounds. "One can always dream."

And that's the last thing I remember before falling into a sleep-fueled fantasy of a firefighter with Tiger Eyes.

Chapter 11

Ridge

I pace back and forth, trying to tame the frustration and helplessness that's been consuming me for the past hour.

Listen, I know this has to happen. It's been six days, and they have to do it before her memory clouds. Before reality and make-believe weave together. Before her truth is jaded by the news reports.

But did it have to be today?

I mean, she's already exhausted. It's been a big day. They removed her urinary catheter, and she went for her first walk. And I missed it. I should've been here to help, but I had my first appointment with the psychiatrist this morning.

All White Sky firefighters are required to attend a minimum of ten mandatory counseling sessions after a traumatic event of this magnitude and be cleared by both the doctor and their respective chief before going back on active duty. Right now, our firehouse is being staffed by volunteers from all over the state. Brothers-in-arms are using their much-needed and hard-earned vacation time to take care of our community. I doubt we'll ever be able to repay them. So, naturally, I want to be cleared for duty as soon as humanly possible.

Because I want to do my job.

It's what I'm trained for. It's what I'm made for.

I just wanna work. And spend my time with Orah.

Well, Orah and Tabby, I mean. Not just Orah. That would be weird, right?

But even after I'm cleared for active duty, I'm still not done with the sessions. I'm one of the select few who's got to keep going for a full six months. I guess that happens when you see people get blown up and shot. When you see your friends mutate from *whole people* to just *pieces of people*. Fucking lucky me.

I shouldn't be so cynical.

And don't get me wrong, I'm not bashing the mental health profession.

It's needed. It's helped countless people.

It's just... I don't wanna talk. I wanna *do*. My way of helping myself is helping others. I need to be back on the job and focused solely on it. That's the only way to help myself, to clear my mind of the horrible images that keep playing on a loop, twenty-four hours a day.

Those images are seared into my soul. For all of eternity. They're waiting on me when I close my eyes. Like a hungry sin eater just hiding in the shadows, waiting for me to give up and curl into a ball so it can devour every vile thought that has ever run rampant in my head. These images wanna consume me; they're starving for me.

And when I blink open? They're still there.

I'm leaning against the window in the waiting room, lost in my thoughts, watching the people in the parking lot below when Ann startles me. "Ridge? They're finally done."

About damn time.

"Who all was it?"

She rubs her tired eyes. "All of them. Just like you said. Five of them crowded around her bed. There was barely enough space for everyone in the room. They even recorded it." She sighs, "But at least there was an attorney there. Someone the state has assigned as a victim's advocate. She seems really nice."

We walk down the hall, passing by Tabby's room. I take a quick look in and see her sleeping. Her interview was today, too, before Orah's. Of course, there wasn't much that Tabby could tell them.

Ann nods in Tabby's direction. "I keep thinking maybe it would've been easier if she didn't remember everything, you know?" She's obviously talking about Orah and not Tabby.

We stop walking, wanting to finish our conversation before we make it to Orah's room.

"She remembers it all? There's no...gaps?"

"No gaps. Not until she collapsed. She remembers the pain." She glances up at me, her eyes glistening. "She remembers reaching for you."

Yeah, I remember that too. And it still guts me.

Unable to think about that, I steer us back to the interview. "You stayed with her, right? During the interview, I mean? I know those guys are just doing their jobs, but sometimes they can come across as a little pushy."

"We both stayed with her. My heart broke ten-thousand times listening to her. I was afraid John couldn't make it. That's his little girl, you know?" Her vocals fall, lowering to a quiet, yet devastated, hum. "Someone tried to kill his baby."

I can't even imagine.

I know I'm young, but I also know that I want kids someday. I can't fathom what these parents are going through. Not just John and Ann, but all of them. Especially the parents whose kids didn't make it out of the theater that night.

"Did she say anything that you didn't already know? Something that she hadn't already told you?"

Her brow crinkles, and she rubs her hand around her neck in nervous habit. "Just one or two things." Her tone is cautious, clipped, and worried.

I decide to not ask about it anymore. Something was obviously said that upset Ann more than she already was.

"John's with her now?" I ask, nodding to Orah's half-closed door.

"No...he...he needed some fresh air," she stutters in defeat, her reply cracking with heartbreak.

Plastering a forced smile on her face, she takes the last few steps and pushes the door open. "Hon? Ridge is here to see you." She spins back to me, a soft giggle working in tangent with her happy façade. "She was worried that you'd get tired of waiting and leave."

Orah's turned away from us, looking out the window, her beautiful face hidden from me.

"Not me." I walk in the hospital room, taking my place in front of the same chair I sat in yesterday. "I once waited thirty-one hours in line for something."

"In line for what?" Orah asks, not turning her head.

"Ummm." I side-glance at Ann, not necessarily wanting to tell the truth in her presence.

It only takes her a millisecond to sense my hesitation. She's a mom. She understands the stupid shit kids want to hide. "Let me give y'all some peace and quiet for a little bit. I'm gonna find John and see if he wants to grab a bite to eat. We'll bring something back for y'all."

"Oh, I'm fine, ma'am," I decline, hating for her to go to extra trouble for me.

"Nonsense, you're a boy. Boys can always eat."

I take my place in the chair. Orah waits until she hears the soft click of the hospital door before she turns to me. Her eyes are red and swollen, but she's not crying. I can feel what she feels. And My Brave Girl is done crying for the day.

I notice the scab on her forehead has come off, leaving fresh pink skin underneath. I can't help but wonder if it's going to leave a scar.

Like everything else.

"In line for what?" she repeats.

I move to sit back, but quickly think better of it, and instead lean forward, resting my forearms on my legs. "Well, after our high school graduation, my best friend and I convinced our parents that we were mature enough to handle a week-long trip to Miami all on our own. Now, keep in mind, boys mature much slower than girls. I mean, we still thought it was hilarious to shut off all the lights and lock the door to the bathroom when my little brother was taking a shower at night." Her smile is barely perceptible, but at least I see something. "Anyway, there's this super trendy, way-too-damn expensive bar that's on the beach. Each year, they host a Hawaiian Tropic bikini contest."

"You waited in line thirty-one hours to see a bunch of women in bikinis?" Her eyebrow hitches. "You just said the bar was on the beach. Couldn't you just look outside and see hundreds of women in a bikini?"

"I guess I should add that we were also stupid when I said we were immature." I can't stop my chuckle. "I even remember the name on my fake ID. Clifford Clingman."

And for that admission? I'm awarded a full-blown laugh.

And it melts my fucking heart.

"You had a fake ID? Did you get caught? Did you get in trouble?"

"Oh, we got caught," I concede, tongue-in-cheek. "But we didn't get in any trouble. My best friend is a football player and was the top high school recruit in the U.S. When the bartender turned us over to the bouncer, he recognized my friend. He was this huge dude, used to play football himself. He actually felt bad when he found out we waited in line so long; he gave us free beer and took us backstage to meet the...contestants."

"And by *contestants* you mean the bikini models. Covered in tanning oil and doing body shots."

I could be imagining it, but I swear there's a small undertone of jealousy in her voice. It's pretty cute.

I can't fight the smirk crawling across my face. "If I remember correctly, I was a perfect gentleman. Body shots aren't really my style."

She studies me, her smile slowly fading. Her syllables are slow and spaced out. "What is your style, Ridge?"

My breath catches in my chest. I'm mesmerized by the way her gray eyes shine like silver glitter from the rays of sunshine trailing through the blinds. "Definitely not body shots off a pile of strange women, no matter how good-looking they may be. I'm more of a one-woman kind of guy. I find monogamy incredibly..."

And then I want to cut the tongue out of my mouth for nearly saying what I was going to say. Talk about fucking inappropriate.

Saying the word *sexy* to a seventeen-year-old could land a man in jail in some countries.

She frowns, sad I'm not continuing my thought. "Incredibly what?"

"Nice," I blurt, trying to save myself.

She blinks, her face void of emotion. I can feel her soaking in my words, absorbing them, digesting them, wondering what I was really going to say. Eventually, her eyes wander from my face and land on my shirt, reading the name of the beach bar where I bartend part time on my days off. I've got about five hundred of these T-shirts and wear one nearly every single day.

"Take off your shirt," she orders.

My heart stops beating, and I'm fairly certain it falls into my stomach. "Wh—what?"

"You distracted me yesterday. I wanna see your injury. You had blood on your shoulder. Show me what happened."

And just like that, my heart starts beating again, like an engine turning over after a dead battery. "Oh." I shake my head and shrug. "It's nothing." And that's true. It's nothing. Nothing at all compared to what she's been through, what Tabby's been through.

"Can I be the judge of that?"

She looks so innocent, lying there in the hospital bed, staring at me with big doe eyes, with tubes still snaking out from underneath her hospital gown like kite string.

How can I deny her?

I have the exact same feeling I had when I broke protocol and let her use my radio.

For some strange reason, I'm not sure if I'll ever be able to deny Zipporah Smith. I'm not even sure the word 'no' is a part of my vocabulary when it comes to her.

Standing up, I slide my left arm from my T-shirt and lean over her bed. Her gaze lasers into me, burrowing into my flesh with an ardent intensity. It makes me feel funny. Prickly or some shit.

I really hope my boxer briefs aren't peeking out from the top of my cargo shorts. But they usually do. It would be really weird for me to stop what I'm doing and pull on my pants, so I just try to ignore that thought.

She begs me closer with a curl of her finger.

Our eyes meet. It's a little too close for comfort, so I jerk my head and look at the ceiling instead. I have no idea why I feel both comfortable and *un*comfortable around her, all at the same time. I'm guessing it's just because what we went through was intimate on so many levels.

Not *that* kind of intimate, of course. But you know what I mean. We were placed in a situation where we only had each other. There's really nothing more intimate than that.

Despite the insignificance of my injury, she still gasps.

I did have to clean the area today and apply a new dressing. The only waterproof bandage I had was a clear one, so I'm guessing she's gasping at the twenty-five stitches decorating the top of my shoulder like blurry, little black flies trapped underneath cellophane. Her fingers reach for me, but stop short of touching my skin.

"Ridge," she whispers. I can smell her breath, and it smells like mouthwash and not the standard hospital funk. "That's so many stitches."

"Says the girl with staples running across her torso."

Her pink fingernails hover over her lower chest. "You saw? When?"

"No, I didn't see your staples."

"Then, how do you know I have staples?"

"I'm a paramedic, Orah. I know your diaphragm repair couldn't have been done laparoscopically."

She purses her lips, turning over different scenarios in her mind. "And..." The one simple word, drawn over five syllables, is a warning, a declaration for me to come clean.

God, how'd You make such a smart girl?

Tucking my arm back into my shirt, I stand straight and finally tug on the belt loops of my shorts, confirming my fear that my boxer briefs have been showing. "Well, your parents added me to your HIPPA forms. So...I may have had a couple of conversations with your doctor."

She cocks her head to the side. "And..."

I snort on a chuckle. "And the surgeons and the nurses." I hold my breath, waiting to see her reaction. But she doesn't give much away. "Are you mad?"

"Why would I be mad?" Her curiosity is genuine, sincere.

"I don't want you to feel like I'm invading your privacy."

A devious little smile plays at the corner of her mouth. "I'm pretty sure I lost all privacy with you when y'all cut my bra off."

I can't help but laugh at her joke.

A millisecond later, worry crashes through my body like a damn freight train.

What if she thinks I'm some kind of perv?

I'm a total professional. Shit like that doesn't faze me when I'm in the zone. I mean, it would take a really disgusting person to interweave breasts from a medical exam with tits from a sexual encounter.

A fucking sicko.

"Orah, I'm a complete professional. I'm trained. And I take that seriously. You know I would never—"

She cuts me off midsentence, reaching out and slipping her hand into mine. "Relax, Ridge. It was a joke. Don't forget I *saw* you." Her thumb rubs back and forth across one of the many healing cuts I have on my knuckle. "I saw you with Tabby. You're amazing. There's no one else I would have wanted to save me."

Her affirmation soothes my worry, calming me like aloe on a sunburn. "I didn't save you."

"I beg to differ."

I really didn't. She almost died.

Not wanting the back and forth on that, I play it off. "Eh, how do you know I was even there? Maybe someone else worked on you."

"Of course, it was you. I saw your face, Ridge. I saw your face right before I blacked out. I knew you were there for me. I knew I didn't have to worry. I knew you would take care of me, protect me." Her gaze shifts, meandering to our clasped hands. "I knew even if I died, you wouldn't let me go without doing everything you could to save me."

Flames erupt throughout my body, striking a series of matches all the way from my head to my toes.

All I want in life is to one day be the hero that she thinks I am. Be the man who can save her from anything and everything.

Be the man who is *her* everything.

And then I realize what I just thought. And how fucking wrong that is.

Slinking my hand away from hers, I shuffle on my feet, trying to think of something to block those runaway thoughts from my mind and trying not to look at her confused face. Confused and saddened because, once again, I pulled away from her. Away from her touch.

I crane my neck, trying to see to her other side. "How's the drainage today?"

Carefully leaning, she looks down at the collection chamber hooked to the side of the bed. "I can't see it from here." She squirms to get out of bed, but I stop her.

"I'll check it." Making my way around to her right side, I squat down and check her outputs. They're minimal. Which is excellent news, especially given the energy she's exerted today, with walking and being interviewed. "Looks good." I push up from the floor and turn to head back to my seat when her bone-chilling exclamation freezes me in my tracks.

"Ridge! Stop!"

Scared she's hurting, I quickly spin around, scanning my eyes across her torso, looking for the culprit of her sudden pain.

"What's that?" she asks, her head bobbing to look at something behind me.

I glance behind my shoulder. "What's what?"

Frustrated, she reaches for my waist. Grabbing my T-shirt, she tugs me. "That. On your back. What's on your back?"

Shit.

"Oh. It's nothing."

We lock eyes. Again.

Her grip tightens, wringing my shirt in her grasp. Her knuckles brush against my sensitive skin. "Show me." Her command is more of a challenge.

She's challenging me. Wanting to know if I'll brush her off or be honest with her.

Not wanting to disappoint her, I have no choice but to show her the truth.

Feeling my willingness to cooperate, she gives my shirt back to me. Slowly turning around, I pull it up, showing her the black and blue horror of my back. Now that the bruises have really settled into my muscles, even a shower is painful. This morning the normal spatter of water felt like I was being hit by a thousand sledgehammers.

She inhales so deeply it almost sounds like she's choking. "Oh, Ridge. What happened?"

I clear my throat, fighting visions of Battles and Hartselle. "Umm. I was in the hallway when one of the explosives detonated. I was really close to it. It slammed me into the wall. You know, before I made it to the supply room."

I can hear her breathing, waiting for me to continue.

"I'm lucky. The devices were crude. The shrapnel didn't project as far as normal." I lower my shirt, careful not to rub my fingers down the more tender areas.

That notion repeats in my mind.

I'm lucky.

"Like me," she chirps.

"What?"

She nibbles on the bottom of her lip. "They said something must have gone wrong with the gun. I heard them say that my gunshot should've been..."

A *kill shot*.

She doesn't finish her thought, but it's only because she can see that I already know.

"I'm lucky in another way too," she adds.

"What's that?"

"I'm lucky that you came into that room. That you found us." She softly exhales. "That you found me."

I stare at her.

My Brave Girl.

With her battered and broken body hidden by the hospital gown. With her raven hair framing her face. With bronzed freckles dotting the bridge of her nose. And with storm-cloud eyes watching my every move.

And I think it's pretty clear to see.

I'm the lucky one.

Chapter 12

Orah

I drag a French fry through the mixture of ketchup and mayonnaise, smiling to myself as I chomp on it, so very happy Momma stayed true to her word and brought back some food for everyone.

Tabby gingerly walked over from her room and the three of us sat around talking and eating while our parents went down to the cafeteria to enjoy their takeout, away from the stench of the alcohol wipes and starched hospital sheets and floor wax.

Seeing as how I am the world's slowest eater, both Tabby and Ridge finished before me. And when Tabby started yawning, Ridge helped her back to her room, cradling her body against his and pushing her IV pole alongside them.

With a smile on his face.

Even though I know his back must be killing him. How could it not? It's the color of an eggplant. An eggplant that rotted two weeks ago, if I'm being truthful.

But despite the bruising, I could still see *everything*.

Every hard line. Every muscle. I could even make out the plump roundness of the top of his butt, because his cargo shorts hang deliciously low on his waist.

And don't even get me started on his stomach and chest.

Not unless you want my heart monitor to explode.

"What are you smiling about?"

His query catches me by surprise, and I wonder if he knows I was thinking about him.

Which, of course, I shouldn't be. I should be ashamed of myself.

Thinking of a cute boy is what landed me in this hospital bed. Although, using the phrase *cute boy* to describe Ridge is like calling a great white shark an ornery fish.

"Hmm?" I ask, trying to feign innocence.

"I said what are you smiling about?" he asks again while perching on the edge of his seat.

I pick up my last fry and wave it at him. "Just savoring my last bite."

He grunts, pushing himself from the chair to gather my trash and throw it away. "Well, savor it, you did. I must admit I've seen caterpillars eat quicker than you."

"Hey! There's nothing wrong with taking time to enjoy your food. Why would I want to rush through something so good? Good things take time. Sometimes, a really, really long time."

He sits back down, cocking his head to the side as he studies me. Sometimes, his stare is so intense, it gives me chill bumps. "I've never thought of it that way. Good point."

Suddenly, a nagging feeling gnaws at me, irritating me like that sensation that you've left home with a candle burning or with the garage door wide open. "How did you know I liked French fries?"

His brow wrinkles in question.

"Yesterday. You teased about saying French fries were the most disgusting food and trying to outlaw them. How did you know French fries are my favorite?"

His Tiger Eyes dart around, looking for something to latch onto. He shrugs, "Everybody loves French fries."

And once again, I can feel what he feels. Not only is he lying, but he's embarrassed. And something else is there too...

Sympathy? Pity?

"Ridge." I sound like a mother scolding her child.

His hand travels the familiar path down his face. One. Two. His sigh is heavy and unsure. "I looked at your social media."

Oh. Holy. Hell.

Shame covers me like a blanket, weighing me down, making me feel inadequate. Of course, it's nothing like the indignity I experienced earlier today. What I put Dad through. But still, that girl? That silly, trivial, fake, bitchy, mean, make-believe girl was a completely different person. My life changed Friday night.

It changed.

And I changed.

"Oh." That's the only word my stupid brain can come up with.

"Orah, I'm sorry for invading your privacy. I just..." He pauses, searching for diplomatic, yet detached, language. Fortunately, he changes course, settling on the simple truth. "I finally got some time to myself late Saturday night. I laid there in bed, trying to fall asleep, and I couldn't. All I could do was think about you and Tabby and my brothers. The brothers I work with, I mean. My co-workers." He looks to see if I'm following along. "I had no idea what happened to you. After I left you here, I was in the dark. I felt so damn helpless. I just... I just felt like I needed to be close to you. I tossed and turned and eventually gave in to temptation. So, I looked you up."

"And what did you think? About my posts? About me?"

I can't believe I just asked that.

I trace my finger around the tape securing my IV to the back of my right hand and wrist.

One. Two. Three. Four. Five.

"Well, they were...I mean, it's...well, you looked beautiful in every single picture."

I'm surprised when his neck reddens a smidge. I'm guessing he's a little self-conscious, that he thinks such a remark is inappropriate.

Because I'm the victim he saved.

Because in his eyes, I'm just a teenager.

But I'm not. That childhood ended in a split second. Actually, it ended quicker than a split second.

I once read that bullets travel faster than the speed of sound. So that's how fast it ended. Faster than the speed of sound.

And that knowledge breaks my heart.

Trying to ease his discomfort, I smile and reach for him, grateful when he takes my left hand in his. "And what did you really think?" I ask.

He presses his lips together. The movement makes his jaw flex. "I meant what I said," he affirms, gifting me with his humble adoration.

Now, it's my turn to blush. I can feel the heat shading my cheeks pink. "Thank you. But I'm not talking about my looks; I'm talking about everything else. About my content."

For a moment, he doesn't say anything, so I give his hand a soft squeeze, urging him to be open, to be forthright.

His sigh is heavy. "Well, are you talking about your content before Friday night? Or are you talking about some of the horrific comments that happened since then?"

The words come out of my mouth without me filtering them. "What if they're one in the same."

His frown makes him look so much younger. Like a little boy who just got told his birthday party was canceled. "One in the same?" he asks in disbelief. "How can you say that? *She must've done something to deserve it'*—you think someone making that shitty and gruesome comment is the same as you posting pictures in a skimpy dress in front of a line of guys who all pretend like they're crawling to you? On what planet is that the same?"

I nibble on my lip, wondering who said that. Really, I guess the possibilities are endless. Everyone loves to love you when you're on top of the world. But when you fall? Well, those very same people are the first ones to jump on your back and stomp your face in the dirt.

But didn't I do the same thing to people?

Didn't I try to ride the coattails of others' misfortunes to make myself feel better about myself? To make myself feel more powerful?

Wasn't that what Friday night was about?

Taking power away from those who thought they wielded it over me and forcing myself to be in control? They all thought I was something I wasn't, so why not empower myself to be whoever-the-hell I wanted. I made the decision to do it. I wanted to be in control of the when, the where, and the how.

The *who*...

Yet by making that decision, I turned myself into the very 'thing' they claimed I was. I wasn't giving myself any authority *over them*; I was submitting *to them*. In all honesty, I caved into the pressure and served myself to them on a fucking silver platter.

And I hate myself for it.

More importantly, Tabby should hate me.

But she doesn't.

And Dad said he didn't hate me. Momma said she didn't hate me. Even Mr. Emmett and Mrs. Laurie said they didn't hate me.

But Ridge? Once he knows the truth, how could he not hate me?

Between my blurry tears and hiccupped sobs during the interview, I saw the way those investigators and police and government people looked at one another today. Despite their empathy for my injuries—regardless of their compassion for the trauma I endured—there's still a small part of them that's disgusted by my actions. Hidden behind their stoic faces was a snake of disapproval, slithering around, weaving thoughts of repulsion into the crevices of their brains.

And the worst part, they said there will most likely be state and federal congressional inquiry hearings on the events at the movie theater. And some, if not all, of my truths may be forced into the light of day. They promised, though, that parts of my testimony could be sealed. They said no one would know, save for the small group who might be present when the time comes. And they said my identity would be withheld from the public record since I was a minor at the time of the attack.

Who the hell do they think they're kidding. Secrets can't stay secret in this day and time. And my identity is already public, just like Tabby's. It took what? Only three hours from when the first shot rang out before comments pinpointing me as a victim hit my accounts.

When I woke up in the hospital, social media was the furthest thing from my mind. Which, I think, shocked my parents. Normally, the phone is glued to my palm. I even pee with it in one hand. But I didn't even wanna think about it. I already had too much to think about. My physical pain. My concern for Tabby. My worry for Ridge.

My shame. My self-hate. My regret.

Plus, my phone wasn't even here. It was laying in the blown-to-smithereens corridor of the movie theater. Both of our phones were. Just like normal teenagers, Tabby and I had our cell phones in our hands that night.

Before I fell. Before she came back for me. Before I told them no. Before bullets ripped through our bodies.

And trust me, as I crawled and twisted and pulled and stumbled with Tabby in my arms, picking up our discarded cell phones was not at the top of my priority list.

So when Dad asked for the usernames and passwords for all of my accounts on Sunday afternoon, after I woke, I instantly knew things were bad.

Turns out, I don't really have ninety-eight-thousand *friends* after all.

I refused to give him the information until he showed me what was happening. After just a couple of minutes of scrolling, I mumbled my details, and he deleted and deactivated every account.

Supposedly, a local cell phone company is donating some huge pile of new smartphones and accessories to all those affected by this... this, well, you know. I think they're dropping them by the hospital tomorrow. From what I understand, even those who didn't lose their cell phones at the movie theater are having to turn them over as evidence.

So, hey, my best friend may be missing her uterus, but it's all okay, because she's gonna be rocking the newest generation device.

Yeah, note my fucking sarcasm.

I'm shocked, and wrenched from my deep thoughts, when I feel Ridge's fingers trail down the side of my face. It sends a spark of life directly into my heart and even makes the back of my throat tickle. "Where are you?" he asks.

"Huh?"

His face clouds with concern. "Wherever you went, you don't have to go there again."

I can't stop the disenchanted snort that rumbles from my lips. "Don't I? We both know that's a lie. I'll have to go there, over and over and over. How many times in my life will I have to go there, Ridge? A hundred? A thousand? A million? Because this world won't ever let me forget it. They'll force me back there, time and time again. Because to them, I'll always be the 'pretty girl from Insta who nearly got killed in the'..." I allow my sentence to fade, unsure of how to complete it.

What do I call it? A massacre? A mass shooting? An act of domestic terrorism? Hell on earth?

His eyes narrow, and he squeezes my hand a little too hard. I'd almost forgot he still had a possessive hold around me. His warmth and grip are like a comforting second skin.

"You won't be that to me." His whisper is strong yet weak. It fills my heart with both love and heartbreak.

That's the thing, Ridge, I will be that. Once you know the truth.

Chapter 13

Ridge

It's way past dark by the time I pull into the parking lot of my apartment complex. Every time I drive to and from the hospital in Tallahassee, I'm flabbergasted to think about us making the drive in only thirty minutes Friday night. Hopping out and locking the door, I take a step in the direction of the crosswalk that leads across to the beach, before quickly changing my mind and reversing course to my apartment. A walk to clear my head would be nice, but I'm exhausted. And starving. And in all honesty, I don't know if my head will ever be clear again.

So, that may be a lost cause.

I take the stairs two at a time, making my way to my second-story apartment.

"Well, damn. I was thinking about sending a search party out for you, brother. Cullen told me your dad left some chicken casserole and other shit in the fridge. I've been seriously contemplating breaking your door down to get to it."

And there, lounged back in one of the two Adirondack chairs on my front deck, is the football phenom known as Holt Hill. AKA my best friend since... well, forever.

He jumps up and wraps me in a hug. And not one of those half-ass guy hugs either, but a real hug. A hug that makes the air whoosh from my lungs in a loud, exaggerated, and grunted puff. Hugs reserved for brothers, for family. If I were more of a pussy, I'd collapse in a pile of tears right now. Instead, I just burst out laughing.

"What the hell are you doing here?" I have to tilt my head to the side to avoid knocking ballcaps with him. It might've taken me years to catch up, but I've really given the bastard a run for his money. My six-foot-two frame only pales in comparison to his by one measly inch now. And he'd never admit it, but his quarterback body is trained to be a little leaner; so, my bulked-up muscles from running constant drills with a hundred-pound hose while wearing sixty-pound gear has me, for once in my life, with a larger bicep circumference than him.

He gives me one last shoulder slap before pulling away. It hurts like a motherfucker on my tender and bruised skin, but I don't dare tell him that. At least he didn't hit me on the shoulder with stitches.

"I talked to C this morning. He told me that he and your parents were leaving today. I figured you may need some company from this amazing guy," he says, hooking his thumbs back at his smiling face. He gives me the once over, dropping both the smile from his face and the macho pretenses. "Seriously, man, you know I've been wanting to see you. I didn't wanna intrude on your family time, though. Plus, I know you have a one-bedroom, so I figured things were already a tight squeeze with the three of them visiting." He shakes his head and clears his throat, fighting back the same emotion I feel. "Fuck, Ridge. You scared the shit out of me."

Pulling me back into an embrace, we spend the next few minutes hugging and pretending that tears aren't streaming down our faces—even though they are. Because, you know, I don't mind talking to Holt about my feelings, but I try to draw the line at him handing me handkerchiefs.

We finally separate, each looking down at the ground, sniffling our noses and fiddling with the hats on our heads. "C'mon," I urge, "let's raid the fridge."

True to the rumor, my dad filled the fridge and freezer with all of his greatest hits. There's not one available inch of real estate that's not covered in homemade delicacies. I have no idea how I'll eat it all before it goes bad. And I can't stand the thought of tossing anything; my dad is an amazing chef. He's been doing catering on the side for years, and his business has really grown in our hometown. In fact, he and Mom have been talking about him hanging up his hat at the normal eight-to-five and doing his catering full time. I know that's a dream of his, and I hope he can make it a reality. He deserves it.

As we scoop food onto our plates for heating in the microwave, Holt sniffs the air. "Sweetie Dana must've cleaned too," he yammers, referring to Mom's first name. "It smells way better in here than it did Saturday."

"Jackass," I quip back, licking my spoon clean. "I don't smell."

"I didn't say *you* smelled. But this apartment has been known to smell like rancid asshole."

I knock him out of the way so I can use the microwave first. "Says the guy who once had a mushroom growing inside of his football cleat."

"Hey! You know Mrs. Tucker's dog took a big ol' dump in my shoe, and then it rained. That had nothing to do with me."

We both laugh at the memory and spend the next few minutes getting ready to eat, setting places in front of the barstools at my small kitchen island. I'm about to swallow my first forkful when his previous statement actually registers with me. "Wait. What do you mean it smells better than Saturday. You were here? On Saturday?"

He toys with his paper napkin, tugging it left and right. Giving a deep sigh, he tosses me a look. "I tried to get to you, brother."

"What?" I'm glad my question is only one syllable, because that one syllable has a hard enough time being heard. Because it's choked and strangled, not wanting to leave my mouth.

"As soon as I saw the news, I jumped in the truck. I knew I could get here hours before anyone else." He shakes his head back and forth. "I had to get to you. I had to know what happened, if you were okay." He shoves his palms into his eyes, like he's physically trying to press the memories out of his skull. "I couldn't let your parents get here and fucking find out you..." His voice fades with the horror of his own thoughts. Growling, he slams a fist down on the countertop, making our plates bounce. "The fucking thought that something might've happened to you and that some stranger would look Jeff and Dana and Cullen in the faces and just blurt out this disgusting thing..." He stabs his fingers through his hair. "You wouldn't have wanted that. I *know you*, and you wouldn't have wanted it. There's no way I would fucking allow it."

And there you have it.

My best friend was worried I was dead. And he couldn't live with himself if some stranger told my family I was gone. In some sterile room. In some sterile meeting. Fueled by sterile words, where they offered condolences for a couple of minutes before moving on to the next family whose hearts they would have to destroy.

If my parents were gonna lose a son, if Cullen was gonna lose a brother, my best friend was ready to bear the responsibility and be the one who broke their hearts. He was ready to take their moments of hate and sadness and rage and shoulder that burden himself.

He picks up his fork and stabs around at his food. "They had the roads blocked, though. The interstate part was clear, but once I got off on the exit, I could only drive for about fifteen miles before they had everyone taking detours. I told the police who I was, what I was doing, that I was looking for you. But they wouldn't let me pass because I wasn't family. A couple of them finally recognized who I was." He shrugs. "I reckon they're football fans. They got through to some people on the radio, and they told me that you had just come out of a hostage situation, but that you were still working the scene."

I think I need something more to drink than this bottled water.

Getting up, I grab us both a beer from the fridge. Tossing the caps in the trash, I slide a cold bottle in front of Holt, and he guzzles half of it in one swallow.

He nods, nonverbally thanking me before continuing. "I drove back up to the exit, looped around, and waited for your parents at a gas station. Dana hopped in with me and C stayed with your dad. We drove back to the roadblock, and once your parents submitted the proper identification, we were allowed to drive here and wait for you. We had a police escort, though. We weren't allowed to drive anywhere close to the theater or the fire station. We had to come straight here and promise not to leave."

"But you weren't here? When I finally got home on Saturday you weren't here?"

He gives a carefree little snort. "Nah. Like I said, didn't wanna intrude on family time."

But he *is* my family.

Of course, I don't say that. I don't have to. He already knows.

"Plus, I had to get back to Ella." He smirks around a mouthful of food. "She wasn't exactly happy with how I left her."

"And how did you leave her?"

Holt's cousin Ella, who is basically my family, too, is currently attending the same college as Holt. She's in the first year of her graduate program, something or other with forensics.

He pops a shoulder in the air like it's no big deal. "I might've pulled her out of my truck—kicking and screaming—and then called the offensive line to go sit on her apartment to make sure she didn't sneak out."

Okay, that's terrible.

And actually kinda funny.

"Holy hell, I bet she didn't like that," I cackle.

Holt answers with a dramatic eye roll. "You got that right." His good humor fades, and he hits me with facts I already know. "There's no way I was gonna let her come with me. Not knowing what I may find? No, not happening. That girl has been through enough heartache. I'll be damned if I willingly put her through more pain than necessary."

"And what about now?" I turn my head to the door, like I'm expecting her to bust through at any second.

Because, knowing the 'real' Ella, she may.

He tangles a hand through his hair, and a low growl rumbles deep in his chest. "The fuckwad had some kind of law school event he wanted her to go to."

Fuckwad being Ella's douche husband.

I dip my head in agreement. "You did the right thing. She didn't need to see me like that." I work my shoulders, grimacing through the pain of my stitches pulling against my skin. "Like this..."

We both still for a moment, before turning our attention back to our food. We're nearly done with the meal before I speak again. "How long are you staying?"

"Through the weekend. Then I gotta drive back home to get ready for the draft. It starts next Thursday."

"You're still going there for it? To Nashville?" Nashville is this year's host city for the draft.

"Yeah. Mom, Dad, Raylee, and I will drive up there." He huffs, "I'd love to just stay home for it, but you know I won't allow cameras in my house." He wafts a hand around, "I don't understand why they need to film my reaction anyway. Whether or not Mom cries has nothing to do with my play on the field. And it's not like my on-camera-smile count has shit to do with me throwing or running the ball." He glances at me and stabs the air between us with his finger. "And just let one of those snide-ass commentators make some remark about how hot Raylee is. I'll beat his ass and get myself thrown out of the NFL before I even sign on the dotted line." He furrows his brow, realizing he just made a roundabout admission about his own sister being hot. "After I throw up, of course."

Oh, please. Who does he think he's kidding. Holt treats both Raylee and Ella like princesses.

Hell, we all do. They deserve it.

Well, minus the offensive line kidnapping, of course.

I take a swig of my beer. "That's just the way it is. You better buckle up, brother, because you're about to have a whole lifetime in the limelight." Everyone's predicting that he'll be a first-round pick, with one of the highest compensation packages ever offered.

He frowns, picking at his mac and cheese with his fork. When he doesn't comment, I switch gears. "You can be out of school for that long?"

"Yeah. I mean, the professors knew I was leaving on Monday to drive home. I just talked to them and my coaches and got permission to skip today and tomorrow too. Everything that needs to be done, I can do online."

"What did you tell them?" I ask. "To get out of class? What did you say about me?"

He wipes his mouth and leans against the backrest of the barstool. "I told them the truth. That my best friend is a damn hero. That he saved lives during the movie theater attack. That he's injured and hurting and saying he's fine."

"I *am* fine," I protest.

"There's a big difference between being fine and being happy."

Am I happy? I'm happy Orah's alive. I'm happy Tabby's alive. Hell, I'm happy I'm alive. But is that enough to sustain me for the rest of my life? Just being happy that we survived…

When I don't say anything, he nods to my plate. "Finished?"

"Yeah."

Holt grabs our plates, trashes the crumbs, and loads the dishwasher. After grabbing us a fresh beer, he leans back on the kitchen counter, facing me. "Show me your back."

My eyebrows lift into my hairline. "What? Why?"

"C'mon, man, don't play stupid. Cullen told me it looks like an M1 Abrams rolled over you."

I snort. "C plays too many video games. That's a horrible comparison."

He cocks a brow, not amused. Grumbling, I stand from my barstool, turn around, and lift my shirt. I clench my teeth together, locking my jaw, not the least bit excited to hear his reaction.

"What the fuck, Ridge!"

Tugging my shirt down, I snatch my beer off the counter and wander over to the couch. I plop down, not giving him the satisfaction of my pained scowl when the couch fabric feels like it's shredding my back into confetti. "It's fine. It'll heal."

"Well, hell yeah, I know it'll heal, but you let me pound your back out there like I was trying to flatten out a chicken cutlet," he grunts, flopping a hand in the direction of my balcony.

I toss him a look of confusion. "When have you ever pounded a chicken cutlet?"

He pouts, trying to defend himself. "I've cooked before."

I pin him with a stare.

"Stop changing the subject, you idiot." Grabbing his own beer, he takes a seat in the recliner caddy-corner to me. "What the hell happened to your back and shoulder?"

"I was really close to the first explosive. It blew me into the wall."

"That's the blast that killed your buddy?"

I guess he and C *have* been talking. "Yeah."

"And then the shooting started?"

I nod.

Instead of immediately jumping in and asking another question, Holt gives me time to marinate in my thoughts, soak in them, slather them in my soul and decide what I feel comfortable sharing. But I guess I need to get more comfortable sharing everything with those I love. I mean, I recited all of the gory details for the authorities, but I put up an invisible wall during that. I shielded myself from experiencing any feelings with the words that flowed from my mouth. I was a complete professional, forcing myself to recount the details of Friday night and Saturday morning as if it were an everyday, run-of-the-mill call. And anytime my subconscious started to absorb what was being said, started to play the visions of the night back to me like a movie, I just took a deep breath, scrubbed my face, and tapped my chin.

One. Two.

I can't do that with my family. If I do, I may change the trajectory of my relationship with them forever. And I don't want that.

I wanna grow old with a wife by my side, surrounded by my entire family.

And Holt may be my best friend, but let's face it, like I said, he's family.

"It looked different. I've seen a lot of bad stuff as a paramedic and firefighter. People with horrific wounds. Blood and guts and tissue and bones. Death."

I take another drink of my beer, letting the coolness drench my throat. "But Friday night was completely different. Nothing could've prepared me for it. For seeing my friend just...disintegrate before my eyes." I cast a glance in his direction, gauging how much verity my friend can handle. "One of his legs nearly blew off, Holt. His intestines were falling out of his abdominal cavity, and half his face was burned beyond recognition. I know the police said the explosives were crude and didn't detonate properly and didn't cause the amount of damage those fuckers wanted." I shrug, "I guess that's why I'm still here." I twist the beer bottle between my fingers. "But it sure as shit seemed like a lot of damage to me, to all the people who died. And then, there was that one brief second when I was lying on the floor, slammed up against the wall, trying to figure out if I was even alive or dead, that Hartselle and I locked eyes. He was still standing up, on the other side of Battles. He wasn't unscathed. It looked like the shrapnel got half his ear. But I'll never forget the look in his eyes right before they shot him. That one second is frozen in time, suspended and dangling in front of me like a window I'm forced to stare out of. Twenty-four hours a day." I sigh so deeply my chest hurts. "And then, they shot him in the head, and his brain matter blasted on the wall, mixing with Battles's blood."

"How many people died? How many of your brothers?"

"You know how many died. You've seen the news."

"I know, but I want you to say it." His command is quiet and firm.

I put the bottle down on the table because, for some stupid reason, my hand starts shaking, bouncing up and down, like I'm shivering in a snowstorm. "Twenty. Not counting the...perpetrators. Five of those were first responders. Three were firefighters—Battles, Hartselle, and Reynolds—my brothers. Reynolds was on the team entering from the other side of the hallway.

"A patrol car drove up right when they were starting to make entry. Two cops entered with that team. Other 911 calls were starting to come in about shots fired. So they made entry with Reynolds and the others. The officers tried to get them to stay back. Protocol is an active shooter takes precedence over fire, you know? The cops just wanted to make sure the scene was safe and secure. They didn't want anyone to be in danger."

I bite on my bottom lip, thinking about the bravery of my friends. "Apparently, the fire alarm that was pulled was on that side of the building, just about ten feet inside from the door. We have computer systems that tell us that kind of thing. So, Chief was about to radio to order me not to go any farther. They were gonna go in just enough to work on the alarm while the police did their thing."

"So the other two first responders who died were the two officers?"

I nod, looking down at my hand and stretching my fingers, trying to stave off the shaking. One of those officers just had a kid. Like three weeks ago. But I can't bring myself to say that out loud, though. "And there are eighteen injury casualties. I'm not even counting the injuries like mine, anyone who got fixed up at the hospital or triage tent within a couple of hours. I'm talking about serious injuries, life-threatening injuries."

The kind of injury that Orah is dealing with right now.

Orah and Tabby.

"You wanna tell me what happened in that room? What happened with her?"

"Her?" My voice hitches with my questioned response. "There were two of them in that room with me."

He gives me a small nod. I guess that's his way of acknowledging his mistake.

"Orah and Tabby."

"And they were here on Spring Break?" he asks.

"Yeah. Some shitty Spring Break, huh?" I don't really feel like smiling, but I give a quick one anyway, trying to diffuse some of the unusual tension that's recently flooded the room. "I don't know what you want me to say. I did what I was trained to do. I stabilized Tabby the best I could with the supplies I had. And then I prayed."

"And what about the other girl? Orah?"

I hang my head in shame, internally beating myself for the five-hundredth time this week. My spirit is even more bruised than my back. "I messed up with her." I drag my hand down my face and tap my chin. One. Two. "Bad."

"How do you mean?"

"I should've checked her for injuries. I should've triaged her better. I took for granted her only injury was a sprained ankle." I shake my head vigorously, mentally picturing my brain sliding from one side of my skull to the other. "I'm a freakin' failure. I allowed myself to get distracted. And those distractions nearly killed her."

"You weren't distracted. There's no damn way. I know...because I've seen you work. You're focused and driven and made for this, Ridge. And even on the one-in-a-million chance you were distracted, that's not what nearly took her life." He waits for me to look at him before he continues. "It was those assholes, those bastards, who decided to go to Hell and slaughter innocent people on their way there. They're the ones who nearly killed Orah."

We sit for a long time. The only noise filling the room is the clock on the wall, giving a soft tick to pass the seconds.

"How old is this girl?" My head snaps up, and I hit him with a gaze. He corrects himself, without me having to ask him to do it. "I mean, how old are *they*?"

I pick up my beer from the coffee table and down the rest of it in one gulp. "Seventeen." I'm not sure why answering that question makes me so damn uncomfortable, but it does.

He leans his head back on the recliner cushion and studies the ceiling. "Man, so young. And now, they've gotta spend the rest of their lives fighting this physical, emotional, and mental trauma." He exhales, the sound thrumming like a whistling insect. "That's devastating."

"She's strong enough to fight this. I know she is." His head starts to lift, and I realize I'm a fucking moron. I correct myself before he can ask me to do it. "I mean, *they're* both strong enough to fight this. They've got each other."

And now they've got me.

Ridge

Ilean against the doorway, smiling when she gives a little giggle at the TV. Then, she grimaces and attempts to look down at her stomach, trying to shift her stiff blankets and hospital wires out of the way. I push from the shadows of the hallway, ready to ask if she's okay when I'm interrupted.

The bathroom door, tucked in the corner of her hospital room, on the side opposite from me, drifts open and a guy wanders out, wiping his wet hands on his jeans. "What'd I miss?" he asks.

What the hell?

Who is this dude?

Being a firefighter and a paramedic has gifted me with quick mental reflexes. Disregarding the horrific events of Friday night, I'm normally fairly quick in my assessment of people, places, and things. You gotta be in my line of work.

So, what do I see? What's my assessment?

Well, the guy looks a little too damn comfortable for my taste. Meaning, he seems to be a little *too* familiar with Orah, if you catch my drift. His walk is lazy and loose. And let's not even talk about the fact that once he makes it back to her side, he drops his hand to the bed, fondling her lower leg, giving her shin a playful squeeze over the covers.

She sure as hell hasn't mentioned having a current boyfriend over the past two days we've spent together.

Wait.

Have I lost my fucking mind?

Apparently, I have.

A psychotic break can be the only *reasonable* explanation for why I care about any of those things.

She's just a friend. I shouldn't care about her having some boyfriend. Unless, of course, he's an asshole who's mean to her or abuses her.

She's just a teen. A young adult. I shouldn't care about some dude rubbing her leg. Unless, of course, he's a perv touching her without her consent.

She's just my victim

Wait. Scratch that.

My Brave Girl is no one's victim. She's a survivor. A champion. A hero.

I bite my lip so hard I wouldn't be surprised if I taste blood, chastising myself for just thinking the same thing that's rumbled through my brain a thousand times since Friday night.

Technically, I guess the essence of my thought is innocent enough, given what we went through together. But when coupled with these obviously unhinged and unwarranted feelings of jealousy, it turns the innocuous mantra into something noxious.

My stomach turns with that realization, bringing everything into focus, shifting me into twenty-twenty vision.

She's not *My* Brave Girl; she's just *a* brave girl.

I try to force those modified words into the nooks and crannies of my brain. I imagine them dripping through my skull like a thick molasses. Coating my cells in a truth honey.

A brave girl.

A brave girl.

Not My Brave Girl.

A brave girl.

So can somebody please tell me why thinking that one little word 'a' feels so fucking wrong. Why it feels like a lie, a falsehood. Why I feel like I'm committing psychological perjury by changing out that one simple, damn word.

I need a lobotomy.

Stat.

"Oh, hey, man. Can we help you?"

The guy acknowledges me, dragging me from my internal torment. I'm left surprised and embarrassed, because who knows what kind of dumbass vacant stare I have on my face.

Orah's storm-cloud eyes widen, and a fresh, new smile breaks out, flaming her gorgeous features in happiness. Even just hours from last seeing her, I can tell the healing pink cut on her forehead has faded even more.

She definitely won't scar if she treats it correctly. I make a mental note—in my freakin' sick-as-fuck head—to bring her some of my cream from home. I've got a silicone gel and emu oil mixture that works wonders. The key is using one hundred percent pure emu oil. And this isn't some trick I learned in Fire College or paramedic training; this comes from Gran. So, you know that shit is good.

"Ridge." Orah's greeting is happy and light.

The guy darts his eyes back and forth between the two of us. "This is him?" he asks Orah. "This is the guy?"

Her cheeks pink, and she gives a small, quick nod.

He rounds her hospital bed and walks across the room, holding his hands in front of him like he's gonna... hug me?

Is this strange dude seriously gonna hug me?

Uhhh. Hard pass.

Call me a prick, but wrapping my arms around Orah's boyfriend and caressing his back isn't my idea of a good time.

I nimbly sidestep him, hitting his stomach in the process with the blanket folded in my left hand. For a second, he's dazed, confused by my sudden movement. I use the opportunity to morph the almost-hug into a handshake. "Hey, man," I fume, surprised at the deep raspiness and evident hostility in my tone.

The guy, with brown hair and a short brown beard, drops his gaze to my hand before recovering and quickly shaking it. "Oh, hi."

A beard.

And it's not some pitiful attempt at one either; it's a full-on, manicured lumberjack beard. So, unless we're dealing with a seventeen-year-old with a pituitary problem, this boy is a *man*.

Isn't he a little old for Orah? What the hell are John and Ann thinking letting her date a guy with this much testosterone.

In flustered shame, I rake my right hand down my own face, scratching my scruff that hasn't been trimmed since before the events of last Friday night.

Orah's laugh is loud and boisterous. And although it's music to my ears, because I haven't heard her laugh this loud since we've known each other, it's also concerning because it has her saying 'ouch' and looking down at her stomach again.

Ignoring the guy in front of me, I toss the blanket in my standard chair and hover over her, scanning up and down her body. The need for knowledge overwhelms my need to be polite. I grab the edge of the scratchy hospital sheet and tug it down, holding my breath, praying I don't see anything unusual—blood or fluids—seeping through the fabric of her hospital gown. A calming euphoria rushes through me when I see nothing but the sickly teal color with little blue polka dots. "Why do you keep saying 'ow'?" I ask her.

She lifts an eyebrow, fighting a smirk. "Because my body is fusing together with a cow. It's not exactly comfortable. I'm counting down the seconds until I start mooing."

I roll my eyes. "And now, she thinks she's a comedian." I walk to the other side of the bed, wanting to check her drainage outputs and chest tube site. Satisfied with what I see, I add to her humor-attempted editorialization. "And it's not like you have a T-bone floating around inside of you. It's biologic bovine mesh. It's only made from the pericardium of the cow. It's durable. Your body will absorb it as new collagen and blood vessels grow. Plus, it's less likely to get infected or cause a herniation."

"And what if I told you that I was a little sad eating my cheeseburger yesterday? Like maybe I was going cannibal on my cousin or something?" she jokes.

I snort. "I'd have to call bullshit on that."

A half-chuckle startles me, reminding me that we have an audience.

An audience I'm not too thrilled about.

She holds her hand out, and the guy immediately rushes to her, wrapping his fingers with hers. She smiles at him like he hung the damn moon and stars.

I can't help the frown that tugs down on my mouth. Do John and Ann know just how touchy-feely this guy is with Orah? Maybe I should say something. I mean, she needs to be focused on her healing. Not on making googly-eyes with some ancient bastard.

"Ridge, I'd like you to meet my big brother, Boaz."

I'm pretty sure my poker face is gone.

"Boaz?"

She nods, "I mentioned him before. Remember?"

Well, hell yes, I remember. "Boaz?" I mumble again. I can't believe the thought didn't cross my mind. In the span of a nanosecond, I replay all of the events since I came into the room, and I realize I'm a total imbecile. He wasn't fondling her leg; he was pinching it in a friendly, slightly rough-housing kind of way. My eyes flash to the side of the bed, where they've already dropped hands. Like most brothers and sisters, they may be okay with a quick hand-hold, but anything past the point of a few seconds has them bored, sweaty, and ready to withdraw.

"Yeeeaah?" he drones, drawing the word out.

It takes me a moment to realize he's actually responding to me.

I fumble around, trying to recover. I'm fairly certain I'm not successful, and instead belong on a blooper reel. "It's nice to meet you. I'm sorry about before." All I can do is shrug and nod my head toward the door, marking the location where I botched our proper introduction.

He lifts a shoulder in indifference, giving me grace, pretending he doesn't know what I'm talking about.

Orah's not so forgiving though. "Yeah, you were acting weird when you came in." Her smile fades, and she studies me. "Is everything okay?"

Is everything okay? I was basically ready to tear her brother a new asshole, when I have absolutely no right to do so. All assholes need to remain intact and free from tearing.

I'm not allowed to be jealous over her relationship with anyone. Let alone her relationship with a boy. A girl like her should have a boyfriend. A boyfriend who holds her hand and touches her leg. She's young and vibrant and has her whole life ahead of her now. She deserves to be happy and carefree.

I need to get my warped feelings under control. I need to wrangle them and strangle them and hide them away before the world calls me out for being in the wrong.

Because I *am* wrong.

Being possessive of Orah is not one of my inalienable rights.

"Everything is fine," I spout, finally acknowledging her question. I turn to Boaz, taking the time to recognize some of John's features on his face. "When did you get in?"

"I finally made it late last night. My flight landed about eight." He chuckles. "It's not been an easy week. Living in the middle of nowhere is not conducive to emergency travel plans."

"Middle of nowhere?"

Orah cocks her head. Her raven hair is tied up in a loose ponytail. "Literally. There's not even cell service."

Boaz nods, his face growing serious. "There's a satellite phone number reserved for emergencies. When I heard my name being called over the handheld CB, my heart dropped into my stomach. All the operator told me was that I needed to video call my dad immediately." I must give a questioning look because he clarifies, "No cell service, but we have satellite Internet. Email and web calls are the easiest form of communication."

"Where do you live?"

"Well, technically, I'm stationed out of Fairbanks, but I spend most of my time in Deadhorse or Coldfoot."

"Fairbanks? Alaska?"

"Yep."

"Man," I click my tongue between my teeth, "that's more than a few miles away from Florida."

He folds his arms across his chest. "You can say that again. And I worried about this little brat," he dips his head to Orah, "the entire trip here."

"And I'm assuming the trip took a while?"

He rocks back on his heels and looks at the ceiling, trying to recall his travels. "A short helicopter ride, an eleven-hour car ride, five connecting flights, with four layovers."

Orah beams up at him. "But I'm worth it, right?"

He gives a dramatic eye roll, trying to make the moment light-hearted.

Latching onto his earlier comment, I ask, "You said you were stationed out of Fairbanks? Are you in the service?"

"No. I'm a geologist with the Bureau of Land Management."

Damn. That sounds fancy. "And what about those other towns? Where are they?"

"Coldfoot is between Fairbanks and Deadhorse. And Deadhorse is four-hundred-ninety-five miles north of Fairbanks."

I try to picture a map in my head. "Well, I may not have aced geography class, but wouldn't four-hundred-ninety-five miles north put you in the Arctic Ocean?"

He laughs in good humor. "Basically, yeah. Within a hair's breadth, for sure."

We're interrupted when Ann peeks around the corner. Despite the tiredness etched into her movements, she smiles. "Oh good, you two met."

"We did," Boaz answers Ann before turning back to me. "But I haven't had the chance to say thank you yet." He clears his throat, suddenly fighting emotion that he wasn't necessarily anticipating. "Thank you so much, Ridge. For saving my baby sister. And Tabby."

I open my mouth to deflect, but he puts his hand in the air stopping me. "I know you were just doing your job, what you're trained for, but that doesn't make it any less heroic, any less meaningful, any less impactful. I mean, you cared for them like they were your own...your own flesh and blood. I'll never be able to repay you for that. Thank you."

Cocking my hands on my waist, I chew on the inside of my cheek, unable to do anything but nod.

Ann rubs her son's arm. "The hotel is ready for you to check in. They got the room ready early. How about a shower and a nap?"

His shoulders roll back, and he lobs his head at the ceiling again, groaning. "Oh, hell, yes. Please."

She rounds the bedframe kissing Orah on the forehead. "Honey, we're gonna help Boaz get settled. If it's alright, Dad and I may rest for a little bit ourselves. Take a quick nap. Is that okay?"

"Of course, Momma."

Ann looks at me, asking my intentions with just my name. "Ridge?"

"Yes, ma'am. I'll be here. I'll keep an eye on everything."

She sighs softly, her eyes bouncing back and forth between me and Orah. I can't help but wonder if she really wants to take a nap, or if she's just looking for an easy way to excuse herself, attempting to give Orah and me time to connect. Well, not just Orah and me. Obviously, I'm talking about Tabby too. It's just she's currently having a sponge bath, so it's not like I can include her at this moment in time. As soon as the nurse came in with the bathing gear, I hightailed it out of her room.

And no one can blame us for wanting to connect. What we shared is powerful. Over the past week, it's felt like I'm a dwindling battery, and the only person who can recharge my current is Orah.

Even talking to Holt last night and this morning left me drained and running on empty. It's like my soul starts to starve the minute I leave her presence, and I need her essence to electrocute me, to shock me back into a positive energy balance, lest my heart stops beating.

"Okay, kids, we'll leave y'all to it." And with a wave, she and Boaz leave the room, softly closing the door behind them.

Orah's voice is sweet and sincere. "Will you charge my battery, please?"

My head snaps to hers. My eardrums rattle, making it hard to concentrate. What did she just say?

Is she feeling me? Again...

She grabs a box from the nightstand on her left side and wobbles the new cell phone in my direction. "This new cell phone? Will you charge my battery, please?"

And once again, I'm the fucking weirdo. Because for a brief second, I thought she might've been talking about her heart.

Chapter 15

Orah

He reaches behind the small side table and plugs the phone into the wall outlet.

"I have a new phone number," I say.

He glances at me before pecking around on the screen to make sure the charging emblem is showing—the little bolt of lightning alerting him to the electric current pulsing through it. "You do?"

"Dad was able to log in to the cell provider app and check my voicemails and text messages." I try to sound nonchalant; but I'm not a very good actress, and my breath is staggered and strained. "There's been some calls. He decided it was best to start fresh with a new number."

His jaw tenses. I stare at him, watching the small muscle twitch. It's hard to see past his facial hair, but I can see it, nonetheless. "What kind of calls?" His tone is low and eerie. He sits down in his usual chair, shifting the big puff of gray cloth to the side.

My curiosity piques. "What is that? A jacket?"

He falls back in the seat, spreading his legs wide and cocking his head. It's a predatory move.

Simple and predatory.

Confident.

It does nothing but confirm that Ridge is a man. Not a boy, but a man.

And it breaks my heart, reminding me that I allowed a *boy* to be the catalyst for the near-death experience of my very best friend in the whole entire world.

He slowly shakes his head. "Nope," he barks, bantering with me. "It's my turn to ask a question."

His familiar phrase causes memories from a week ago to flood my mind. It's only early afternoon now, but in a few short hours, it will officially be the one-week 'anniversary'.

Of course, I can't deny him of his request. And I suppose I'll never be able to deny him anything.

I pin him with a stare. "You know what kind of calls."

He glides his tongue around on the inside of his cheek. "John showed you the texts? He let you listen to the voicemails?"

"No. I told him I wanted to, but he wouldn't let me."

He sighs, deeply, and I can't help but wonder if that hurts. If it aches the sore and tender bruises decorating his back. "Good. You don't need that negativity in your life. Evil comes in all shapes and sizes, Orah. Sometimes, it comes disguised as those we used to call friends. Other times, it's a stranger, hidden beneath a mask. All you can see is Mother Teresa, but really, if you search hard enough, you'll find Freddy Krueger is lurking beneath the plastic. Breathing low and soft, just biding his time until he can slice through your happiness."

He's right. Evil does come in all shapes and sizes. Those killers belonged to someone. They were someone's son, someone's grandson, someone's brother, someone's friend. And they were nearly *my* murderers.

Not wanting to delve into my thoughts regarding immorality, I simply add, "Some were just requests for interviews."

One corner of his mouth tugs upward. "You wanna give interviews?"

Just thinking about giving an interview makes me wanna hyperventilate. And throw my IV pole through the window like a javelin.

It makes me wanna collapse and revolt, all at the same time.

I giggle, trying to urge a smile from him. Because I'm greedy and want the gift of his smile ten-thousand times a day. "I'd rather eat the hospital meatloaf."

As soon as he grins, flashing his straight white teeth under his pink-brown lips, my heart fills with warmth. I soak in the feeling for a moment before circling back to my original question. "What's that?" I ask, pointing a finger to his side. "A jacket?"

Standing up, he grabs the pile of cloth and unfolds it. My hand immediately darts out to touch it. It's a large blanket—soft, furry, and beautiful. A gray faux fur with specks and swirls of white, tan, and black. "It's a blanket," he announces, confirming the obvious. "I figured you were getting tired of cuddling with those scratchy, smelly hospital sheets and covers."

"You bought me a blanket?"

His cheeks pink. Just barely. But since I already have his face memorized, I can see the difference. "Well...I..." His voice falls off. It's so innocent and pure. Light and fumbling. It boomerangs a blush to my own cheeks. "I didn't necessarily think you'd want a blanket that smelled like the store. So, this blanket is from my place."

"Your place?"

"Yeah. My mom, you know? She helped me decorate when I moved into my apartment, and she bought some blankets for the living room and bedroom. I just thought...well, I don't know what I thought."

My throat feels dry and thick. So parched it makes my incisions and staples throb. "You brought me a blanket from your house? A blanket that smells like you?"

His eyes widen, and his brow furrows. He's trapped in thought, drowning in reflection. *I can feel him.* And he feels like he's crossed some invisible line that he wasn't supposed to. He thinks he's jumped a barbed-wire fence that was meant to jail him. He blurts out the next sentences so rapidly that his syllables run together like one long word. "Not just you. I brought Tabby a blanket too. I already gave hers to her. It's the same color, same everything. It's no big deal. I can take it back if you don't want it."

His blustering is cute and unassuming, giving me a glimpse of the Ridge of four years ago, when he was just a teenager, when he was just my age. Before turning into a pillar of strength and confidence. Before turning into My Hero.

I shove the hospital blanket down my waist, leaving me covered in just the thin white sheet. "Help me."

My words and actions knock him out of his disheveled and un-Ridge-like stupor. He yanks the hospital bedding off my body, piling it on the floor by the door. And then? Then, he covers me from head to toe in *him*. In the thick, heavy, beautiful blanket that smells like ocean water and detergent and whatever cologne he wears. I smell it every time he leans close to me. And I remember it from our storage room too. Faint traces of it even carried above the blood and gunpowder that suffocated the air last Friday night.

The smell of my terror and his cologne.

Etched into my brain forever. Carved in blood and ash and shrapnel.

"I love it. Thank you." With bated breath, I utter into existence the one thing I told my parents shouldn't be mentioned today. At all. Not even a peep. "It's the best birthday present I've ever gotten."

His jaw drops, and the black circles of his pupils eat away at his Tiger Eyes. "What? Today's your birthday? Are you serious?"

My lip twitches, fighting between a smirk and a frown. "Well, it is. And it isn't."

His nose scrunches, cloaking his features in confusion. "Huh?"

"Yes, today's my eighteenth birthday." His spine straightens, and his excited eagerness floats through the air. I cut him off before he can shower me with congratulations. "But I'm not acknowledging it. I refuse to. No one's allowed to talk about it."

He grunts in displeasure and props a hand on his waist. The action makes his shirt bunch around his belt, giving me a glimpse of his tight, bronzed skin. "What?"

"I refuse to celebrate my birthday while parents are still burying their children." I swallow, and my throat makes a weird tinkling noise. "I'm not gonna eat cake and open gifts while wives are watching their husband's coffins lower into the ground. I'm not gonna throw a bedside party while husbands are picking up their wife's personal possessions from the morgue."

He drags his hand down his face and taps his chin. One. Two.

The motion calms him, centers him, brings him back in control.

With tension in his shoulders and his jaw clenched, he sits back down, propping his forearms on his knees. "Zipporah Smith, your life is something to be acknowledged. Not ignored. You only turn eighteen once." He wafts his hand toward the window, indicating the great, wide world. "And those people out there, those who are dealing with the unthinkable tragedy of what happened last week, would want you to celebrate."

"You don't know that."

"I do."

"How?"

"Because it's what I would want." The statement rushes from him, like a flurry of snowflakes in a blizzard. Wild and chaotic. Frenzied and unhinged.

Closing his eyes, he inhales, taking a moment to stretch the healing muscles of his shoulders and back. His black eyelashes fan across his cheek, drawing attention to his freckles. The air whooshes from him in one big huff. Blinking, he focuses back on me, giving me his undivided attention. "If something had happened to me, I would want you to celebrate every single second of your life. I would want you to throw the best fucking birthday party this hospital has ever seen. I would want you to take epic vacations. And dress in the funniest Halloween costumes. And go to New York City to see the Rockefeller Christmas Tree. And have Taco Tuesdays and family game nights. I...I would want everything for you."

"But what if I don't deserve everything?"

He bobbles his head back and forth. But even through the movement, I can see the thump of his heartbeat as it pulses in his neck. "There's no world, no galaxy, no eternity in which you don't deserve infinite happiness."

I lower my head. Staring at my new favorite blanket, I watch as a teardrop splatters into the middle of a white swirl. Sniffling, I quickly wipe my eyes, determined to dam the flow of tears before they fully start. My heart rumbles in my chest, making my incisions burn. It feels like someone is rubbing hot sauce across my stitched and stapled wounds. I tighten my core, trying to increase the sizzle of the pain.

I focus on it. On the hurt. On the ache. On the scorch. I use it as my homing beacon. I sink into myself, pushing past the scalding discomfort. I envision myself hollowing a tunnel straight into the depths of my soul with a red-hot branding iron.

And once there, I search.

I search high and low for the answers, for my true feelings.

Do I deserve happiness?

Do I deserve a birthday?

Do I deserve a life when so many others lost theirs?

Sensing my withdrawal, Ridge eases back in the chair and busies himself with checking my phone, making sure the charge percentage is still increasing. "My turn," he says, winding his way back to our game of questions, knowing that I won't refuse to play. Because if I did, it may hurt his feelings. And that's something that I simply cannot fathom.

"Your turn, huh?"

"Yep." He pops the word, lingering on the 'p'. When I give a swift nod, he continues. "I remember you said you were the oldest in your class. Is that right?"

He remembers me saying that. For some reason, it makes me feel both incredibly special and incredibly pathetic. "Yeah."

He puffs his cheeks out like he's blowing a balloon. "How'd that come to be? Did your parents start you in school late?"

"No, Mom and Dad decided to hold me back in kindergarten for another year."

"Why?"

"Because I had missed seventy-two days of instruction time. I was out sick."

He jerks in shock, clapping his hand on the armrest of the chair. "Seventy-two days?!"

For a moment, his lively behavior dissipates the fog of my sadness. His mood is playful and curious. Two things I really like when it comes to Ridge. "Yeah, believe it or not, they thought I might have a brain tumor."

His face immediately blanches, his attempt to lighten the mood instantly derailed. "What? Are you serious?"

I scratch where the IV tape is starting to rub my skin raw. "Yeah. It started with dizzy spells and poor coordination. I'd be playing, or even just walking through the room, and I would lose my balance. Then, I started throwing up. Like all the time, for no clear reason at all. My eyes would get blurry, and my head would hurt. For the first few weeks, the pediatrician went through the normal gamut of illnesses. You know...viruses, inner ear infections, things like that. Then, they worried I had meningitis or epilepsy. When all of that was negative, they started thinking I had a brain tumor. Which completely terrified my parents; there was already a history of cancer in our family." I work my fingers over the soft material of the birthday present that isn't my birthday present. "There was a spot on my MRI. The specialists thought it might be medulloblastoma."

"Holy shit, Orah."

I lift one corner of my mouth, trying to ease his concern for the little girl I used to be. "But it wasn't. The subsequent scans didn't show anything. Absolutely nothing at all. The doctors said the original spot must've been an ar..." I slow, trying to remember what they called it. For some reason, the word 'artwork' always comes to mind.

"Artifact." He fills in my blank with ease, once again confirming just how damn intelligent he is.

I nod. "Yes. An artifact."

"So, what was it then? What was making you sick?"

I shrug, fighting the urge to scowl at my traitorous body. I begrudge the fact that my laughter from earlier has already worked its way into the mending nooks and crannies of my torso, making me sore as shit. Whoever said laughter is the best medicine, obviously didn't have a shredded diaphragm and a collapsed lung.

"We're not sure. The symptoms ended up going away on their own. They disappeared as quickly as they came. My parents never got any answers."

"Really? The doctors couldn't come up with anything?"

"No." I shake my head. "But I was totally fine; it was like it had never even happened."

"And you went back to school after that? After you got better?"

"I did, but I had already missed so much. I guess I could've caught up to my peers, but I remember not wanting to listen to my teacher. I suppose I...went on a learning strike," I profess, with a smirk.

He cocks his head. "Why didn't you wanna listen to your teacher?"

"I was mad at her." My proclamation is basic and raw, but it still hurts my heart today as much as it did the day she said it.

There's not a lot I remember from that time. I mean, I was only five years old. But this event is charred into my memory. And all of these years later, I still cling to it, wondering if her snide comment was just an unfortunate result of her having a bad day, or if she was somehow reading the writing on the wall, turning over tarot cards made just for me.

Ridge scoots closer. He drapes an arm across the edge of the bed. His tone is solemn and serious. "What happened, Orah? Why were you mad at her?"

"It was before I was sick enough for Momma and Dad to keep me home," I explain, giving the backstory. "I had walked up to her desk to show her the drawing I did during free time. When I was standing there, I got really dizzy. When I fell down, I accidentally knocked a vase of flowers off the corner of her desk. She had just gotten them delivered to the classroom that morning. I can't remember if it was her birthday or her anniversary or whatever." I flop a hand, edging it closer to his. "But anyway, when I knocked that off the desk, it broke." I battle with the tightness in my chest. "She told me that I was a walking catastrophe."

I suck my bottom lip between my teeth. "And for whatever reason, that remark really stuck with me."

Thick and viscous. Like rubber cement.

And sometimes I worry, it not only stuck *with* me. But *in* me.

Chapter 16

Orah

Ridge pouts in discontent. "You realize there's nothing about you that's catastrophic, right?"

I lean my head back against the pillow and toss a look out the window, staring into the brightness of the spring sun. Until my eyes burn and my nose tickles. Instead of agreeing or disagreeing with his soothing narrative, I weave our conversation back to the original topic. "The only way to placate my parents was to promise that we could do a belated birthday party sometime." I turn back to him and struggle through a smile. "So, see? The momentous occasion of me 'becoming an adult' won't go unnoticed." I snort. "It'll just be noticed a little later than usual."

His throat works on a large gulp of air. "Well, I'm gonna notice it *now*. When it matters the most. So, happy birthday, Zipporah Smith."

"Why does it matter the most now?"

"Because *now, today, this minute* is the truth. Rarely is the truth in black and white. But this? This is written in stone. There's no denying the calendar. You had seventeen years and fifty-one weeks of living. And one week—seven days—of being my hero. Without you, your best friend would have died. Without you, I don't know if I would've made it out of that theater alive. You're my paragon of bravery."

His hero?

I'm the furthest thing from a hero. I'm a sham. A counterfeit. A phony.

Without a doubt, he'll think differently once he knows the reality of my past.

Flustered in my thoughts, lost in my contrition, I mumble a thank you.

Now content that I'm accepting his compliment instead of dodging it, Ridge dives into another question. "Tell me about Boaz. How old is he? I feel like a douche for not asking about him sooner. I'm sorry."

I can't believe he just called himself a douche for not asking about my family tree... especially after everything he's done, which now includes gifting me with my 'un-birthday' birthday present.

"He's twenty-five. He's a really awesome big brother. Smart and kind and selfless." Tendrils of shame creep through me when I think about how I've treated him over the past few years.

"He been in Alaska long?"

"For the past three years. He went to the University of Alaska Fairbanks for graduate school, to get his master's degree. After graduation, he was immediately hired by the Bureau of Land Management. It's rural and remote and hard. But he loves it." I give a little shrug, failing to hide the melancholy in my tone. "I've never even been to visit him."

Ridge bops forward, resting his forearms on his knees again. The sudden movement must pull on his stitches because he sneaks a peek at his shoulder. "Well, it's not like taking a little day trip. That's a visit you have to commit to, that's for sure. You've been busy with school. I'm sure he understands."

I should probably stop talking. Anything else I say on the matter will cast me in a horrible light, but I can't stop myself from sharing my honest history with Ridge. I guess some stupid part of me wants to start ripping the Band-Aid off now, hoping that will make it easier in the end.

But I know it won't.

Because there's nothing easy about the truth of last Friday night.

And no matter what thorns I use to try and pierce Ridge's skin now, nothing will prepare him for the truth. Because the actuality of Friday night is sharp and jagged, filled with brambles. It will slice through him like a sword, cutting to the bone and changing his anatomy.

Changing *our* anatomy. The structure of our friendship. The framework of our connection.

"He understands that I was a bitch," I spew.

Ridge's jaw slacks open in shock. "Orah..."

"It's true. The past few years I haven't given Boaz this version of me." I look down at my new blanket and trace a swirl of black with my finger. "He had the other version of me. The one that existed before Friday night. The one from the pictures and posts and videos." I wait for Ridge to interrupt me, but he doesn't. "I had opportunities to visit him with my parents, but I didn't go. Because that would've interrupted my life. He would email. Telling me about his job, the people he met, the beautiful landscape of Alaska. Half the time I didn't even open them to read them."

I snake my hand closer to the edge of the bed, testing the waters, wanting to see if Ridge is so disgusted by me that he moves away. For right now, he's still sitting forward. "We'd arrange times to web call, and I would ignore the schedule. Heaven forbid, I missed one second of a football game or a Saturday night out. I needed to post about my adventures for all of my followers." I fade into a whisper, half hoping that he won't even be able to hear me. "I spent hours—*hours*—doing my hair and makeup, every single day. I wanted to look perfect. I wanted every girl to be jealous of me, and I wanted every boy to be infatuated with me. I wanted the boys to dream about me, wish they could be with me."

I'm too nervous to even look at him this time. My eyes flutter around the room, not connecting with anything specific. "I acted better than everyone. I was conceited and spoiled and bratty. I was mean to people."

I tap my finger against the bed.

One. Two. Three. Four. Five.

This time I speak even lower. If the universe can't actually hear the words, maybe they don't exist. Maybe I can cleanse the verity of my past by whispering the words into the wind and letting them float far, far away. Where they can't hurt me. Where they can't hurt Momma and Dad and Boaz. Where they can't hurt Tabby. Where they can't hurt Ridge. "I was mean, Ridge. I was really, really mean."

Finally, his fingers lace with mine, giving me what I've silently been pleading for…his touch. In my eyes, Ridge is superhuman. I need some of his strength to seep into me. Because something tells me that the hardest days are yet to come. That there's worse things in store than healing from the bullet that ripped through my body.

"I'm not gonna say what I should probably say." His blunt jargon catches me off guard.

"And what should you probably say?"

"I reckon a normal person would pacify your concern. Tell you that you weren't being mean, that you were just being a normal teenager."

When he pronounces the word *teenager*, his grip loosens, and I worry he may pull his hand away from mine.

I squeeze harder than I should.

Refusing to let him go.

"But I'm not gonna say that," he continues. "I'm not gonna lie or sugarcoat things. Not for you. You deserve my honesty." He glances up to the TV mounted to the wall, watching as a woman removes a fluffy, chocolate cake from an oven. Then, he rakes his free hand through his hair before locking eyes with mine. "Shit, Orah, for all I know, you were mean. Maybe you were conceited and spoiled and bratty, just like you said. I have no idea *who you were* or *what you were like* before last Friday night. All I have are those pictures I saw. And listen, I'm all for a woman being who she wants to be. If you wanna tell thousands of people you bought a pink bra, more power to you."

Yeah. I did do that.

I posted a picture showcasing the skimpy pink bra and panty set I bought.

It got a crap-ton of likes too.

I purchased the lingerie set after making fun of another girl's dirty bra and baggy granny panties in gym class. Really, I made fun of her to make myself feel better. She has a gorgeous body. Fit and trim and curvy. She has the body of a woman. And my body is still trapped between girlhood and womanhood.

Later, I found out that her family's house was foreclosed on, and they had to move into a motel. She was washing her clothes in a bathtub; that's why the stains weren't coming out of her bra.

A nasty fucking bitch.

That's me.

That *was* me.

This time he does tug his hand away from mine, leaving me broken and sad. "But you were a kid, Zipporah. You were too young to responsibly make those decisions. Decisions that should only be made by a consenting and informed adult." His jaw clenches, and I swear, if I listen hard enough, I can hear the grind of his teeth. "You posted videos of your underwear, and you weren't even old enough to vote yet. Do you know how many perverts troll the Internet looking for pictures of girls like you? Girls who *look* like you? They sit there, staring at your face, staring at your body, and..."

His speech drops off, but he doesn't have to finish his sentence for me to know what was supposed to come next.

His chastising makes me feel about two-inches tall. But, in a strange way, it also makes me feel protected. He's wanting to save me all over again. Save me from myself, save me from my own poor judgment.

A lump forms in my throat, choking me. It's hot and fiery, like I swallowed a piece of flaming charcoal. Tears sting my eyes. I widen them, praying the salty drops stay in my body, begging them not to spill out and flood my face.

"What did your parents say about, well, about your persona? I can't imagine they were happy. Didn't they have discussions with you about this kind of stuff?"

And now, I feel about two-centimeters tall, completely shrank down from the inches of a minute ago.

Karma. Someone said this happened to me because of karma. Maybe they're right.

My lonely hand reaches down and pulls the blanket farther up my body. "They didn't know about the posts like that. Anything that might have gotten me into trouble, I posted on my Instagram or TikTok or Snapchat accounts. My parents only have Facebook. I told them I shared the exact same images and captions across all platforms so there was no reason for them to establish accounts on everything to monitor me." I'm afraid to look at him, afraid of what I may see, so I go back to swirling my finger over the different colors etched into the faux fur. "I monitored my more scandalous accounts and blocked my parents' friends. I blocked Boaz too."

"You lied to them? To your parents? To your brother?"

I don't respond. I just sit here wondering if the ache in my chest is from my injuries. Or from the regret of who I used to be. Or from the worry that Ridge will stand up and leave. How can he even bear to look at me right now?

I was already panicking at the thought of leaving him. Scared to leave this hospital and return home, never to see him again. Just the idea of not being near him makes a small piece of my soul die. And these admissions may have signed my death certificate...while my heart is still technically beating.

Not to mention, he just confirmed he thinks of me as nothing more than a child, a silly teenager. I'm not exactly sure how that makes me feel. But I'm fairly certain the answer is not *fine, good, or okay*.

And if confessions about my temperament and personality are this difficult, I can't even imagine what the future will be like. You know, when I have to tell him the other stuff. The stuff that happened exactly one week ago.

I'm sinking into my thoughts, wading through mental quicksand so thick my brain waves can't even fire, when he catches me by surprise, taking my hand in his again.

"Listen to me, Orah." His voice is strong and firm, unwavering. Just like him. "All I know is that the girl in front of me right now—the girl who shielded her best friend's body with her own—isn't mean or selfish. She isn't conceited, spoiled, or bratty. She's..." He pauses, watching as my unshed tears make their appearance, streaking down my face in hot, thick streams. "She's kind and generous. Brave and fierce. Strong and determined. Loving and engaging." Standing up, he leans over me. Gripping my face, he tenderly wipes my cheeks with the palms of his hands. Calloused and rough, they glide across my hospital-chapped skin. He dries my tears, absorbing the moisture from my body into his own. Absorbing my pain, absorbing my hurt. From my eyes into his hands... he consumes my past, determined to clean the ugly with just his fingertips. Determined to be My Hero, yet again.

"Friday night was your catalyst. The fucking worst catalyst known to mankind. Something I wouldn't wish on my worst enemy, not in a thousand lifetimes. But your catalyst, nonetheless. You're a different woman now, Orah. Nothing will ever be the same again. And you know what? That's okay. Fuck those people who said this happened to you for a reason. Fuck them straight to Hell. But we can't hide from the fact that *it did happen*. It happened to you. To me. To Tabby. To my brothers. To all those other families." Shifting his body upright, grimacing against the pain of his healing back and shoulder, he studies me with tender adoration. "We can't hide from it, but we can survive it. Every single day. Together. We can survive it together. Me and you." He opens his mouth and then closes it, unsure if he should forge forward. His Tiger Eyes glisten, intent on telling me what I already know...Ridge is a precious jewel.

Eventually, he gives in and finishes his thought out loud. "You and I were destined to meet, Zipporah. The universe knew we couldn't fight this battle without one another. Fate knew. God knew." He clears his throat and swivels his face to the side. Is... is Ridge crying? "*I knew*. The second I opened that supply room door, I knew we needed each other to fight this." Giving his eyes a pinch with his thumb and forefinger, he turns back to me, pinning me with his stare. "Remember what you said. We're gonna save each other."

Chapter 17

Ridge

Icheck the speedometer, debating slowing down. I mean, I *am* going fifteen miles over the speed limit. With the crazy drivers I've passed on the road today, that's probably not the smartest move. I don't need to add road rage to my repertoire of survived tragedies. Deciding to split the difference, I adjust my cruise control to just eight miles over the speed limit.

My therapy appointment with Dr. Evans ran long this morning. That's right, I said therapy. She not-so-subtly tore my ass a new one when I forgot my manners two sessions ago and referred to my visit as 'seeing the department shrink'. Obviously, and for good reason, Chief Latner lit into me, too, and now I know to choose my language more carefully. All in all, it's going as well as can be expected. I mean, she basically wants me to describe ad nauseum what I saw and felt and heard and experienced when my friends' bodies were torn apart before my eyes. And I have to talk about Orah and Tabby and what happened in that room. And how I thought they were gonna die. She's asked over and over about what I was thinking when Orah called my name and reached for me. When she reached for me and then fell into a crumpled, broken pile, her body rebelling against survival.

Yeah. I don't like to talk about that with Dr. Evans.

Especially since Dr. Evans is free to discuss certain aspects of our sessions with the Chief. That's how he knew about my 'shrink' comment. Don't get me wrong, I signed the release form, and I understand it's their mutual job and responsibility to determine if I'm mentally prepared to return to the rigors of being a firefighter and paramedic...but...

It kinda chafes my ass is all. I mean, what if they twist what I say?

Sometimes, when I try to talk about Orah and what we went through, my words get jumbled up, and I sound...like a fucking sicko.

I'm not stupid.

I know there are boundaries.

I'm the first responder. She's my patient. I'm well aware of the Florence Nightingale effect and how our emotions can cloud our judgment when we're vulnerable.

I'm older. She's younger. Yes, it's only by a few years, and yes, she's now an adult in the eyes of the law; but she's still a junior in high school. I'm not really itching to get on someone's watchdog list for...well, for being whatever the opposite of a cougar is. I think I heard someone use the phrase 'manther' once.

And yeah, I don't wanna be that.

True, she's gorgeous.

True, she's smart and funny and kind.

True, if we're just talking about the fundamentals of biology, I'm physically attracted to her. But, I mean, that's just science. You know, pheromones and shit.

I wouldn't act on that attraction. Like I said, I know there are boundaries.

Yes, Orah and I hold hands, but I've also held hands with Raylee and Ella before. And, trust me, those women are gorgeous, too, but... ewww, gross. No, thank you. They're like the sisters I never had.

So, I consider hand holding to be well within the brick wall of said boundaries. Nothing will ever—and I mean EVER—happen beyond that.

And yes, I was jealous of Boaz when I thought he was some secret boyfriend. But, come on, I'm a dude. Shit like that is normal. It doesn't mean anything.

From the outside looking in, the power dynamic runs in my direction. I'm the person of influence.

But anyone who knows us can see that Orah is the one in control. What the hell am I saying? I mean, Orah *and* Tabby are the ones in control. Those two little ladies have me wrapped around their fingers.

I hope they're in my life forever.

I can't imagine breathing without them.

So, you can see how some of my words might get misconstrued. I mean, Dr. Evans apparently knows witchery because sometimes I get a little verbal diarrhea in our sessions.

But I'm trusting the system.

Really, I've got no choice but to trust it; I've got six months of it whether I want it or not.

I glance at the clock on the dashboard for the umpteenth time, mentally counting how many hours we may have to hang out before she gets sleepy. Now, that we have an official date for her discharge, I'm eager to soak up as much time with her as I can. The hospital is releasing both her and Tabby this coming Saturday. On Friday, they'll remove Orah's chest tube and stitch up the site. They'll also remove her staples.

And then Saturday?

The girls will load into cars with their families and drive away.

Far away.

Turning into the hospital parking lot, I'm pleased to see there's no reporters milling about the front entrance today. That doesn't mean they won't show up at some point, just to have an on-scene introduction for whatever story may be running tonight, but for now, the coast is clear. Once parked, I toss my phone and wallet into the pockets of my cargo shorts and make my way to the building that I've spent more time in lately than my own apartment.

It's Tuesday. Eleven days after my world shifted on its axis.

Holt's company over the weekend was nice. We had some good chats. He's nervous about the draft and his future, so I tried to be a good friend and pull my head out of my ass long enough to calm his concerns. We both know that worrying about a football draft that's bound to make Holt a millionaire ten times over is small potatoes compared to what I went through, but it was nice to focus on someone else for a change. It was nice to worry about a 'problem' that would have been there regardless of what happened that Friday night.

If that call had been nothing more than a simple false alarm trigger, then Holt's fears would still be in my world today, still in my sphere. I think focusing on that eased some of my own anxiety.

In all honesty, Holt was content to keep his worries to himself, but after a gazillion times of him asking me if I wanted to talk about anything—meaning what happened to me and how I'm processing it—he could see I needed a change of topic. He even chewed me out for taking both of the blankets and leaving him with nothing to cover up with but some beach towels. His bitchin' made me laugh. Which felt damn great after that conversation I had with Orah.

Walking toward the automatic doors, I'm shocked when I see a little sprite of red hair and freckles sitting in a wheelchair and leaning her face into the sun. She's dressed in actual clothes today, a baggy sweatshirt and some sweatpants. I'd be concerned that meant they had moved up her discharge date if not for the IV pole hanging on the vertical wheelchair extension. "Planning to make a break for it?"

Tabby's head falls forward, and she blinks rapidly, adjusting her eyes. "That sounds like one hell of an idea." She nods to the parking lot. "I thought that was you in that Jeep. What do you say, let's take off and drive with the top down?" She forcefully morphs her playful smile into a scowl. "I need some fun. You know my last day of vacation kinda got ruined," she deadpans.

It's true, Tabby's family and Orah were set to leave on that Sunday morning. Thirty-six hours is all they had left. Thirty-six hours and the girls could've left White Sky.

Whole and happy and without bullet holes.

And Tabby with the ability to bear children in the future.

I cock my hands on my hips, pretending I'm giving it serious thought. We both know that's a lie. "Well, I reckon your mom and dad might have a vocal—and not too happy—opinion if I steal you away to go galivanting down the Florida coast. We better stay put; I don't wanna get on Emmett's bad side."

She snorts, "As if. Dad has more of a crush on you than Orah does."

What. The. Hell.

I'm not exactly sure what kind of face I make, but Tabby finds it funny as shit. She laughs uncontrollably, her hands immediately dropping to her lower stomach. Between giggles and gasps of air, she scolds me. "Stop making me laugh. That hurts. Ouch."

This time it's my turn to scowl. Needing something to do, I push her wheelchair under the awning, getting her out of the sun. "I'm not doing anything," I mumble.

Great. Great comeback, Ridge. You're really on top of your game.

Once she has control of herself, she flaps her hand behind her, trying to pat my forearm. "Oh, calm down, I was just kidding. But seriously, dude, you should've seen the look on your face."

I choose to ignore her version of events, and instead, look down the hospital corridor when our nearness makes the automatic doors slide open. "What are you doing out here anyway? Where's your parents?"

"We were out here saying goodbye to my grandparents and Dylan. He's missed enough school, so they're taking him home."

I've met Dylan, Tabby's little brother, several times. He's only seven and a fireball of energy. Right after the shooting, Tabby's grandparents caught a flight from South Carolina, and they've been taking care of him since energized little boys and boring hospitals don't mesh well with one another.

"I told Mom I wanted a few more minutes in the sun," she continues. "She just ran inside to use the restroom and get a bottle of water."

"Well, you wanna escort back inside?" I ask.

"Sure. Let me just text Mom. I'll tell her you're bringing me up." She pulls her new cell phone from the kangaroo pocket of her sweatshirt and pecks around on the screen. I wonder if Tabby had to get a new phone number too. I can only assume she did. Orah gave me her new number, but I've yet to call her.

Satisfied with her communication, she tucks the phone away and jacks her nose up in the air. "Onward, Jeeves."

Taking my position, I push her.

"You know, it's not like I'm bedridden. The first couple of days were rough, but I'm walking good now. I told them I didn't need a wheelchair, but they said no."

"It's hospital policy, Tab. They don't want a patient falling."

She sighs. "I'm so ready to be out of here. I miss home. I miss my bed. After this, I hope I never see another hospital as long as I live."

I hope that for her too. More than she'll ever know.

I nod to some nurses I know through the glass partition dividing the hallway from the emergency department. Stopping in front of the elevator, I hit the button for service.

"My stitches come out on Friday." She smacks her lips together. "Well, some of them. I have stitches on the inside, too, but the doctors said those will dissolve over time."

"They will. And there's always a chance that a rogue one may make its way to the skin's surface in a few weeks or months. Don't let that scare you. Just show your parents. They can watch it for infection."

"When do your stitches come out?" she asks. "Orah told me about your shoulder. How come you didn't tell me?"

I just shrug. "It's no big deal. And they came out today. I took them out myself." The elevator door pops open, and I usher us inside, hitting the button for the fifth floor.

"Really? She said it was a lot of stitches." She lobs her head from one side to the other. "Well, I guess that doesn't matter to you. You're a medical mastermind."

I scoff, leaning back against the side wall. "I'm not a medical mastermind, Tabby. I'm just a firefighter who wanted to torture myself with more training, so I took the extra classes."

There's way more to it than that, obviously.

And truth be told, I was fucking dying to get more training.

Training to hopefully save more lives? To hopefully help more people? Hells yes. Sign me up.

I push off the wall, taking my sentry behind her chair when we hit the fifth floor. The girls are still in one of the ICU bays. But at least this area has actual rooms for privacy and not just partitioned curtains. From what I understand, they were in an open-curtain bay area for the first twenty-four hours after their surgeries.

Tabby looks over her shoulder, glancing back at me. We're passing other patients' rooms and the commons area, so she speaks a little lower, trying not to garner too much attention. "She had a nightmare last night, you know?"

My heart sinks low in my stomach. And like a dumbass, I ask the question I already know the answer to. "Who?"

"Orah, dummy. Who else would I be talking about."

Seriously? And Orah thinks *she* was the mean one...

I ignore her name calling. "What happened?"

"Boaz was there. It was his night to stay with her so Mr. John and Mrs. Ann could get some sleep. Anyway, he said she started breathing really, really heavy. And then, all the machines started beeping. You know, they keep putting those stupid, sticky electrical things on our chest at night when we wanna sleep. They get tangled in everything and piss me off."

"Tab..."

For the love of all that's holy, what the hell happened?

"So, yeah, then, she just started screaming. I even heard her in my room. I couldn't tell what she was hollering. But it took a good minute or two for the screaming to stop. My mom was with me. She went running in there to help." She pops a shoulder in a half-shrug.

"Boaz said she barely slept the rest of the night. I think she finally dozed off this morning after the sun came up."

I was afraid of this. Terrified. Scared shitless, to be more exact.

It doesn't take a genius to see that the shooting altered Orah's brain chemistry. I mean, she's freely admitted to feeling like her whole personality has changed. The foundation of her entire being was lifted up and turned a hundred-and-eighty degrees, like a house shifting during a tornado. I was just praying that PTS wouldn't be a byproduct of the storm.

Wishful thinking, right?

I've caught her counting too. I'm not sure if she even realizes that she moves her lips when she does it.

One. Two. Three. Four. Five.

I noticed it last Wednesday when I was first allowed to see her. And I saw her do it again, on the very next day. And last Friday, after our tough conversation, I asked her family about it. They said she'd never done it before. It's not some lingering quirk or habit from when she was a child. I asked if she'd ever had any repetitive behaviors or unique habits.

Nope. Nothing.

Like I said before, I'm no mental health professional. And trust me, Dr. Evans would be happy to attest to that. But... I'm worried. Orah's counting for no reason, and now she's having nightmares.

When we get closer to Tabby's room, three heads peek out from the doorway—Emmett, Laurie, and Ann.

"You missing something?" I tease, giving Tabby one hard push so that she rolls down the last few feet by herself.

The ladies chuckle. "That we are," Laurie adds.

Emmett pretends to cower, acting as if Tabby is going to run him over. "Haha, Dad. Very funny."

He quickly rights himself, reaching out to shake my hand. "How's it going today, Ridge?"

"All good. Thanks." I stand back, giving everyone space to make their way into Tabby's room. "Tab said your parents just left with Dylan."

"Yeah. He's already missed more than a week of school. They're gonna get him settled back into his routine." He checks his watch. "Their flight should be leaving in a couple of hours."

Ann and Laurie fawn over Tabby, trying to help her stand even though she whines that she can do it herself. "Need help transferring back to bed, Tab?" I ask, just wanting to egg her on.

"Sure, Hero. Why don't you get your burly butt over here and sweep a girl off her feet?"

"Tabby!" Laurie whisper-shrieks.

There's no telling how many times in her tenure as a mother Laurie has had to reprimand Tabby using that exact same tone and exclamation. My guess? Tens of thousands.

I can't help but laugh at the joke. Of course, the girl doesn't need my help. She's already jumped in bed and is snuggling with the blanket I brought her.

She leans back against her pillow. Someone's given her a pillow that has purple and green hearts all over it. Her eyes blink slower, telling me she's most likely tired from her adventure outside. "Alright Tab, get some rest. I'll come check on you later."

My eyes immediately find Ann's. I lift my brow in silent question asking if Orah's up to accepting visitors. Her smile brightens, and she gives me a little nod. She says her own goodbye, kissing Tabby on the cheek, and walks up to my side, giving my bicep a little squeeze and gently pushing me in the direction of the door. "You got a minute to talk?"

"Of course. What's up?" Although, I'm pretty sure I know what's up. She wants to tell me about the nightmare.

In the hallway, we huddle against the wall, halfway between the girls' rooms. "She had a rough night. She had a nightmare." Ann rubs her temple. "Well, I guess a night terror would be a more accurate description. They had to give her a sedative to calm her down."

"Does she remember it? Does she remember what she was dreaming about?"

I hold my breath, praying it's not the same nightmare that violently assaults me in my sleep. Yet, somehow, already knowing it is.

"She said everything happened in blurry flashes, that she wasn't exactly sure what she was dreaming about until the end. She remembers the end."

Fuck. "Which was?"

Ann works her mouth left and right in a twitch, before rushing through the tale. "She was reaching for you and calling your name. She said you looked right at her, and then you turned and walked away."

My heart instantly turns to stone, painfully bouncing against my sternum. Like a massive boulder rolling down the side of a mountain. It's a landslide of epic proportion.

That's no ordinary nightmare. That's no mere night terror.

That's the world collapsing. Imploding. Ceasing to exist.

Orah calling to me, reaching for me, needing me.

And me—turning and walking away. Willingly.

Never. It won't happen. I refuse to let it.

I know I have to let her go. I have to let her leave this hospital, leave this state, leave this tragedy.

Leave me.

But that's different.

That's her, turning and walking with her head held high toward the rest of her life. That's My Brave Girl doing exactly what she was meant to do, living a full and happy life.

That's not me, turning my back on her when she needs me.

If she reaches for me, I'll be right there to grab her. To hold her. To support her. To help her fight. Until she's strong enough to turn around and leave me again.

Because that's my job, right?

Heal her and then turn her loose.

"Ridge?" Ann's voice echoes in my ears, making me realize I missed what she said.

"I'm sorry, what?"

She bends closer. "Do you think it'll happen again? Do you think it'll get worse? They said they would prescribe some sleep medication for us to take home." She wiggles her nose. "Something different than the sedative they gave her last night."

"Yeah. Most doctors prescribe non-benzodiazepine hypnotics for home use."

Her eyebrows shoot into her hairline, and she gasps. "Hypnotics?"

I give her shoulder a comforting squeeze. "It's just a word, Ann. It's not a hypnotic like what you're thinking."

Swallowing loudly, she nods.

"She's met with the hospital psychiatrist, right?"

Ann looks over at Orah's slightly ajar door, staring at the fake wood like it's about to open a magical portal. A mystic wormhole that we can all travel through and emerge on the other side, fully healed and in tiptop shape with no mental or emotional baggage weighing us down.

If only.

"Yeah. And we've already got her on the schedule with someone back home too. The victim's advocate attorney arranged it for both of the girls. And us, if we want it."

I gift her a small smile, despite the fact that my stone heart is still crumbling to pieces. "Good. I'll talk to her too. Maybe she'll open up more to me."

"Thank you, Ridge." Before turning and leading the way to Orah's room, Ann wipes a rogue tear from the corner of her eye and steels her shoulders, holding her back ramrod straight.

These parents.

Man… So. Damn. Strong.

I see where Orah gets her strength from now.

Pushing the door the rest of the way, she peeps into the room. "Hon, Ridge is here. I'm gonna run out and grab everybody some food. Sound good?"

"Yes, ma'am." Orah's sweet singsong timbre sprinkles across my senses like a soft spring rain, slowly molding some of the broken stone back together again, making my chest feel less heavy, less painful.

Giving me a little wink, Ann spins on her heels and walks down the hall, bopping into Tabby's room and no doubt asking if they want something to eat as well.

Cocking one foot across the other, I lean against the doorframe, soaking her in. Sunlight streams through the slanted blinds of the hospital window, making her raven hair shimmer. A content smile falls on her face, pulling her mouth into a curve.

Her hand, with her now-chipping pink nail polish, reaches for me. And my name barely has time to spill from her lips before I'm walking toward her.

To Orah.

And with each step, I shove my disturbed thoughts down deep, hiding them forever. Hiding them from everyone. Even myself. Because if I hide them down deep enough, I can pretend they don't exist.

She's not *a brave girl*.

She's My Brave Girl.

All. Fucking. Mine.

Chapter 18

Orah

His sigh is deep and dramatic. Like a little boy who's tired of following his mom around the clothing store shopping for dress pants. "Again with the cooking show?" He squints, staring at the images flashing across the TV. "The caramel swirl in that pan of brownies looks like an ostrich."

I roll my eyes. "It does not."

He looks at me like I've grown three heads. "What! Of course, it does." He stands up, stomps to the mounted television, and then starts pointing. "Head, beak, neck, tailfeathers, legs."

Oh. It does look like an ostrich.

I don't have to verbally concede. Based on his triumphant smile, my concession must be written on my face. "See. Told ya," he teases.

And when I stare for a moment too long—my eyes roaming from his dark brown hair, to his handsome face, and across his hidden, yet chiseled chest—his smile falters. And he rakes his hand down his mouth, tapping his chin in his comforting rhythm.

One. Two.

"Why do you tap your chin?"

"Do you like cooking and baking?"

Our questions overlap one another, vying for the top spot.

Which one will win?

I shimmy in the bed, pulling my gifted blanket tight around me. "Nope. It's my turn to ask a question."

He growls under his breath, the air between us vibrating with the sound. "Huh. I don't know about that." He's not mad, though. Try as he might, he can't hide the smirk tugging against his fake frown.

He walks back to his chair and sits down. I can't help but notice that his back and shoulder don't seem to be causing him as much discomfort today. Clearing his throat, he waves his hand in front of him, giving me permission to proceed.

"You have this habit of running your hand down your face and tapping your chin. Twice. Why? Have you always done that?"

Ridge shifts in his seat, gifting me with a shy chuckle. "You're coming out swinging, huh? Hitting the hard stuff first, I see."

I scoot my hand across the bed, waiting for the moment something happens that makes him wanna grab it. In the meantime, I work my index finger over my thumb, flicking at my chipping nail polish.

"This is the hard stuff?" I ask. "Asking about a habit?"

"I guess not." He folds his hands across the mid-section of his frayed, blue T-shirt. "It started when I was little. Four, I think. It's like...I couldn't get the words I wanted to say to come out of my mouth. Everything was all jumbled inside of my brain. Most of the time, I knew what I wanted to say, but I couldn't get my tongue to get on board. And sometimes, I wasn't sure what I wanted to say, I was only sure of the emotion I wanted to convey. It's like I wanted to *give* my feelings to someone, but I wasn't sure how to do that with just words."

His Tiger Eyes find mine, locking me in place, freezing me with an intimacy that we weren't—that we aren't—meant to share. Yet we do.

I can feel what you feel.

And it's true.

Every freakin' word.

And if it's so true, why does it feel so forbidden?

"Anyway, one of the kids at daycare started making fun of me, calling me stupid because of my delayed responses. My grandpa could see I was struggling. I'd get frustrated and upset. He told me that sometimes a person's mind just needs a little jumpstart. He said it was like turning a key in an ignition. I needed an action to bring my brain to life. I needed a moment to compose myself, center myself, calm myself. He said that if I did some sort of movement that made me look like I was thinking, then people wouldn't notice the pause." His hands flap up and then fall back down to his torso. "There you go. Tap. Tap."

"So tapping your chin calms you?"

He licks his lips. "Just like counting to five calms you."

My heart skips in my chest, like a skidding rock jumping across a pond.

I'm glad they unhooked some of the monitors, or else I'd be shrilling and buzzing and beeping. "Wh—what?" Even my syllables skip. Scared because there's no hiding from the truth.

He fidgets in his seat, moving one hand to the edge of the hospital bed. "I've seen you. I don't think you realize that your lips move when you do it." His fingers tap my favorite blanket, matching the cadence of every whispered number. "One. Two. Three. Four. Five."

Oh my gosh. How can I explain it away? This deficiency. Because that's what it is, right?

"I asked your parents. They said you've never done it before. It's not some old habit."

My tripping heart thunders into a frenzied momentum, racing against a whole new set of horrors I might not be able to stop. Ever.

They're talking about me? Behind my back? What have they told him? Surely, if they'd told him *everything*, he would've stopped coming to see me. He would treat me differently. He wouldn't look at me with tenderness in his eyes.

"Orah, look at me." His utterance is an edict, a demand for me to follow.

I'm shaking. My head feels disconnected from my body. Not having any other choice but to surrender to his command, my eyes swing to his. Without hesitation, he grabs my hand, holding it tight.

"Stop." His order is hot and fiery.

"Stop counting?" I'm his complete opposite. My tone is cold and shivering, tumbling through the air like a falling snowflake.

"No. Stop…" He breaks, trying to grasp what he wants to say. Maybe he wants his fingers back so he can tap his chin. "Wrapping yourself in shame. It's not your cloak. It's not your second skin. It doesn't belong anywhere on you."

Shame.

Oh my god. He knows.

"Orah, I don't know what happened to you. But I can *feel* you. Something else happened that night, and you're hiding it from me. Hiding it from yourself. I'm not gonna pressure you into telling me. You'll tell me when you're ready." He gifts a soft smile, barely winding his lip under the growing mustache of his newly forming beard. "Or, maybe you'll never tell me. And that's okay. Because I can still fight for you—fight with you—without having to know every detail."

"What if I'm not worth fighting for?"

His back straightens, like he's a marionette and someone pulled his strings. Once again, he's squeezing my hand too tightly. But that's okay. His strength never hurts me.

His strength *will never* hurt me.

"Fuck that shit, Zipporah. You're always worth fighting for."

I move my right hand, wanting to reach across and trace my fingers down his cheek. Tenderly, lovingly. But my dumbass IV gets caught on the hospital bed railing and yanks my hand back, pinching and burning the skin around my port. I break our gaze, turning to stare at the stupid, offending tangle of plastic cords and tubing. I've never been so mad at inanimate objects before.

Unfortunately, Ridge slides his hand away from mine, leaving my left hand empty and vacant.

He clears his throat and shifts in the chair. "I mean, I'll aways fight for my patients. Fight for my friends."

Patient.

Friend.

Teenager.

All words I hate when Ridge says them about me.

"So, tell me," he continues, using a more business-like tone, "why the number five? Why not three, ten, or fifteen. Why five?"

"The gunshots stopped for a second, and I started counting. I counted to five, and then you opened the door." I thin my lips together, working the cherry-flavored lip balm Momma brought me. "You came to save us. So, I didn't have to count past five anymore."

He sucks a harsh breath into his lungs. Instead of dwelling on the honesty of the statement hanging in the air between us, acknowledging the faith I've had in him since the moment that supply room door opened, he volleys the conversation back to me with his original question. "My turn. Do you like cooking and baking?"

"I don't know. I've never done it before."

He grins in confusion, making himself look so young. "But you like watching the shows?"

"I've never watched them before. Before now, I mean." I give a little shrug. "I just don't feel like watching the stuff I watched before. You know..." I trail off, wondering if he remembers my comment that night about always liking action movies. He must. Because he gives me a knowing, little nod. "I tried watching the regular cooking shows. You know, the ones with 'real' lunch and dinner food," I clarify with a one-handed air quote. "But I like the desserts better." My eyes flitter back up to the screen, where the host has moved on to some kind of trifle. "They look so yummy, don't you think?" She pours a whipped cream over the top, using a spatula to form pretty mountain peaks. "Maybe I could do that. Be a baker. Some kind of dessert maker or something."

"My dad is an amazing cook. Absolutely freakin' amazing. He does catering on the side. His business has really grown, and he's been tossing around the idea of going full time. Right now, he's an underwriter for a commercial insurance company." He leans forward knocking my covered leg with his hand and giving a low chuckle. "But he hates doing cakes and desserts. He likes the 'real' food," he specifies, mocking me with the same air quotes. "Maybe one day, y'all can tag team it."

"A job offer before I even bake my first cupcake? How lucky." I add a little wink to my teasing. "What about your mom? What does she do?"

"She's an admin assistant for an interior design company. And my little brother just started college. He's thinking about studying hospitality management, but right now, I think he's majoring in beer pong and grab-ass."

I burst out laughing, unable to stop the snort that follows.

I can't help but think how different the two brothers must be.

Grab-ass versus monogamy.

And call me an idiot, but I don't think Ridge was gonna tell me the other day that monogamy is 'nice'.

What would a relationship with Ridge be like?

If he considered me an adult, I mean. His equal, his partner.

A relationship with Ridge would be many, many things. And trust me, *nice* would be too tame of a word.

Sexy. Powerful. Lustful. Soul-shattering. Those are the words I think about when I picture Ridge. And me. Together.

And then I remember that I shouldn't be allowed to think such things. My raging, wild hormones and all-encompassing need to give a big fuck-you to the entirety of my school population led me to the worst night of my life.

And then...the best night. Because I met *him.*

Can't something—or someone—be two things at once?

Can't I be sorry, be regretful and still be hopeful for my future?

Can't a small part of me still be allowed to think that I deserve happiness, joy, and companionship?

"So, you haven't watched the news?" His question breaks my wayward thoughts.

He's kidding, right? "No. Definitely not." I'm getting hot so I toss half of my left leg out from underneath the blanket and bed sheet. My gown rides up, and when my bare thigh accidentally brushes against his fingertips, he chokes on a gasp and sits back in his chair like his ass is on fire, wedging his fists together in a ball. I pretend his reaction doesn't make my heart bleed. "Don't they say ignorance is bliss?"

"Yeah, well, whoever '*they*' are, can go screw themselves. *They* haven't been through what we've been through. And ignorance takes away our power. I refuse to let you give away any more of your strength. No one's taking dominion over you ever again, Zipporah." He leans close, but he keeps his hands firmly in his sphere of movement, not crossing the invisible line that's meant to keep us separated. "Repeat after me."

Is he really wanting me to do some kind of empowerment chant? Seriously? "Seriously, Ridge?"

"Yep."

He doesn't elaborate, so I just give him a small nod, conceding to his request without even fighting it. "Okay. I'm ready."

"I went to the movies, and there was a mass casualty incident."

My eyes snap to his, pinning him in place with my shock and abhorrence. What? He wants me to do what? Has he lost his mind? I clamp my lips together and vigorously shake my head, moaning around the sound no.

"Yes."

"No."

"Yes, Orah. This is your life. Fucking take it back and live it."

Tears immediately start streaming down my face, burning my already-dry skin, pooling in the crevice of my mouth, catching in the sticky beeswax of my lip balm. "I can't."

I'm surprised he can even understand me. My refusal is meek and mild, nothing more than a mumble of unintelligible half-syllables.

"You can. And you will."

I'm not sure how long we sit there like that. Me with my silent tears falling down my face. And him with his Tiger Eyes brimming with defiance and eagerness.

My chest hurts. And it's not just from the bullet wound and surgery and staples and mesh and tubes and bandages. It's from my spirit—my essence, my life force—trying to weave its way into my DNA, trying to make me whole.

Eventually, my mouth creaks open, and a voice that doesn't even sound like mine starts talking. "I went to the movies, and there was a mass casualty incident."

I stare at the blanket, focusing on a black swirl that looks like a heart with a line down the middle.

A broken heart.

"Two men killed twenty people."

"Two men killed twenty people."

"They injured eighteen others. With serious injuries. Just like mine."

"They injured eighteen others. With serious injuries. Just like mine."

"My best friend was shot."

"My best friend was shot."

His hand reaches for mine. With soft but purposeful intention, our fingers lace together. "I was shot."

"I...I...I was shot."

His thumb charts a path across the back of my hand. The movement is slow and intimate. Mesmerizing. "I nearly died."

I glance over at him. With more gentleness than I deserve, his free hand traces across my cheeks, wiping away my tears.

When I don't repeat his words, he stands up. Hunching over me, he slides his calloused palm from my jaw around to the back of my neck. And then he lowers his forehead to mine. His hot breath dances across my eyelids, making me dream of the things I've *always loved.* Sunshine and flowers. Oceans and mountains. And the things I love *now.* Cupcakes and cookies.

And him.

"Say it."

"I...I...nearly died."

"But I didn't."

"But I didn't."

"I'm glad I lived."

"I'm glad I lived."

"My future can be whatever I want it to be. With whoever I want it to be. That power is mine."

I tip my head. My lips brush against the hair lining his chin. He smells like soap and saltwater and life. "My future can be whatever I want it to be. With who—"

"Alright, kids. We've got more food than an army can eat." My mom's announcement filters down the hallway, followed by the snickers and chuckles of my dad and brother.

And in the second before they round the corner, emerging into my hospital room, Ridge steps away from me, divorcing me from the joyous visions of *him* being my life. Of him being the 'whoever' in that mantra.

He snags his hand down his face and taps his chin. One. Two. His condolence is eerie and chilling and completely debilitating. "I'm so sorry, Orah."

And why is he apologizing?

Because he doesn't feel the same way?

Or because he does.

Chapter 19

Ridge

It shouldn't be this hard.

Saying goodbye.

Especially to someone I only met fifteen days ago.

But it is.

Tabby and her parents pulled out about twenty minutes ago. And now, it's just Orah and me. Sitting outside in the early May sun. There was a news van outside in the main parking lot earlier. The hospital security team chased them away, reminding them that the patients being discharged were protected by law. Just as with everything else, somehow the information was leaked that the 'two teenage victims visiting from South Carolina' were leaving today. Just to play it safe, though, we're sitting in a secluded alcove of the interior courtyard, with the hospital buildings themselves playing bodyguard to prying eyes. Her parents are inside finishing the last little bit of paperwork, and Boaz is at the hotel, packing the last of their stuff.

Yesterday was an exhilarating and tiring day. Her staples and chest tube were removed. Finally. She has stitches, obviously, from where the tube was, but they were able to use absorbable stitches. So, technically, there won't be anything else to remove from her body.

They also discontinued her IVs, giving her the first touch of unencumbered freedom since I wheeled her stretcher into the trauma bay of the ER. Despite her exhaustion and sore body, she wanted to shower. With her stitches tightly covered in a waterproof bandage, of course. She said nothing had ever felt so good. And she dressed in normal clothes. Ann laid out two outfits on the hospital bed, and I watched as Orah bypassed the blue shirt and cream-colored lounge pants, instead reaching for the black shirt and black comfy shorts. I sat with her as she blow-dried her hair, and when the repetitive movements of holding her hand above her head and working a hairbrush began to make her side and torso sore, I took over.

Well, undoubtedly, I'm never gonna be a hairdresser. And I probably pulled enough hair out of her scalp to make a wig for a small child. But she never complained. Not once. She just smiled and thanked me.

And then, she wanted to walk.

And so, we did.

With the nurses giving a little leeway to the wheelchair policy since I was with her, knowing I would catch her if she were to fall.

We came down to this same courtyard at dusk, meandering left and right, weaving through the flowers and small water fountains that are supposed to be calming and relaxing. Yeah, they weren't exactly doing their job.

My body was hyper-alert, aware of every single thing Orah was doing. Every single thing she was thinking. Every single thing she was feeling.

I was aware of the way her coconut scent carried on the breeze. I was aware of the way the muscle lines, carved into her lean legs, flexed with each step. I was aware of the way her storm-cloud eyes watched me, eating me alive like prey to her predator. I was aware of the way her knuckles brushed against mine while she mindlessly picked at her chipping pink nail polish.

I was aware of every breath, every whisper, every heartbeat, every unspoken wish.

And that's when I realized the rest of my life would be spent in purgatory. Loving someone I wasn't supposed to love. Denying my feelings *for* her. Denying them *to* her. And denying them to everyone around me.

Because what would people think?

If they knew the truth.

I'm twenty-two. She's barely eighteen.

I'm her paramedic. She's my patient.

I'm a man. She's a teenager.

And we live three states away from one another.

"Ridge, did you hear me?" Her sweet voice tosses me deeper into the abyss.

"I'm sorry, what?"

She tugs on the collar of her shirt. She's wearing a different black one today. This one is sleeveless with a lower neck line. "I put the salve you brought me on this little cut. From where you put the needle in my chest." She leans forward, showing me how the ointment glistens on the small strip of pink skin. She shuffles, unknowingly giving me a quick flash of her black bra.

The paramedic in me wants to take a closer look at the wound I created. Touch it, make sure there's nothing unusual about it, study it to see if I need to do anything different next time. But the man who realizes he's in love with the girl in front of him knows he can't do that.

It wouldn't be right.

"You packed it? Just let me know when you start to run out, and I'll send you more. You need to massage it into the skin, twice a day, where the staples were. It'll help with the healing."

"I packed it," she confirms. Then, she nods at my shoulder. "I didn't take yours, did I? I mean, you still have some for your shoulder, right? Are you using it?"

I can't help my grin. "Of course, I'm using it. My gran would tan my hide if I didn't."

She stands up from where she's sitting beside me on a stone bench—a respectable distance away, I might add—and moves in front of me.

Right in front of me.

It takes me by surprise, and I have to straddle my legs wider so I'm not…you know, clenching her hips with my thighs.

Talk about fucking inappropriate.

"Orah, what are you—"

"Show me," she demands, completely interrupting me. "Let me see your shoulder."

I lift an eyebrow and give her a noncommittal chuckle. "You don't believe me?"

"I'll always believe you, Ridge."

I can't even formulate a response. I don't deserve the trust and confidence that she puts in me.

Fortunately, she's distracted from paralyzing me with her gaze when a small group of nurses come out the side door, giggling and chattering.

I scoot back a little, trying to drag myself out of her magnetic pull. "I can't whip my shirt off, Orah. We're surrounded by people."

She scrunches her nose and gives a barely-there sigh. "I'll just have to take a peek then."

In no more time than it takes me to blink, she reaches her hand into the collar of my T-shirt, lifting it from my skin. She bends down and peeks inside the darkened cavern of my shirt, scattering her peppermint breath across my healing left shoulder. Her fingertips trace the pink, jagged, and slightly bubbled scar, gently spreading whatever ointment may be left over from my morning application further into my skin.

My vision blurs, and my thoughts grow heavy and fuzzy. I'm functioning in a drunk fog. Drunk simply by her innocent touch, her innocent eyes, her innocent heart.

Satisfied with her perusal of my flesh, she adjusts my shirt, making it even around my neck. "There," she says, like everything she just did to me is simple and uncomplicated.

When it's so far from it.

Her eyes dart to my chest, reading the logo written across it. "Clifford Clingman must really like this bar." One corner of her mouth lifts. "His closet is filled with nothing but their T-shirts."

I give a little cough, making sure I have enough power to even speak. "Cliff just drinks at the bar. I'm the one who works there."

"You work at a bar?"

I tap the emblem on the breast pocket. "Belly's Beachside. I bartend there part time, when I'm not on shift at the station."

Her brow crinkles. "Belly's?"

"His last name is Bellinger. Everyone calls him Belly."

She nods, giving me a breathy little "Mmmm."

She really needs to sit back down.

My body is tense and taut. Even my damn leg hairs are standing at attention, trying to get closer to her.

"When do you go back to work? I mean, regular work? At the firehouse?"

"Should be toward the end of next week. My mandatory ten sessions will be done on Thursday." I decide to reiterate what she already knows about my required counseling, hoping it takes away any stigma or fear she may have about doing the same thing once she makes it home. "I'll still have the other sessions, for a full six months, but I should be cleared for duty sometime after Thursday."

She shuffles on her feet, cocking her body from left to right and worrying the hem of her shorts between her thumb and index finger. "I'll worry about you."

"There's no reason to worry. I'll be fine."

"You don't know that."

How am I supposed to respond. Because it's true. I have no idea what will happen. On the next call. Or the one after that. Or the one after that. But this is in my bones, in my soul. It's what I'm meant to do.

"Orah, I—"

"Okay, honey," Ann's interruption resonates in my ear. "We're ready. We should get on the road. We have a long drive."

Shit. I didn't even see John and Ann walk up. How long have they been standing there?

As soon as Orah gives me room, I jump up and shove my hands in my pockets, cursing the redness that I know colors my cheeks.

John holds out his hand. "Ridge...thank you." Our shake only lasts for half a second before he pulls me into a hug. Gripping me tightly, he pats my back with one hand, timing the pounding with his words. "You will always have a place with us. Come visit. Anytime."

Ann snakes her arms around me next, hugging and sniffling. "Oh no," she mumbles. Pulling back a smidge, she fumbles into her pocket for a wrinkled, used tissue. "I knew I was gonna be a blubbering mess." She wipes her nose before tossing her arms back around my neck, rubbing her wet and snotty Kleenex all over the side of my face in the process. I'm about to laugh when she squeezes me tighter, instantly making me emotional. The gratitude oozing from her soft, motherly tone warms my heart, making me feel all gooey inside. Like a chocolate chip cookie fresh out of the oven. "Thank you. Thank you so much, Ridge. You have been our saving grace over these past two weeks." Stepping away from me, she tucks herself against John's side, popping the tattered tissue at me as she talks. "You stay in touch. I mean it." She laughs, "You may regret giving us your phone number."

I just chuckle and shake my head. "Never."

And then... it's *our* time.

Our time for goodbye.

Fuck.

My jaw clenches, pressing my teeth together and sending a shooting pain through my tongue. What the hell am I supposed to say? It feels like my mouth is glued shut. I can't even pry my damn lips open.

I steal a glance at her. Her eyes are glazed and hazy, darting at the ground around me, refusing to land on my face. Refusing to look at me.

Her body trembles. She's shaking from head to toe. Shivering like the sun just died, leaving us in a cold and frozen and empty land. It's almost imperceptible. I'm not even sure her parents notice it.

But I notice it.

Even the hair swinging from her ponytail pulsates.

I want nothing more than to scoop her into my arms and hide her away from the rest of the world. Keep her safe and sound in my embrace for all eternity. Until the sun that she thinks is dead comes back alive. Until it resurrects and shines, pouring heat and happiness over us.

Her lips move on a silent prayer.

One. Two. Three. Four. Five.

She takes a wobbled step forward.

I do the same.

And then, she reaches out and wraps her arms around me. Her forearms cross around the back of my neck.

But...she's not even touching me. Not really. Her hands are barely grazing me. Her embrace is light and airy, like walking through the damp mist on a foggy morning.

So...I do the same. My hands skim across her waist and around the small of her back. My caress is nothing more than...

Than fucking business casual.

It's like I'm hugging my great-aunt's step-niece at a funeral.

That's how remote and distant this feels.

"Thank you, Ridge." She's monotone and stoic.

I toss a look behind her, searching for John and Ann. Their faces are serious, their brows pinched together.

Are they mad at me?

Am I doing something wrong?

I take a small step back, placing distance between us so that there's not even the remotest of possibilities that our bodies will press against one another.

Her hands fall to her side, limp and floppy, like she doesn't even have the strength—or desire—to keep touching me. She croaks her last word, and turns and walks away. "Bye."

"B—bye." By the time the fumbled noise leaves my mouth, she's already five paces away from me, drudging behind John and Ann like a zombie.

What. The. Fuck. Just. Happened.

No. No. No. No. No.

This...this can't be happening. Not like this.

Is this what she really wants?

Do I mean nothing to her?

Of course, I mean nothing to her.

I'm just some guy who helped her when she was in a really tough situation. It was just my job. Nothing more.

It was just my job.

She's only my patient. Nothing more.

She's ready to leave.

Ready to leave me.

It. Was. Just. My. Job.

My ears start ringing. The decibel is so high-pitched it feels like someone is stabbing my eardrum with an icepick. Numbness shoots down the side of my face, running from my cheek to my jugular. My vision pinholes; everything in my periphery blurs into faded colors and wavy lines. My muscles violently twitch and spasm, making my legs feel like they're about to give out. Like I'm about to collapse, right here and right now. Electrical shocks bounce from one side of my brain to the other, playing ping pong with my thoughts.

And my heart.

Oh, my fucking heart.

It feels like it's ripping in two. Like it's splitting my chest wide open, filleting my body, right down the middle.

It feels like it's searching.

Searching for the missing piece.

Searching for the goodbye that shouldn't really be a goodbye.

I stumble. My hand darts out, grabbing for the stone bench to steady myself.

I can feel what you feel.

My eyes tunnel a line to Orah, not paying attention to anything or anyone else. Not the flowers or the decorative fountain. Not the handful of other people—visitors, patients, doctors, and nurses. Not the squirrels running up and down the trunk of the one lone tree, anchored in the corner of this fake oasis.

Only her.

My Brave Girl.

Walking away. Being brave. Being exactly what I want her to be.

Head held high. Back ramrod straight.

I can feel what you feel.

And in that second, her steps slow. She bends at the waist. One hand wraps around her stomach, and the other hand flies to her mouth.

Her devastated cry is silent. A muted scream meant for no one but herself.

But I can fucking feel it. I feel it pulse against my skin like an echo in a cave.

I can feel her tears streaming down my own face, even though we're fifty feet away from one another.

And I know.

This isn't how it ends.

Chapter 20

Orah

Tears flood my eyes.

They scald my skin like rivers of lava. Leaving ash and devastation in their wake.

I blink rapidly, praying that my parents don't turn around. I don't want them to see me dying.

Because that's what it feels like.

Because he let me go.

He said goodbye and let me go.

I'm just his patient.

A teenager.

A victim.

And so, he let me go.

Oh, this hurts. This hurts so fucking bad.

My stomach spasms, lurching me forward at the waist.

My mouth opens, literally aching for me to release my sobs. I want to bellow. Loud and wild and animalistic. I want to shatter the sun with my wail. I wanna scream so loud that the fiery sphere breaks into a million pieces and rains to the earth like yellow confetti.

I push the back of my hand against my mouth, biting hard, begging myself to be quiet.

And then it happens.

A scream.

A scream that shatters not only the sun, but the moon and stars too.

Except it doesn't come from me.

"Orah!"

I spin around, instantly drawn to his desperate intensity.

He's bent at an awkward angle, with one hand splayed across the stone bench where we'd been sitting. He rights himself. My body mimics his. Rebelling against the desire to fall to the ground and curl into a ball, I straighten, wanting to be strong. For him.

Our eyes lock. I might not can see the swirls of brown in his Tiger Eyes from all the way across the courtyard, but that's okay. Because I have them memorized.

My hand slides down my chin, spreading my tears and saliva. My throat constricts, like there's an invisible villain strangling me into submission. I'm not even sure I can speak.

So, I don't.

I mouth just one word. One simple word. Something that for seventeen years and fifty-one weeks was just a *word*.

But that word changed. Fifteen days ago.

Now it's a name.

A plea.

A prayer.

"Ridge."

He immediately reacts.

He takes off in a sprint, racing directly toward me. And I mean, *directly* toward me. He isn't taking the path of least resistance. He isn't following the twists and turns of the paved and winding walking path. Oh, hell no. He's coming straight for me. Jumping over benches, dodging pedestrians, and pushing abandoned wheelchairs out of the way.

I put one foot in front of the other, willing myself to run.

Wanting to meet him.

Wanting to ease his burden.

Wanting to *give* more than I *take*.

For once.

Somewhere behind me, my mom's warning falls on deaf ears. "Orah, be careful! You'll hurt yourself."

Ridge apparently thinks the same thing. Because he picks up his speed and gives me a head shake. It's his nonverbal warning, telling me not to run. His nonverbal affirmation, telling me that he'll come for me.

He'll. Always. Come.

The moment we're within arms' reach, I launch into him with so much force, he has no choice but to spin me around. I'm filled with euphoria, blinded to the pinching pain from my last stitched wound stretching beyond the point of comfort. My arms circle his neck. I'm not hitched high enough to wrap my legs around his waist, so instead, I settle for hooking my left leg around the back of his right thigh. One of his hands presses into the small of my back, begging my body to be closer to his. His other hand slides around my neck, his fingertips tangling in my hair, haphazardly tugging strands out of my ponytail.

I bury my face against his neck, drenching his skin with my salty tears. And even though I shouldn't, even though it's wrong, even though it's against the unwritten rules, I nuzzle my chin beneath the collar of his shirt, planting one soft and slobbery kiss on his healing scar.

I tell myself that it's okay.

Because the fold of my arms and crook of my elbows hide my actions. My kiss is secreted away from everyone. Concealed. Disguised.

Does he even know?

Can he feel me?

Feel my lips?

He bends his head, fogging his own hot breath across the shell of my ear, sending chills down my spine. "I'm sorry. I'm so fucking sorry." He swallows. The noise vibrates through my chest. "This isn't goodbye. I'll always be here. I'll always be here to help you fight, to help you heal."

My voice breaks, sputtering from me in a flurry of fragments and splinters. "How...how...am I...supposed to do this...without you?"

"You aren't. You don't have to." He nestles his nose against my hair, inhaling my scent. "I'm just a phone call away. I'll always answer you, Orah. Always. And if you need me, I'll drop everything and come running."

I let that promise soak into my core.

And I don't respond.

Because we both know it's not *exactly* true. That's not the way the world works. He won't be able to answer every single time I call. And he definitely won't be able to drop every important thing in his life to come to my aide every time I need him. He won't be able to calm every worry, soothe every nightmare, nurse every wound.

And I'm talking about both wounds. The ones you can see and the ones you can't.

And on top of everything, I'm so damn scared. Scared that once he knows the truth about me, he won't *ever* answer the phone, won't *ever* come running.

Well, he may run.

But it certainly won't be *to* me; it'll be *away* from me.

I'm not sure how long we stay together, molded in our embrace, but it's long enough for my tears to break and my howls to subside.

Slowly, he dips down. My right foot lands on steady ground. I want nothing more than to stay cocooned in his arms, entangled around him, like a vine growing between branches. But I know I can't.

Because no matter what's happening in this particular moment, that's not who we are, right?

We're not boyfriend and girlfriend.

We're not partners.

We're not lovers.

And so, I slink my body down his, begrudgingly standing on my own two feet. I lift my head and draw a gulping breath into my lungs, wincing when the expansion hurts my healing torso.

Ridge cradles my face between his hands and wipes my cheeks with his calloused thumbs. His palms are huge, and he's able to cleanse me with just a couple of tender strokes. "Hey." His heated whisper dances between us, lazy and slow. "I looked up your name."

"Wh–what?" I choke.

"I looked up Zipporah. It means 'little bird'. Did you know that?"

I nod, making his hands slide up and down. "I knew that."

He smiles gently, giving me a little chuckle. "Of course, you did."

Unable to stop myself, I lift my fingers and trace them down his handsome face. Down the slant of his nose, past the mustache part of his facial hair, across his pink lips. I land on his chin. His short beard had grown past the point of being prickly; its texture is soft and thick. I tap his chin.

One. Two.

"It's grown," I purr with a rumbled sniffle. "Your beard. I like it."

"Maybe I like it too." His Tiger Eyes dart back and forth, bouncing from my hair to my eyes to my lips. Sighing, he lifts his gaze, looking behind me, acknowledging my parents. "I'm so sorry. I just... I couldn't let her go. Please forgive me."

Forgive him?

What does that mean?

I can hear my mom's hushed whimper as she quietly cries. Dad gives a cough, clearing his throat before speaking. "There's nothing to apologize for, Ridge. We understand."

And with that, the boy I love gives me a quick peck on the top of the head and then steps away, releasing me from his hold.

I inch forward, wanting him back.

But he shifts, adding the distance I was trying to erase.

"My turn," he laments somberly.

Somehow, I think this question is gonna hurt. So I close my eyes and count.

One. Two. Three. Four. Five.

And then, I open my eyes, determined to be as brave as he needs me to be.

"It's time to say goodbye, Little Bird. I need you to turn and walk away. I need you to do that for me. Can you do that?"

Another tear spills onto my reddened and raw face. I swipe it away, wondering why fate is so cruel.

When I don't say anything, he hangs his head, refusing to look me in the eye. "I need you to save me now, Orah. Can you do that?"

He wants me to save him by walking away…

I'd want that too.

Because being with me will bring him nothing but pain.

So, I turn, shuffling my unwilling body. And with each and every step, I wonder why saving him feels a lot like dying.

For the both of us.

Chapter 21

Orah

My home doesn't even feel like home.

I sit on the edge of my bed, repulsed by the things I see.

Books, movies, clothes, pictures.

My closet is filled with skirts that are too short and tops that are too tight. And why are there so many colors? Pink and orange and blue and green. Light and airy and pastel.

I used to think those colors were beautiful.

Now, I only think one thing.

Blood.

Those colors don't hide blood. They highlight it.

And I've seen enough blood.

The bulletin board above my desk is a collage of my life *before*. Concert ticket stubs. Mardi Gras beads from the masquerade-themed Homecoming dance. Dried flower petals from a rose that some random hot guy gave me at the mall. And pictures. Sure, there are photos of me and Tabby, of me and my family, but there's also photos of me with others.

With the boys who wanted to touch me, kiss me, be with me. Who thought I owed them something because I flirted and posed next to them in slightly provocative ways.

With the girls who wanted to be friends with me in public. Who, in private, secretly wished I would fall on my face and have all my front teeth knocked out.

I've known some of them since elementary school. We've gone to the same birthday parties, sat next to one another in the lunchroom, sang songs together in the school Christmas program. And they are some of the same ones who said I got what I deserved.

Even the carousel of the home screen on my smart TV is filled with downloads of action movies. Blood. Gore. Violence.

Yeah. Been there, done that.

My hand creeps across my purple and white bedspread, searching for the comfort of my new favorite blanket.

How am I supposed to sleep surrounded by these demons? The demons of my past, of the girl who used to be. It's true the girl I am now has a whole new set of demons, and many would say the horrors of my old life pale in comparison to the horrors of my new life.

But aren't all devils still devils?

Evil can still be evil, without us trying to compare monstrosities. There's no need to crown a winner.

When it comes to pain and trauma, misery is an equal opportunist.

Grabbing my trash can, I purge my teenage sanctuary of the things I no longer am.

A homecoming queen.

A social influencer.

A clotheshorse.

A movie buff.

A cocktease.

A bitch.

A brat.

And more importantly...

A bad daughter.

A bad sibling.

A bad friend.

Of course, I can't actually fit all of the stuff in my tiny trash can, so I stack everything in neat little piles outside of my room, in the hallway, making sure there's no obstruction and enough room to pass in case I need to run from something.

I've changed into my pajamas and snuggled into bed, when Boaz taps the doorframe. I couldn't decide whether to leave the door open or closed.

What would be best?

Is the danger outside of my room greater than the danger inside of my room?

Stuffing his hands in his pockets, he crosses to me. I scoot over so he has room to sit. He scrunches his face when he sees my blanket. "Want me to take that thing down to the wash? It probably smells like hospital funk."

It smells like *him*.

I shake my head. "I'll wash it in a few days. It smells fine for right now."

My big brother's a smart guy, a man of science. But it doesn't take a rocket scientist to know why I don't want to wash it. Giving me grace, he just smiles and says okay.

"What's with all the stuff outside of your room?"

"It's stuff I don't need anymore."

"Well, I reckon you didn't *need* any of that stuff to begin with. I think a better turn of phrase would be 'it's stuff you don't *want* anymore', right?"

I wiggle on my pillow, considering his philosophic words. "Yeah, I don't want it anymore."

"And what *do* you want, Orah?"

"I wanna be a better sister." He opens his mouth to defend me, but I interrupt him. "I've been so mean to you the past few years, Boaz. How in the world did you put up with me?"

Shrugging, he lifts an arm, reaching around and scratching the back of his head. "Well, I figured it was just a phase. I knew some-how, someway, you'd find your way back to being the sweet, kind, loving little girl I grew up with. I just had to have faith." He pats my hand. "I just wish it had happened a different way. I hate that this happened to you. If I could take this pain away from you I would. In a heartbeat."

"I wouldn't wish violence on my worst enemy." His gaze follows mine, wandering over to my bulletin board, where the only remaining pictures are of him, my parents, and Tabby. "And I made a lot of enemies," I croak out a pained admission.

"It was teenage bullshit, Orah. None of that matters now. None of that makes you a bad person."

Oh, if he only knew.

I'm not sure what possesses me to tell him some of my secrets. They just start pouring from my lips before I can even stop them. "I once lied about Corinne cheating on a math test. I wanted to get her in trouble, get her grounded. Because Neal had tickets to sit in one of the fancy skyboxes at the North Carolina Bearcats game, and I wanted to go." I nod at the wall, like I can see past it to the stack of trinkets in the hallway. "That's how I ended up with the football signed by half the team. And then, I wouldn't even talk to Neal the next week at school."

Boaz opens his mouth, furrows his brow, and then chomps, closing his teeth with a clacking sound.

"And I catfished someone once. Well, I'm not really sure if catfished is the right term. I guess it would be more accurate to say that I misled them, but I promised them that I would promote their product—these homemade candles—if they sent me a bunch of free samples. I made a couple of posts, just to meet the very minimum of my obligation. Pictures of me scantily clad with the candles in the background. Of course, no one paid attention to the candles because my ass was halfway hanging out of my shorts. And then I turned around and sold the candles so I could buy a vintage purse from the consignment boutique downtown. The same purse that Lillian wanted for her birthday. They only had one, and I bought it before her parents could get it for her."

Boaz hops up from the bed. Cocking his hands on his hips, he stares at me. "What the hell, Orah? Are you serious?"

Instead of confirming his appalled dismay, I give him another truth, wishing it were a falsehood. "And last Spring Break, I told Mom and Dad that I was spending the day at the lake with Anna Leigh and her family. Really, I spent the day there with a group of thirty-year-old guys. Some of them follow me on social media, and they paid for me to make an appearance."

Boaz turns into a man I've never seen before. His eyes widen, and his jaw tics in fury. The muscles in his shoulders tense. "What. The. Fuck." He takes a step toward me, pointing a finger in my direction, accentuating his every word with a jab. "You better be kidding, Zipporah Smith. Please, tell me you're kidding."

My reply is so quiet, I can't even hear it in my own head. "I'm not."

"Last Spring Break you were fucking sixteen years old. Sixteen!" He turns around, refusing to look at me.

Tears immediately spring to my eyes, and my battered heart struggles to beat. I hate the pain I'm causing him. I hate the pain I've caused my parents. The pain I've caused Tabby. The pain I'll one day cause Ridge.

Dragging shaky hands through his hair, he spins back around. "They didn't..." He trails off, physically pained by the thought of what could have happened in a scenario like that. What typically does happen.

A sixteen-year-old girl surrounded by ten men. Alone. On a party boat. In the middle of a lake. All for one-thousand dollars. There is so, so much that could've gone wrong in that story. I was a complete and total lunatic to ever think that was a good idea. Actually, I wasn't a lunatic at all. I was a self-centered little girl living in her own little bubble. Some could call it naïve, I guess. But I associate innocence with the ideology of naïveté. And there was nothing innocent about my decision to make that appearance.

And what's even worse, I forced Tabby to help me with my lie. I asked her to lie to her own parents and help cover for me. She told her parents she was spending the day with Anna Leigh too. Because why would I ever go to the lake for a day of fun without Tabby.

Instead, she spent her day and early evening huddled in a secluded corner of the bookstore.

"I mean, you weren't..." Boaz struggles to continue. "You weren't hurt, were you? Did they take advantage of you?"

I sit up in bed, struggling against my still-sore muscles. "No. They didn't do anything. A couple of the guys were really nice. Married, with kids. They kept the others in line. It was mainly just me serving them drinks in a bikini."

"Boaz." Momma catches us both off guard. She's leaning against the doorframe watching our interaction. Despite the forced calmness in her tone and the forced tranquility settled on her features, it's easy to see the hurt suffocating her soul. Hurt put there by me. Hurt caused by me.

And I'll never be able to forgive myself.

He looks back and forth between the two of us. "You know about this?" he asks her, the hitch of disbelief in his cadence is hard to miss.

"Some of it," she announces bluntly. Making her way into my bedroom, she sits next to me, taking over the spot Boaz vacated. "The Corinne-Neal thing is new to me." She reaches out, tucking a loose hair behind my ear. "I can call her parents and tell them Corinne never cheated."

I do my best to blink back the unshed tears that are making my vision blurry. "No, Momma, that's on me. I'll take care of it."

Boaz tosses his hands in the air, "What the hell is going on? Does someone care to explain it to me?"

"That bullet tore through more than just your sister's body, son. It tore through her soul. There's nothing more to explain."

He answers on the first ring.

In fact, it was a half-ring. I can't help but smile, thinking that, maybe, he was waiting with his phone in his hand, just wishing for me to call.

That's probably not the case, but that doesn't mean I can't think it.

"Hey." The sound of him immediately pacifies the panic that's been coursing through my body since my conversation with Boaz.

"Hey."

"It's late. I was starting to think you'd fallen asleep. Of course, no one can blame you for being tired. The car ride couldn't have been easy."

"It wasn't so bad. Normally, Dad likes to shout a few choice words at the other drivers, but he kept it pretty tame today. I can only assume it was for my benefit," I jest with a chuckle.

We're both quiet for a second so I fill the space. "Tabby's home safe."

"Yeah, she texted me a few hours ago."

They texted?

Maybe he wants me to text instead. Maybe he doesn't like talking on the phone. "Oh, I...I can text you instead. If you prefer that over talking on the phone."

"Stop, Little Bird. If I didn't wanna hear your voice, I'd tell you."

Well, I highly doubt that. Ridge is too nice to say something like that.

"What did you do tonight after getting home? There must've been something on your list. Eating ice cream directly from the carton? Going for a walk in your neighborhood? Taking a bubble bath?" His last comment comes out slowly, like he realized too late that he shouldn't be talking about me taking a bath.

"I cleaned my room."

He laughs, deep and low. It sounds a little different from normal. I wonder if he's lying down. "Are you serious?"

"I guess you could call it more of a...purification."

"Purification?"

"I don't wanna be the person I was before. And I can't do that with all the same stuff floating around me like glitter in a snow globe."

"You can be whoever you wanna be, Orah. The girl from before, the girl from now. Or someone new and undefined. Someone even you couldn't predict. I'll support you. And whoever you wanna become...just tell me how to get you there. I'll do whatever needs to be done."

"How'd you get to be so nice?"

This time his laugh is even more guttural, and I *know* he's lying down because I hear him turning over. "Nice? Just ask my brother. He may have very different words to describe me."

I doubt that.

"Of course, you're nice. You risk your life every single day to help the people around you. You risked your life for *me*." I lift my head, pulling the ponytail holder from my hair, before settling back against my pillow again. "What made you wanna become a firefighter? Become a paramedic?"

"Well, when I was in high school, a really bad storm came through. It completely decimated the majority of our neighborhood. Our house was one of the few that was spared. It was just unbelievable. To see that kind of destruction. And to know that one person could be fine and just a hundred feet away, someone else could be... not fine."

I hear him pulling his lip between his teeth. I close my eyes just so I can picture him.

"People were trapped in their homes. Trees were down everywhere. There was flooding and mayhem and chaos." He sniffs. "We spent two days helping, anywhere and everywhere we could. After that I knew what I wanted to do. There was no question in my mind as to what my future was supposed to be."

"That sounds horrible. What was the name of the hurricane?"

"Oh, it wasn't a—"

"Orah, I'm heading to bed. Did you take your antibiotic?"

Ridge must hear my mom's interruption because he stops talking.

I nod. "Yes, ma'am."

She smiles and wiggles her fingers in a sleepy goodbye. "If you need anything at all, just let me know."

And then, Dad walks up behind her and gives her shoulder a loving squeeze. "Let us both know. We're just down the hall, honey. We're right there. We'll sleep with the door open."

"Thank you, Dad."

They wrap their arms around one another and head down the hallway toward their bedroom. I know they have to be exhausted. Well, beyond exhausted is probably a better description. And they both have to return to work on Monday. Although, Momma's job is going to let her work from home for the next few weeks as I 'reacclimate to my life'.

Ridge clears his throat. "I should let you go. You need your sleep."

Please don't let me go.

"What if I can't sleep?"

"Meaning what? You're not tired? Or you're worried about all the things you'll think about as you try to fall asleep? Or you're worried about having a nightmare?"

"Maybe all of the above."

"Then, you'll get your parents. Or you'll call me."

"I can call you? What if it's the middle of the night?"

"I told you I would always answer your call. I meant it."

I bite the inside of my cheek, wishing I could stay silent. "But you won't *always* be able to answer." I finally clear the air, saying the unspeakable thing we were both thinking today in the hospital courtyard. "What about when you're at work? When they send you out on a call? Into a burning building? Into the middle of a car crash? Or into another, you know, people with guns."

"That won't happen again," he confidently and swiftly promises.

"You don't know that."

He's quiet for a moment, just soaking in my forthright rebuttal. "I refuse to think like that. I can't let them steal my happiness, Little Bird. They've already taken enough."

He's right.

They've taken everything.

He just doesn't know it yet.

Chapter 22

Ridge

"**R**idge!"

Belly's boisterous laugh, along with the smell of the ocean air and stale beer, consumes my senses. And instantly, I know I made the right decision. I give him a quick handshake, and before our fingers even break, Dottie, his wife, is pulling me into a hug. "Sweet mercy, we've missed you like crazy around here."

I kiss the side of her temple. Looking over her head, I scan the bar, nodding and giving a one-handed wave to several of the regulars who are hollering my name and holding their drinks in the air to welcome me back. "I've missed you guys too." And it's true, I have.

I didn't think it was appropriate to work at the bar while I wasn't cleared for active duty. And if I'm being honest, I couldn't even bring myself to walk across the street and just have a beer as a patron. Every time I thought about doing it, I backed out. It felt like I was cheating, cheating on the life I'm supposed to be living as a first responder.

When she doesn't make a move to untangle herself from my side, Belly gives his wife a little tug. "Geez Louise, Dottie, you're gonna suffocate the boy before he can even pour his first beer."

Tears brim her eyes, and she studies me with motherly suspicion. Giving me a small frown, she wags her white bar towel in my direction, wafting the drying mix of beer and liquor in my face. "You look thin. Have you been eating?"

Logging into the computer system, I click to start my timecard. "I've been eating just fine." When I turn around, she's still analyzing me. I chuckle, tucking her back against my side. She's a little sprite of a spunky woman. Right down to her sun-bleached gray hair and sun-beaten brown face. In true Dottie fashion, she once told me sunscreen was for the weak of heart. Naturally, I harassed her daily until she made an appointment with the dermatologist for a mole and skin cancer check. "I promise, my appetite is just fine. I haven't lost any weight. But even if I had, it would just be because of my depression over not seeing you."

She reaches up, patting my cheek. "My boy's still a flirt, Belly. That didn't change these past few weeks."

Belly hands me a fresh towel and my favorite bottle opener. "Nah, he don't know how to flirt. If he did, he would take all those women up on their offers to have a no-strings attached, one-night romp in the hay." He leans across the bar, dropping an overflowing draft in front of Tim, one of the locals who runs a fishing charter. "But the boy's basically a monk."

I stuff the bottle opener in my back pocket and give him a playful, but major eye roll. "Hardy har. Don't worry about me, Bel." I know just what to say to make him and Dottie cackle and howl. And of course, bar humor mirrors the same things Holt, C, and I talked about all through middle and high school. "This python in my pants has never gone hungry."

Sure enough, they all bowl over laughing, even Tim and a couple of men and women I don't know or recognize—who probably don't even understand why my appearance at work tonight is such a cause for teasing and celebration.

Belly snorts. "Python? Please. I heard that thing was nothing more than a salamander."

After forty years in the beach bar business, Dottie can give as good as she gets. "Oh Bel, trust me, there wasn't no salamander in the room with us last night." And just for good measure, she gives me an exaggerated wink. "Ain't that right, baby?"

And with that, Tim shoots beer out of his nose, and I nearly shit my pants because I'm laughing so hard. After he settles down, Belly leans against the counter and points in the direction of the back of the bar, where the rolling doors open to the beach patio. "Well, Romeo, let's see how you handle that dime piece who's been asking about you."

I squint, trying to see to the back of the dimly lit bar. "What? Who are you talking about?" I ask.

He just gives me a shrug. I turn to Dottie, but she ignores me, focusing instead on adding fresh ingredients to the blender for a Bushwacker.

Well, okay.

Strolling to the back, I flip through my internal Rolodex, wondering who in the world could be here? What woman? And a good-looking woman at that?

Shit, who's the last woman I slept with?

Amanda.

And it's been over six months since our relationship ended. I mean, sure, it didn't end bad…but it still ended. I can't imagine her randomly showing up. Plus, I heard she moved to Mississippi.

And when the fleeting thought that the unexpected visitor may be Orah passes through my mind, a heat blossoms in my chest, making my heart thunder a little harder. And making me fucking curse myself.

Because I shouldn't *want* Orah to be here.

I shouldn't *want* to see her.

Not to mention, she's three years from being twenty-one. I'd hate to have to kick Belly's ass on my first night back.

I don't see anybody I recognize inside the bar, so I round the corner, making my way to the outdoor patio.

And then, pure happiness explodes throughout my entire body. Popping loud like a bursting balloon, it's an audible noise that cracks against my brain.

She senses me and slowly turns in my direction. Instantly, her stiff back loosens—just a smidge—and her guarded smile widens—a whole bunch. "Hey, there, stranger."

"Stranger, my ass," I balk. Hauling Ella into my arms, I hug her, tightly and intensely.

She buries her head against my shoulder, sniffling and refusing to shed tears. "You had us worried."

I sigh, rubbing her back in a slow and intentional pattern. "Oh, c'mon, now. You should know I have no intention of leaving y'all. Of leaving you. Of leaving our family."

Pulling away, she shades her eyes against the setting sun and studies me. "Sometimes our intentions don't align with reality."

And she knows that better than anyone.

I peck the top of her head and point to the table, nonverbally telling her to sit back down. "Well, this time, they did align. So, I'd say I'm pretty lucky." Needing to wet my throat, I reach across and steal a sip from her glass of iced water. With a teasing grin, I rave, "What the hell are you doing here?" Of course, I already know what she's doing here.

"Doing an in-person wellness check. The same thing I've been trying to do for the past three weeks."

"No football players sitting on your apartment this weekend?"

She leans forward, pointing a perfectly manicured finger in my face. "Listen, *he* may be your best friend, but *he's* currently in the doghouse with me. In fact, he's not even in the doghouse. He's out in the rain. Cold and wet and covered in fleas."

Obviously, she's still a little mad at her cousin, the famous and newly NFL-drafted, Holt Hill. "Well, he's gonna have the money now to build his own doghouse. A fucking doggie mansion." I cock my head, words tumbling through my brain. "A hound lounge."

Ella sits back in her seat and rolls her eyes, mumbling under her breath, "Oh my gosh, y'all are so stupid."

I ignore her balking comeback, because, hello, she loves me.

"And no asswipe this weekend?" I ask.

She bites the corner of her mouth, fighting against a smile. "My *husband* has a bachelor party in Key West this weekend."

I wanna poke holes in my eardrums every time she refers to that asshole as her husband.

Dottie surprises me by tapping me on the shoulder and setting a beer down in front of me. "Dottie, what are you doing? I already clocked in."

"And you'll stay clocked in. Catch up with Ella first." She waves her hand behind her to the people sitting at the inside bar. "Those tightwad tippers ain't going nowhere. They'll still be here in an hour."

Laughing at her own joke, she turns on her heels and disappears through the lifted rolling doors.

Yeah, so Belly and Dottie already know Ella. Apparently, they all wanted to have a little fun at my expense. Although, I'm not quite sure if Ella knew the plan was for Belly to let me think a hot, young, single woman was sitting at the bar pining for me. "How'd you know I was working?"

"Raylee told me. We talked last night. She said you received your active-duty clearance. You start back on Monday?"

"Yep. Chief called to give me the news a couple of hours after my therapy session yesterday."

"Are you sure you're ready to go back? I mean, it's only been three weeks. No one would blame you if you needed to take longer. You know, to process it all. To grieve."

I shake my head. "No, I need to be out there. I need to be doing what makes me happy. Hell, I would've gone back on the third day if they'd let me. This has been the longest three weeks of my life."

In all honesty, it's been the longest *one* week. Because tomorrow will be one week since Orah left.

One week since her stormy, gray eyes stared into mine.

One week since I felt her slender fingers connect with mine.

One week since I felt her frenzied heartbeat drum in rhythm to mine.

She gives me a little nod, before taking a sip of her water and turning to stare at the ocean waves. They crest high and reckless, clashing with the orange beams of the blazing sun as it sinks into the horizon. "Do you wanna talk about it? About what happened in that room?" Her eyes dart back over to me, and her empathy is tangible. It's a tactile ribbon tying the two of us together. Her tragedies and mine. Different, yet the same. Because when loss is involved, no one pain is greater than the other.

That's why love and loss are two sides of the same coin. They're the only elements in this world where millimeters are the same as miles.

I know some people will disagree with me. They'll say I'm being too simplistic, too unrealistic. They'll say love comes in varying degrees. That it can be measured differently. That not all love is equal.

They'll say, *'Well, I loved my first girlfriend or boyfriend. With my whole heart. But I'm older now. And married. And I love my spouse more'.*

But what if that first love wasn't actually *love*? What if you just liked the shit out of that person? What if you liked them and wanted them and desired them? And your brain confused that with love. Even though, deep down, your heart knew the difference?

Because how can you love someone with your whole heart, but then love someone else *more*?

Because how can you love someone *just a little*?

I mean, sure, I joke that Mom loves me more, but I know that's not the truth. She doesn't love me more than Cullen.

And look at my grandfather. Gran wasn't Pop's first wife. He married Vivian when they were both twenty. He once told me their love was wild and fast and free. And when she died at the age of twenty-two, from complications from her pediatric COPD, he thought he would never love again. And four years later, he met Gran. I once asked him who he loved more, Gran or Vivian. He's the one who told me that love didn't work that way. He said love's not a race with one person crossing the finish line before the other, declaring themselves the winner. He said that both women are the loves of his life, that his heart expanded into infinity and both women own every inch.

He didn't love one *just a little*. He loved both...*with all*.

And maybe I'm too young to call bullshit, but I want to believe in that.

Because if I don't believe in it, then my purgatory for loving Orah just got a hell of a lot worse.

Because that means I'll never know happiness the way I want.

I already know I'll spend the rest of my life loving her. My Brave Girl. My Little Bird. But if I can't love anyone else even remotely close to the way I love her?

Then, that's worse than purgatory.

That's pure Hell.

Because I'm already loving her and losing her at the exact same time.

Every millimeter. Every mile.

Ella's voice is whispered but firm, snapping me out of my spiral. "Do you wanna tell me what happened to that girl? *With* that girl?"

And unlike my conversation with Holt, unlike the conversations I've had with my parents, my brother, and everyone else in my extended family...I don't correct Ella. I don't remind her there were two girls in that room with me.

Because she's had a mile of love and a mile of loss.

She's walked that path. Fucking crawled it. On her hands and knees.

And she knows a fellow traveler when she sees one.

I only work for a few hours, with Belly and Dottie sending me home a little after eleven.

Ella is already parked in the parking lot of the apartment complex, so I'm able to grab her bag on our walk home. Being the gentleman, I promptly give her the bedroom, and together, we even put fresh sheets on the bed. Trust me, my momma didn't raise no fool. Ella and I may have grown up together, but I draw the line at her sleeping on my dried morning wood leakage.

And I'm not saying that's happened.

But, I mean, it *has* been more than six months since my dick was in something other than my hand.

We chat for a few more minutes, but it's not long before she's yawning. Once she turns in, I flip on the TV, turn the volume down low, and stack the couch with a pillow and a blanket. A new blanket I had to buy at the store. And just like every other night for the past week, I clutch my cell phone against my chest, wondering if or when Orah will call.

Will she need me tonight?

That thought scares me almost as much as her *not* needing me.

We've talked every single day—during the day.

And three different nights.

And two of those nights, she was full of fear, speaking with a shaky, clipped tongue. Wobbly and weak. Like a thin piece of tin shaking during a hurricane. Bending, denting, and wavering.

It's the nightmares.

Nightmares she refuses to fully acknowledge. Nightmares she refuses to treat with sleep medication. Nightmares she pretends are nothing more than the insomnia of a teenager who's not currently going to school.

After a while, my eyes grow heavy. Between slow and languid blinks, I watch a woman spread cream cheese frosting over some kind of homemade cinnamon roll.

When my phone buzzes with the incoming call—*her* incoming call—it launches my heart into a sprint. It knocks against my ribcage in a wild, irregular pattern. My ears buzz, like I'm driving up a mountain or diving to the bottom of a swimming pool. I quickly open and close my mouth, trying to pop them, not wanting to miss a single word that she has to say.

Because everything she has to say is important.

Important to me.

"Orah," I croak, while trying to clear my throat.

"Oh, no," she mutters, quiet and still. "I woke you."

"You didn't. I'm on the couch. I just sound funny because I'm lying down."

"Are you sure?"

I blink, trying to focus on the TV. "Yeah, I was watching that cinnamon roll episode you told me about."

She sucks in an excited little breath. "Doesn't it look delicious?"

"Yeah. Did you work on the chocolate chip cookies? Did you figure it out?"

"Ridge!" She's trying to keep her giddiness contained to an after-midnight-appropriate volume, and it makes her squeak. "I figured it out today. They were so good. Oh my gosh, like, the best I've ever had. Tabby said the same thing. My granny too."

I lean back, smiling at the ceiling like a damn moron. "Well, what did you do different? What made them so good?"

"A little bit of cream cheese. Not a lot, just a little. And I upped the brown sugar a smidge. And I let the dough sit for twelve hours before I shaped them and baked them."

And because my moronic behavior didn't resolve itself in the past five seconds, I blurt out, "I can't wait to taste them."

She pauses for a moment. "I...I can't wait to bake some for you."

When I don't immediately respond, she switches topics. "How was your first shift back at the bar?"

"It was really good. Belly and Dottie were happy to see me. And several of the regulars were there. I didn't stay as late as normal. They had me clock out a little after eleven. Oh, and—"

"Ridge?" Ella peeks around the corner of the hallway. "Are you okay? I thought I heard..." She trails off when she realizes I have the phone up to my ear.

In a split second, horror washes over me. Not only because of the pained gasp that erupts from deep in Orah's chest, but because I'm ashamed for Ella to know I was talking to Orah. Not because I'm embarrassed about Orah, but because I'm embarrassed about my own behavior when it comes to her.

It's just blaring confirmation that those feelings I have to deny may one day shatter everything I hold dear.

I shuffle into a seated position, quickly answering Ella. "It's fine. I'm just on the phone."

Lifting her chin in the air, she gives a little nod before disappearing back into the bedroom.

"Orah?"

She's completely mute. Speechless. Voiceless. Frozen.

Fucking hell.

Why does it feel like I'm crushing her. We're seven hours away from one another, yet it feels like I'm standing right beside her, pushing her to the ground, and stomping on her heart with my boot.

"Little Bird, it's not what you think. I promise."

And so, what if it was?

Technically, I'm a twenty-two-year-old, single man, right?

Yeah. Too bad the word 'technically' doesn't take into consideration how my soul feels.

"You're with a woman? You picked up a girl at the bar?" Her swallow is loud and laborious.

"No. I didn't." I'm firm and steadfast, determined for her to hear the truth in my tone. "That's my...cousin." True, Ella's not my cousin, by blood or marriage, but that doesn't make her any less my family. "She's visiting for the weekend. She hasn't seen me since before... well, since before that night. She's in her first year of grad school at the University of Florida. She drove over and surprised me at the bar."

"Your cousin?" She repeats slowly, like she's trying to decipher a foreign language.

"My family, yes. She's staying in the bedroom. I'm taking the couch for the weekend."

"Oh."

If I close my eyes, I can picture her lips moving.

One. Two. Three. Four. Five.

Sure enough, after I count to five, she continues, "Oh, okay." I hear her wiggling in bed, and she gifts me with a throaty giggle. Her words are mumbled, almost like she's talking to herself and not me. "Why did that hurt so much?" And then, what she said out loud actually sinks into her brain, making her gasp again. Even louder. Even more shocked. "Oh my god, I don't know why I said that. Please ignore me. I have no idea what...I mean, you know...I just..." She fumbles around, trying to justify her obvious jealousy.

Is it possible she's denying her feelings too? Is her jealousy about more than just our bond? Does she need me for more than just her healing? Does she need me for more than just our friendship?

Does she need me the way I need her?

And what if the roles were reversed? What the hell will I do the first time she tells me she has a date? Has a guy over? Has a boyfriend? A boy her own age, I might add.

Yeah, I don't think I'm prepared for that.

Shit, I don't even wanna think about it.

"Ridge, are you there? Did I lose you?"

"No, you didn't lose me."

But maybe it's better for everyone if she does.

Losing me might be the only thing that saves us both.

Chapter 23

Orah

"For the love of all that's holy..." Tabby groans as she licks her fingers clean. "This newfound obsession of yours with baking, plus these new hormones I'm on," she breaks off again, leaning forward to swirl her finger in the leftover frosting rimming the bowl, "are gonna be the reason I have to wear a Hefty trash bag as a bathing suit next time we go to the lake."

Well, that statement is shitty on so many levels.

First, it's a reminder, that based on the current state of my healing torso, my father's name should be Victor Frankenstein and not John Smith. These scars are gonna be with me for life. And more than visible in any bikini.

Second and most importantly, it's a reminder that I got my best friend shot. And now, she's having to take hormones to ward off surgical menopause.

I take some of the extra bowls and measuring cups over to the sink and start rinsing them. "It doesn't matter what you wear. You're still the most beautiful girl anywhere we go. Beautiful, inside and out."

It's a little too quiet, so I glance up in her direction.

She's staring at me like I'm a little green alien with ten eyeballs and foot-long antennae. "You realize the Orah of a month ago would never say something like that. She'd have a smartass quip."

"Fine." Sighing, I flip off the faucet and dramatically wipe my hands on my apron. "You're still the most beautiful girl anywhere we go. Beautiful, inside and out." I pause, giving a lift to one eyebrow. "Bitch."

Immediately, we break out in laughter, cackling like that one word is the funniest thing we've ever heard.

"You know I hate that word, Zipporah." Momma walks into the kitchen, lugging her work bag in one hand and her purse in the other. She's trying to scold me, but when she sees the infectious smiles stretched across our faces, she just rolls her eyes and gives me a quick kiss on the cheek. "You sure you're okay with me going into work for a few hours?"

"Yes, I'm fine."

"Don't worry, Mrs. Ann. I'm here to keep her out of trouble."

"Oh, please," Momma chides, while stuffing a water bottle down in her bag, "the two of you together *are* trouble."

And with that, she walks away, leaving Tabby in a fit of giggles.

I force myself to smile.

Why do innocent little comments like that cut like a double-edge sword now? Things that didn't bother me before, bother me now. I know my mom meant absolutely nothing by that remark. It was a joke, spoken in teasing affection. It's something she's probably said a hundred times before.

But now? All I can think is...*you're right. I'm the worst kind of trouble.*

Tabby leans back against her barstool. "What's up with the face?"

"What face?"

She points a finger at me and then whirls it around in the air, looping circle after circle. "This face. This frown." She furrows her brow. I can only assume it's supposed to be a mirror image of my own, so I do my best to relax myself. Faking confidence, I lean against the countertop, lazily crossing one foot over the other.

My reward? A snort.

"You realize you only smile, truly smile, when you're cooking or talking to the Hero." She wobbles her head. "Or talking *about him.* Or *texting him.*"

Well, this really isn't what I want to spend my day doing—dissecting my unrequited love for Ridge Conway. So, instead, I dissect the other part of her analysis. "I like baking and dessert making. That's technically different than cooking."

"Oh please, Orah, the only thing you knew about desserts four weeks ago was that you had to open the plastic wrap before eating the candy bar. I'm glad cooking desserts makes you happy, but don't try to steer the conversation around the main point I'm trying to make."

One. Two. Three. Four. Five.

I fold my hands in front of me, trying to hide the shakiness. "Which is?"

I'm waiting for her to speak Ridge's name. But instead, she says, "You."

"Me?"

"Yes, you."

I push away from the countertop and busy myself with cleaning the flour spots and smears on the granite. "Don't be silly. I'm fine."

She hops down from her stool, taking her frosting bowl to the dishwasher. "Really? You think I don't see the differences? That your parents don't see them? Even Boaz notices. And he's looking at you through a computer screen." Grabbing a paper towel and the spray bottle of cleaner, she works behind me, disinfecting after I wipe down. "The clothes. The hair. The touching and moving things. The counting."

I wear dark clothes. If something happens, I don't wanna look down and see blood the way I did that night.

I wear my hair pulled back. Never loose. If tragedy strikes again, I don't wanna have a black curtain of blood-soaked hair dragging across my face. I can't forget that feeling; I can't forget that smell.

I touch. I move. I touch again. Sometimes, things just aren't in the right place. They need to be in the right place. I can't think when they aren't. My brain stops turning. And that's not good because I need my wits about me. What if I attract another catastrophe? I need to be able to think, clear and unencumbered. And how the fuck can I do that when people move my TV remote or leave the hand towel off the towel ring.

My five seconds. Sometimes, I need my five seconds more than I need air to breathe. Five seconds and no gunshots. Five seconds and Ridge will save me. Five seconds for my heart to beat, proving I'm still alive. That I survived, that I made it.

I lick my lips, trying to ease the dryness. My whisper is low and slow. I angle my head away from hers, halfway hoping that she can't hear me. "Dr. Crandall says that it's fine to have coping mechanisms."

"I don't think avoiding the root of the problem is what she means by coping mechanism."

"I'm not avoiding anything," I retort, with a little more accusation and hatefulness to my tone.

"You are when you refuse to tell her, or anyone else, the truth about that night."

I toss the rag down and spin to face her head on. "The truth? I think plenty of people know the truth. You, Mom, Dad, Boaz, your parents, and all those law and attorney people. And soon, the whole damn world will know it too. When that congressional inquiry hearing is done and we have to testify, *everyone* will know what I did. And the truth won't be about the assholes who tried to kill us. It'll be about me. And what I did. And then, you'll realize that you need to hate me." My hands fly up, wiping the sudden and fast-falling tears that are spilling from my eyes. "You need to hate me and run as far away from me as possible, Tab. Because *I* did this to you. I put you in that theater. And then I put that bullet in your belly. I took away your chances of being a mother!"

"Stop being a martyr, Orah. You didn't fire that gun!"

"But I might as well have!"

Tabby vehemently shakes her head, whipping her red hair across her face. "You're so damn stubborn. You refuse to listen to reason. You're worried about what he's gonna think. I know you are. He won't think any less of you, Orah. Hell, he was a teenager once too!"

"I...I don't know what you're talking about." Well, that lie doesn't even make any sense.

"You know *what* I'm talking about and you know *who* I'm talking about." She reaches out and grabs my hands, linking her fingers with mine. "Tell Ridge what happened. Maybe it will help your nightmares. It's him you're reaching for. It's him you're calling out for. Maybe telling him the truth will stop the nightmares."

I look down, mesmerized by Tabby's pink nail polish.

She painted her nails. And she painted them pink.

Will I ever want to paint my nails again?

And if I do, will I want to paint them pink?

My polish didn't chip that night, but I could still see the blood caked underneath my nail bed. I guess black or navy or gray polish could hide that. Not pink. Not white.

"And what if the nightmares don't stop?" I question.

"But what if they do?"

"But what if they don't," I pop back.

"Then, maybe it's time for you to try the sleeping pills and anxiety pills the doctor prescribed."

Feigning concession, I just nod at my best friend. Because she doesn't need to know that pills are another thing to add to the list. The list of quirks and differences that separate this Orah from the Orah of a month ago.

What if the pills take away my ability to think, my ability to react quickly, my ability to protect myself.

If something bad happens again, don't I need to be quick and resourceful, swift and mindful?

Because I'm here. And Ridge is there.

He won't be around to help me next time.

He answers on the first ring.

I was hoping he would. His shift ended at seven this morning, but he had to stay for the memorial afterward. He told me he might work at the bar tonight, but I had a feeling he would be exhausted. Mentally, emotionally, physically.

The one-month memorial.

The memorial they invited me and Tabby to. Like it's some sort of party or wedding that we just couldn't wait to attend. Trust me, excitement was the last thing I was feeling when the governor's office called my parents to extend their 'hopes that our schedules could accommodate the visit'.

Oh yeah, I can't wait to be on the televised memorial.

Where everyone is piled together, with absolutely no hopes of the news media being able to blur our faces.

Count me in.

NOT.

Just because I once had ninety-eight-thousand *friends* and was fine flashing my butt cheeks via a slow-motion skip in a short, pleated skirt doesn't mean I'm fine with strangers seeing me now. Seeing me, judging me, knowing me.

Don't get me wrong, I understand the essence of the memorial, and I want to honor those who sacrificed their lives to help. Honor those who were killed, those who were injured. And I would have gone, if it had been a closed memorial. But this was wide open. To every Tom and Dick and Harry who printed out a sticker with the word 'Press' on it. And I know because Tabby was telling me that some social media influencers were using their online status to secure press credentials. All in hopes of seeing me. Their rising competition, who a month ago was gathering new followers every single hour, and who has now fallen from grace.

So, instead, I asked my advocate attorney, Mrs. Levenson, to provide me with a list of names and addresses for the next of kin for everyone who was killed. I'll write letters to them expressing my condolences. My real condolences. Not just a simple handshake and somber smile for the cameras. Because I know, without a doubt, that's all I would have been able to muster, when surrounded by a herd of people, flashing cameras, and low-talking anchormen.

But that's not Ridge.

He would be expected to attend.

He would *want* to attend.

He could never imagine being anywhere else, but right there. Right in the middle of it.

I can see him now...hugging people, enveloping them in his arms. Speaking assurances and encouragement. Giving them strength to fight, strength to continue living.

Because that's what Ridge does.

He's a hero in more ways than one.

And maybe that's why I call him. Late at night. Wishing for him to be My Hero, over and over again.

And each time, he delivers.

For. Now.

Instead of saying 'hello', he moans into the phone. "Mmmm." The guttural noise makes my belly flutter, and a deep heat blossoms in my groin. "This time you did catch me sleeping."

"Oh!" I'm completely flustered. And it's not only because I don't want to keep him awake if he's tired, but also because I'm embarrassed by the amount of desire that one forbidden sound has thrust through my body. "I...I should let you sleep. I didn't mean to wake you."

Didn't I?

I called at one in the morning.

"Little Bird, if you hang up this phone, I'll call you right back. I wouldn't answer if I didn't wanna hear your voice. I've told you that. Many times."

"Sorry." In habit, the word rolls off my tongue.

He gifts me with a husky chuckle. Easy and lazy, lush and sensual. If you were to ask me right now, I'd say that laugh is the best gift I've ever been given.

My fingers curl around the edge of my favorite blanket. Well, maybe the laugh is my second favorite present.

Tugging the fuzzy material to my nose, I inhale so deeply it hurts. His scent has long been replaced with the smells of my own house. My coconut shampoo. My apple-scented lotion. And now, the aromas that constantly hang in the air from my newfound hobby. Cookies, breads, and brownies.

Maybe I'll tackle pies next.

Cakes will come last.

If ever.

Have you seen what people do to their cakes? It's pure artwork. Nothing short of gorgeous, breathtaking pieces of art.

I wanna make *art*, but I also want my art to taste good. Actually, I want it to taste *damn good*. Can I do that without fondant? All of the baking shows use fondant, and, no, thank you. I've had fondant several times in the past, and I can confidently say I'd rather eat wax paper dipped in Elmer's glue.

He sighs, casting his sexy laugh to the side. "So much for our pact not to apologize to each other, huh?"

"Maybe some pacts are meant to be broken."

"Maybe."

I'm not sure how to respond, so I don't. Sometimes, our phone calls aren't filled with a lot of talking. Sometimes we sit in silence. It doesn't seem to bother Ridge, and I'm glad. Because there's times when I just wanna sit and listen to him breathe. I want him to lull me to sleep with the rhythmic sound of his inhales and exhales. In and out. In and out. Knowing that he's alive? That his heart is pumping? That his warm breath is scattering across the phone and traveling hundreds of miles to play a symphony for my ears? Well, that's enough to put me to sleep.

Without any nightmares.

And nothing but dreams.

"My turn." That announcement displaces the quiet and sends a shiver down my spine. "Did you have a nightmare?" he asks.

"Why would you think that?"

"Because I can feel what you feel. And we sit here, night after night, talking about anything, everything, nothing. And you never say what needs to be said."

My body tenses, prickling with fear and frustration. It's like my blood is filled with tiny little spikes, and they're poking a path down every vein and artery. "And you always say what needs to be said?"

What the hell.

Why did I blurt that out? With such defiance and...and...accusation?

Before I can even apologize for such a catty comment—that obviously makes no sense whatsoever, because, I mean, we're *just friends*—he stuns me.

"You know I can't."

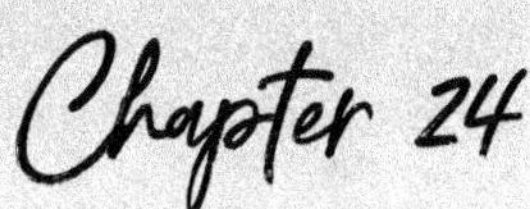

Chapter 24

Ridge

What the hell.

Why did I blurt that out? With such recklessness and...and... adoration?

Because trust me, if I played those four simple words back to myself over a recording, I'm pretty damn positive the *adoration* would be easy to hear.

My stupid-as-shit lovesick attitude is gonna get me into so much trouble.

This is what I get for letting my guard down, letting myself pretend that I can be her friend, her champion, her companion. I can't be any of those things while I'm madly in love with the girl.

And fuck me. Because I know I won't be able to stop. I won't be able to stop answering her calls, responding to her texts, dreaming about her, thinking about her, praying about her.

Praying *for* her.

Praying that someday, somehow, our lives will change, and she can be mine forever. That I can kiss her, touch her, make love to her, and make her my wife.

Allow my heart to expand into infinity and fill up with only one woman—her. My Brave Girl. My Little Bird.

But those prayers will most likely never be answered.

Because it would never change the past. It would never change how we met. It would never change the fact that I was in a position of authority when I met her. And loving her would be wrong.

Wouldn't it?

And if it's not wrong, then why does it feel so wrong at certain times? It sure felt wrong the other night. When my hand moved underneath the sheets and wrapped around my hard-as-fuck dick. Pumping myself, I nearly broke when my mind flashed with nothing but images of Orah.

Her smile. Her laugh. Her soul. Her bravery.

Needless to say, I cursed myself, jumped out of bed, and went for a run on the beach.

In the middle of the night. For five miles. With my erect cock rubbing a blister on my stomach. Yeah, that little fucker decided to play the rebellion card and taunt me with the fact that I couldn't get release the way I wanted.

You can bet your bottom dollar that I won't be suggesting boner jogging as an Olympic sport anytime soon. I could barely walk the next day.

"What?" Her gasped reaction forces me to pull my head out of my ass. "What do you mean by that?"

"I...I didn't mean anything by it."

"What aren't you saying?"

I twist the truth. "It was just a knee-jerk response, Orah. I didn't mean anything by it."

"What aren't you telling me, Ridge? Do you...I mean, are you..."

What I wouldn't give to hear, *'Do you love me too? Are you con-sumed with me the exact same way I'm consumed with you?'* But that would be selfish of me.

And what if Orah is in love with me? The exact same way I love her?

Well, I can't let myself think like that. Because that would be the ultimate blessing *and* curse.

Triumph and failure.

Pleasure and misery.

Heaven and Hell.

When she takes too long to gather her thoughts, I jump in, immediately interrupting with a pile of bullshit so thick even a bulldozer couldn't plow through it. "Orah, you know what I meant. Sometimes we can't say what needs to be said because healing takes time. People who have gone through a trauma like you need to run the marathon, not the sprint."

"You mean like us."

"Huh?"

"It wasn't just me who went through that, Ridge. You were there too. You had the same experience as me. Your body is decorated with scars too." She swallows. "It was us. We went through it together."

"With Tabby," I add, trying and most likely failing to rebuild our boundaries.

"Yeah," she repeats, parroting me. "With Tabby."

Now that I'm fully awake, I toss the covers off me and sit up on the side of the bed. "She visited today, didn't she?"

"Yeah."

"Y'all bake?"

"Uh-huh."

I snort and stab my hand through my hair in frustration. She's still trapped in her mind, still thinking about my vague and ambiguous proclamation. Which, let's be real, should've stayed as an inner monologue. "Well, are you gonna tell me what delicacy you baked, or do I have to start guessing?"

"No. It's my turn," she bops, with a little more force and power behind her. "Tell me what happened today. At the memorial. Are you okay?"

Shit.

I'm so glad she wasn't there.

Some dumbasses thought it was a good idea to parade around outside the barrier, but still within view, with posters decorated with leaked pictures of the fallen victims on them. And in bright red letters across each one, it said '*Fake*'.

Trust me, there was nothing fake about it.

"You didn't watch any of the news coverage?"

She's still got a thing about the news, so I'm pretty sure the answer is no.

"No." I can hear her fidgeting around. "I wanted to see you. In your Class A uniform. But I didn't wanna see anything else."

I guess I could offer to send her a picture of me in full dress, but that would probably tear down another brick of the boundary wall. So, instead, I just keep my mouth shut about that. Besides, if the congressional inquiry hearing happens, she'll see me dressed up then. According to Chief Latner, the latest scuttle is that they're looking to do a field hearing in Tallahassee. Which, I suppose, is good news given the circumstances. If it has to happen, I'd much rather Orah be in Tallahassee than plopped down in the middle of urban Washington, D.C.

I stand up and walk out into the kitchen. "Well, today was everything you're probably thinking it was. It was good and bad. The best of both worlds. I was able to honor my brothers, speak to some of the injured, and hug kids who lost their dads. But today was also a reminder of all the bad that's out in the world. A reminder that no one is immune to tragedy. True, the majority of people will never experience the kind of tragedy that we did, but they still have their own demons wreaking havoc and stealing happiness. Car accidents, cancer, addiction, natural disasters." I grab a bottle of water from the fridge and take a quick drink. "Despite my desire to help everybody—every single person I meet—that's not feasible or realistic. So, I did the best I could. And today, that was wiping the tears of a mother who will never see her son again."

"Do you think I'm weak for not going?"

Blasphemy.

"Zipporah, I've never met anyone stronger. And I doubt I ever will."

If I strain hard enough, I can hear her numbers muttering into existence.

One. Two. Three. Four. Five.

I sit down on the couch and prop my feet on the coffee table. "My turn. What did you bake? And did Tabby help or hinder?"

My tease earns me a cute little giggle. "Maybe a little bit of both. I reckon helping and hindering go hand-in-hand with Tabby."

I think back to Tabby's last text messages to me.

Tabby: My dad is making me watch Backdraft. Have you ever had sex on top of the fire truck? On that rolled up hose thing? It looks extremely uncomfortable.

Me: Inappropriate on so many levels, Tab. I'm not answering that.

Tabby: I'll take that as a yes.

Me: Then, I'll correct you. No. End of discussion.

Tabby: Good to know. You're a stud, but a prude.

Tabby: By the way, your girl has me worried. I think her nightmares are worse. And she still won't take any meds.

Me: She's not 'my girl', Tabby.

Tabby: Whatever you say, Hero.

Me: And I'm talking to her about the importance of following her doctor's instructions. It just takes time. She's still scared.

Tabby: I found a pair of high heels in the back of her closet. She freakin' loved those shoes. They made her legs look hella awesome. Anyway, when I pulled them out of her closet, she made me throw them in the trash. Like the outside trash can. She wouldn't even let me sell them and get her some money. Those shoes were expensive.

Me: She's afraid something will happen, and she'll need to run. She blames her shoes for twisting her ankle that night. She only wants to wear flat shoes now.

Tabby: She didn't tell me that. She just yelled at me to throw them away. Why wouldn't she tell me?

Me: Give her time. And by the way, she didn't come out and tell me that. I just know.

Tabby: And she started crying the other day when she couldn't find a recipe that she printed out. She burst into tears and cried and cried and cried.

Me: She's still dealing with pain. Physical and emotional. Friday will mark one month. That's not a lot of time given what y'all went through. Why do you think school administrators told you both not to worry about coming back to school this semester? Everyone knows, it takes time.

Tabby: I just wish I could help her more. But I don't remember anything. I have this big empty box where memories should be. I can't connect to her. Not like you.

Me: I'll take care of it.

What I meant was… I'll take care of her. Of all parts of Orah. The parts that Orah thinks are broken. Even though, they aren't. Not even close.

I'm fairly certain Tabby understood that my sentiment had more depth, more underlying meaning, but she didn't call me out. She didn't tell me to get a grip and get a life. So, there we are, Tabby Morrison, helper and hinderer extraordinaire.

"We did sticky buns. With extra stick."

"Extra stick?"

Her tone lightens, giving me a jolt of happiness. "I doubled the gooey caramel glaze. Although…"

"Although what?"

She snickers, and her lips graze against the phone, muffling it for a second. "It was so gooey and sticky that it literally pulled off one of Dad's crowns."

"Like a tooth crown?!"

"Yep. And, with it now being the weekend, he can't see the dentist until Monday."

Smiling, I take another sip of water. "Well, I'd definitely say the sticky part of the recipe was a success. Poor John."

"Tabby took the extras home. Dylan was having a sleepover tonight."

"So you decided it was a good idea to pump all the seven-year-olds with sugary pastries?"

"Well, I have to make sure Tabby stays entertained somehow, don't I?"

I lean my head back on the couch, wishing I could be there with her, wishing I could see all of the fabulous desserts she's learning to create. Taste them. Savor them.

And then congratulate the hell out of her.

Encourage her.

Because I think this hobby is helping. In its own special way, it's doing something that I can't do.

That no one can do.

"I wish you had been here. To taste them, I mean. I might be biased, but I think they were really good. I had to force myself to stop at two."

Not wanting to venture back down into the territory where the lines of our relationship blur, I field the banter with good humor. "If I had been there, I probably would've lost my mind. You forget, I've seen how slow you eat. Add extra sticky into the mix, and I'm surprised you even finished your serving before the Fourth of July."

"Hey!" Her tone is light and airy. Just the way it should be for a teenager on an extended break from school. "I'm not that slow of an eater. Believe it or not, but this time I wasn't even the last one to finish."

I lick my lips. "Who was last? John? You realize you only beat him because his teeth were falling out of his head. Literally."

She gives me a spicy little grunt. "That's completely irrelevant."

I can't stop my laugh. I don't even have to close my eyes to visualize her. Taking small little tears from the dessert bread, popping them into her mouth, and then rolling them over her tongue. All before she even bites down.

When my cackle dies, the distance between us thickens.

The telltale sound of her moving underneath her own sheets swirls an intimacy in the air. "My turn," she banters, grasping control of our exchange. "Let's see...tell me something about your brother."

"My brother?"

"Mmm-hmmm."

"He's a great kid." A flame of embarrassment creeps up my neck. Here I am, calling Cullen a kid, when Orah is even younger than him.

"How old is he?"

"He turned nineteen back in March. He's actually going to a community college in Southern Georgia right now. He should be graduating from there in the fall. Then, he'll transfer to a university to finish out a bachelor's degree."

"Is he like you? Are y'all similar?"

A vine of jealousy winds its way into the nooks and crannies of my mind, suffocating all areas of reason and rationale and logic. It's a fucking kudzu, strangling me of my sane thoughts.

Is she wanting to know if he's like me so she can be with him? Seek him out? Date him?

I mean, he is closer to her own age.

There's only one year and one month between the two of them. If anyone is counting.

I drag my hand down my face and tap my chin.

One. Two.

And when that doesn't calm my tsunami of unsuitable feelings, I jump up from the couch and head to the front balcony, hoping that some fresh air will do the trick.

She must hear the door open and close.

"Ridge? Are you okay? Are you leaving?"

"I'm good. I'm just sitting outside, getting some night air."

"Oh. Okay."

I settle into one of the chairs and quickly realize this was a horrible damn decision. Apparently, my neighbor—yet again—decided to try his hand at cooking the spoils from his deep-sea fishing excursion. And instead of taking the fish guts straight to the dumpster like a normal person, he's left them in a plastic grocery bag by his front door. Needless to say, the nighttime breeze is wafting the scent straight into my nostrils.

Instead of retreating inside, I force myself back into the chair, determined to pay penance for my jealousy and improper thoughts of Orah via red grouper nasal torture. "Alrighty, well, C is like me in a lot of ways, but he's also different from me. He's getting a little more serious now that he's older, but when he was a child? Oh god, that kid was goofy. And wild and free-spirited. It's like the only fear he had was living a dull life. He would do anything for money and a dare. And that included eating weird shit. I'm surprised he didn't spend half his life in the hospital getting his stomach pumped." I rub my fingers across my mouth, fighting the urge to simultaneously laugh and throw up when I think back on our youth. "Bugs. His own boogers. Cheese pizza that got left out on the back porch overnight, during a rainstorm. A milkshake made with orange sherbert, fried Brussel sprouts, and sardines."

"Ughhh. That all makes me sick just thinking about it," Orah sputters in exaggerated disgust.

"And it wasn't just the food thing. The night before his first day of middle school, we dared him to shave part of his head. Just one lawnmower line, right down the middle. And when he was in high school, we dared him to spend the whole day at the beach wearing a thong bikini bottom. It was all fun and games until he randomly ran into a girl he had a crush on and his right nut popped out when they were standing there talking. Not to mention, his ass cheeks got so sunburned, he developed actual water blisters. One popped, got infected, and Mom had to take him to the doctor for antibiotics."

Orah snickers, sending a flirty little whisp of air my way. "That's horrible. Oh my gosh, why would he willingly agree to dares like that? That poor boy."

"Poor boy!?" I guffaw, raising my voice. "You know how much allowance money that kid won from me?"

"Sounds like you may not be the best gambler."

"No, I guess not, huh?"

"So, he was the wild heathen who is slowly making his way toward settling down," she murmurs, marinating thoughtfully on her analysis. "Is that what makes you alike? The settling down? Maturity?"

"Maturity? Is that your way of telling me I'm old?" I joke.

"No. Something tells me Ridge Conway only gets better with age."

Chapter 25

Orah

The hushed discussion and fleeting looks confirm that something's going on.

Wanting to shield myself from whatever news my parents are about to deliver, I spin around and lean a hip against the countertop, slowly folding the mixture together. I know that's not going to make a difference in the end result, but for a few blissful and ignorant moments, I can stare into the depths of this cupcake batter and pretend my world isn't about to implode.

Turns out the head in the sand method isn't all that effective.

Despite my best efforts to remain unaffected, my heart speeds up, ratcheting my anxiety tenfold. A cold sweat breaks out on the back of my neck. Acid swirls in my stomach, swishing back and forth like giant ocean waves.

"Honey?" Dad's affectionate, yet wary, term of endearment rumbles against my eardrums.

Planting a forced smile on my face, I spin back around, pretending like I'm oblivious to the tension fogging the room. Sometimes I feel like I can actually see it.

See the tension. See the unease. See the fear.

See it all circling around me.

A dense fog driven into creation by those surrounding me.

It reminds me of when the mosquito trucks used to come through the neighborhood, spreading stinky and smoky chemicals into the air.

And I had to walk through that poisonous smog just yesterday.

I went to the grocery store with my granny, and I spent the whole time fighting a haze that was so heavy I could barely move. People I knew stared at me. Strangers I didn't know gawked at me. The general public has become my judge, jury, and executioner. And when I walked past Aria Anniston as she stood in the middle of the cake mix aisle, she leaned over and fake-whispered to the boy she was with that I was a slut who had a five-way with four guys in the parking lot after the school musical this past February.

Well, not only did Aria Anniston graduate two years ago—so she wasn't even home from college during February—but the musical was *Mary Poppins*. What kind of weirdo wants to have a fivesome after watching that? Not to mention, the school had carnival games, hot chocolate, and popcorn for everyone in the parking lot afterward. So, she's proposing what? That I tossed a baseball at weighted milk jugs and then immediately dropped my panties?

Granny noticed something was wrong with me, but I refused to talk with her about it. So, instead of gabbing about all the ways my past is still terrorizing me, we went to her house and baked white chocolate snickerdoodle cookies.

I guess that's one other benefit of me being a different person now... I'm reconnecting with my grandmother. Just like I am with my parents, with Boaz. When I was young, Granny and I were so close. I loved nothing more than visiting her, spending the night with her. Of course, as the lures of being a popular girl, an emerging social influencer, captured me in the jaw with a long and rusty fishhook, I left her behind.

Behind and alone.

She loved me.

But I walked away from her, every chance I got.

And just like everyone else, she has forgiven me. She's given me more grace and leeway than I deserve.

In fact, she's been letting me go through all of the old family recipes, gathering the tasty secrets passed down throughout the generations. And I can't wait to make them all.

Drawing me back into the room, into the kitchen, where bad news is about to be delivered, Dad forges forward. "So, we got a phone call this morning from Mrs. Levenson. The congressional inquiry is happening. A date's been set. It'll be a field hearing in Tallahassee at the state capitol."

I set the mixing bowl on the counter before I drop it. "Wh— when?"

"September."

Five months after my life nearly ended, I will have to testify about it. To a whole room full of people who won't understand. And my words will be preserved for all eternity, catalogued and filed away for people to examine and scrutinize any single time they want.

My racing heart accelerates even more, making it hard to breathe, hard to think, hard to survive.

"They think it'll last two weeks," he continues. "They're separating everyone into blocks. So you and Tabby and Ridge will all be in the same block."

My vision blurs around the edges. Splaying my hands across the counter, I wiggle my finger, tracing the blended and swirled colors of the granite. I wish I were upstairs, hiding under my favorite blanket and tracing its lines of white, tan, and black instead. "Who else is in our block?" My voice is scratchy and weak. "Is...is *he* in our block?"

Dad's face hardens. His eyes dart around the room. It's clear to see he's uncomfortable. He opens his mouth to answer, but nothing comes out. Instead, he clears his throat and tries again. "Yes."

I'm gonna throw up.

How could I have been so stupid?

How could I have let this happen?

That day was one poor decision after another.

And what's even worse? It was all my idea.

"He's asked for your contact information again," Momma adds. "Mrs. Levenson just told him it wouldn't be appropriate for the two of you to talk at this juncture, that new conversations may sway your memories and taint your inquiry testimony."

Oh my god. Is she serious?

Please, no.

No. No. No. No. No.

One. Two. Three. Four. Five.

I lick my lips, suddenly aware of how dry my mouth is. I close my eyes, watching black spots dance across my eyelids. This can't be happening. It feels like someone is stabbing me in the lungs, puncturing another hole deep inside my body. "I...I can't talk to people?" Even my stutter feels like it's physically assaulting me. "R—Ridge?" If I can't talk to him, I'll cease to exist. "Tabby?"

Momma pushes from the kitchen table, and I open my eyes so I can follow her hurried movements. She rushes to my side, gently grazing her hand across the side of my face and hair. "Oh no, honey. You can talk to them, absolutely. Mrs. Levenson just said that to protect you. She knows that you don't want to talk to that Levi boy."

My stomach lurches again with the knowledge that his name has been spoken into existence in the midst of our kitchen. In the middle of the room that has become my sanctuary from the bad thoughts that want to devour my brain.

He's concerned about his future, I get that.

But I already explained to the attorneys and all the police and federal investigators that everything that happened in that room happened because of me. Not Levi.

I slowly nod, trying my best to be brave and accept my fate like an adult. "So, it's happening. I'll have to tell my story again. Publicly. And everyone will know."

Mom shakes her head vigorously. "No, like they said, you were a minor and because of...well, you know," she clicks her tongue against her teeth before continuing, "certain things will be sealed."

I try to smile again, but I can feel the wobble of my lip.

I'm about to fucking lose it.

We both know *sealed* is just a word.

My identity was supposed to be *sealed*, and we all know how that turned out.

But we can pretend.

We can pretend that the word equals reality. We can make believe that the local police haven't had to come over and force the news crews to leave our front yard. We can feign innocence about the mail that's addressed to me, and that Mom and Dad throw away before I see it. And we can act all naïve to the fact that Boaz had a black eye on our web call three days ago.

My brother got hurt.

Because of me.

After I left the room, I spied on the rest of Boaz's call with my parents. Apparently, one of the oil workers used to follow me. And he made some comments to Boaz about my appearance. And how it's a shame that the movie theater attack messed up my body.

Because he missed it.

It being my body.

He missed gawking at me. Looking at me. Jerking off to me.

Needless to say, my brother laid the guy flat on his ass and was then taken down by two of the douchebag's friends.

But, by all means, let's pretend that the word *sealed* will protect me.

I blink, fighting against my tears. "Yeah. You're right, Momma." I try to inhale, but the air gets stuck in my throat, making a weird gulping sound. I glance at the clock on the stove.

7:30 p.m.

I lean across and set the still-full mixing bowl in the kitchen sink. Other ingredients are scattered across the kitchen, but I don't have the energy to put them away. "Is it okay if I clean the kitchen tomorrow? I think I wanna go to bed."

Dad walks over to me. The tenderness etched across his face makes me weak, and a tear spills over. "Talk to us, Zipporah. Tell us what you're thinking, what you're feeling. Let us help you."

One. Two. Three. Four. Five.

I inch forward, allowing him to fold me into his embrace. The tightness of his hug makes me crumble, and even more tears start to fall. And then he begins to sway, from one side to the other. Like I'm a baby and he's rocking me. It's the epitome of fatherly love. "Oh, sweetheart..." His tone is calm and comforting, like sunshine after a rainstorm. "We're gonna get through this. There's nothing that you can say or do that will change how we feel about you. You and your brother are the reasons we live and breathe and smile. We're a family, and nothing will ever change that."

Momma rubs my back, gently scratching her nails up and down my spine. She used to do the same thing when I was little.

Dad pulls back a smidge, forcing me to emerge from my hidden position. My face is soaked and flushed and snotty. He wipes me clean with his hands. "We've all been given a second chance at life, Orah. A lot of families from that night weren't as lucky as us. And we'll do anything to help you. To heal you. To give you a life filled with all the happiness you deserve. Because you deserve it, sweetie."

God help me, it sure doesn't feel like I deserve it.

I roll over, and hold my breath, waiting for the clock on my nightstand to turn from 5:15 to 5:16.

Another night.

Another night with no sleep.

It doesn't matter that I skedaddled from the kitchen, washed my face, brushed my teeth, and got into bed before most eight-year-olds. It doesn't matter that I silently cried myself into an exhausted stupor. And it doesn't matter that I *wanted* to go to sleep—despite the fact that I was almost one hundred percent certain a nightmare would wake me.

None of that matters because once again, my body refuses to give in.

I suppose it's trying to protect me from my mind, from the images I see when I sleep. But the shitty thing is that the images I see when I'm awake are just as horrific. Just as terrifying. Just as scary.

Normally, I would've reached for the phone a few hours ago and called Ridge. But he's on active duty tonight. And I'm trying to honor that, trying to honor his desire to serve and help.

It's not right for me to occupy his time when he's working.

What if he's in the middle of a burning building? Right now, what if he's surrounded by fire and smoke and damage and carnage?

Wouldn't I feel it?

If I can feel him, wouldn't I feel those things too? Burning me, scalding me, suffocating me?

I flop onto my back and kick off the covers. Refusing to part with my favorite blanket, I finagle it into a ball beside me, holding onto it like it's some kind of giant, blob-like teddy bear. Small streams of bluish-white light filter in from the blinds. It's a smushed combination of the streetlight at the end of the driveway and the bright, full moon that's slowly dimming as the sun gets ready to rise. In the glow, I watch the ceiling fan spin around and around and around. One of the blades has a piece of lint on it. I try to time my blinks with the dusty blade passing over my nose.

Blink. Blink. Blink. Blink. Blink.

One. Two. Three. Four. Five.

Everything about me feels sore and swollen and achy.

I'm so damn tired.

Shit, I'm more than tired.

I'm... drained.

I feel like there's nothing left of me.

I'm the kindling that refuses to catch fire. I'm the engine that refuses to crank. I'm the tire that refuses to hold air.

I'm the cracked glass. And I'm about to shatter. One wrong move will explode me into a million jagged shards.

And what happens then? No one will be able to pick me up without hurting themselves. Without slicing their skin. Without bleeding.

"You need sleep."

I'm so weary that Momma's sudden appearance doesn't even surprise me. Normally, I'd yelp, and my heart would erupt into a galloped sprint.

Now?

Yeah. Nothing.

Even my heart is too exhausted to be frenzied.

"I know," I mumble.

She pads over to my bed and nudges her finger in the air, non-verbally telling me to scoot over. I make room for her, and she climbs in next to me. Together, we lie on our backs.

I wonder if she sees the dust too.

"I bet you haven't slept more than three hours a night in the past two months." Her observation of the truth demolishes me.

Two months.

Yeah. Tomorrow is the two-month 'anniversary'.

"That's not true. When I was in the hospital I slept more than I was awake."

"That's because they had you on medication." She turns, staring at my profile. "It's not healthy, Orah. Your body needs sleep. It can't heal without it. Physically, emotionally. You're gonna keep struggling until your body gets the rest that it needs."

"I know."

She whimpers, choking back her sobs. "I'm so scared, honey."

My cracks splinter.

Shifting onto my side, I study my mother. This woman who has given everything for me. Worry lines that weren't there months ago decorate her forehead. Her skin is ashy and pale, and her hair looks more brittle than I remember.

Casualties.

Those two assholes created a domino effect. Everyone who died, everyone who was injured, has family, friends, and loved ones. Our wounds are slowly killing them as well.

Those two boys knocked the first domino, and the run is still going. Blocks are still falling. Every single second of every single day.

How long will they topple?

Will it ever stop?

I reach out and trace her face, feeling her tears drench my fingertips.

"Okay, Momma. I'll try a sleeping pill."

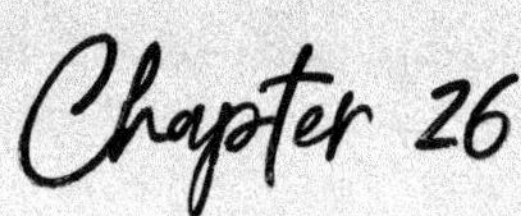

Chapter 26

Ridge

I hate big weddings.

Don't get me wrong, I know most people love them. And if that's your thing, good for you. But for me? Nope. No, thank you. I'd rather recreate and drink C's sherbert/sprout/sardine milkshake.

I know I shouldn't look a gift horse in the mouth. I mean, where would Dad's catering business be without huge weddings? Down the shitter, that's for sure. But I just don't understand them.

The pomp, the circumstance, the money.

Holy shit, the money. Money that could be spent for a down payment on a new house. A new vehicle. A dream vacation for the whole family. Heck, even a donation to the Children's Hospital.

Maybe that's just the guy in me. I reckon most guys are like me; they don't like big weddings.

On the tail end of that thought, I hear a huge ruckus at the front of the dance floor. I crane my head, wanting to see what's going on, but refusing to move and lose my place in the mile-long bar line.

Kip's standing on the small stage, in front of the cover band, shaking his ass to and fro. Lifting his bourbon and Coke high in the air, he waits for everyone to whoop and holler before he downs the drink in two swallows and tosses the plastic cup somewhere over the drummer's head. Then, he turns around and does a fucking back flip right off the stage. He lands on his feet but quickly stumbles, getting swallowed by the pile of guys and girls quickly getting drunk.

Well, I take back my previous thought.

Obviously, these dudes all love weddings. Love with a capital L. In flashing lights. With lasers shooting out of it.

I guess that makes me the weirdo in this scenario.

It's also pretty damn obvious, based on their state of inebriation, that the groom and other members of the bridal party were 'sipping Grandma's secret sauce' before the ceremony even began.

Because trust me, they didn't just start a few minutes ago. Based on these lines for the drink stations, I'll be lucky to have two beers in me before I walk back to the hotel tonight.

Kip and I went to Fire College together. Like most of the other guys, he was attracted to the big cities. So, that's how I find myself spending the weekend in Atlanta. Tonight—Friday night—is the wedding. And then tomorrow night is a housewarming party at his and Brianna's new condo in the middle of downtown. And then they leave for a two-week honeymoon in Fiji.

How the hell he is affording all of that on a fireman's salary, I'll never know.

Shuffling forward as the line barely moves, I stab my hand through my hair. My shift ended at seven this morning. I went home and took a nap, threw my stuff in a bag, and drove up here, giving myself just enough time to check into the hotel, change clothes, and walk over to the elaborate event center. I didn't want to get here too early because I'm not exactly abiding by the dress code. It's a black-tie event. Because, of course, why wouldn't it be? But the last thing I wanted to do was pay to rent a damn tux or buy some fancy new suit. Hell, I even hate wearing ties. That's why I'm dressed in simple black slacks and a white button-up.

With my sleeves rolled up.

Because it's hot as shit in here with five-hundred people dancing, eating, and partying.

Not to mention, my guilt could be a partial culprit for the sweat that's starting to roll down my back.

Guilt for not telling Orah where I am.

I didn't even tell her I was going out of town. So, if she calls, I'm gonna have to find a secluded corner where the noise is somewhat muted. Although, based on the way everybody's yelling out the lyrics to "Uptown Funk", the only place that'll be quiet will be my hotel room, which is two blocks over.

And why didn't I tell her?

Why didn't I tell her that for two-and-a-half days, the distance between us has been sliced and diced, taking me from seven hours away from her to just three hours away from her?

Well, that's the million-dollar question, isn't it?

I guess I didn't tell her because my thoughts inevitably trail to… I'm only three hours away from seeing her smile. From smelling her coconut shampoo. From wrapping her in my arms and feeling her body next to mine.

And I shouldn't think like that.

I know I shouldn't.

I made the mistake of mentioning mine and Orah's ongoing phone conversations to Dr. Evans during our last session. And she may be one hell of a doctor, but her poker face sucks. And it was easy to see that she disapproves of me having a…platonic relationship… with one of my former patients. Her frigid stare made me feel about two-inches tall.

Shame slithered through me, hissing and biting and poisoning me.

Tainting every feeling I have about My Brave Girl.

Even the pure and innocent and virtuous ones.

And the sad and unfortunate truth—the thing that makes Dr. Evans's judgment pack an even more powerful punch—is the fact that deep in my heart, deep in my mind, deep in my soul, those random thoughts of her smile and her shampoo and her body consume me.

And those are the things that I don't consider pure and innocent and virtuous.

And I'm not even talking about the treacherous path of sex. I fucking refuse to think about Orah and sex. Together. So, I'm not talking about that.

I'm talking about life and love and forevers.

And that's why I didn't tell her I was coming to Atlanta. It would probably be better for me to move to California and set up shop there, putting days and days of distance between us instead of just one measly tank of gas.

Fuck. Me.

Maybe I just need to get laid.

True, I prefer relationships to one-night stands, but that doesn't mean I haven't had a quick shag for shits and giggles.

And maybe that's just what I need tonight.

Hell, isn't that what young, single people do at weddings?

They hook up with someone to forget the troubles weighing them down?

They get naked with a stranger and attempt to fuck away the visions of the person they're not supposed to be with? The visions of the person who is wrecking their lives, driving them insane with desire and want and hunger.

I've already had my fair share of eyes on me. I guess I could just pick one of them.

Not the bridesmaid, though. She has black hair.

No one with black hair.

Finally, it's my time at the bar, and I make the split-second decision to follow through on my asinine plan of finding a lady for the night.

Needing liquid courage, I order a double shot of whiskey in addition to my beer. I fish through my pocket and stuff a couple of bucks into the tip jar, and then sneak away to the far side of the massive ballroom, seeking a modicum of privacy to down my shot. For some reason, just looking at the small plastic cup makes me angry.

I wanna crush it in my fist and watch the brown liquid slide through my fingers and pool onto the glazed concrete floor.

Instead, I turn it up and chug it.

In one deep, burning swallow.

"You must really hate weddings if you're already having to double fist?"

I jerk to the side, following the voice that carries just above the pounding noise of the band. She emerges from the shadow of the back corner and slowly makes her way to my side. I'm only five steps away from her, but she takes her sweet-ass time closing that short distance, doing her best to sashay her hips from side to side. It takes me less than a second to size her up, to realize she thinks of herself as a piece of art.

And she wants me to regard her.

To appraise her.

To bid on her.

And then, take her home.

She brings her acrylic wine glass up to her red-painted lips and takes a seductive drink, giving me a glimpse of her tongue as it flicks the rim. "Unless it's the opposite. Maybe you love weddings, and you're just eager to catch up with everyone else." She nods her head to the pile of people dancing. "I'm fairly certain Kip and his grooms-men floated a keg before the ceremony."

There's a side table not too far away. I give the empty shot glass a toss, and it lands on a pile of cocktail napkins that someone left behind. Turning back to the woman, I do exactly as she wants.

I eye fuck her.

Six ways from Sunday.

She's pretty. Blonde. Blue eyes. Nice body. Heavy makeup. Short dress.

Stiletto heels.

Heels that wouldn't be good for running if something were to happen.

Stop it, Ridge.

I work my jaw back and forth, trying to loosen the hell up. Lifting my own beer bottle to my mouth, I take a swig. Her eyes dart to my arms and widen in delight when I twist my hand in just the right way to make the vein in my forearm jump. Giving a shrug, I flirt back. "Which do you think it is? Love or hate?"

I shuffle on my feet, refusing to give in to the urge to walk away, to pretend she isn't there, to pretend this one-minute encounter hasn't made her intentions perfectly clear.

And this is one of the many reasons why I'm not a fan of the hook up.

There's this weird, instantaneous feeling that erupts in the air when the person standing in front of you, the person whom you've never even met before, wants sex. It's this bizarre dynamic of tension and slack.

It's like...well, growing up, we had this little dog named Ralphie. Man, Mom loved that pup. Anytime we sat down at the dinner table, Ralphie would stand on his back two legs, put his front paws and chin on the table, and beg for food. He'd look at you with these sweet, glistening, little puppy eyes. Here this dog was, begging you for a tiny scrap. This animal was giving you all the power. The power to decide what he could and couldn't have.

But guess what? That gift of power was only temporary.

When Ralphie saw he wasn't getting anything from you, he'd turn back around, completely ignore you, and eat his own dog food. He took back his power. Boom. Just like that.

I don't know, that's probably a stupid way to describe it.

But, sometimes, that's what a one-night stand feels like for me.

Temporary and not worth the trouble.

Because she—whoever *she* might be—can turn around and leave. She can find comfort and satisfaction in something—in *someone*—else.

Well, I want the power for more than one night.

I want a girl who wants me just as badly as I want her. Day after day. Night after night.

I wanna be the only man who can bring my woman comfort and satisfaction. No other. Just me.

I wanna control my lover for-fucking-ever.

And more importantly, I want her to control me right back.

Control. Me.

I bite the inside of my cheek. This is ridiculous. *I'm* being ridiculous. I have no idea why I'm making such a big deal out of this. Normal guys have casual sex. Hell, I believe in love at first sight, why can't I believe in copulation at first sight.

She tilts her head and hums. "Mmmm. Love or hate? Maybe, a little bit of both."

I give her a smile. "I guess you're right..." I tilt my response, indicating I want her to fill in the blank with her name.

"Kate."

"Kate," I repeat. The syllable feels wrong on my tongue.

"And you are?"

"Ridge."

She flashes a sparkling smile. "Well, Ridge, are you a friend of the bride, the groom, or both?"

"Kip and I went to Fire College together."

Her eyes flash. "A firefighter? I knew I liked you."

Well, that's a stupid thing to say. What if I were an accountant or a trash man or a teacher? She wouldn't like me then? I do my best to shrug off the corrosive and ignorant fodder, even though it chafes my ass. "Yes, ma'am. A firefighter. And what about you, Kate? What do you do?"

"I'm a stylist." She leans close. Like she's about to tell me a huge secret. Like she singlehandedly holds the key to the eleven secret herbs and spices for Colonel Sanders's chicken. "For the movie studios."

I pop an eyebrow. "Really?"

"Atlanta is a thriving production metropolis. All of the major studios film here." She glances around the room, pretending to blush. "You wouldn't believe some of the people I've met, some of the people I've worked with." She tosses her hair, wafting her perfume in the air. The scent is strong and floral. "Who's your favorite actor or actress?"

I thin my lips together. "I don't really have a favorite," I grant, drawing out my reply, just so it seems like I'm actively trying to think about an answer to her question.

She strokes a finger across her collarbone. "Oh, come on, everybody has a favorite."

I shake my head. When she just keeps nodding, trying to press me for a name, I blurt out the first one that comes to mind.

Her smile brightens. "Oh, I'm very familiar with him. I haven't worked with him on set, but I did meet him at an industry event. Let's just say," she peeps around to make sure we're still alone, "the rumors are true."

And with a giggle, she takes another sip of wine.

What the hell is that supposed to mean? Do I look like someone who reads tabloid magazines in my time off? Why on earth would I pay attention to the rumors of some Hollywood action movie star? A guy I'm never gonna meet?

I jiggle my empty beer bottle. "Looks like the line has died down some. I'm gonna get another beer. Would you like some more wine?"

"Absolutely." And when I walk away, she falls in sync with my steps. "I'll come with you, Ridge."

Standing back in line puts us closer to the action and the blaring roar of the band. The pulse of the music makes my temple throb, ripping a pounding headache through my brain. I do my best to ignore the pain and instead bend closer to her ear. "So, Kate, you didn't say, are you here for Kip or Brianna?"

"Brianna and I were sorority sisters."

"Nice. And, obviously, you live here in Atlanta?"

"I do. I have a loft in Midtown." She wraps a hand around my bicep. Leaning on one foot, she pretends to adjust the strap on her stiletto. "What about you?"

"I live in a small resort town on the central west coast of Florida."

When she settles her foot back on the ground, I take a meandering step forward, wondering if she'll let her hand fall back to her side.

She doesn't. She holds on.

"A small town? Really? I would've pictured you as a big city guy. Fighting fires during the day and prowling the clubs at night."

Clubs?

Yeah, no.

A nightclub with overpriced, watered-down drinks and VIP booths and cover charges? Nah, I'll take a draft beer and Belly's relentless teasing over that any day of the week.

"No. Big cities really aren't for me."

"So, what you're telling me is that as soon as the wedding festivities are done, you're heading back to your small, little Florida town? No obligations keeping you here?"

Ahhh. There it is.

Extra confirmation, as if I needed any, that she only wants me for the night.

One night. No strings attached. Non-committal sex.

I...I can do this. Right?

I mean, it's what I *need* to do, right? To prove to myself that I'm not tied to Orah. I'm not in love with her. I'm not bound to her.

I just think I am.

And this will prove that. Won't it?

I bump against her and graze my nose across her hair. Again, with the floral. Roses? Whatever it is, it smells too fake. "Trying to get rid of me already, Kate? Before the fun even begins?"

She squeezes my bicep tighter, digging her nails into my skin. When I straighten, her eyes slither down my face and focus on my lips. "Never." She nibbles the side of her mouth. "I just like knowing upfront how much time I have to *play*." And with that, she whispers the word 'play', moaning it in auditory foreplay, obviously trying to get me to jizz in my pants.

At the bar, I take her wine glass from her and hand it over, requesting a refill from the bartender. And then I order a fresh beer for myself. I would order two, but double fisting now that I've got a woman on my arm might seem a little odd.

We continue our flirting while we wander around the ballroom. We small talk with others; we share a plate of hors d'oeuvres. We dance to the slow songs, our bodies pressed against one another, tight and firm, with her fingernails scratching across my neck and tugging at my hair, giving us a precursor for what is to come.

And when everybody starts wigging out like they've never in their entire lives heard "Shout" by The Isley Brothers, I twirl her around and shake my ass like this is the best night I've ever had.

I even let her feed me a slice of cake, pretending it doesn't skeeve me out when she clunks the fork against my front teeth.

Hours.

Hours go by.

And with each passing minute, my nerves get bigger, angrier, more defiant.

They flame and fire in my stomach, sending rancid acid shooting up my throat. Even my beers don't tame the burn.

Maybe I'm meant to feel it. Meant to ache. Meant to hurt.

Because...maybe what I'm doing is wrong.

But you know what? I'm still gonna do it.

Because isn't loving what can't be mine worse?

Chapter 27

Ridge

My hand is quaking when I tap her key card against the lock and open the door to her hotel room.

As luck would have it, Kate's staying in the same hotel as me.

I guess that makes me really lucky, huh?

I glance around. The bed is ruffled, but still made. There's make-up bags and hair supplies on the side table, a bulging suitcase on the floor by the window, and a scattering of discarded clothes and shoes on the floor. I toss the key on the wet bar as she moves the Do Not Disturb sign from the inside of the door handle to the outside.

Shit's getting real now.

I shove my hands into my pockets, disgusted by their tremble.

Apparently, I can run into a raging inferno or attack an armed gunman, just fine, but having sex with a good-looking woman? It gives me the shivers.

She tosses her small clutch onto the top shelf of the closet and snakes her arms around my neck. I tug my hands from my pockets and plant them on her waist, fumbling when my right thumb gets caught in my pocket lining and bends at a weird angle. Her breasts plump against my torso. She angles her hip, forcing my legs apart. And then she grinds into me.

I'm scared I won't be turned on enough to get an erection.

And *terrified I will.*

She pushes onto her tiptoes and suckles my earlobe between her lips. Grinding. Sucking. Grinding. Sucking. I can smell the staleness of the wine on her breath. Her words are hot and too loud for my eardrum. "I'm not really big on kissing. That okay with you?"

Yep.

Her right hand lowers. Down my chest. Down my stomach. And it lands on my dick.

Welp. I'm hard.

What can I say? It's been over seven months.

I'm not a monk.

She giggles and bites my neck. When she starts to suck too hard, intentionally trying to give me a hickey, I jerk my head to the side. I definitely don't want to spend the next few days walking around with a love bite on my body.

Because this isn't love.

Planting my mouth on her ear, I return the favor of the nibbles and licks. Except I think she has hairspray residue all over her ear. It tastes like chemicals. Like rubbing alcohol and baby powder and... funky stuff. It makes the back of my throat tickle.

Fortunately, I don't have to poison myself for too long because she shifts her head, focusing her eyes on the massive bulge in my trousers. Her left hand joins her right, and she squeezes my cock and balls.

Uh. Yeah. That pinches. Her long fingernails tweak my nut sac skin in the wrong kind of way.

Oh well, beggars can't be choosers, I suppose.

And I'm begging, aren't I?

Begging her to make me forget the things—the person—I'm not supposed to be thinking about.

Her hands slide up to my abdomen, and she yanks my shirt away from my belt. "Take it off," she orders. "I'm tired of waiting. I've been wanting to sit on your cock all night long."

For whatever reason, that announcement provides me with a visual that kickstarts my stupid brain into making at least one smart decision tonight. "Wait. Kate, I don't have a condom."

She smiles. Her skin is flushed, and she has lipstick smears on her white teeth. "Oh, firefighter, I have a whole box." She tosses her head in the direction of the nightstand.

Sure enough, there's a huge blue box of condoms sitting right next to the complimentary hotel notepad and ink pen.

Huh. I wonder if her level of preparedness is supposed to make me feel better or worse.

Laughing, she dips her fingers into the collar of my shirt and tugs. Immediately, two small buttons pop off. They fly into the abyss of the room, and I can't even hear where they land because we're on carpet.

What the hell?

I need this shirt.

"Hey!"

My protest just makes her laugh harder. Eager to keep the remainder of my shirt in usable format, I make quick work of my buttons and strip, tossing the shirt behind me on the TV table.

Even the dim lights of the room don't dull her satisfaction. Her pupils dilate, and she sighs. Reaching out, her hands roam my muscles. And when her fingertips trace the scar on my left shoulder, I hiss.

She moans. She thinks her touch excites me.

Fucking shut up, Ridge.

Her touch does excite you.

It. Does.

You're about to have sex with a beautiful woman. *Shut the fuck up and enjoy it.*

She leans forward, taking my left nipple in her mouth. And then, she playfully bites down, scraping her teeth across my flesh.

I guess I should start taking her clothes off.

Yeah. That's what I should do.

I loop my fingers in the straps of her dress, dragging them down her bare shoulders.

Ow!

Damn. She's actually chewing on my nipple now.

Shit. That's making my skin raw.

It's a nipple, woman. Not a piece of saltwater taffy.

Entering my campaign to end the nip carnage, I growl, "Let me see you." Happy to oblige, she pulls away, abruptly ending her assault on Ridge's Tit Town. Although, she does leave the townsfolk covered in slobber and spit.

Grabbing her straps, she shimmies out of her dress. Most men would die to have a girl like this in front of them. She's wearing nothing but a strapless black bra, black panties, and her black high heels.

And she really does have a great body. Curvy and luscious.

She grabs my belt, intent on removing the barrier between us. And before I can dwell on the consequences, she drops to her knees, taking my boxer briefs with her.

There I am. With my slacks and underwear tucked around my dress shoes and my church socks—black with red diamonds—still standing at attention right below the curve of my calf muscle.

Her fingernails dig into my thighs.

My engorged dick bobs in her face.

"Oh, hell, yeah," she moans. She looks up at me, her eyes blinking slow and heavy. She's weighted down with desire and lust. I know because she's rubbing her thighs together. And then she gives me a bold and wicked smile. "This cock is a fucking monster. I knew I was making the right choice."

Ummm. Thanks.

She inches forward.

Inch. Inch. Inch.

Her tongue flickers out, and she presses the very tip of it to my wet slit. The touch is so light that if I wasn't watching it, I wouldn't believe it was happening.

But it is happening, and my body reacts to the image.

I shudder.

And that makes Kate very, very happy.

She pulls back just a smidge, and then opens her mouth like she's about to swallow a flaming sword at the circus.

And then...

A cell phone shatters the quiet.

It's loud and jarring and foreign.

It makes my brain feel wobbly, like a thousand marbles are rolling from side to side, clanking against my eardrums in the process.

She gasps in surprise and then grimaces, her face twisting in knots as she stares at my pants, which are still tangled around my feet. "What the hell, *Ridge*? You didn't silence it?" The way she articulates my name makes my stomach turn.

Uhhh, obviously-the-fuck-not, *Kate*.

Of course, I don't say that.

Because despite my state of undress with the stranger named Kate, I try to be a gentleman when warranted. And if anything warrants it, I think this does.

I shoot down, grab my boxer briefs and pants and wrangle them up my body, trying to ignore her huffs and puffs. Promptly zipping, but leaving my button and belt undone, I reach in my pocket and fish out my deafening phone. By the time I get ahold of it, it's stopped ringing. I flip it over so I can read the home screen, mentally preparing myself to either rip Cullen or Holt a new asshole, or rip *myself* a new asshole *if and when* I see Orah's name...

And that's when my heart drops.

Forget dropping.

It stops.

It stops beating completely.

It dies, taking all of my humanity with it. And leaving an empty void where it once thundered in my chest.

This time, there's no hiding the quiver of my hands. My fingers shake like I've been wandering through a blizzard for hours on end. I punch the screen, returning the missed call.

Kate flaps her hands, smacking them against her thighs. "You're actually calling someone? In the middle of *this*?" She's still on her knees, face-level with my now-flaccid dick, so when she wiggles her finger back and forth between our bodies—indicating *this*—her red fingernail bounces off her boobs and hits me in the groin.

I spin around just so I don't have to look at her.

The phone rings only once. "Ridge?"

"Ann? What's wrong? Is everything okay?"

It's after midnight. There's no way she's calling me just to say hi, just to check in.

The after-midnight calls come directly from Orah. Not her momma.

She speaks in a frantic frenzy, filled with distress and distemper. "I'm sorry to call so late. I really am. I just...we didn't know what else to do."

"It's fine. What's going on? Where's Orah?"

"Ridge!" I'm vaguely aware of Kate standing up and ripping at my shoulder—my scarred shoulder—trying to get my attention. "Hang up the phone. Now."

Ann hears it. She falters. "Oh. Oh, no. I...I interrupted. You're with someone."

I'm probably reading something into it that isn't there, but I think I hear disappointment in her tone. And it claws at the barren cavern where my heart used to sit, scratching at the walls and marring the surface.

Shame isn't even the right word. There's not a word in the existence of the human race that describes how inadequate and remorseful I feel.

I shake my head, even though she can't see it, and lie. "No. No, it's not like that. I'm just at a wedding."

"A wedding?"

"Uh-huh, yeah. Now, tell me what's going on. Where's Orah?"

Kate folds her arms across her chest and slaughters me with her eyes. Further cementing my asshole status, I hold up a finger, nonverbally telling her I need a minute, and rush out of the room and into the hallway of the hotel. Because nothing screams class, like a shirtless man with undone pants wandering around the corridor of the tenth floor of an expensive, Atlanta hotel in the middle of the night.

"She's sleeping," Ann says.

"She's sleeping? Orah's asleep?" I ask twice, wanting to make sense of her statement.

"Yes, but she's been asleep for a really long time."

Wild panic courses through my body, making me shake even more. "What do you mean she's been asleep for a really long time?"

I hear John talking in the background. It sounds like someone else is there too. Another woman. Tabby's mom, maybe?

"Ann!" I urge her.

"It's been over sixteen hours."

"Sixteen hours?! When's the last time she slept? Is she saying anything when you try to wake her up? Or does she just roll over and go back to sleep?"

There's more conversation on the other side of the line. Conversation I'm not privy to, and it's driving me insane. "Ann, you gotta tell me what's going on." I stalk up and down the hallway. Every step is like an electric shock, a pounding jolt that's trying to resuscitate not only my heart, but my entire world.

"Okay. So, she's not been sleeping well. You know that. I mean, she calls you all hours of the night. It's the nightmares and the fear and the anxiety. It's just too much for her. Well, we finally convinced her to try the sleeping medication the doctor prescribed. I know we should've waited until nighttime to give it to her. You know, so we could try and establish a normal sleeping pattern? But she was just so tired. Exhaustion is not even the right word for it, Ridge. We couldn't stand to see our baby like that."

I lean against the wall and scrape my hand down my face, tapping my chin. One. Two.

"Okay. So, when did you give it to her? And what did you give her?"

"She took the pill at seven this morning. But she didn't fall asleep until about eight." There's a muffled noise. Either she pulled the phone away from her, or she partially covered it with her hand. "John, get me that bottle." After a second, she comes back and reads the prescription name and dosage to me.

I'm already shaking my head, slapping my skull back and forth against the wall. "That's the lowest strength. There shouldn't be any major problems or complications with a dose that small."

The little bit of knowledge I now have gives me back a small shred of my sanity. I take a deep breath, trying to calm my frazzled nerves and overstimulated brain cells. "It's probably just allowed her to relax for once, to stop the racing thoughts about that night. She may spend a whole twenty-four hours napping. Who knows... Her body will tell her when she's had enough sleep." I balance the phone between my chin and shoulder and work my button and belt, fastening them. "What's she doing when you try to wake her?" I once again ask the question that Ann didn't answer. "What's she saying? That she's still sleepy?"

"That's what I'm trying to tell you, Ridge. We can't *get* her to wake up. At all. We shake her, yell at her, move her. And nothing happens."

Apparently, those electrical shocks did their job. Because my heart roars to life, ripping into a violent rhythm that shakes my ribcage. "Wh–what?"

"We can't even get her to open her eyes." Ann gives a sharp little inhale and then rushes through the rest of her explanation in a hushed tone. "Ridge, she...she's not even waking up to use the bathroom. She's peed on herself. Twice. And we've completely changed her clothes and the bedding both times. She didn't even make a sound."

"Is she struggling to breathe?"

"No. She's breathing normal. And we've checked her pulse several times. Each time has been in the fifties. The Internet said that was normal for when someone is sleeping."

I'm a paramedic, not a doctor, so it's not like I sit around reading medical journals for fun, but I do know that certain people can have sensitivities to certain medications. Not allergies, but sensitivities. Maybe that's happening to Orah. Her body can't process the prescription the way it's meant to, and it's having an exaggerated effect on her. Making her sleep for double and triple the time of a 'normal' person.

"We called the doctor," Ann continues. "But with it being the weekend, we had to leave a message with the answering service. I don't know when she'll call us back." There's more muffled noise, more jumbled talking and discussions. "I think, maybe, we should take her to the hospital. What do you think?"

What do I think?

I think if My Brave Girl wakes up in a hospital again, while having absolutely no clue how or why she's there, she's gonna freak the fuck out.

And that's the last thing I want to happen.

Not to Orah.

"No, don't carry her to the hospital. But if she starts having difficulty breathing or her heart rate drops or spikes, then call an ambulance."

"But—"

I interrupt Ann, already making my way back to Kate's hotel door. "Listen, I'm on my way. Give me ten minutes, and I'll be on the road."

There's a brief pause. I can hear the confusion and turmoil pouring out of her like a waterfall after a hard rain. "Ridge, that's really nice of you, but I don't think we can wait seven hours. If she doesn't wake up in the next little bit, we've gotta do something. We're scared."

"It's not gonna be seven hours. I'm in Atlanta. I'll be there in less than three hours."

"You're in Atlanta?"

"Yeah. My friend's wedding was here."

"Are...are you sure?"

"Of course, I'm sure." There is absolutely nothing that could keep me away from Zipporah Smith right now.

If I had to crawl to South Carolina on my hands and knees, I'd do it.

Obviously, I'm not looking forward to explaining this to Kate, but maybe a little humiliation is just what I need. What I deserve. "Listen, I'm on my way. I left your address at home, so text it to me, okay? I'll be there before you know it. And if there's any change with Orah, any change at all, call me, okay?"

"Okay. See you soon."

As soon as I hang up the phone, my worry and anxiety take root, growing deep in the bedrock of my soul. Like grass growing in the smallest crack of the sidewalk, it splits me wide open and springs up, making its presence known, refusing to die even though it should.

Again, I drag my hand down my face and tap my chin.

Tap all I want, nothing is gonna ease this blooming weed of apprehension until Orah is awake and in my arms.

I take a few deep breaths, trying to center myself. I've gotta at least get my shakes under control. I can't drive like this. And I sure as shit can't apologize to the woman who just had her tongue on my cock while I'm like this.

And like the dumbass I am, I push on the door, expecting it to crack open. Nope. This is a hotel door that automatically locks as soon as it's shut. So, I have to knock.

I have to knock on the door so I can get my shirt to cover the nipple that Kate tried to saw off with her incisors so I can drive three hours to check on the girl I'm secretly in love with who won't wake up and has a diaphragm healing around bovine mesh.

Kate opens the door with a scowl plastered across her pretty face. Turning, she walks away and sits on the edge of the bed.

"Kate, I'm so very sorry. That was a call I couldn't ignore. It's a... family friend. She has health issues and is having a reaction to some medication." Her snarl doesn't soften. "I've got to leave for South Carolina. Right now." I grab my shirt from the TV stand and slide my arms through the sleeves. "I probably didn't mention this, but I'm a paramedic too. They need my help."

She rolls her eyes. "Whatever." She stands up, fishes her handbag out of the closet, and dramatically waves her hand at the door, indicating I should go first. It's then I notice that she's completely re-dressed. In the dress that was crumpled on the floor just ten minutes ago. I tilt my head, studying her. She's also reapplied fresh lipstick, and that sickly floral perfume scent is even stronger now.

She put on fresh perfume?

"You're going out?"

She looks at me like I'm the lamest dude to ever walk the face of the earth. "Yeah, Ridge. I am. I texted a friend and the after-party is still going on. I'm headed back down there."

Of course, she is.

Those condoms won't use themselves.

I button my shirt and give it a quick push, tucking one side in. I'm freakin' dying to race down to my fourth-floor room, throw my crap in my bag, and hit the road. But it's the middle of the night. I can't very well let her go traipsing around this big-ass city all by herself in the dark. "Listen, let me walk you back to the venue. You don't need to be out there by yourself."

She cocks a hand on her hip. "Are you serious right now?"

I furrow my brow. "Of course, I'm serious."

She growls. Literally growls. "You," she rages with an accusing finger-point in my face. "All of the prime DNA went into your good looks, hot body, and massive cock. Because you sure don't have any intelligence floating around in that empty brain of yours. I live literally two-and-a-half miles from this place. I do my fair share of walking alone at night through this city." She thins her lips. "I. Got. This."

"Your place is only two miles away? Why the hell would you pay for a hotel room?" I flop my hand toward the bed. "This place is four-hundred dollars a night."

Discreetly, and almost imperceptibly, her eyes flicker to the condoms on the nightstand.

Oh, say no more. She doesn't want her one-night stands seeing where she lives. Being all up in her business. Hanging out more time than necessary.

Hey, I get it. After spending this time with Kate, I wouldn't want *her* to be in *my* apartment either.

Heading out the door, I decide nothing would be more torturous than waiting for the elevator with her by my side. Racing to the end of the hall, I take the stairs, two at a time, down to my room.

Well, this night was an epic failure. My grand visions of putting Orah behind me by getting in between the sheets with someone else backfired.

And outside of my all-consuming concern for Orah, the only thing I can think is...if I never run across another '*Kate*' as long as I live, I'll be a happy man.

Chapter 28

Ridge

I'm almost true to my word.

It's seventeen minutes before I'm tossing my overstuffed and discombobulated duffle bag in the back of my Jeep. Not ten. It took longer than I thought it would to check out of the hotel. The front desk clerk couldn't comprehend the fact that I was allowing a family emergency to take precedence over the ten-percent discount I got for booking under the wedding party block for a minimum of two nights. Eventually, I told him to keep the damn money because I had to get on the road.

I'm tossing the car in reverse when I catch my reflection in the rearview mirror. My eyes are a little glossy and red, and I'm quickly reminded of the laissez-faire attitude I forced upon myself so I could venture into that room with Kate and whip my dick out. And that make-believe, cavalier horniness was the result of seven light beers and the double shot. And a few sips of Kate's wine when she wouldn't shut up about me trying it. I started drinking close to seven hours ago, and my last drink was more than an hour ago. Reaching over into the glove box, I grab my breathalyzer machine.

Yeah, I'm that guy.

And you'd be that guy too after responding to your first drunk driver fatality.

Shit. What am I gonna do if I blow over the magic number? I wonder how much a three-hour Uber would cost?

Did I drink enough water? Eat enough pigs in a blanket?

When the machine beeps, I utter a silent prayer and look at the numbers.

.039.

I close my eyes and give thanks for the answered prayer.

The drive to South Carolina is a nightmare. Agonizingly slow, powered by small bursts of blurred mania. It feels like a vise is gripping my heart, squeezing and strangling the blood from the one single organ that's keeping me alive. My only saving grace is that the wretched feeling ebbs and flows, never staying constant, never quite killing me. Because when I think I'm about to explode, just when I think I'm about to be decimated, a calm rushes over me, reminding me that everything's gonna be fine.

She's gonna be fine.

I'm gonna be fine.

We're gonna be fine.

We've been through something way worse than a reaction or sensitivity to medication. We've been through Hell. Literally. We've seen the fiery blaze. We've felt the molten heat. We stood in the middle of it, counting the flames. And we emerged on the other side—alive. Together. Whole.

Scalded. But not incinerated.

I'm about thirty minutes out from her house when my phone rings. I slow my speed just a smidge and pull into the right lane, trying to refocus my brain so I can have a conversation. My only greeting is her name. "Ann?"

Her sobs echo through my Bluetooth. "R—Ridge?"

My hands clutch the steering wheel in an unforgiving grip. "What happened? What's wrong?"

"She woke up."

If she woke up, how come Ann doesn't sound happy?

"She's awake? How is she? Why are you crying?"

"Something's not right." She coughs, choking on her weeping gasps and moans. "She...she..." She stutters around her hiccups.

"She what?"

Before Ann can finish, I hear a disturbing flurry of activity on the other side of the line. Muffled voices. Shrieks. Wails.

"I think she's sick," Ann enunciates, trying to be heard over the ruckus.

"Sick? Sick how? Describe it to me." There's a lump in my throat the size of a boulder. I can barely get the words out.

"She woke up about twenty minutes ago. For a few minutes, everything seemed fine. We had her sitting in the living room, drinking some water. I was about to fix her something to eat. And then," she staggers over a sniffle, "then, she just started shaking. Shaking like she was really, really cold, but she's not. She's actually sweating. And she's breathing funny, like she's about to hyperventilate. We tried to give her more water, but she threw it up. She keeps saying her chest hurts. Her eyes are jumpy and wiggly, like..."

Swerving back into the left lane, I speed up, racing past the eighteen wheelers hauling in the middle of the night. "Like what?"

"Like she can't even focus on us. It's like she's staring straight through us, like she's seeing a ghost or something." There's more noise and crying, amplifying my nerves, making me even more desperate to get to her.

It sounds like Ann drops the phone.

"Ann? Ann!"

All of a sudden, a new voice jumps across the distance. "Ridge?"

"John? John, what's happening?"

He swallows so loudly it's audible. Audible over everything else, even the slam of my own heartbeat.

"She...she..." He can't even speak.

"She what?!"

"She's sitting in the corner right now. Talking to herself."

"Talking to herself? What's she saying?"

"Something about saving."

I stop breathing. I inhale, and it's held prisoner, captured deep in the recesses of my lungs. "Saving what?"

He's quiet for a few beats. I assume he's trying to decipher her words. "She's saying, 'I can help you. And then you can help me. We can save each other.'"

A machete slices into my body, flaying the wide chasm that's already divided my chest in two.

It's *her* words.

Her words from that night.

The first words she spoke to me when I ran into that supply closet and changed the trajectory of both of our lives.

"Should we call an ambulance?"

I punch the gas. I'm actually going so fast now, the only smart thing to do is to put my flashers on. "It sounds like she's having a panic attack." I wanna tap my chin, but I need both hands to drive. "Listen, I'll be there in twenty or less. I have my jump bag with me. I've got medicine."

He repeats the information to Ann and whoever else may be there, and then he whispers a plea before ending the call. "Hurry."

Hurry.

Hurry.

Hurry.

Raindrops start to fall, plopping against the windshield in a scattered pattern. The weather dances with me, synchronizing itself to my pace. I drive faster; the drops fall harder. My windshield wipers work double time, flashing back and forth, creating a smear of water. I blink rapidly trying to ward off the reflective glare from my headlights bouncing off the waterlogged asphalt. By the time I turn off the interstate exit, the rain is pelting my Jeep in thick sheets, powered by giant gusts of wind. It's so loud; I can barely hear the navigation instructions blaring from my speakers.

After an eternity...

An eternity of living and dying...

An eternity of plowing through red lights and racing past stop signs...

An eternity of convincing myself that Orah's health problems are happening as karma for the things I did just hours ago...

I pull into the circular driveway of a one-story brick house, with a large front porch, and lights blaring from every window.

Putting on my game face, I force myself into my role. The role I'm meant to do, the role I want to do, the role I'm lucky enough to be a part of.

I'm observant. That's part of my role.

Through the midnight skies and colored pyramids of summer raindrops, I see all sorts of things.

I see the black mailbox with the name 'Smith' written in pretty cursive letters.

I see the hydrangea bushes, glistening with water, their pink and white blooms drooped for a nighttime slumber.

I see the open front door with a large wooden sign leaning next to it that reads, "Shoo...unless you have cookies, Christmas presents, or a winning lotto ticket. If that's the case, C'mon In!"

I see all of those things. But they don't give me cause to worry. What worries me is the image of John, Ann, and an older woman whom I don't know running out of the open front door and down the three porch steps.

But they aren't running toward me.

Oh, no.

They're running toward *her*.

My Brave Girl is standing in the middle of the pouring rain, at the juncture of where the walkway meets the circular drive, staring up at her house.

I fling the Jeep into park and jump out so fast, I don't even kill the engine. I've barely cleared the driver-side door when I call her name.

Call *to* her.

Call *for* her.

"Orah!"

The movement of her body is slow. Dream-like and lazy. Disconnected and disjointed. Heavy and filled with burden.

Her every motion is blanketed by terror. It's so real, so tangible, I can feel it breaking my bones, snapping them into piercing, little shards.

I can feel what you feel.

My own steps falter, and I slide a hand across the hood of my car just so I can steady myself. The rain batters me, soaking me from top to bottom. My hair, my beard, my clothes. My white dress shirt clings to me. The fabric is thin, but it might as well be a fur coat. It's suffocating the breath from my lungs.

Through the darkness, I watch as she turns to face me. I put one foot in front of the other. My legs feel like they're filled with lead. Just like me, she's drenched. Her raven hair blends with the darkness of the night. Her black sweatshirt swallows her body, and her heather-gray shorts cling to her thighs.

She blinks. And blinks again.

And then...she *sees* me. She sees past the hurt and dread and anxiety that's clouding her vision. She sees me standing in front of her, begging her with my heart, begging her with my unspoken words, to follow me out of this Hell.

Let me break the chains, Orah.

Let me extinguish the flames.

Let me silence the screams.

One. Two. Three. Four. Five.

It takes five seconds for my name to burst from her mouth in a soul-gutting sob. "Ridge!"

She races toward me, and the second she starts moving, my own body does too. I'm no longer weighted down. I'm no longer cemented to the ground. I mimic her actions, running and stomping through the puddles.

She dominates me.

I'm the marionette tied to the string that only Orah controls.

She jumps into my embrace, a tangle of arms and legs and sleek skin. I haul her higher, getting a better grip, and she immediately wraps her legs around my waist and buries her face into the crook of my neck.

Her cries are like a living nightmare. Something I pray I never hear again after tonight. Her body violently shudders, racked with wails so profound it's like she's weeping for every man, woman, and child who's ever experienced a trauma. A scream rips from the depths of her healing lungs, wild and animalistic. It's followed by short, frenzied breaths wrapped around even more sobs. She tries to quiet herself. Opening her mouth, she bites down on my scarred left shoulder, wanting nothing more than to stifle the unwanted feelings surging through her and holding her hostage.

Her chest is pressed against mine, and even through the layers of clothes, I can feel her heartbeat pummeling against me, beating the shit out of my battered spirit.

It's way too fucking fast.

I press my lips against her knotted hair. Gone is the coconut scent. It's nothing but a mix of sweat and ozone. "I'm here, Little Bird." I kiss her temple. "I'm. Right. Here."

I lift my head. John is standing in the rain on the bottom porch step, watching us. Ann and the other woman are huddled under the porch roof, holding onto one another as tightly as me and Orah. I quickly walk their way, eager to ease My Brave Girl's pain.

Well, her physical pain, that is.

The emotional pain won't start to heal until she finally speaks her truth.

I give a quick nod to John, squinting against the stinging rain, which is now blowing sideways. "Get my jump bag out of the back. It's pushed up underneath the seat. And my cell phone is in the front." I don't include instructions for him to turn off the ignition or shut the still-open driver-side door; I think John's smart enough to figure those things out on his own.

I cross the threshold, entering the house like I have every right to be there, like it's my home and not Orah's. Ann scuttles behind us, fawning her hands across Orah's back. The comforting gesture does nothing to soothe Orah's hysteric cries and hurried breaths. "You have a big bathtub?" I ask her.

She nods. "The largest is in our bathroom. The master bathroom, I mean."

I bob my head, nonverbally requesting her to lead the way. I follow behind her, barging through the living room and down the hallway, holding Orah close, wanting to make sure I don't accidentally ram her body into a random piece of furniture. We're dripping everywhere, creating a trail of crumbs—rainwater, dirt, and leaves. Turning into a large bedroom, my eyes bounce from the disheveled king-size bed to the dresser to the dimly lit bathroom on the far side.

The white and tan bathroom is large, with a long vanity with two sinks, a tile shower, and a toilet in a small water closet. Tucked in the corner is a huge garden tub. "Turn it on. Make it a little hotter than normal," I tell Ann.

There's a dressing bench set flushed against the wall next to the tub. I shift Orah in my arms, turning her sideways, and sit down. Her face rubs across my neck, sliding down the wet mixture of rain and snot and saliva. She nestles against my chest. Her feral cries have somewhat quieted. Not because she's settling down, but because they are strangled before they can even escape her body. Suffocated by her frantic and delirious attempts to suck oxygen into her lungs. I fling her matted hair out of the way and press my fingers against her carotid. I check my watch and count the powerful beats as they slap against the pads of my fingers.

Shit.

She's got to calm the fuck down.

John bursts into the room. He sets my bag and phone beside me on the bench, and without hesitation, wraps his arms around his wife, trying to be her calm in the middle of this calamity. Ann clutches his soaking wet shirt. She fists the fabric so hard that water pours out of it, flooding the light brown rug underneath their feet. The older woman peeks from around the doorframe. She's got brown hair with a slice of light gray framing her face on both sides. She frowns in worry and wipes her runny nose. John reaches in her direction, "Mom…" She grips his hand and allows herself to be tugged into a three-person hug.

John's mom.

Orah's granny.

Keeping one arm locked around Orah, I open the jump bag, making quick work of tearing into the sterile syringe and drawing the medicine from the correct vial.

I'm lucky; White Sky allows all paramedics to carry a fully stocked and government-issued jump bag on our person, even when we're off duty. We're not allowed to carry narcotics in our clone bag, but we've got everything else. Our superiors never want us to feel like our hands are tied when it comes to helping someone, to offering life-rendering aid. The overwhelming urge to help doesn't stop just because we haven't punched the clock on our timecard.

But… we *do* have to file a report and account for any medications and supplies that we use while off duty. So, the fact that I'm in South Carolina and about to administer meds to the young woman I was locked in a storage room with during a mass casualty incident is gonna be a little hard to explain.

But I can't think about that now.

Right now, the only thing that matters is Orah.

My Brave Girl.

My Little Bird.

"I'm gonna give her some medicine to help ease the panic attack. A shot of lorazepam."

"That'll help?" John asks.

"It should, yeah."

Ann worries her fingers, twisting them back and forth in a cat's cradle. "And if it doesn't?"

The last thing I want is to subject Orah to another hospital stay. Especially a hospital stay that's happening within the wee hours of the two-month anniversary of her nearly dying. My eyes flicker to the three people in front of me. The heat from the hot water is steaming the mirrors and mingling with the summer chill that's clinging to our saturated clothes. "We'll cross that bridge when we come to it."

I push Orah's shorts up her thigh. In one swift and fluid movement, I do the intramuscular injection. She doesn't flinch at the pain. Doesn't grimace or wince. The pain in her mind is so much worse than just a little pinprick to the leg.

I toss the used needle on the counter. Begrudgingly, I make a move to stand up. It's like I can't bear to be torn away from Orah's embrace for even one single second. "Stand her up."

They take her from my arms and do their best to balance her. Which is hard to do because she's still shaking like a leaf, and her legs wobble, like she's using muscles that have lain dormant for years.

I rip my shirt off, not even taking time to mess with the buttons. Of course, my mind flashes to my encounter with Kate.

Not all of my buttons are on this bathroom floor. Two of them are in her hotel room.

And that thought alone guts me.

"Take her clothes off."

John and Ann share a look. "You...you want us to get her naked?" Ann asks in a verbal stumble, filled with surprise.

What? Of course not.

I shake my head. "No, absolutely not. Leave her undergarments on. I...I can't see her."

I guess I should word that differently. But it's true. I *can't* see her. Yes, I'm a professional. But I'm in love with my patient; it's not right.

While John and Ann manhandle Orah, working to strip her from her heavy, waterlogged clothing, I toe off my shoes and socks. I slide my belt from my slacks and toss it on the building clothing pile.

John hugs Orah's trembling body next to his, holding her up as Ann drags her shorts down her legs.

And then, Orah's standing there in her black panties and a black tank top.

"I have to leave her tank top on," Ann explains. "She's not wearing a bra."

"That's fine." Reaching over, I turn the water off on the now-filled bathtub. Dipping my hand, I test it. Sure enough, it's a little on the hot side, but she'll need the extra heat now that the storm water has chilled her to the bone.

I step into the tub—while still in my pants—and hold out my hands for Orah. Tears are streaming down her beautiful face, cutting a path across her rosy cheeks and chapped lips. Her gray eyes are wide, frozen with fear and hollow with sadness. And her teeth are chattering so hard, there's a very good possibility that she may chip them.

It fucking breaks my heart.

John takes small baby steps with her. "C'mon, honey. You'll feel better once the medicine kicks in. Let's get you cleaned up."

I don't think there's any way that she'll be able to actually step over the side of the tub; her body is too shaky and loose. "I got it," I tell John. Sliding one hand behind her back and the other behind her knees, I dip down and lift her. For a moment, I hold her, wishing that my touch alone could heal her. Because I would give anything if that were the case.

Fuck my moral compass. I'd never leave her side.

Right or wrong be damned.

Eternity could come and go, and she would still be in my arms. Safe and sound and loved and cherished.

Setting her on her feet, I gently guide us into the water, taking care to make sure she doesn't slip or fall. I sink into the tub and settle her between my legs. As soon as the back of her head falls against my chest, her face turns, scattering her gasping breaths across my bare skin.

I hold out my hand. "My phone."

Ann grabs it and drops it, quickly apologizing. I try to extinguish some of the boiling tension that's draining us all, leaving us exhausted and evaporated, running on empty. I give her a little smile. "Thanks, Ann. You're doing great."

Thumbing through my apps, I open the meditation one and click on a green noise playlist. The room is instantly filled with the overlapping sounds of muted ocean waves, chirping insects, and a crackling fire.

Orah's granny has shifted position back to the doorway. Beside her is the light switch. "Ma'am? Could you turn out the lights, please?" She flips the switch, casting the bathroom into darkness. It's not pitch black, though; there's still light filtering in from the bedroom.

For a few minutes, everyone stands around, watching from the shadows as I take a bath with their daughter, with their granddaughter.

Eventually, Orah starts to calm. Her sobs turn into sniffles. Her teeth stop clanking together. And her hyperventilating gasps wane into a normal rhythm.

The relief we're all feeling is palpable. It's like we were falling into quicksand, just waiting to be swallowed alive, and suddenly, someone has thrown us a rope. It's a gift we worried would never come.

Her granny is the first to speak. "Maybe we should give them a moment?"

"Oh, I...uh..." From the edge of the darkness, I watch Ann turn to John. She's not sure what to do.

He takes her by the hand and leads her out of the room. "We'll be in the bedroom, Ridge. Just holler when you're ready."

I nod as he turns, and I wrap my arms around Orah's stomach, fixing her in my grasp. "I'm here, Zipporah." Lowering my head, I kiss her forehead. "Remember, Little Bird, we're gonna save each other."

Chapter 29

Orah

I tiptoe down the hallway, trailing my finger next to me on the white-painted chair rail that divides the wall into two colors—ivory and taupe. I pause outside of Boaz's room, staring at the small slit where the door didn't close all the way.

Ridge is still sleeping, having been gifted with the glory of my brother's vacant, king-size bed instead of the double bed that sits in the guest room.

I guess it's no surprise that I woke first, considering how much sleep I've had over the past thirty-plus hours. First, there was the sleeping pill. Then, there was the subsequent nap after my panic attack subsided. The slumber was a consequence of both the exhaustion of suffering through it and the medication that Ridge gave me.

I woke about three hours ago, took a long shower, and had an even longer talk with my parents. And now, I'm eager to talk to Ridge.

Well, not exactly *eager*, but you know what I mean.

Now that I've made the decision to tell him the truth about that night, I'm anxious. I need to do it quickly before I chicken out.

Yes, I'm terrified of what he will think of me. Yes, I'm terrified that he'll walk out of my life, never to be seen again. But I can't keep this locked inside anymore. It's eating me alive. I think last night/ this morning was evidence of that.

And don't misconstrue what I'm saying…it's not like I'm gonna call up the news crew and start doing interviews about what happened. I still don't want people to know.

But Ridge isn't *people*.

He's the part of me that I didn't even know was missing.

I didn't realize part of me was lost. But it was. I was just trying to fill the void with status and possessions and internet fame.

Little did I know, I had a gaping wound long before that bullet tore through me. And every single second of every single day, I was leaking more of myself into the abyss. My happiness. My sense of self-worth. My kindness. My humor. My joy.

Leak. Leak. Leak.

Drip. Drip. Drip.

Ooze. Ooze. Ooze.

I was transforming into nothing but an empty shell.

But then he opened the door. And dammed the weeping injury.

My life actually started the night I was supposed to die.

But that doesn't necessarily mean it's gonna be easier than it was before. Oh, no. I suppose an authentic life worth living is hardly ever easy.

I push on the door, and it creaks. He's sprawled across the bed, one leg underneath the covers and one leg above. His right arm is overhead, draped across the pillow. He's dressed in a T-shirt and gym shorts. Over in the corner of the room, a duffle bag is open with a spattering of clothes spread around it. I guess he brought in his bag and got fresh, dry clothes.

Mom and Dad told me everything that Ridge did. I wish I could remember the bath. I wish I could remember what he looks like without a shirt on. As my brief glimpses of him from the hospital are nothing more than faded memories. I wish I could remember what it felt like to be in his arms with almost nothing between us. But everything is hazy and blurry. It's like a dream.

Once again, he turned my nightmare into a dream, and I don't even remember it.

I pad across the floor, and before I lose my nerve, I crawl into bed with him, tugging the comforter up around me. I lay on my side and fold my hands underneath the pillow, watching him as he sleeps.

He's always observant, always aware of his surroundings, so I'm not really surprised when he senses my presence—or the presence of someone—and starts to wake up. He shuffles around, giving a husky moan that reverberates low in my stomach and sends a hot tickle across my pelvis. He flips his hand and rubs his eyes, eventually popping them open to stare at the ceiling.

It's only a split second before he turns and sees me.

"Oh, shit!" He bolts upright and bounces across the mattress, taking the comforter and sheets with him. His eyes widen in shock like I'm a venomous snake about to strike. He's perched on the very edge of the bed. One wrong move, and he'll roll right off and onto the floor.

I cover my mouth, trying to stifle my giggle.

He furrows his brow and glances behind his shoulder to the open door. "What?!" His voice is laced with sleep and confusion. He looks back at me. Then back at the door. "Where are your parents?"

"Momma went to the grocery store, and Dad is taking a nap."

His eyes roam across my face, and then slowly travel the length of my body. It's not like I'm wearing anything scandalous, just an oversized black T-shirt that I confiscated from Boaz's closet a few days ago and short black shorts.

But the way I feel when his eyes are on me like that?

It's more than sexual. He makes me feel valuable. Priceless. Powerful.

In. Control.

He clears his throat and scrubs his hand down his face before tapping his chin. "Should...should we be in here? Alone?"

Should we?

Probably not.

But do I wanna be anywhere else?

Absolutely not.

"It's okay. They know we have a lot to talk about. They know we need privacy."

He jabs a hand through his hair, making his wild bed head even more crazed. His dark brown strands poke in every single direction. He squints, looking at the small lines of sunlight as they peek through the window blinds. "What time is it?"

"A little after two." I slide my hand across the fitted sheet and pat the area where he had been sleeping. "Lie back down. Let's talk."

For a moment, I think he's going to say no, but then he wiggles his body, settling back down. Of course, he doesn't settle in the *exact* same spot; that would put him too close to me. Put him in a position that he obviously thinks is too scandalous...based off the way he basically had a cow when he saw me lying next to him.

Did he freak out because he doesn't want me that close?

Or because he does?

Grabbing the stolen comforter and sheet, he flops the covers in my direction, blanketing my bare legs, hiding them from view. Then, he kicks both of his legs free so that I'm the only one under the cocoon of the bedding. Lastly, he punches the pillow beneath his head, fluffing it so that he's resting a little higher. He's lying on his side, facing me, but the natural shape of his masculine body and the tilt of Boaz's punched pillow have him towering over me.

Finally, he exhales a melodramatic sigh.

I snort. "Comfy?" I riff around a grin.

He cocks an eyebrow, fighting his own smile. "Orah Smith, what would you like to talk about?"

I'm sure he thinks I wanna talk about last night. But I can't talk about last night without talking about *that* night.

I pause, contemplating changing my mind. I could get up, run out of this room, and continue to hide the truth from him. But the fact remains, he *will* find out what I did, and I would much rather him hear about it from me while we're alone in my house than in the middle of our congressional inquiry, surrounded by politicians and lawyers.

My stomach somersaults, making me queasy. My heart beats, erratic and chaotic. Its frenzied pattern matches the jumbled thoughts as they zigzag from one side of my brain to the other. There's no organization; it's like my body is a literal junk drawer—ink pens, batteries, scissors, a screwdriver, and all those crappy little things you save, never knowing when you may need them...the twist ties from the bread bags, the silicone packets from the vitamin bottles, and a suitcase key for a suitcase that you don't even remember owning.

I'm not sure what to say first, which horrible truth to deliver.

So, I randomly pick one and blurt it out.

"I lost my virginity on the night of the attack."

The good humor instantly falls from Ridge's face. His lips slack open, giving me a glance of his pink tongue. Confusion and concern color him in equal parts.

He doesn't say anything.

One. Two. Three. Four. Fi—

"Wh–what?" he babbles.

Underneath my pillow, I squeeze my fingernails into my palms, wondering if I'm strong enough to draw blood. If I can focus on causing a visual pain, maybe it can help me with the pain that I can't see.

After a second, I give up.

Because I need to start focusing on the pain that's hidden deep in my heart, deep in my soul. The pain that's hidden away from this man in front of me. The man I owe my life to. The man I love.

Isn't that the only way to stop the nightmares? To stop the fear? To stop the suffocating regret?

"I'm ready to tell you about that night. I mean, if you want me to?" My offer hitches up at the end. Suddenly, I'm overcome with a new terror...

What if he doesn't care?

In the hospital he said he knew that I was hiding something. He said he wanted to know. He said he would always fight for me.

But people say a lot of things.

People change. Feelings change. Even the truth changes.

One person's truth can be another person's lie.

So, maybe he doesn't even care about *my* truth anymore.

His hand shifts to the middle of the bed, entering no-man's land between our bodies. He turns his palm upward, and curls his fingers, inviting me to hold his hand.

And I do.

"I want you to. Your words have a home in my heart."

Heat blossoms across my face. The sincerity in his tone calms my nerves and soothes my rattled anxiety.

I think his bluntness shocks him, though. He drags a hand down his scruff and taps his chin.

Taking a deep breath, which barely even hurts anymore, I start at the beginning. "You saw my social media before it was deleted. You saw some of the comments. I think a pretty wide consensus was that I was sexually active. Perhaps even promiscuous." He nibbles on the inside of his cheek. The motion twitches the mustached hair of his beard, tweaking it left and right. "But that wasn't the case. I was a virgin. I mean, I had never even gone to..." I shift my head downward, pretending to use the mattress to scratch my forehead when I'm really just trying to hide my eyes from his gaze. "Well, you know, third base." My speech is muffled, and hot air bounces back in my face.

One. Two. Three. Four. Five.

I right myself. His features are etched in seriousness, solemn and thoughtful. Steeling my resolve, I continue. "I know it sounds stupid, but I had had enough of it. The petty remarks. The snarky looks. The jealous whispers. The laughing behind my back. One day, I just snapped, I decided that I needed to control the narrative. I needed to control my destiny. Of course, looking back now, the smart move would've been to delete my accounts and ignore everyone, but instead I decided to have sex."

I try to plow through the word. Try to speak it proudly. Bravely. Boldly. Even though nothing about my decision to have sex was proud or brave or bold; it was peer pressure. Pure and simple.

It wasn't *me* making that decision. It was my anger and bitterness. My resentment and cattiness.

My bitchiness.

I wasn't in love. I wasn't some curious young woman wanting to experience sexual exploration. I wasn't a mature, young adult ready to cross the line into the next, and natural, phase of affection and passion.

I was a teenager with a chip on my shoulder the size of Saturn.

If I was gonna get in trouble for eating a cookie, when no cookie was in my possession to begin with... then, guess what? I was gonna steal a whole fucking truckload of cookies.

I'll. Show. You.

You're accusing me of sleeping with nearly every single boy in my high school, so guess what? I'm gonna get a college guy. A good-looking, self-assured college guy. Someone who can give me a really good time.

Of course, a 'really good time' is definitely not what I got.

His jaw tenses, and the artery in his neck thrums against his skin.

His heartbeat.

Tap. Tap. Tap. Tap. Tap.

I squeeze his hand. And when he squeezes mine back, I keep going. "I knew I didn't want it to be with anyone from my school, anyone I knew. So, that left one choice..."

"Spring Break in a completely different state," he croaks, filling in the blanks.

"Yeah," I nod. "I met him on the beach that day, that Friday. Tabby and I had gone for a long walk, and we ran into him and his friend. He actually recognized me. Believe it or not, he was a follower. He and a bunch of his classmates." I decide to bypass the intricate details, and I leave him with a simple, "We flirted, and I made my intentions pretty clear."

He sucks in a breath and holds it.

I immediately mirror him. Panic sparks inside of me, setting my nerve-endings on fire. My feet start to go numb, buzzing with the sensation of a thousand pins and needles.

He shakes his head, "No, Orah, breathe." He exhales. And then waits for me to do the same. Mesmerizing me with his Tiger Eyes, he commands me to do it again.

In. Out.

In. Out.

"It's all good. *We're* all good." He gives me an encouraging nod.

"The boys invited Tabby and me to a party that night, but obviously, her parents would never approve that. But I knew I could talk her parents into taking us to the movies."

"Those boys met you there?"

I wish I could give a different answer. "Yeah. And poor Tabby, she didn't even wanna go. She didn't like the other guy at all. But just like so many other times in our life, she gave in." Tears sting my eyes. "Because she loved me."

Ridge repositions our connected hands higher on the bed, moving them from waist-high to chest-high. His fingers are beautiful. Long and firm and strong, covered in calluses.

"Because she *loves* you." He corrects my use of past tense. "She still loves you."

My throat burns, and I try to swallow past the emotion.

"I...I knew that room was there. I knew before the shooting started." I blink, and a tear slides down my face, landing on the pillow. "I knew because that's where he took me."

Ridge's grip tightens on my hand.

"I thought we'd sneak out of the theater and then come back before it was time for Tabby's parents to pick us up. I thought he would take me somewhere. That party or his house or a hotel. But he didn't. He took me into that supply room." I choke on a sob. Not wanting to sever my connection with Ridge, I pull my other hand from underneath the pillow and cover my mouth, trying to shove the cries back inside my body.

He tenses. Everywhere. It's an energy so significant that it immediately makes me tremble. His anger...

I can feel it. I can see it. I can hear it.

It's like the hissing and crackling of a high-voltage power line.

There's a five-line power pole that runs through the woods at the back of our neighborhood. It runs adjacent to the dead-end street; a street where the developer ran out of funds and decided to stop building. Of course, that's where we would all go to ride our bikes, play kickball, and build tree forts. The noise used to scare me—the humming and popping. One time, I even saw the conductor glowing, flashing with a faint, neon blue halo around it. I was terrified it was about to catch fire. After all, Momma's blow dryer had caught fire once. I had been in the bathroom with her, and it flashed with that same blue color, right before a flame shot out of it.

But Dad told me there was nothing to worry about.

He called it corona discharge.

Something about the relationship between the conductor and the air surrounding it. I can't remember everything he said, but it's something about the conductor having such a strong electric field that it strips the electrons from the surrounding air, creating ions.

I don't really remember what electrons and ions are, but I know that's how I feel.

Ridge is so powerful that just his presence is stripping me of my basic elements, my basic chemistry.

And I'm creating light. And hissing. And crackling.

I am the reaction. Simply because *he* exists.

His clipped and savage snarl is filled with gravel and pain. "He fucking forced himself on you?"

Lifting the top sheet, I quickly dry my face and wipe my runny nose. "No, he didn't force himself on me. I didn't tell him no. In fact...I...I told him I wanted it."

And when he closes his eyes, blocking me from his view, my heart shatters into a million pieces. Pieces so small, so intricate they can never be put back together.

But then, because this is Ridge, because this is My Hero, he opens his eyes and with his other hand, he reaches across and wipes the tears from my red and tender cheeks. His fingertips linger, tracing across my jawline and down to my neck. Across my collarbone and back up to my nose. And with every millimeter he maps, he glues a piece of me back together.

Although, after telling him this story, I don't know if I'll ever be whole again. Parts of me are too mangled. Too torn. Too pulverized.

But I do know that an incomplete Orah—with Ridge in her life—is better than a whole Orah without him.

Chapter 30

Orah

Slowly, he pulls his wandering hand back across to his side of the bed. "I'm here, Little Bird. Say what you need to say."

My revelation is low and quiet, nothing more than a feather in the breeze. "It wasn't what I thought it would be. It was nothing like the fantasy I built in my head. I thought because it was *my* decision, *my* choice, that I would be happy about it." Memories flash through my mind, bright and prominent. It reminds me of the little red view-finder I had in preschool. But instead of images of animals and flowers and landscapes, I'm seeing me.

Me…with my shorts around my platform wedges.

Me…bent over the desk, scared that every pounding thrust would send the papers and laptop careening to the floor.

Me…worried that someone would walk in and find us.

Me…trying to turn my head, just so I could catch a glimpse of his face, try to connect. Try to feel something other than pain.

Honesty flows from me, and in a way I'm so relieved to be breaking the chains of my secrets, that I'm not even embarrassed by the virgin words I'm saying. Virgin…because I haven't spoken them to anyone. Not my parents. Not Boaz. Not Tabby. Not my doctors. And certainly not the lawyers and investigators. "But I wasn't happy. Even though it was my decision, I wasn't happy at all. He led me into that room and shut the door. I looked for a lock, but there wasn't one. I told him that we should leave, go find somewhere different. He said we just had to hurry."

Ridge blinks, and one lone tear falls down his handsome face, trapping in his facial hair. But I don't acknowledge it.

Because I can feel what he feels.

And if I concede to those feelings, if I allow them to consume me, I'll never make it through this.

"He didn't touch me. He didn't tell me I was beautiful. He didn't even kiss me. He just turned me around, asked if I was ready, and when I said yes..." I don't have to color between the lines, Ridge knows what happened next.

I look down at Boaz's bedspread and wish we were in my room. At least then, I'd have my favorite blanket to look at. I could zone out and get lost in the swirls. "There was a clock on the wall. I watched it. The entire time. I didn't know what else to do. I didn't know what to do with my body. And I had no idea what he was doing with his. I didn't even see him...his...you know." I don't know if the situation calls for using the word penis, dick, cock, or private part. Since I prefer not to think about any of those words when it comes to Levi, I just leave that part of the sentence out. "He had already turned me around and pulled my shorts down when I heard him opening the condom. So, I just balled my hands into fists," I squeeze his hand tighter to demonstrate, "and I watched the clock. Tick, tick, tick. For one minute and thirty-one seconds, I stared at that clock." I can't help the cynical chuckle that pops from my mouth. "I guess I should be glad that he didn't last longer."

I shake my head in denial, thinking about the finality of it all. "It's crazy to think that something so important, something that literally changes the fundamental physiology of your body can be done in less than two minutes."

Ridge's jaw twitches, and he grinds his teeth. "He's a fucking rapist."

"He's not. I told you it was my idea. I told you he asked me right before…well, you know…and I said *yes*."

"That doesn't matter, Orah. Consent is more than just a word. He should've seen the signs, seen that you were uncomfortable. Seen that you didn't want what you thought you did. Seen that your body didn't match your voice." His pupils widen, eating away at the dark brown iris, leaving me with more of the light brown-yellow rim. "A man would look his woman in the eyes and *feel* what she wants. He would know without a doubt that her word was her oath—her desire, her passion. A real man pays attention to his girl."

A flurry of possessive heat stirs low in my belly. Possessiveness for this man lying across from me. And it makes me mourn.

Mourn what my first time should have been like.

I give him a soft smile. "But he wasn't a man. Just a boy. And I wasn't his girl."

We're both quiet for a while. I'm not even sure if Ridge realizes that he's taken to working his thumb around our clasped hands, across the back of my knuckles and down the inside of my wrist.

He breaks the silence first. "I don't remember seeing a clock."

"Huh?"

"In that room—*our* room—I don't remember seeing a clock on the wall."

"That's because I threw it away. When we finished, he walked out and just left me standing there. I took the clock off the wall and threw it in the big trash can in the corridor."

I wish I could've paid better attention that night. But my eyes were blurry with tears I knew I had to hide from Tabby. She thought I was just hooking up with the guy, having a little make-out session. She had no clue I was losing my virginity while she was watching a movie and trying to stop Levi's friend, Colby, from eating all of her Sour Patch Kids. Maybe if I wasn't lost in my own thoughts and pain, I could've noticed something was wrong. I could've seen the small, unattended black backpacks, leaned and concealed against the large strip of black baseboard molding. Seen them hidden behind the cardboard movie cutouts. Seen them draped across the disheveled section of the concession counter, mixed in with the napkins and extra popcorn seasoning.

Maybe if I'd not been lost in my own maze of despair, I could've noticed the backpacks. Before they exploded and started killing people.

I still don't know everything that happened, and I still avoid the news like the plague, but the police specifically asked me if I had seen those. Considering I was one of the small handful of patrons not in the auditoriums when shit started to go down, it was a valid question.

"He left you? Just left you standing there?" he growls.

"Yeah."

Ridge is about to rage, when he realizes that he may be raging against someone who might have walked away from *me,* but might not have ever walked away from the *movie theater itself.* "What happened to him? Was he injured or..."

I shake my head. "No. Nothing happened to him. As soon as he got what he wanted, he texted his friend, and they left the theater. I had to walk back into that movie auditorium by myself with Tabby trying to whisper a hundred different questions to me. Was he a good kisser? Did he get my number? Are we starting some kind of long-distance relationship? Did he touch me under my shirt?" I give a little sniffle, trying to clear my now-stuffy nose. "I couldn't bring myself to tell her what happened. So, I lied and told her that we just kissed and that he got called away by his family."

"I can't believe you went through that. I'm so sorry, Orah. I wish it had been different." His genuine and heartwarming empathy fills him with anguish, and his gorgeous lips quiver, ever so slightly. "I wish your first time had been...beautiful. Not ugly."

Oh, it gets so much uglier.

He smirks, trying to make light of his promise, even though I can hear the truth behind it. "And if I ever see the little fucker, I'll bash his brains in." He pauses for a second, wondering if he should ask the next question. Eventually, he relents. "What's his name?"

I could tell him that it doesn't matter, that it's all in the past; but Levi is scheduled to testify during the same block of time as us, so there's a very good possibility that we may run into one another. I need to prepare Ridge for that as much as I need to prepare myself.

"Levi Sills. He's gonna be at the inquiry at the same time as us." I level Ridge with a look that's meant to be stern and no-nonsense. "So, it's probably best if your head-bashing fantasies stay just like that. As fantasies, not reality."

He gives me a cynical grunt. "Huh. We'll see." He scrunches his forehead in thought. "Sills." His face contorts into a look of repulsion as the name works across his tongue. "He's from White Sky?"

"No. He goes to a school in Georgetown."

"Georgetown? Like the neighborhood in Washington, D.C.?"

"Yeah. He was born and raised there. I guess his dad is into politics. What's those things called?" I try to pluck the acronym from my mushed brain. "A PAC. His father is involved with a PAC."

"A political action committee?"

I nod. "Yeah. And I guess his grandfather is some big real estate guy and owns a massive amount of rental property in Florida, including several houses in White Sky."

His eyes roll back in his head. "Duncan Sills. That's why the last name sounded so familiar. We've had a couple of calls at some of his rental spots. Minor injuries, smoke alarms. That kind of thing."

I give a sad little shrug. "Well, I guess the majority of the houses in the bigger party cities were already rented. That's why Levi and his friend, Colby, went to White Sky for their Spring Break."

"Did you know he followed you on social media? Had you interacted with him before?"

"I logged on after we met each other, and I saw where he followed me; but I didn't know beforehand, no."

"So, he really *was* a stranger."

Ridge's observation of the undeniable facts hits hard. Not only that, but his tone hitches a little on the end. And that tilt is like a machete slicing through my already fragile heart.

"He was a complete stranger," I confirm. "I...I don't know if that makes it better or worse."

"Worse." The sentence barely leaves my mouth before he's verbally shoving his one-word condemnation in my face with a tone of disgust that he's never directed at me before.

Never.

Oh my god. That hurts.

One. Two. Three. Four. Five.

"Oh, shit..." His face immediately softens, and he reaches his free hand back across the chasm of the bed and strokes the side of my cheek with his rough-hewn palm. I nearly pull away from his touch, but his fingers lace around the back of my head, holding me hostage. "Oh, Little Bird, I didn't mean it the way that it sounded. It came out all wrong. I wasn't talking about you or about what happened to you that night. Or about any choices you made or didn't make. I was talking about *me*, about my own experiences, about my own choices." His fingertips massage into my scalp. "I would never think less of you because of what happened. I *will never* think less of you. *Never.*"

My tongue vibrates with anxiety, making it hard to talk. "Your experience? Your choice? You've slept with a stranger?"

I'm so stupid. Of course, he has; he's a grown man.

Tall, dark, and handsome.

A gorgeous grown man with muscles for days and a sexy beard.

And, hello, he saves people for a living.

He slowly unravels his hand from my hair and moves it back to his side of the bed. And for a moment, his other hand loosens its grip against my own, and I'm devastated by the fact that he's about to stop holding my hand. But then he clamps down again, determined to be my strength throughout the entirety of this confession... in my brother's bed. In the middle of the afternoon. After a horrific panic attack.

"Yes. And it's happened more than once, Zipporah. I've had a few one-night stands."

"And that's how you know you prefer monogamy?"

He nods, so very slowly. "I prefer to be in a relationship with a woman before we have sex."

My utterance is a penance for the past and a prayer for the future. "I wish it hadn't been with a stranger."

Chapter 31

Ridge

"**I** wish it hadn't been with a stranger." Her declaration is breathy and intimate, making my body feel things it shouldn't fucking be feeling.

Things I've never felt before.

And it's not just my body.

It's everywhere.

In my heart. In my soul. On planes that I didn't even know existed. My love for her is written in the stars.

And my desire for her has created new galaxies and universes.

I'm rewarded—and punished—with visions of me and Orah making a life together, creating a family together, growing old together.

And trust me, it's a punishment of the worst kind, because it's teasing me with something that can never be.

Needing to re-focus, I ask the first question that pops in my head. "You haven't talked to him since?"

"No. He tried to call, but I have the new phone number, so he couldn't reach me."

"How do you know he tried to call?"

"He, and his lawyer, have both reached out to Mrs. Levenson, trying to get my new contact information. Since he wasn't there during the actual attack, he wasn't assigned an advocate attorney," she explains. "But I have no desire to speak to him. It's not like he wants to check on me. Not like he wants to be my friend or my boyfriend or anything like that." Her nose scrunches like she smells something bad. "He's just worried about getting prosecuted."

Prosecuted?

She gives a little shrug, holding my hand tighter in the process so she doesn't disrupt our physical connection. "At least, that's what Tabby said when he reached out to her. He messaged her as soon as she reactivated her social media account."

"He's scared about being prosecuted?" A solar flare of anger surges through my blood, setting it afire like lava. "So he knows what he did was wrong. He knows, and he's trying to cover his tracks."

There's no pleading ignorance.

No claiming that he didn't see the signs, that he didn't feel Orah's nonverbal distress. Sense her hesitancy. Notice her fear. Witness her anxiety over losing this part of herself to an inconsiderate asshole such as himself.

Because with the right person, losing your virginity isn't *losing* anything at all. It's finding something you didn't even know was missing.

"He knows it was wrong, but not in the way *you're* thinking."

I trap my bottom lip between my teeth. "What's that supposed to mean?"

Her face softens. It reminds me of the face my mom would make when she would have to tell us that fun was no longer on the calendar of events for the day... *It's raining; you can't go swimming. It's getting late; you don't have time for ice cream. It's closed; you can't go to the toy store.*

"In the state of Florida, the age of consent is eighteen. Remember, I wasn't eighteen that night. My birthday was one week after that night."

Oh, you gotta be fucking kidding me.

A technicality?

He's worried about getting into trouble over something like numbers all the while he treated Orah like a piece of garbage. Like some dispensable piece of trash that he could use when and how he wanted with no regard whatsoever to her feelings, to her body, to her psyche.

Orah will never be dispensable. Never. Not to me.

She's the one thing I can't live without.

And the one thing I'm not allowed to live WITH.

I'll tell you one thing, this Levi boy better hope our paths never cross, at the inquiry or otherwise. Because if they do, I'm gonna break his arms and shove them up his ass. "I hope they throw the book at him. They can try him as an adult, right? If he's more concerned about the damn numbers than the morality of the situation, then he's gonna have a rude awakening when his entitled little ass realizes that being eighteen makes him an adult in the eyes of the law. They aren't gonna care if he's a high school senior who has to report to a student council meeting." I click my tongue against the inside of my cheek. "What's the maximum punishment he can get?"

"I told Mrs. Levenson that I don't want to pursue charges."

"What?" Did I just hear her right? "But he should be held accountable for what he did, Orah. Just looking at the birthdates on the licenses should be enough for the prosecutor to come after him, right? Is there a 'Romeo and Juliet Law' that lessens the penalty? Because he deserves the max."

"No, Ridge. It's not like that. I begged Mrs. Levenson for her help. She talked to the district attorney on my behalf, and they both agreed to honor my wishes, that with everything else that happened that night, mine and Levi's...date...should be the least of everyone's worries."

A fresh and violent fury pulses in my body, pounding against my temples like a sledgehammer to the skull. "Date? That wasn't a date, Zipporah; that was statutory rape."

"Those are just words, Ridge."

"Well, words carry infinite power when they contain the truth."

She gnaws on her own bottom lip, thinking. It's clear to see she's wondering if her 'yes' contained a morsel of truth.

I can tell you right now…it didn't.

She sighs and works the side of her face against the pillow. "I'm already gonna have to talk about what happened in that room with him at the congressional hearing. I really don't wanna have to relive it over and over just so he can get punished for a decision I made. Is ruining his college career gonna make me feel better about the whole situation? No. It won't erase anything."

What. The. Fuck.

"Excuse me? Did you just say college?"

Her eyebrows shoot high, and her storm-cloud eyes pale a shade.

The answer to my own question flashes through my brain, solving the riddle that I didn't even know was a cryptic play on words. "He goes to *a* school in Georgetown? Do you mean he goes *to* Georgetown? As in Georgetown University?"

She stares at me. And for a moment, I'm captivated by her innocence and beauty.

Then I quickly snap back to the task at hand. Which is figuring out how to make this fucking weasel pay for hurting My Brave Girl. Although, there's no penance sufficient enough for cowards who use the weapon of rape. They take an act that's meant to be shared in love, and they warp it into a dangerous armament, meant to destroy the body and kill the soul.

I growl in frustration. "Exactly how old is this guy?"

She gives a slow bob, barely moving her head. I'm not exactly sure what that means.

When she doesn't offer any other information, I pin her with a glare. "Okay, my turn," I say, steering the conversation to our familiar game of questions.

Her trepidation fades for the briefest of moments, and she gifts me with a sly grin and a snort. "I think you've already had a turn."

"Nope." I pop the syllable through my lips like I'm blowing a bubble and shake my head. "Now, how old is this guy?" I ask again. "Eighteen? Nineteen? Twenty?"

She frowns. And I can tell that she's debating lying.

I can feel the framework of the fabrication as it forms, her mind intricately weaving the falsehood and wondering how long she'll be able to look me in the eyes and deceive me with her dishonesty.

And I can feel when it all falls apart. When her heart realizes that this conversation is supposed to be her catalyst, her Big Bang, her breakthrough. It's supposed to be the moment she faces the truth of what happened to her. To Tabby. To me.

To everyone.

She inhales. "He's twenty-four."

What. The. Actual. Fuck.

Needless to say, I nearly shit the bed. Literally.

"Twenty-four!" I jolt upright, making her bounce against the mattress. The sudden movement breaks our connection, and my hands flail through the air. "That's older than me, Orah!"

Her cheeks pink in embarrassment, and my body immediately responds to her flushed color.

And it responds in the correct way. The right way.

And what's the right way? Shame.

I'm ashamed by my reaction.

The last thing My Brave Girl needs is my inability to control my shock. I want to be her rock. Her strength. Her peace. Her cornerstone.

I wanna be the firm foundation she uses to grow her future.

I snake my hand down my face and tap my chin, trying to calm my frayed nerves. And trying to pacify my overwhelming longing to punch Levi's teeth so far back in his throat that he's shitting molars for the next five years.

"I'm sorry, Orah. I'm acting like a complete buffoon. I'm just so...so...fucking livid that he would prey on you like that. If he followed you on social media, he knew your age. He knew you were still in high school. He knew you were seventeen. That's..." I'm shaking so badly, I can barely speak. "That's predatory behavior." I swing a foot on the floor and shift to look at her. "Open the damn dictionary to despicable, and his picture would be right there." I swipe my thumb and forefinger across my pinched eyes, creating a mash of black and yellow spots that dance across my closed eyelids. "How the hell is the asshole twenty-four? Did he fail a couple of years? Start college late?"

"He's in law school."

Isn't that just lovely.

Not only is he a son of a bitch, but he's a schmuck. What kind of wannabe lawyer violates the law, and the trust of a young woman, in such a horrific way. "You're serious?"

"Yes."

Maybe I can reach out to the dean and get him kicked out of school. Because there's no way this guy should ever be tasked with advising, defending, or representing people in legal matters.

He should be behind bars.

"Ridge?"

Her voice is sincere and pure, still filled with light and hope, despite what happened to her. Despite the fear that ravages her body. Despite the disquiet that permeates her spirit.

Orah's been living with a parasite.

Secrets are the worst kind of invader. They're vile and heinous, attacking anything and everything in their path. They feed on peace and happiness, destroying joy as soon as it appears. And this secret has been preventing her from healing the way she should.

And I'll do anything to help her. Anything to soothe the ache that's draining her, leaving her empty and vulnerable. Leaving her susceptible to the evil darkness of anxiety...the same darkness she was fighting during the height of her panic attack.

If I need to be the clean slate, the blank canvas, that she marks with the regrets of her past, then so be it. I'll take it all. Every hidden secret, every obsessive thought, every guilt-filled memory. I'll dirty myself, over and over and over, if it means that she can have even one minute of unadulterated happiness.

I only wish she knew the truth.

And the truth is that nothing about her past is dirty; nothing about her decision to have sex is filthy.

My blank canvas will still be blank, still be white as snow. Orah may pull away and see mud and grease, scratches and dents. But all of that disorder lives only in her mind. The truth is...you can't sully anything when you're made of Angel's wings.

Instead of replying with a simple 'yeah', I lean across and skirt my fingertip over her forehead, mapping the area where her scratch was. It's fully healed, without any trace of what happened.

I'm sure the same can't be said of her torso.

Closing her eyes, she takes a deep breath, giving herself a moment to absorb the warmth of my touch. After a count of five, her eyelids spring open. "There's more."

More.

One simple syllable.

How can one simple syllable fill me with so much fear. And anger.

"What do you mean? That Levi guy did something else?" A vise wraps around my heart, tight and unforgiving. "Tell me what he did, and I'll take care of it."

What I mean is...I'll take care of *him.*

It'll be hard for him to tap the 'follow' button on all those social media accounts when he's nursing ten broken fingers.

She frowns. "Not him. The...the shooters," she stutters.

I fidget a little, pulling my hands onto my lap. My one foot is still planted on the hardwood floor. I squeeze my toes against the grain. My reply is low, whispered with the love that I'll never be able to speak out loud. "I'm proud of you, Little Bird. It's time you talk about that night. You're dragging around a burden that shouldn't be yours to carry. Those assholes chained you to a two-ton weight. And it's time to cut the chain, break the lock. It's the only way to stop the nightmares, to move forward, to live your life."

"You don't understand, Ridge. They chained me to the weight— just like they chained everyone else who was in the theater that night—but *I'm* the one who chained the weight to Tabby. Not them. *Me.*"

I shake my head. "Orah, no—"

"Yes." She interrupts me. There's no wobble in her decree. It's firm and strong. "Lie down, Ridge. I want you to hold me."

"What?" I croak.

She gifts me a quick, tender smile. "I need to tell you everything. Every single thing. I'm terrified of you knowing the truth, but I'm even more terrified of you finding it out from someone other than me." She swallows, making her throat bob. "I'll have to talk about all of this during the inquiry, and I can't stand the thought of blindsiding you. You deserve to know what happened, and you deserve to make the decision."

"What decision?"

"The decision of whether or not you still wanna be my friend."

Chapter 32

Ridge

In the span of one-tenth of a second, I've gone stir crazy.

I've grown twisty and restless. My body's twitching, my foot's tapping, and my brain is sizzling. All because I want to collapse into the sheets, tug her against me, and never let go. I wanna feel the heat of her body as it presses into mine. I wanna bury my nose in her hair and inhale the scent of her shampoo. I wanna draw my lips back and forth across her jawline, charting a course that leaves her with a tickle in the back of her throat and a yearning low in her belly. I wanna tell her that nothing, not one single damn thing, could ever make me stop being her friend.

But, *none* of those things are appropriate.

Because *all* of those things cross the line of actual friendship.

So, instead, I jump out of the bed, leaving her wide-eyed and worried. I cross the room in record time and grab my tennis shoes from the bottom of my duffle bag. She's scrambling into a seated position when I tap the footboard of her brother's bedframe with my knuckles. "Go get your sneakers on. Wait for me in your room. I'll come get you in a minute."

Her brow crinkles. "What? What are we doing? Where are we going?"

I give her a little wink. "You'll see."

I traipse out of the bedroom, down the hallway, past the small formal sitting room and kitchen, and into the family room. John's sitting in a recliner, blankly staring out the window. The television is tuned to a golf game, but the volume is low. The conversation of the announcers is barely a blip in the quiet of the room. I sit on the couch and slide my feet into my laced and well-worn shoes.

There's a tree outside of the window, and we both watch as a bird lands on a bottom limb. It pecks at something and immediately takes off in flight again. "She finally tell you about that night?" he asks, studying the distance like he can still see the animal flying.

I lean back against the couch cushions. "I'm guessing we're at the halfway point. She said she needs to talk to me about the shooters."

He slowly turns to look at me. "She told you about that boy, well, that man? About what he did?"

His tone is filled with venom, and his face is filled with sorrow. It's fucking heartbreaking. I can't imagine what this whole ordeal has been like for him. My father once told me that one of life's greatest tragedies is being a dad who can't fix what's broken. And trust me, he wasn't talking about toys and furniture and appliances. "Yes, sir."

"He used her and walked away. Left her standing there, scared and confused. What kind of person does that? What kind of man?"

"He's not a man. He's a fucking rapist, John. A predator. And he deserves to be in jail." I sit up, balancing my forearms on my knees. "Isn't there something you can do? Put some pressure on the attorneys, on the DA?"

"She doesn't want it, Ridge. She doesn't want any of the focus to be taken away from the other victims of that night." His head falls back. Closing his eyes for a brief moment, he sighs. "She doesn't want everyone to know what happened. She said it's bad enough that all of the lawyers and police and government people know. She doesn't want the news reporters to find out. Because of her age and the nature of the...incident...Mrs. Levenson assures us that portions of the inquiry hearing can be sealed, even if the media try to submit a FOIA request."

"Yeah, I know certain things are exempt from the Freedom of Information Act, but I'm not sure about the specifics."

John looks past me and down the hallway, obviously checking for Orah.

"She's waiting for me in her bedroom," I answer his unasked question.

"Do you know he offered a payout? If she retracted her statement about them having sex? If she told investigators that all they did was kiss and that she lied about her age—that she told him she was older than she was—that he would pay her."

"Wh–what?" My ears start to ring.

"Yeah. Fifty thousand." He makes a sucking sound with his teeth. "He messaged Tabby on some private app thing that hides conversations and automatically deletes them after they've been read. She immediately told Emmett about it."

"Bribery! On top of everything else..." I shake my head. Every millimeter of movement makes the anger festering in my soul grow deeper. It takes root, planting itself for eternity.

"Yeah. His attorney claimed it was a mistake. Said that Tabby misunderstood the conversation. Said his only goal was to offer financial assistance to Orah so she could receive the best aftercare for her injuries." He squirms in his seat. "People deserve to know the truth about that rich little fucker," he growls.

"I agree. I'm not above paying him a visit." I clench my jaw and toss my hand in the air. "D.C. is what? Seven or eight hours from here? I could have the shitbag in the emergency room before the eleven o'clock news even comes on."

John quirks a smile and gives me a little chuckle. "That'd be nice, huh?"

He thinks I'm kidding.

Yeah, not so much.

My parents raised me to know that violence is wrong. But somehow, I think they'd allow an exception in the case of Levi Sills.

If I close my eyes, I can picture wrath pouring into me, threatening to fill me up, threatening to drown all of the good that's inside of me.

Because I wanna hurt him.

I wanna hurt him for taking what wasn't his. He stole from Zipporah. And nothing will ever make that right.

He tosses a nod to my laced tennis shoes. "Something I need to know?"

It takes a surprising amount of strength to push aside the hate so I can continue with my conversation. "Yes, sir. When I was driving last night, I saw signs for a national park near here. The pictures on the billboard showed a trail with a wooden boardwalk?"

"Yeah. Congaree. It's about thirty minutes away."

"Not too strenuous?"

He shakes his head. "Not if you do the Boardwalk Loop Trail. It's fairly easy."

"Something Orah could handle?"

Confusion settles in his features. "You wanna take her hiking? *Now*? In the middle of..." He slows and circles his hand in the air, trying to formulate the right word. "Your talk."

"Yes, sir. I think some fresh air would do her good." I rake my hand down my face. One. Two. "I think she needs a little break before she tells me the rest. I want her to feel in control, and that might be hard to do here."

"Here?"

I don't want to hurt John's feelings, but I also don't want to hide the truth from him. "Here. In her childhood home. Surrounded by all the memories of her youth. With her parents hovering just down the hall."

His lips thin, his jaw tics, and he closes his eyes. Tightly. After just a second, he exhales, long and laborious. "As much as that hurts to hear, I understand where you're coming from. And you may even be right." He turns to look back out the window. "I guess every young person has a milestone that catapults them into adulthood. A turning point that shifts them from needing their parents to needing someone else. An event that makes them wanna take the reins themselves and gallop at their own pace." When he turns back to me, his eyes glisten with unshed tears. "But never in a million years did I think my baby's event would be this."

"I wish it wasn't this, John."

Eventually, I stand from the couch, and I'm about to leave the room when a nagging feeling pulls at my heartstrings, reminding me to do the right thing, to be the honorable man. To be the complete opposite of Levi. "I laid in bed with Orah." I stab a hand through my unkempt bedhead and quickly clarify my admission. "Not like that. I mean, I laid next to her while she talked. Nothing happened between us. But I...I just wanted you to know."

"I know," he claps back, matter-of-factly.

I'm pretty sure my eyes widen like saucers. "You know?"

His good-humored snort is followed by a wide grin. The movement crinkles his eyes and makes one of those stubborn tears fall. He quickly wipes it away. "Y'all left Boaz's bedroom door wide open. I saw you."

"Oh." What the hell did he see? I try to think back, wondering if I did anything that crossed the line. I know I felt *things* that crossed the line, but I don't think I physically did anything that would be inappropriate.

Says the guy who took a bath with his daughter in the middle of the night. Shirtless. While she was in a thin tank top and panties.

I curse myself for thinking that way. I did what had to be done. To calm her, to soothe her. And I would do it all over again. I'll do it for the rest of my life if that's what she needs.

"Ridge, it's okay." His simple statement is firm yet gentle, fatherly in every facet.

"I would never disrespect you or Ann. Or Orah," I explain.

"The fact that you are here right now speaks volumes about your character, son. We know that you would never disrespect us or our daughter. We trust you."

"Ridge?" Her sweetness coats my eardrums in honey.

I turn to see her leaning against the doorframe. Still clad in her black T-shirt and shorts, she's now added black sneakers to the ensemble. Her stormy eyes dart from me to her father and then back again. "Is everything okay?"

I hold out my hand. Without any trepidation or hesitation, she scurries across the room and folds her fingers against mine. And when she looks up at me, her fear and turmoil fade. Because she can feel me. She can feel the unshakeable and unbreakable faith I have in her. "We're gonna make everything perfect, Little Bird. Me and you."

Chapter 33

Orah

"The largest intact expanse of old-growth bottomland in the Southeast." Ridge knuckle-taps the plaque he's reading from. "I think this is the hundredth sign talking about the 'old-growth bottomland'. They're really fond of saying the word bottomland."

I peek over his shoulder and point to the sentence, making sure he acknowledges the rest of it. "*Hardwood forest* bottomland."

Giving me a side-glance, he dramatically rolls his eyes. "Excuse me, Little Bird, how could I already forget what the other ninety-nine signs told me." He spins around, and his torso brushes against me, sending chills through my sweaty and sticky body.

Wearing all black might calm me, but it's not very conducive to the southern heat and humidity. Despite the trees shading us, the early evening sun is still blazing, giving just a small glimpse of what's to come for July and August.

Ridge nods to the wooden bench tucked against the small alcove of the boardwalk. "Wanna sit?"

What he means is *wanna talk...*

Ridge and I used the drive out here from my house to pretend we were 'normal' people. People who didn't have front row seats to the most horrific actions of our fellow mankind. We were just a normal boy and girl, riding in a Jeep with the windows down, while the summer breeze engulfed us in the smell of honeysuckle. A normal boy and girl talking about the little things. No major revelations. Just our favorite candy bars and songs. Which Dr. Seuss book made us giggle the most before bedtime. Which school lunch did we actually like. And of course, which fast food restaurant has the best French fries.

When we arrived, Ridge quickly chose a green-dot, easy trail for us. I haven't been to the National Park since I was little. I think I was about seven the last time I was here. Granny, Boaz, and I spent the day together, running and playing and hiking. We ate peanut butter and jelly sandwiches and then stopped for ice cream on the way home.

And something about that pleasant memory has made this new memory—the memory I'm making with My Hero—even more significant, more important.

The walk hasn't been strenuous, but that hasn't stopped Ridge from doting on me, from treating me like I'm the most precious gift that's ever come into his world. And it's not his obvious actions that choke me with emotion; it's the things that he thinks I don't notice.

But I do.

Because I notice everything he does.

I notice every shy smile. Every tap of his chin. Every blink of his Tiger Eyes.

And I notice how he places himself in front of me, walking ahead of me with slightly outstretched arms, protecting me from the unknown, every single time people pass us from the oncoming direction on the trail. If someone changes their direction, if they step one millimeter too close to me—or what Ridge perceives as *too close* to me—he's there, blocking their trajectory.

And I notice how when fresh sweat starts to form on his brow, he tugs the small backpack from his shoulder, digs through the contents, and hands me a fresh wet wipe, telling me to reach under my shirt and clean my scar. He says I'm still healing, and that sweat can irritate the skin. And I notice how, as soon as his fingers brush against mine, depositing the cleaning wipe into my palm, he turns around, giving me privacy, being the gentleman, despite the fact that he's basically seen me naked.

And covered in blood.

Sitting next to one another, he pulls our shared water bottle from his pack, and we both take a hearty swig. Spreading his legs, he sighs, taking a moment to study the scene before us. Tall trees, swampy water, broken stumps, and bright green ferns.

Nerves flicker in my stomach, flashing high and low, burning like a match.

"Your turn," he chirps, simply and without fanfare.

He's giving me the control, allowing me to decide how I handle the continuance of our conversation. He's giving me the grace to make the decision myself. I can dip a toe into the shallow end or jump directly from the high dive.

As much as I'd like to cannonball, loud and proud from the ten-meter platform, I think a slow and easy dunk is all my heart can take.

"When do you go back to work?"

"I was supposed to report for shift tomorrow morning, but I called one of the guys and swapped. My next tour will start Monday morning at seven."

"Oh, Ridge, I'm sorry. I shouldn't have occupied your time today. You needed to leave for work, and I kept you."

"I stayed because I wanted to." He hooks his clasped hands between his knees. "I'm healing, too, Orah. Little by little, day by day. But the fact remains, as long as you're hurting, I'm hurting. When you're scared, I shatter. When you cry, I drown. When you can't breathe, I suffocate." He doesn't turn to look at me, but that doesn't make his utterance any less powerful. Any less impactful.

All I can do is nod.

I close my eyes and imagine myself swimming through the thick, viscous water of my past. Strong arms, strong legs. Kick after kick. Stroke after stroke.

I might not be ready for the swan dive, but I need to be brave enough to go under, to sink beneath the glassy surface and not arise until I'm...free.

"I tried to watch the movie. I tried to pretend that everything was fine, that I was happy with my time alone with Levi, happy that I made the adult decision to rendezvous with a stranger." I lick my lips. "But it wasn't that easy." I glance at his handsome profile. "Because I was in pain." He slowly turns his head, capturing me in his gaze. "Down there." My eyes flicker to my lap, and then I whisper the words into existence, corralling the truth between our bodies. "He made me bleed."

Ridge gasps, strangling himself with a heartbroken and staggered breath.

I guess I'm not being very practical. I suppose a majority of women bleed when they lose their virginity. Perhaps saying *Levi* made me bleed is being too harsh? Too unfair?

Because he wasn't the only one who made me bleed that night.

But, I guess not all blood runs red and pours outside of the body.

And that's something to consider.

Because Levi also made my soul bleed.

"I knew I needed to...fix...what I could. The last thing I wanted was for Tabby's parents to pick us up and see my shorts covered in blood." I can feel the redness of embarrassment flush my cheeks, but I refuse to cower or back down. I told myself I would give Ridge the full truth, and that's what he's gonna get. Not to mention, he's a professional. And I recognize that. I recognize it and respect it. "Plus, I didn't need Tabby to see it. She already knew that I had my period the week before Spring Break. Our cycles are typically in sync, and we were both worried that we would be on our periods during vacation. We were relieved to see that wouldn't be the case."

A horrible thought crashes down on me, churning a torrent of water over my head.

Our cycles are typically in sync.

Turns out, my best friend isn't going to have a menstrual cycle anymore.

Because she had a hysterectomy. At the age of seventeen. Because of me.

He must sense my wandering mind because his hand slides across the wooden bench, and his fingertips graze against my thigh. Ever so softly. Ever so gently. In fact, if I weren't watching him do it, I don't know that I would even feel it happening.

"I told Tabby that I wasn't feeling well, that something I ate was making me nauseous. We went down to the concession stand to get a Coke, and then we went to the restroom. She fluffed her hair and washed her hands and talked about us getting part-time jobs for the summer. All the while, I was having a silent meltdown in the bathroom stall." My heartbeat speeds. A faint buzzing noise starts to grow in my head, making the inside of my ears itch. "I didn't have a tampon or a pad or anything, so I just folded up some toilet paper and tried to stick it inside of me. But that didn't really work because I was so swollen. It hurt to even touch myself. Everything burned and throbbed. It felt like I was covered in a thousand papercuts." Before that moment, I never thought that ninety-one seconds could cause so much damage. I give a little shrug, "Anyway, I had to settle for just wadding the toilet paper in a big pile in my panties." I sniffle, trying to keep my tears at bay. "I plastered a smile on my face, told Tabby I was feeling better and asked to borrow her lip gloss."

I'm physically looking at the trees, watching as the sun creeps lower in the horizon, teasing the pending night. But all I can *see* is mine and Tabby's reflections, staring back from the mirrors in the movie theater bathroom.

With the cracked tile above the sink.

With the leaky soap dispenser.

And the crinkled paper towels on the floor from people too busy to clean up their own trash after missing the garbage can.

"He...he was that rough with you?"

My hand falls to my side, and Ridge immediately takes it in his own. And when he inches our joined hands toward the middle of the space between us, trying to play it safe again, I firmly tuck our fingers back against the warmness of my thigh.

"He wasn't anything with me, Ridge. Not rough, not gentle. He just...existed." I swallow, gulping away the sob that's begging to escape. "Besides, it's not like he hit me or anything."

"A man doesn't have to hit you to cause you misery," he answers. "You...you..." he quivers, shaking like a tin roof in the middle of a rainstorm, "couldn't even touch yourself. That's not right, Orah." He hangs his head. "It's so fucking wrong."

Streaks of sunlight highlight his facial hair, sprinkling the brown with flashes of red. Unable to stop myself, I lean over and plant a soft kiss on his jaw, right on the sensitive area beneath his earlobe. The flurry of my breath sends a shiver through his body.

I know it does. Because I see it in the shake of his shoulder.

Looking back up, he gifts me a loving smile. "I'm the one who's supposed to be making you feel better."

"You do make me feel better. Just by being here, by listening to me, by giving me the power to tell my story."

I only pray that this story doesn't end with him walking out of my life. I don't want the credits to roll before the second act begins.

Wiping a rogue tear, I quickly continue, determined to forge forward. "Everything changed when we were walking back to our seats. That's when we saw them. The bad guys."

Unfortunately, I've learned their names. I didn't willingly seek out the information; I saw it on some of the paperwork I had to sign for Mrs. Levenson.

But speaking their names just seems wrong.

If I say their names, will I give them new life?

"I don't wanna say their names."

"Then don't." Ridge's response is simple and finite.

I nod, despising the sudden headache that's now pounding against my skull, hammering a tortuous and constant rhythm. "They were in the hallway, huddled around one of the fire alarms. At first, I thought they were wearing Halloween costumes." My heartbeat speeds up even further. "And then we realized they weren't."

Ridge shuffles, scooting a little closer to me.

"They turned and saw us. I'll never forget the look on their faces. It's like it happened in slow motion. For a split second, they were surprised. Then, they smiled. In perfect tandem. Slow and intentional." I squeeze my eyes shut. The intense pressure behind my eyelids is a bittersweet feeling. It's a physical pain I welcome. I wholly embrace it because I'm so tired of the aches that can't be seen. The suffering that's not a part of my skin and bones and muscles.

But my reprieve is short-lived because I'm immediately bombarded with the playback of that moment. And fucking terrifying doesn't even come close to describing it.

"When they took a step in our direction, we turned and ran. But I didn't get far." I lift my foot in the air and wiggle it back and forth. "Because of those stupid shoes. Those damn heels." My chest constricts, making my healing scar vibrate and hum. It's like I can feel an evil energy seeping out of my stapled and stitched wounds. "I fell."

My tears are flowing freely now, scalding a hot path down my flushed face. "She came back for me."

One. Two. Three. Four. Five.

"Tabby could've gotten away, but she came back for me."

And when Ridge pulls me into his arms, I let go. I sob and cry and scream. My heartbeat violently thrashes against my ribs, and my brain feels like it's being squished in a vise. The pressure is so fierce it completely muffles the ringing in my ears. I drag my hands under his shirt and scrape my fingernails across his sticky back, wishing I could brand my grief into his body. Because I need someone to help me carry this load. And the only person I want is him. And perhaps, if I can carve a part of myself into him, then he'll never be able to leave me. The rest of the story won't matter. The truth of what's coming will be inconsequential. Because he'll already be fated as mine.

His body engraved with my markings.

His blood underneath my fingernails.

My tears soak his shoulder, seeping my sorrow into his own healed scar from that night. His hands rake across my hair, and he hushes me with a low, soothing voice. He peppers kisses along my forehead. And I know the exact path he's blazing...

Where my cut was.

The cut I can no longer see when I look at my reflection.

The cut I can *always* see *despite* my reflection.

Slowly, my tears begin to taper, and I'm vaguely aware of him telling some passing strangers that we're fine, that there's nothing to be concerned with. Eventually, I pull away from his embrace, feeling both ashamed and empowered by my outburst. He reaches into the backpack and grabs a fresh wet wipe. But this time, instead of handing it to me, he does all the work. With heartbreaking compassion and masculine power, he cleans my face, wiping away the salt and grime, the sweat and dirt. His eyes never leave mine, and there's a possessiveness hanging in the small slit of space between us. It's animalistic and feral, basic and pure.

And somehow, I know that I'll never be lucky enough to actually hear him say the words that match this feeling...

We belong to each other.

You're. Fucking. Mine.

He tosses the used wipe into the bag and settles an arm across the back of the bench. Our bodies shifted while he was comforting me, and we're both fully facing one another, each with a leg hitched up on the wooden seat. "Do you need some water?" he asks.

I shake my head. "No."

He scruffs a hand down his face and taps his chin—one, two—trying to quiet some of his own demons.

I pick back up where I left off. "She came back for me. She could've gotten away, she could've ran to the other end of the hall and out the exit doors, but she came back because of me."

"You can't think like that, Orah. Those guys had guns. You can't outrun semi-automatic fire. And what if one of the explosives detonated when she was running past? Then Tabby might not be here at all. Maybe you saved her life by her coming back for you."

Instead of taking time to agree or disagree with him, I continue, slowly walking toward the high-dive that will submerge me into the deepest waters. "We were scrambling to get up, and before we knew it, they were standing over us. With guns pointed in our faces."

He mumbles a curse.

"The boy with black hair said he knew what I was."

Ridge furrows his brow in confusion.

"He saw me and Levi. He heard us. He knew what we had done. He knew what happened in that room. He called me a whore."

His back stiffens into a rod, and his jaw tightens, the muscles in his face twitch with tension.

"He said that girls like me didn't deserve to breathe the same air as him, but that he'd be willing to let my friend go. As long as I gave him the same treatment. He said he'd trade me. 'A quick fuck for the life of my friend' is what he said."

My nose is already running again, and I give it a quick wipe with my fingers. I must smear snot across my face because Ridge wipes my cheek with the pad of his thumb and then just brushes it off on his shirt.

I guess under some circumstances the scene would be funny. But this isn't most circumstances. Ridge's face is crimsoned in anger, and his one foot planted on the boardwalk is now vigorously bouncing. Up and down. Up and down. A thousand miles a minute.

"I'll never forget the way Tabby looked at me in that moment. With equal parts of disgust and hope." I lick my dry and cracked lips. "I...I was actually angry that she was finding out the truth. I was mad that she knew about me and Levi." I clear my throat, begging my body not to wear out before I finish. "I told him no. I told him that I wouldn't touch him if he were the last guy on earth."

"Bird..." His tormented moan is charcoal and glass, charred and shattered.

"He didn't say anything back. He just stood there laughing. And for just a second, I thought they were gonna let us go. But I was wrong. Because that's when the blond boy pulled the trigger."

Chapter 34

Ridge

I swirl my spoon around in the milk, watching as it splashes up the sides of my cereal bowl. One of the guys made lasagna earlier, but I didn't feel like eating.

Because all I've been doing since I got back last Sunday night is thinking about Orah. And Tabby. And how I wanna kill the stranger named Levi Sills. Literally. Not figuratively. And then, I nearly have a mental breakdown wondering how thoughts like that make me different from the shooters.

How can I denounce something bad, yet still *wanna do* something bad myself.

At yesterday's appointment, Dr. Evans said that it's only human nature to want bad things for people who have wronged us. For people who hurt other people. For people who take advantage of the vulnerable. For abusers. For murderers. For rapists.

But she said the difference between me and the shooters was that I would never follow through on my desires.

I guess she's right.

I wouldn't actually end Levi's life if he were to walk through the doors of the station right now, but I sure as hell would fuck him up. Broken ribs, missing teeth, a cracked nose.

And I would enjoy every single minute of it.

What Orah went through…

Not only with him, but with the shooters as well.

It goes without saying, My Brave Girl further cemented her status as the strongest woman to ever exist. After the offenders shot Tabby—and Orah, even though Orah didn't realize it—they hurried back to their position in the corner of the hallway where they pulled the fire alarm. Orah watched as they scurried up the steps into the projection room, leaving her and Tabby bleeding out. She quickly set to work, scrambling to pull her best friend's broken body into the supply room. She said it felt like hours, but it must've only been seconds, because by the time the group of preteens made it out of the auditorium where the video game movie was showing, none of them saw bodies in the corridor.

"Conway!" Chief Latner's bellowing scream echoes through my brain.

Shit. I knew this was coming.

When I returned to shift on Monday, I had no choice but to file my off-duty incident report and catalog my depleted medications and supplies. I mean, our off-duty jump bags are subject to random searches. It's a form of accountability, and the last thing I ever want to do is jeopardize one of my brother-in-arms' ability to help someone, to have access to lifesaving equipment at the tip of their fingers.

I stand from the table and make my way toward his office. We round the kitchen doorframe at the same time, nearly running into one another. It flusters him, and he tosses a hand over his head. The offending paperwork in his grasp floats to the ground, scattering around our feet. I bend, quickly scooping it into a pile and handing it back to him. He yanks it away with such force, he slices a papercut into the webbing between my thumb and forefinger. "Give me that!"

We garner the attention of everyone in the vicinity. I'm non-verbally questioned with furrowed brows and widened eyes. Everybody's wondering what the hell I did to get the doghouse treatment.

Chief stabs a finger in the air. "Get your ass in my office. Now."

I walk ahead of him, with my head held high, refusing to show fear or shame. Because if given the chance, I wouldn't hesitate; I would do it all again.

Over and over and over.

Chief slams the door and makes his way around to the business-end of his desk. I plant myself in front of the two visitor chairs. To the naked eye, I'm calm, cool, and collected. My spine is pulled long and tight, my body the perfect mixture of respect and confidence.

Of course, no one can see how fast I'm tapping the toes of my right foot. I'm slapping them up and down, quick as hummingbird wings, against the firmness of my steel-toed boots.

He tosses the papers down on his desk and cocks his hands on his hips, squeezing his bulky waist. He nods his head at the haphazard stack of documents. "You care to tell me what the fuck that is?"

"Sir?"

That poorly timed attempt to be a dumbfounded, yet polite, oaf earns me a scowl. He volleys the next statements to me in short bursts, lifting his voice like he's truly questioning the validity of my report, even though he already knows it's true. "You were in South Carolina? Using White Sky meds and equipment? On the movie theater girl? In the middle of the night? In the middle of her fucking home?"

"Yes, sir."

He sucks in a deep and haggard breath. "Please tell me you're kidding? Please tell me you didn't drive all the way from here to South Carolina to treat an emergency medical condition?"

"I didn't drive from Florida. I was already in Atlanta. My friend's wedding was last weekend."

He presses his fingertips into his closed eyelids, smushing so hard I worry his eyeballs might pop out. "Ridge, you're not a doctor; you're a paramedic. And you're not even that full time. You're a firefighter. Those people should've called 911, not you. You're not legally qualified to give out medical advice like that. Don't you understand your actions put this entire department at risk?"

Those people.

They're not *those* people. They're *my* people.

He shakes his head. "Why'd they even call you?"

I open my mouth, but I'm not exactly sure what to say. How do I describe mine and Orah's relationship? Without sounding like a pervert, that is...

I guess my silence strikes him as guilt.

"Oh, holy shit!" He's so on edge, he even does a little jump with his exclamation. "Please don't tell me you're sleeping with her? She's a patient! Have you lost your damn mind?!"

My stance breaks, and I hold my hands in the air like I'm a bad guy surrendering to the police. "What? No, of course not. I would never do that. Nothing inappropriate has even happened between the two of us."

Huh. That's not exactly true, is it?

He tilts his head, eyeing me with suspicion and silently questioning my honesty.

"I swear, Chief. We are not in a sexual relationship. It's not like that."

Well, I may not have a medical degree hanging on the wall, but I apparently graduated summa cum laude in dumbass-ery.

Because the way I phrased my denial did nothing but raise more questions.

I can see it. Plain as day. It's like a wallpaper of question marks has been plastered to his face.

"Not like that?" His speech is slow and measured. And obviously rhetorical, so I don't answer. Eventually he sighs, his shoulders collapsing against his torso. He sits down in his rolling chair and leans his head back, staring at the ceiling. "It's my fault, really..."

Breaking formation, I slide into the chair closest to me, perching on the end of it. "Chief?"

"I should've listened to Dr. Evans."

"Wh—what?" I stutter.

"She told me that you were forming an attachment to the movie theater girl."

That *girl* has a name...

Nerves tick in my chest, click-clacking around, matching the cadence of the clock behind him. It's nestled between framed photographs of his family.

He sits up and studies me. "She said that you were still talking to her. Said that you try to avoid direct conversations about her, but that you've let it slip once or twice. That you've talked about struggles that the girl is currently facing. Problems and fears. She said it's obvious that the two of you have a bond."

I drag my hand down my face. One. Two.

A bond.

Is that what it's called? When you love someone so much it hurts to even exist when they aren't near.

Because seeing her again—seeing her in person, feeling her in my arms, smelling her shampoo, tasting the salt of her skin while I gently kiss her forehead—it's made me wanna hit the pause button on my life. Freeze my heartbeats. Halt my breathing. Stop the blood pumping through my veins.

Because I don't wanna experience the joy of living without Orah by my side.

"An infatuation," he chides.

All I can muster is a raised eyebrow.

"That's what she called it." He gives a little shrug. "And just to be completely forthcoming, which is more than I can say of your behavior toward me and this department as of late, she did say not all infatuations are bad."

"It's complicated, Chief."

"You think I don't know that, Ridge?" He slides forward, propping his forearms on his desk. "But those complications are exactly why this can't go on."

The room starts to spin, and I beg myself to get a grip. To find control. To be strong.

I run into fucking burning buildings. Why the hell am I spiraling over a simple discussion with my superior?

I reckon because it's not so simple.

His observation carries a punch, slapping me with the truth I already know. "It's not right, son."

I give him a sheepish nod.

"The two of you met under the most intense of circumstances. That can cloud reality. It can distort the authenticity of your feelings. It makes everything more intimate."

I hang my head, fearful to speak my feelings to him, of all people. To the man who's nurtured my passion for helping those around me. Who believed in me. Who's been like a second father. Who gave me more than just a job...he made my dreams come true. "And what if our feelings aren't clouded? What if they aren't distorted? What if..." I drop my protest, allowing it to dissolve, leaving my love for Orah trapped in the confines of my body.

His eyes flare in anger. "They better fucking be clouded. Distorted. Not real. Because she's a patient, a victim. And you know we have restrictions about that in our Code of Conduct." His jaw tenses to the point of breaking his teeth, and he leans even closer, tapping his forefinger against the edge of his desk calendar. "She's. Also. A. Minor."

I don't really think it's appropriate to point out the fact that Orah turned eighteen one week after the attack. That's only one small rung of this broken ladder.

"Ridge, you've put this department in a horrible position. What if the press were to find out about this? Think of the optics? 'Firefighter saves young girl from the movie theater attack and then grooms her for a relationship. Exploits her damaged body and mind for his own pleasure'. You'd be vilified from the Atlantic to the Pacific."

Shit. It sounds even worse when he speaks aloud some of the same fears that have bounced around in my own head.

"The mayor wants you gone. He wants me to fire you."

In less than a second, my slouch is gone. I'm wired straight like a coat hanger is sticking out of my collar. "What?! Chief, please, I—"

He cuts me off, holding up his hand, lacing his features with compassion. "I'm not doing it."

Relief courses through me.

If I'm not a firefighter, who am I?

If I'm not helping people, saving them, then what would I become?

I know without a doubt I would lose myself. I would disintegrate into nothing, with my ashes scattering to the wind.

"Thank you," I humbly accept his goodwill.

"Don't thank me yet." His tempered empathy quickly fades. "Because it stops now. Whatever's going on between the two of you? It ends. Do you understand?"

It. Ends.

"The last thing we need, that *you* need, is a scandal," he pointedly declares.

"I...I..." How am I supposed to concede to that? To leaving her? When she only just agreed to start taking her anxiety meds? When she still has so much healing to do?

His timbre is low and calm. "Son, you just saw your brothers die. Right before your very eyes. You were held hostage. Stuck in a room with two girls who barely survived. What you saw that night...what we all saw..." He reclines back in his chair and rocks. The squeaky noise resonates in my ears, as loud as a bullhorn. "Maybe I put you back on active duty too soon."

"No, you didn't. This job, being a firefighter, is my purpose. I'm not whole without it."

"Well, then, we need to make this right."

I clear my throat, cursing myself when the sound cracks. It reminds me of when I was in middle school and my voice changed, switching from boyhood to manhood. "Yes, sir."

"How many times have you seen each other since she left the hospital?"

"Just the once. Just this past weekend, and I wouldn't have even seen her then had it not been for the emergency," I clarify. "Everything else has been phone conversations."

"And her parents are aware of y'all talking on the phone? They know about it? Condone it?"

"Yes."

"And that's why they called you Friday night? When she had the sleeping pill interaction and subsequent panic attack? You have a relationship with them too?"

"I think everyone from that night is connected. We went through something that others can't comprehend."

He takes my reply with a grain of salt and instead asks me another question. "What about the other girl? Tabitha…" He shuffles some of the papers on his desk, searching for Tabby's last name.

"Morrison," I say, not wanting to play ignorant to the fact that I know whose blood decorated my hands and clothes and body that night.

And of course, the crimson stains didn't all come from the fiery, silly redhead. But from her best friend as well.

The girl I love.

The girl I thought I had more time with.

But now, my deepest and darkest secrets have come to light. There's no more hiding, no more running, no more pretending.

Now, she's the girl I have *no* more time with…

"Yes, Morrison. Have you seen her? Do you talk with her? Dr. Evans said you haven't mentioned her in the past few weeks."

"We text some." The words taste bitter on my tongue. Like burnt coffee grinds.

He rubs both hands across his face, like he's trying to scrub my idiocy from his pores. "Well, obviously that stops too."

"Yes, Chief."

"So, we're in agreement? No more visits. No more phone calls. No more texts. Not even a fucking carrier pigeon. Right, Ridge?"

Despite my best efforts to be firm and strong, to be unwavering and unbending, I break. I fold against myself, collapsing into a pile of weakness. I pretend my plea is all about the wellbeing of my patient, of Orah. In reality, it's an excuse. Because I'm completely and utterly defenseless when it comes to Zipporah Smith. "I can't stop now."

His eyes harden, and his face reddens. "Excuse me?"

"We still have the congressional inquiry. We still have to testify about what happened. If I cut off all communication with her now, she...she won't recover from it. At least not in time for that. I *know* her, Chief. I know how she thinks. I...I can feel what she feels. And if I stop right now, she'll spiral." I stand up, unable to sit still anymore. With heavy foot, I pace back and forth. "She's the strongest person I know, but I promised her that I would be there for her. That I would help her heal and grow and survive. I promised her I wouldn't abandon her."

He slaps the desk and jumps up from his own chair, sending it skittering across the plastic floormat. "You did what?"

"I'll walk away, Chief. I promise. After the hearing."

He wobbles his head back and forth, wondering how ferociously and with what speed he should tear me a new asshole.

I point my finger in the general direction of Tallahassee. "You know how those politicians are. The lawyers? The government officials? The police? The governor? The mayor?" Yeah, the fucking mayor. Who couldn't wait to shake my hand and pose for pictures during the ceremony with me, but now wants my head on the chopping block. "Just think what kind of attention it will attract if she freezes, if she refuses to testify. We don't want the focus on us, or even Orah or Tabby. We want the focus to be on what can be done to prevent future tragedies like this from ever happening again."

I can see the moment he gives in, the moment he decides to make a deal with the beast he knows instead of the one he doesn't. "So, three more months? And then it ends?"

"That's right. Yes, sir."

"And in these three months, you'll slow your contact with her? With them? You won't say or do anything that puts yourself or this department in jeopardy? You'll keep things strictly professional? You won't engage more than necessary?"

Four syllables. Four syllables that splinter my heart. "Absolutely."

Spinning around, he mumbles a curse and a string of incoherent garble. Finally, he turns back to me. "This arrangement stays between the two of us, got it? And Ridge, I'm fucking serious, if this doesn't stop the minute the congressional hearing is over, I'll fire you. And I'll make sure every department in the Southeast knows how fast and loose you like to play with ethics."

Resigning to my fate, I lean across and hold out my hand, offering it to my mentor, to my Chief, to my friend. And he shakes it. Probably against his better judgment. But at least the action gives me some small hope for redemption.

Once dismissed, I pause at the doorway, unable to shake the nagging desire for him to know, without a doubt, that I spoke the truth earlier. I need him to know that I didn't take advantage of Orah. "Sir? I didn't cross *that* line. I swear to you."

He just lifts a brow. "Didn't you? From where I'm standing, *every* line has been crossed."

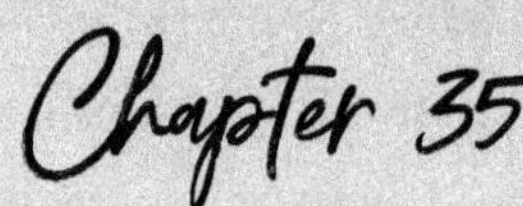

Chapter 35

Ridge

It's been a rough two months.

Trying to thread the needle of right and wrong with Orah. Being available for her calls and texts, but not *too* available. Being friendly, but not *too* friendly.

Listening to her.

Calming her.

Encouraging her.

Cursing her nightmares and fighting her demons.

Loving her from a distance. In as much of a strictly platonic way as I can muster.

And that's why what I'm about to do is so fucking dreadful. It's downright sinful.

With this one decision, I've violated every promise I made to the Chief. Every promise I made to myself.

Because I'm sitting outside of her house.

I turn the small jewelry box over and over in my hand. My thumb traces the silver swirls decorating the white paper. Silver and white. It looks like it should be a wedding or anniversary present. Not a birthday present.

I should've asked the lady to wrap it in something different.

I don't wanna give the wrong impression.

Holy shit. My mind is warped.

Who cares what the wrapping paper looks like? It's *me*. I'm the one giving the wrong impression, not the box. I'm the one who just drove seven hours to deliver a birthday gift. On a day that's not even her actual birthday.

True, I was invited to this intimate gathering, but I told Orah that I wouldn't be able to come. I reckon a part of me knew I was lying when I said I couldn't get away from work.

Back in the hospital, I told her this event was something to be celebrated. Something to be applauded. Something to be thankful for. And under mounting pressure from her family, she finally agreed to commemorate the milestone that hit exactly one week after she almost died.

Her eighteenth birthday.

The pounding on my driver's side window scares the shit out of me, and my free hand immediately curls into a fist, ready to pummel the danger that awaits me.

"Why are you sitting in here like some crazy stalker?"

Tabby's red hair is pulled back in a ponytail with short, fuzzy strands pointing in all directions, courtesy of the August heat.

Rolling my eyes, I open the Jeep door, climb out, and quickly tuck the small present into the pocket of my cargo shorts. I'm not even done with my hideaway when Tabby flings her arms around my neck, bouncing her body against mine in a pile of arms and legs. "It's been a hot minute, Hero."

I can't stop the giddy smile that engulfs my entire face. Relishing the happiness, I quickly kiss the top of her head. "I hate when people say 'hot minute'. It sounds stupid."

Pulling away, she furrows a brow and hooks her thumb at her chest. "Not me. I don't sound stupid. I sound cool."

"Whatever you say, Tab," I snicker on a sarcastic scoff. "And by the way, I'm not a stalker; I just pulled up."

She jabs a finger in my face. "Liar. You've been sitting out here for ten minutes. I saw you pull up from the bathroom window when I was peeing."

I cock my head. "You pee with the front blinds open?"

"No, smartass. I heard a car and then peeked out of the blinds." She folds her arms across her chest. "And stop deflecting. Why were you sitting out here all alone?"

I rock back on my heels, adding yet another lie to my heavy-hitting arsenal. At this rate, I'm packing more fibs in my soul than clowns in a clown car. "I was having to do something on my phone."

She frowns. "Why are you being weird?"

"I'm not being weird."

She bobbles her head up and down. "Yeah, you are. Orah told me you'd been acting funny. What's wrong with you?"

A cold sweat breaks out across the back of my neck. "Funny? I've not been acting funny."

She dramatically rolls her eyes. "I'm not gonna waste time on your foolishness." She grabs my hand and starts pulling me behind her. "Not when there's cupcakes inside."

The gathering may be small, but that doesn't stop the excited chatter and bombardment of hugs when Tabby drags me through the front door and immediately into the kitchen where everyone is gathered around the kitchen island, filling plates with food.

Despite the people surrounding me, my eyes instantly find *hers*. She's like my homing beacon, always guiding me out of the darkness and into the light. She's standing with her back against the wall over by the kitchen table, speaking to her grandmother. Granny, who's already fork-deep in mac and cheese, flickers her gaze between the two of us, monitoring our actions. Monitoring our *reactions*. And for that reason, I begrudgingly turn my focus back to those in front of me—John and Ann, Emmett and Laurie, and of course, Tabby's younger brother Dylan, who keeps trying to jump in my face, excited to show me the small Lego he just built. It's shaped like a Space Shuttle, and one of his voracious jumps sends the tail wing flying off the back of it. It hits the refrigerator and breaks into a couple of pieces.

"Oh, damn!" he hollers, before sliding across the floor on his knees to inspect the damage.

It's a tile floor. Little dude is probably gonna have bruises on his kneecaps.

Laurie blows a raspberry. "Don't say damn, Dylan."

"Why not? Tabby gets to say it."

Tabby purses her lips and pretends not to sense the incoming debacle.

"Your sister is seventeen, not seven. And school starts next week. You say that word in class, you'll get sent to the principal's office," Emmett explains.

"But Tabby—" he starts.

Tabby bends to help him pick up the pieces. "I'm smart enough not to say it in school, Dyl."

He scrunches his nose like he's thinking real hard. "Well, I reckon I'm smart enough not to say it in school too." He folds his arms across his little chest, mimicking the stance Tabby gave me outside just a few minutes ago. "So, I'll 'damn-it-up' at home, just like you do, and then keep my mouth shut at school." He loosens his arms and pretends to zip his lips with his finger.

And of course, we all try not to laugh. Which is pretty hard to do.

Laurie just sighs and slaps her hands against her thighs. "Let's just talk about this at home, okay?"

And before I can turn around, I *feel* her. Her presence slowly grows stronger, telling me that she's inching closer. One small step at a time.

Of course, her baby steps are inconsequential.

Zipporah Smith slammed her way into my heart in less time that it takes a person to blink. The second I heard her in that storage room I was a goner.

I turn to face her, and I'd be lying, yet again, if I said her glowing smile and sparkling storm-cloud eyes didn't drug me. I'm sluggish and dreamy and fucking addicted to every part of her.

The seen and the unseen.

The vocal and the silent.

The whole and the incomplete.

I'm not sure who the Orah before the movie theater attack would've become, who she would've turned into if never trapped in that room.

But this Orah?

She's the reason. The reason for everything I am or will ever be.

The grin on her face twitches, overcome with mischief. "Did you lie to me, Ridge?"

"What?"

"*Someone* told me *he* couldn't come to this little gathering because Belly had no one else to work the bar." She mocks me, with a light and airy tone. Just the kind of sound I love to hear from My Brave Girl.

I shrug a shoulder. "Eh, he found someone else. I mean, we're talking about pouring stale beer, not solving the Collatz conjecture."

A giggle erupts from her perfect mouth. "Ah, Mrs. Fulton would love you. She had a whole bulletin board on that in math class last year."

And... cold water is poured on me. A daggum tsunami of it.

Orah's still in high school.

I'm. Infatuated. With. A. High. School. Student.

Yeah, Chief was totally right about all of those lines. Apparently, I set them ablaze with a flamethrower. And then I plowed right through the charred remains with a bulldozer.

She wraps her fingers around my forearm, giving it a quick squeeze. And then her fingertips trace one of the veins that runs from my elbow down to my wrist. Her whisper is soft, yet intense. "Wherever you went, I need you to come back." She takes a step closer. "Give me a hug, Ridge."

Pushing my worries to the far recesses of my brain, I fold her in my arms. She fits against me like she always does. Perfectly. "Happy Birthday that isn't your birthday, Bird."

She nuzzles against my shoulder, using her nose to shift the collar of my T-shirt. Taking a deep breath, she inhales my scent, skirting hot air and moisture across my scar. Silently, I beg her to kiss it. To kiss me.

Because when she does that, it's innocent enough not to make me spiral. Spiral into thoughts of what a shitty person I am.

But it's also scandalous enough to alleviate the urges coursing through my body. The urges I'll never be able to fully satisfy with anyone else but her. I think my last attempted tryst proved that. After the disaster with Wedding Kate, I haven't tried again. I think the universe agrees that fucking Orah out of my system is an epically horrendous idea.

And then, that same universe tosses me a bone.

Her lips gently peck against the waxy, pink skin of my healed scar.

The caress of her mouth against my flesh sends a cascading waterfall of chills from the top of my head to the bottom of my toes. I squeeze her tightly, finding my home in her embrace.

Eventually, we separate, and I bend down to the table, giving Orah's grandmother a quick hug from the side.

She pats my cheek, scratching her finger across my trimmed beard. "It's good to see you again, Ridge."

"You, too, ma'am."

"Ridge," John starts, "you better make a plate before Emmett eats it all." He gives a playful nod to his friend's non-existent stomach.

Emmett snorts and drops what looks like half a stick of butter into his baked potato. "Hardy har, John. I didn't know you'd taken to stand-up comedy."

I take stock of my surroundings. Ann, Laurie, and Tabby have joined Granny at the kitchen table and are already eating. After a polite chuckle, I answer John. "No, it's alright. I didn't mean to interrupt your supper. I know I'm just showing up out of nowhere." I side-glance at Orah. "I told Orah I couldn't come."

"Ridge, you know you're always welcome here. You don't need a formal invitation. Plus, we've got more than enough food," Ann protests, pointing at me with her fork. "So you better eat."

I can't help but smile. Not to mention, the food smells damn great. And I *am* hungry. "Yes, ma'am."

Grazing my hand across the small of Orah's back, I lead her to the kitchen island, positioning her in front of the spread of food. I grab one of the blue and brown plates and wave it in front of her. "You first."

She's dressed in a fitted black top that highlights the lines of her collarbone. Her raven hair is pulled high into a messy bun, and the curve of her neck calls to me. Like a siren to a sailor, it's a dreamy and melodic harmony made only for my ears. And because of that, the small jewelry box in my pocket burns like a fire, scalding my thigh.

She gives me a wicked little smile. "If you insist." And with a devious sway to her hips, she spins around and starts fiddling with something on the opposite counter.

"Uhhh, is that an air fryer?" I ask.

She gifts me a non-committal grunt and then reaches into the machine and pulls out the cooking basket. With one quick flip of her wrist, she fills her plate with golden French fries. They're so hot, steam is still rolling off the crinkles.

"French fries!" I turn back to the kitchen island. "There's a whole pan of baked potatoes right here," I announce with a laugh.

Taking her place beside me—and in front of the barbequed chicken—she cocks her head to the side, giving me a dose of sassiness. "Well, it's my birthday. Can't I have whatever I want?"

I snatch a fry off her plate and pop it in my mouth. "I don't know. Can you?"

Her eyes widen, and her playfulness falters, favoring something deeper, more meaningful.

Well, shit. I'm a fucking idiot.

That was me...shamelessly flirting. It rolled off my tongue with no effort whatsoever.

Why? Because My Brave Girl is in a good mood. Her demons are still there, but in this very moment, they aren't tormenting her. And that makes me happy.

"Ridge? Want one?"

John draws me away from my staring contest with Orah. He dangles a beer in my direction.

Yeah, can I have twenty?

"I'd better not. I can't stay long. I have to report for shift at seven in the morning."

Orah's grip on her plate weakens, and it bangs against the countertop with a loud ting. I glance around us, making sure it didn't chip and send any porcelain shards scattering in the direction of her bare feet.

"You're not staying the night?"

The disappointment in her question rips at my heart, clawing at it like a rabid animal.

I shake my head. Everyone is watching us, boring little tunnels into my skin with their laser eyes. "I can't," I mutter apologetically. "I'm needed at the station."

She blinks in rapid fire, trying to stave off her tears. "But…but… you'll get sleepy on the drive back. It's dangerous."

I give her a wide smile and discreetly tap her thigh with my fingers. "That's what Red Bull and Nerd Clusters are for."

My response is unexpected, and a lighthearted giggle bursts from her, giving me a temporary reprieve from the ache of knowing that this will be one of the last times I see her.

And like I said, I shouldn't even be seeing her now.

If Chief Latner finds out, or Dr. Evans or anyone from the mayor's office, my whole career, my whole livelihood, will literally implode.

I didn't even tell my parents or Cullen or Holt that I was making this un-birthday trip. They all know about my June visit to see Orah, how I left the wedding and drove in the middle of the night because I was worried about her reaction to the sleep medication. And they all know about the panic attack that I walked into upon my arrival. Of course, I didn't divulge anything that Orah told me in confidence; it's not my place. She trusts me to hold her secrets, and I would never violate that trust.

And I didn't tell my parents about the subsequent ass-chewing and the threat to derail my career if I didn't follow through on the Chief's ultimatum.

Well, I guess I'm being unfair.

It's not like Chief Latner is doing this because he's some sort of egotistical asswipe. He's doing what has to be done to protect the department. And me. And more importantly, Orah.

And that's what I told C and Holt when I gave them the watered-down version of everything and asked them to keep some of it from my parents. Of course, it came as no surprise to them that I had kept in contact with Orah. That we were having conversations in the middle of the night when she couldn't sleep. That we were protecting each other from the all-consuming memories of blood and violence and death. And that we were encouraging each other with the precious gifts of time and new beginnings and fresh starts. I told Holt that I feel like I have a noose around my neck and that every decision I make causes me to slip. Inch by inch, I'm strangling. And I have no one to blame but myself.

"Well then, you better start eating, Hero," Tabby teases, forcing our attention back to the spread in front of us. "Because your girl is hiding her cupcakes in the fridge in the garage, and she won't let anyone even *look* at them until dinner is over."

And with that, everyone returns to eating and making idle chit-chat, acting like Tabby's comment about Orah being '*my girl*' is simple fact and nothing out of the ordinary.

If only they knew...

Come September, nothing will ever be ordinary for me again.

"You really liked them?"

We're sitting on the porch steps, listening to the summer crickets and cicadas as they serenade the night. The front porch light brightens one side of her beautiful face, casting her in a haunting and breathtaking glow. "No lie, Little Bird, those were the best cupcakes I've ever tasted." I knock her with my shoulder. "I scarfed down three of them before you even finished one."

She cocks an eyebrow. "Is that supposed to be a compliment about my baking? Or a dig about how slow I eat?"

"Maybe a little bit of both."

Her laugh carries through the dark, and she returns the favor, bumping me with her own shoulder. "Asshole."

Her taunt is breathy and sultry, instantly making me reach for the jewelry box in my cargo shorts. Because the smart thing would be to forget the gift. Jump in my Jeep and drive away.

But the way her voice just assaulted my heart—and my libido—has me fumbling for the small, square box and not even regretting it. "I got something for you."

"Oh, Ridge, you already gave me a gift."

I snort. "The blanket doesn't count."

My free hand is resting on my thigh, just above my knee, and when she slides her own hand on top of mine, I nearly grow too emotional to speak. Her slender fingers splay across my knuckles, and with a gentle shift, she moves so that her thumb and forefinger can softly caress my leg.

"I'm not talking about the blanket. You gave me the gift of life. The gift of friendship. The gift of *you*."

I can't talk. So I just hold the box between the two of us and nod to it.

She glances from me to the box and then back again. Wordlessly, she moves her hand away from my leg and takes it, studying it like she can see straight through the wrapping paper and into what's inside.

After several seconds, I clear my throat, trying to replace the emptiness I feel from her missing hand. "Unless you developed X-ray vision since I last saw you, there's only one way to know what's inside."

She cocks her head studying me. "Maybe I don't want it to be over."

"Wh–what?" I stutter.

"My birthday that's not my birthday. Maybe I don't want it to be over. If I open this, you'll leave."

It hurts to even swallow. "I'll leave regardless."

She stares at me, losing herself in my eyes. My eyes that—fuck me—are collecting unshed tears. Because apparently, I have no control over my feelings. She reaches across the chasm that's separating us and snakes her forefinger down my nose and past my lips. Landing on my chin, she gives me two little taps.

One. Two.

"I suppose you will."

And when one of those bastard tears escapes, she turns back to the jewelry box, giving me a moment to wipe my face and collect myself.

I can feel what you feel.

Can she feel me pulling away? Can she see the horrific lies that I'm gonna spend the rest of my life living?

The lie that I don't care about her? That I don't love her? That she was nothing more to me than just another patient? Just another victim? Just another survivor?

She tugs the bow and rips into the package, placing all of the trash on her other side. And when she opens the box, she gasps.

It's not a bulky necklace by any means. That's why they were able to fit it into a small, square box instead of one of those huge, rectangle ones. The linked chain is delicate but strong. Just like her. And the little bird charm immediately garners her attention.

Surprisingly, there are a lot of 'bird' necklaces out there on the Internet. But none that I found piqued my interest. So, I had the local jeweler custom-design this one. The chain and charm itself are 18-carat rose gold. I just couldn't stop thinking about how good the color would look with her raven hair and storm-cloud eyes.

And because I respect Zipporah, and I respect the choices and changes she needs to undergo to heal, the bird is black, decorated with black diamonds. Except for its eye.

Which is Tiger's Eye.

The jeweler thought I was a senseless moron when I requested it. Because who in their right mind would set a common, inexpensive, semiprecious stone in the heart of pricey jewels—jewels that took one hell of a chunk out of my savings account. But even he had to concede that the swirls of brown highlighted both the rose gold and the black diamonds in the very best of ways.

Her fingers tremble as she traces the bird, lightly brushing her touch across each and every gem. "Ridge, I...I can't accept this. It's too beautiful, too expensive." She turns to face me. Her eyes have found the tears that I refused to shed, the tears that I locked behind closed doors as soon as I had a chance to wipe my face. They flow down her cheeks, freely and with wild abandon. "It's too much. I don't deserve it."

I should hold her. I should comfort her. But instead, I take the box from her, free the necklace, and twirl my finger, motioning for her to spin around. Securing the necklace around her neck, I gently kiss her left shoulder, mimicking the exact action done to me just a few short hours ago. "You deserve everything I can never give you, Zipporah."

And without another word, I cross the driveway, hop in my Jeep, and drive away.

I'm thirty minutes down the road, when my phone pings with a text message.

Little Bird: Maybe I don't want everything. Maybe all I need is all you have to give.

Chapter 36

Orah

Islam the door to the bathroom stall and fling myself, fully clothed, onto the toilet seat.

When I feel the dampness of someone else's pee soaking through my black leggings, vomit rushes from my stomach and into my mouth. Grabbing the small trash can, I hurl the contents of my meager breakfast onto the pile of toilet paper squares used as Kleenexes and the discarded tampon applicators. Then, I make the poor decision to open my closed eyes. And when I catch a glimpse of someone's bloody pad, I retch even more.

I puke until my stomach is sore and nothing but spittle of yellow bile makes an appearance.

The exertion has my healed scar throbbing in phantom pain and a sizzling ache running the length of my breastbone. Cold sweat dots my brow, and the baby hairs on the back of my neck cling to my skin. My heart batters against my ribcage, violently and aggressively, making it hard to even hear the thoughts in my own head.

With a shaky hand, I set the trash can on the floor and clean my face. I layer the used toilet paper right on top of my barf, vowing to dispose of the hazardous waste myself. There's no way I should force the custodial staff to clean up after me; they have enough on their plates.

And then, I laugh.

An unexpected and maniacal chuckle rips from my mouth, making me cough and choke on the acidic mucus still left behind in my throat.

Well, that's definitely something the Old Orah never would've thought.

The me of four months ago would've never given a second thought to the exhaustive and brutal work of our school's janitorial team.

In fact, if I remember correctly, it was just eight months ago that I overflowed one of the toilets in D Wing because I flushed— well, attempted to flush—Stefanie's favorite scarf. She told a group of girls that I gave head to Keagan in the flatbed of his truck while he fingered my ass.

What *is* true is that I flirted with Keagen and flashed him my bra in exchange for him getting his older brother to buy me a six-pack of wine coolers. That Friday night, Tabby and I got drunk, watched eighties rom-coms, and ate our weight in cheddar popcorn.

And it just so happens that Stefanie is one of the many reasons I'm currently having a breakdown in the secluded bathroom of the auditorium during lunch period. It won't be secluded for long, though; the afternoon drama classes will be bursting through the doors in about thirty minutes.

This first day back has been terrible.

So much worse than I ever thought it could be.

And if my reaction to the events of today is this bad, I can only imagine how much worse it would've been if I had still been refusing to take my prescribed anxiety medication. Because overwhelming can't even properly describe it.

Every single day of my high school career, I have walked through a metal detector. I should be used to it. But today brought a whole new paranoia. We used to always laugh about how much stuff the metal detectors missed. Not to mention, they were down for maintenance just as much as they were up and running.

But today…I was obsessed.

The speed at which they allowed the students to pass through blew my mind. There was no way they were catching all of the contraband. They didn't even pull Declan for a side search, and I know for a fact he brought a hunting knife to school two years ago.

Then, there's the crowds.

Holy shit, the fucking crowds.

Crowds of kids, crowds of teachers, crowds of strangers I've never even seen before. Everyone loud and yelling and crammed into the long, skinny hallways, during every single class change. It's too noisy to hear someone call for help. It's too congested to have a clear path to run in the event of an emergency. If something bad happens, all of us would be sitting ducks just ripe for the plucking.

The easiest carnival game ever invented.

And don't even get me started on Mrs. Carrington. I had her last year, too, so this wasn't my first rodeo with her. She's so concerned with being the cool, hip teacher that she blatantly ignores the safety regulations that are supposed to be enforced throughout our school. She wants kids to listen to their own bodies and use the restroom when and where they see fit. She thinks it's an antiquated ideology for her students to have to ask permission to go to the bathroom during class. Which I get. Hey, I'm all for it. It's embarrassing to have to announce to the whole classroom when you need to go pee. But she's way too lenient on the situation. She leaves the hall passes hanging by the door and lets kids come and go as they please. And of course, she made twenty hall passes. Yeah, twenty. So, at any given time twenty of her thirty students may be out wandering the halls, doing the sloth-shuffle to and from the restroom. But of course, she then claims it's too distracting to our learning for her to stop teaching her lesson and open the auto-locking door for any returning kids. Her solution? The magnetic strip that prevents the lock from latching. And the school board banned those. All of our school doors have auto locks that engage as soon as the tardy bell rings and runs throughout the entirety of the period.

What am I supposed to do if a shooter comes in the building? Or a man with a knife? Or a woman with a bomb? What am I supposed to do if he or she gets to Mrs. Carrington's door before the alert is sounded over the intercom? Before she has a chance to pull the magnet and allow the door to lock?

I mean, does she not remember what happened to Micah Wood in seventh grade? His parents were in the middle of a custody dispute, and the estranged father snuck into math class and tried to kidnap Micah.

Naturally, I was a nervous wreck during her whole class.

Then, there was the lunch bell fiasco.

The lunch bell sounds different than the class period bells. It's a different tone, deeper and more resonant. Apparently, it reminds me of a fire alarm. Because when the first lunch bell went off, I jumped up from my assigned advanced physics table, which was in the front of the classroom, and basically sprinted toward the back of the room where the chemistry lab is. My vision was blurry, my ears were ringing, and my feet felt like they were made of lead. I only stopped when Quinton stood from his seat at the back and got in front of me, blocking my path. With a frown, he gently shook my shoulders, speaking words I couldn't even understand. After a few seconds, the oppressive fog lifted, and he spun me around to face Mr. Lawrence, who sternly reminded me that our class didn't take lunch until third bell, so I needed to sit down.

And then he remembered what happened to me. I could see the memory slowly settling over his features like syrup being poured over a pancake. Bright red embarrassment scalded his cheeks, and he mumbled a sincere apology, telling me that I was free to go to the nurse if needed.

He's always been nice to me, kind and generous, so I instantly forgave him. His apology and humbling behavior warmed my heart.

And then...the snickering and giggling from Stefanie and her friends immediately froze it. My blood turned frigid and icy, clogging my pumping heart with bitterness and anger.

And it wasn't just them.

I heard the whispers. I felt the stares. I saw the looks of fake pity. And I tasted the joy in the air. The delight of those triumphing over my demise, over my fall from status. Because people love to measure their bliss by using the anguish of others. The misery of their nemesis is the Mendoza Line for their own happiness.

I reach for the comfort of my necklace and graze my fingers over the charm, slowly counting the rows of small diamonds.

One. Two. Three. Four. Five.

One. Two. Three. Four. Five.

One. Two. Three. Four. Five.

Fumbling for my backpack on the floor, I pilfer through the small interior pocket until I find my phone. I snuck in with it. While Tabby and everyone else was locking their phones in the required lockers, I quietly stood to the side, pretending I didn't even bring mine with me. So, technically, I'm the one breaking the school board code now and not Mrs. Carrington. In fact, just having the phone in my hand could land me in suspension.

He answers before the first ring is even finished.

"Orah? How is the first day? Are you okay?"

My voice is creaky and weak. It reminds me of a broken door just hanging by the hinges. "It's my turn."

He pauses. I can hear the low rumble of his breath through the phone. "Okay. Ask me anything."

I think for a quick moment. "What was your favorite day of high school?" I shift my body and settle my cheek against the coolness of the side partition of the bathroom stall. And of course, I do my best not to think about what germs may be on there.

"My best day?"

"Uh-huh."

"That's easy. The first day of my senior year."

Interesting. So, his best day has been my worst day.

"The school system we went to had a primary school that went to second grade, an elementary school that went to fifth grade, a middle school that went to eighth grade, and the high school. So, high school was the only time that Sea and I technically went to the same school. We had the same lunch period, and I'll never forget seeing him across the huge lunchroom, looking around, completely nervous about who he was gonna sit with. Most of his buddies had a different lunch time," he explains. "That look on his face…that wasn't what I was used to. He always seemed so fearless. And there he was…vulnerable and exposed. I remember standing up and yelling his name. When he saw me waving him over to our table, this sense of relief just flooded him. And he smiled. Right at me. Like he was proud that I was his brother."

I grab another piece of toilet paper and wipe at the tears as they stream down my face.

When I don't immediately respond, he sighs. "My turn," he demands. "What's going on? Are you safe? Where's Tabby?"

Sniffling, I sit up from my reclined position on the commode and tap my black tennis shoe against the tile floor. "Tabby and I only have one class together, and it's at the end of the day."

"I see. So, you've been navigating the day by yourself?"

A cynical chuckle heaves from my lungs. "Not successfully, I haven't."

"Do you wanna tell me what happened?"

"What hasn't happened, Ridge? I feel like a caged animal. Everything is scary, everything is overwhelming."

"And?"

"And they're staring. And whispering. And talking about me. One girl even asked to see my gunshot wound. She said it was the only way to put the rumor to rest that I faked the whole thing."

"Shit…" He mumbles under his breath. And if I listen closely enough, I can hear him tapping his chin. "Well, I know you haven't had class with Tab yet, but have you been able to talk to her? Is she having a bad day too?"

"We aren't supposed to have our cell phones. We're required to lock them up when we enter the building, but I snuck mine in my backpack. All that to say, I haven't been able to talk to her. Not in person or by phone." I rub my eyes with a ball of toilet paper, trying to capture the crumbled remnants of my mascara. "But…"

"But what?"

"But I saw her."

"You saw her? When?"

"I was in American lit. When I looked out the window, I saw her on the quad. She was with her class doing some kind of experiment with paper airplanes."

"And?"

"And she was smiling, laughing. She…she seemed happy, Ridge." I shake my head, hating the jealousy that's swirling low in my stomach. "How can she be so comfortable here? How can we be so different?"

"You already know the answer to that, Little Bird. There's no one-size-fits-all when it comes to healing. Everyone has to follow their own path. Not to mention, Tabby still doesn't remember what happened. The last thing she remembers is the two of you being in the restroom. You? You remember it all. You saw it all, felt it all."

"Remembering is the punishment I deserve. Maybe, if I'd just done what he wanted—let him have his way with me—he would've let us go."

"Zipporah." My name pours from his lips in a sweet, intoxicating mixture of compassion and reverence.

That sound alone suppresses my fears. It pacifies my feelings of inadequacy. It gives me hope. Hope that I can one day look in the mirror and see the girl that he sees.

The *survivor* that he sees.

The *woman* that he sees.

I used to pray that he would one day see me as more than just a silly teenager. More than just a victim. More than just his patient.

And now? Now, I know I'm *more*.

I've known it for a while. And he has too.

We belong to each other. Destiny marked us as one. Our fate was carved in bullets and blood, in bondage and liberation.

I stiffen my back and roll my shoulders. Closing my eyes, I picture long and sturdy tendrils of bravery, building and growing throughout my body, weaving and winding their way through every muscle, every bone, every organ.

One day, we'll both be brave enough.

Brave enough to admit out loud how we feel. Brave enough to kiss and love and start a life together.

One day.

Because I can feel what he feels.

And My Hero may never admit it, but sometimes he's as scared as me.

Chapter 37

Ridge

"When's your parents coming in? Tomorrow?" Belly tosses a look back at me as he sets two frozen drinks with little pink umbrellas in front of two middle-aged women.

I shake my head. "No."

He reclines against the bar. "I thought your timeslot for testifying was Thursday? Didn't you say you have to be there by eight that morning? They'll have to leave in the middle of the night to get here on time."

"They're not coming."

He straightens, overcome with sudden concern. "What? Why? Is somebody sick?"

"No, it's nothing like that. I told them not to come."

His bushy eyebrows fold together. "Huh? Why would you do that?"

I glance around, making sure no one is eavesdropping on our private conversation. "Because I'll get too emotional if they're sitting there listening to me, listening to every horrific little detail." I turn and wipe some spilled beer from the bar top. "I need to keep things as professional as possible. I'll be in my Class A, representing the department." I toss a guy a wave as he throws a tip in the jar and heads out the door. "If any of my family is there, I'll be focused on them. The attention should be on the real victims, the real survivors. I don't wanna distract from that."

"Damn, son, you realize you were a victim, too, right?" He points to my shoulder. "You had all them stitches. You had that bruise that covered your whole backside. It's not like you were sitting around drinking margaritas and watching everything happen to someone else. It was happening to you."

I shrug. "Eh, but I'm trained for that kind of stuff."

I do my best not to let his statement affect me. But that seems to be a losing battle. Because every single thought or comment or memory about that night or the pending congressional inquiry has me thinking of Orah, and how I'm so close to losing her.

I'm down to less than two days.

Less than forty-eight hours.

Gone are the months.

Gone are the days.

And before I know it, it will be only minutes.

I have no idea how I'm gonna end things. I've gone back and forth a thousand times in my head. I've contemplated acting like everything is normal and then ghosting her. But that just seems fucking harsh.

I've contemplated telling her the truth, but I don't want her to think that I'm choosing my job over her.

Even though, I guess that's what I'm doing.

But it has to be done. Dr. Evans is right. Chief Latner is right.

Our relationship is based on one single event. It's tied in an ugly bow, knotted together by ribbons of stress and trauma and fear and anxiety. Maybe her feelings for me aren't even real; maybe they're just clouded by her gratefulness that I was there.

If another firefighter had slammed into that room, would the two of them have the kind of bond that we have? Would they talk and laugh and cry and comfort?

Would he love her the way I love her?

Would she love him?

What if I were lying in the hallway and Battles had been in the room with her?

Would it have been him gifting her a diamond necklace? Him playing midnight question games? Him searching for the joy that only her laugh can bring?

Orah and her family—including Boaz, who flew in from Alaska two days ago—and Tabby and her parents, arrived in Tallahassee today. They had meetings scheduled with the advocate attorney. She asked me to come spend the day with her tomorrow. I told her I couldn't, that I had things to do at the station to prepare for the inquiry. That's just another lie that I told her. We did all of our final prep interviews last week.

A guy at the end of the bar, toward the back, holds his mug in the air, indicating that he's ready for a refill on his draft. I'm setting the craft APA in front of him when Dottie comes around, dramatically rolling her head. "About damn time."

"What?"

She flops her hand in the direction of the outdoor patio. "Those two numbnuts are finally ready to close their tab."

One of the wooden pillars of the rolling door is in my line of sight so I can't catch a good view, but it looks like two young guys. I know the patio has been somewhat crowded tonight, but it's not been overwhelming. So Dottie's been handling the table service by herself. Outside of grabbing supplies and dropping a new keg, I haven't left my post behind the bar.

That exasperated rant piques Belly's interest. All teasing aside, the man is still head over heels for his wife and very protective of her. "Dot, those boys say something to you?"

She just grunts and wraps her arms around him. "Calm down, Bel. You know I've heard it all before. Besides, I can hold my own."

Well, now *my* interest is piqued. What did they say to my girl Dottie? "Dottie, what did they do?"

Our regular, Tim, is sitting across from us. He was engrossed in the nightly news playing from the TV hanging on the wall behind us, but now he seems to be completely rapt by our conversation. "They were out on the beach before they came in here a few hours ago. I saw them hitting on some girls."

Belly snorts on a laugh, making himself cough. "Uh-oh. Alert the presses. Boys are hitting on girls at the beach."

Dottie slaps his arm.

Tim slants forward, wiping the beer from his mustache before elaborating. "One of them was Foster Tucker's daughter."

Dottie gasps. "Foster Tucker's daughter? That girl's in middle school. She's in my niece Sharon's art class."

"I know. I hollered at her and told her she better run up the road to her daddy's store. Told her it was getting late." He narrows his eyes. "One of them guys had his arm around her and everything. Thought I saw him grab her bottom." He makes a sucking noise with his teeth. "But I can't be for sure."

"Damn. You call Foster and tell him?"

"No, not yet." He takes another sip of his beer, worry and confusion etched into his sunburnt face. "What if I misread the situation?"

An ominous cloud forms over my head, covering me in a dark and inexplicable anger. Rage vibrates throughout my body. It's like I can actually feel it oozing from my bone marrow. A murky, toxic sludge that poisons me, leaving me nothing but a rotting shell.

My grumble is disenchanted and disillusioned, haunted and chilling. "You said they're closing their tab. Where's their credit card info?"

Dottie slides over to the register and taps on the computer screen, pulling up the card pre-authorization. She takes a step back once the data is displayed. I breathe deep and close my eyes, begging my intuition to be wrong, praying my instinct is incorrect. My eyes pop open, and I exhale.

Levin M. Sills.

Levi Motherfucking Sills.

My chest constricts, with my lungs squeezing the very life from my beating heart. A shrill buzz echoes in my ears. So loud, so powerful, it makes the back of my skull throb and itch. My fingers clutch the countertop so tightly, my knuckles turn white.

"Ridge? What's wrong?"

Dottie's voice is nothing more than a wah-wah-wah sound, pulsing around me like a nightclub strobe light.

My appearance must be cause for concern to everybody because Belly rips me away from the computer and shakes my shoulders. "What the hell is wrong? Are you okay? Talk to us." Tim stands on the bar's footrest, towering over and crowding our space.

I clear my throat, trying to force the words into the world. "I know that guy. He...he hurt someone I care about."

Belly drops his hands and just stares at me. In a foggy blur of adrenaline and outrage, I watch as his eyes dart from the guys on the patio to Dottie to me and then back to Dottie. In an unspoken language, honed by years of life, love, hardship, and reality, Dottie gives him a simple nod. He sniffles and tugs on the worn leather belt holding up his tattered cargo shorts. "Well, then, go do what you gotta do."

And then it happens.

My training kicks in.

A calm floods my body, washing away the venomous drip. It leaves me fresh and focused and driven.

I feel like I'm about to enter a burning building.

Like I'm about to triage a patient.

Like I'm about to enter a movie theater under attack.

I tense my jaw and tap the bar with my clenched fist. "Don't run his card. I'll pay for their drinks. I'll be damned if I let his money taint this bar. We're not taking a single dime from him."

Tim's mouth falls open in shock. Belly tosses a rag over his shoulder. "You ain't payin' for shit, son. We'll call it a walkout."

Tim taunts. "I think you mean a *toss out*," he wisecracks, attempting a poorly timed joke.

Turning on my heels, I stomp through the bar, allowing the heaviness of my footfall to sink into my psyche.

One. Two.

One. Two.

One. Two.

I round the corner and walk across the patio, respectfully smiling and waving to the group of older ladies who catcall to me in good humor, all the while giggling and laughing. They come in twice a month to drink wine and play gin rummy. A couple of them are football fans, and I once convinced Holt to play a few rounds of cards with them. They were all devastated when he politely declined Francine's request for strip poker.

I stop in front of Levi's table. And for a moment, the repugnant little shits don't even have the decency to look at me. They see my Belly's Beachside T-shirt and quickly size me up as the low man on the totem pole.

"Levi?"

I shouldn't be surprised when the blond holds out his hand, flashing a watch that probably costs more than my parents' home. "Dude." He widens his eyes and wiggles his head, emphasizing his obvious displeasure with me. "Do you have my receipt? We've got someplace to be." He casts a scheming look at the guy next to him, and they both cackle and snort, leaving very little to the imagination.

The shitheads are up to no good, and they want me to know it.

But just in case I didn't pick up on the innuendo wafting through the air like rancid fish guts, he adds, "And a girl to be in between." He scoots into his friend's personal space and not so subtly adds, "And I gotta finish it all before she reports back to homeroom."

The guy winks. "Something to be said for a teacher's pet."

And with that, they both collapse in a fit of laughter. The other guy slaps his palm on the table, and a near-empty plastic beer cup tumbles on its side, spilling draft across the weathered wood.

It's just my luck they would be drunk.

Red-cheeked. Glassy-eyed. Slurred speech.

It's too damn bad.

Because I really want him to have a clear memory of me pounding his face with my fist.

I stretch my neck, popping it left and right.

I just need him to give me a reason. I'm a firefighter after all. An unprovoked attack could lose me the very job that I'm trying so hard to keep.

But defending myself?

Well, that's a different story, isn't it?

I flick my chin at the other guy. "Colby, I presume?"

They send each other a questioning look before the other guy answers, drawing his syllable out over his beer-bloated tongue. "Yeeeahhh?"

I prop my hands on my hips and spew a non-committal grunt in response.

Levi rolls his eyes. "Damn, didn't you hear us?" He makes a writing motion with his right hand. "Just give me the ticket to sign. We're done."

"No ticket," I say.

"No ticket? What? Your credit card machine broken or something?" He flops back in his chair and gives me a condescending grin. "Well, you're shit out of luck, buddy. Because I don't carry cash on me. Only plastic."

"Nope. Credit card machine is fine."

Colby flings his hands in the air. "What's the holdup then?"

I shift my arms, folding them across my broad chest. "We don't want your money. It's not good here."

Levi's smile brightens. "Ahhh. So, you know who my grandfather is, huh? You're wanting to get on his good side? See if he'll give you some sort of deal on property or something?" He pretends to look around and then curls his forefinger like he wants to tell me a secret. "Bad news... my grandfather doesn't have a good side."

"I don't give a tiny rat's ass about your grandfather. This is about you."

He's fascinated by that comment. He tries to sit up straight. His spine refuses to cooperate, though, and he undulates like a snake. "What about me?"

I avoid responding and instead drag my hand down my face, stalling for dramatic effect. "Well, you're in town for the inquiry, right? The congressional field hearing about the movie theater attack?"

His jaw clenches, and Colby nervously clutches the armrests on his chair. It only takes Levi a split second to recover. He frowns. "I don't know what you're talking about."

"Sure, you do. You were there." Leaning down, I plant my hands on the table, making a little extra effort to swish the spilled beer back in Colby's direction. He scoots his chair out of the way when some droplets land on his leg. I lower my volume to a whisper and lace it with a tone of friendly tease. I even toss in a smile for good measure. You know, for any witnesses who may be watching us. "C'mon, Levi. You can't pretend no one will find out. You're an adult. Your name is part of the official record. They're only shielding the names of minors because they're required to." I furrow a brow and pretend to study him. "But you're not a minor, are you? You think those swarms of reporters don't already have stories written about you? They're just waiting to get some pictures. They'll be slathered all over that building like butter on a biscuit." I push even closer. "I heard the judge or senators or governor or police—or whoever is making the big decisions—is allowing a handful of news crews into the actual hearing rooms." Standing up straight, I gift him a sympathetic sigh.

He falls for my fake sincerity and lowers his guard. "Man, I tried to get out of it. We weren't even there when the shit went down. We had already left."

"Really?"

"Yeah." A sly smirk decorates his face. "And I don't have to worry about those reporters." He hooks a thumb at Colby. "Neither of us do."

"Oh, yeah? And why's that?" I ask.

He scoffs, acting like my sheer stupidity is beneath him. "Uhhh, hello? My *father*. I'm from D.C., buddy. My father has dirt on everybody. You won't find my name or picture in shit." He shrugs. "Or if you do, it won't be for long. We'll take care of it. The facts are controlled by the people with money." He rubs his fingers together. "And it just so happens my family's pockets run deep."

I pull a towel from my own back pocket, right the plastic cup, and start wiping the mess. I make eye contact with a few guys a couple of tables away and give them a friendly smile and head nod before turning back to Levi. "Well, I guess that's par for the course, isn't it?"

He cocks an eyebrow. "What is?"

"The bad guys rarely get what's coming to them."

Levi blinks his bloodshot eyes. "Huh?"

"You, Levi. I'm talking about you." I laugh, a little too loudly, before lowering to a hushed rumble. Dropping the chummy façade, I spit my accusation in his direction, hurling it with loathing and disgust. "You like spending time with the girls, huh? Young ones? I wonder how many 'facts' your daddy has already buried. Hard to be a lawyer with that many tombed secrets pulling you into the grave. A fall like that could break your fucking neck."

His face blanches, draining of color. And once his half-functioning brain actually processes the meaning behind my threat, his pupils widen, giving me a glimpse into the hollow Hell of his soul. "What the fuck did you just say to me?"

"You heard me. You're a fucking rapist. A predator." I scrape my teeth across my bottom lip. "And one day, I'm gonna make sure the whole world knows it too."

I watch as his hands curl into fists. His torso shakes with anger. A palpable hum electrifies the air, making the hairs on my forearms stand. I shift to my tiptoes, readying myself for whatever may come.

And I hope it comes soon.

I'm betting on the little pissant having zero patience, zero self-control, zero humility. But an ego as big as the fucking moon.

I toss the damp rag over my shoulder. "In the meantime, word of advice, I hear shaving your pubes can make your cock look bigger. Maybe then you won't be so insecure about your miniscule dick. I mean, there's gotta be a reason why you do what you do. Why you prey on young girls?" I flick my eyes toward his lap. "It's a small pecker situation, right?"

And then I allow every hateful thought, every vicious feeling, every malignant vision to course through my body with the power of a hurricane. My bones quake. My muscles tighten. My blood boils.

I feel violent and wild and explosive.

Leaning back down, I spread my palms across the table and prop myself just inches from his face. "But your cock isn't the real problem, is it?" I pause for a beat before answering my own question. "No." I shake my head back and forth. It's a threatening, yet barely noticeable movement. "Your perverted brain is the issue. Your fucking black heart. Your rotten and putrid soul." I slow my speech, accentuating each syllable with repulsion and abhorrence. "You. Are. A. Disease." I lob a cynical chuckle. "Don't you think it's time you screw someone who's at least old enough to vote, you pathetic fuck?"

And...that does it.

Levi launches himself across the table. He's clumsy and sloppy, nothing but a chaotic jumble of arms and legs, hands and feet. I nimbly jump out of his way. The fumbled inertia of his own body topples both the table and him onto the floor. His head whips in my direction. Pure evil radiates from his pores. It's thick and potent. It's suffocating any goodness, any redeeming qualities that might once have been a part of his DNA. Like bitter raindrops falling on my tongue, I can taste his immorality as it hangs in the air.

I move toward him with an outstretched hand. To the naked eye, it looks like I'm offering assistance, offering to help pull him up off the splintered and sand-beaten patio decking. But then, I angle my body away from the prying eyes of the other patrons and give him a come-hither motion with my fingers. "C'mon, motherfucker. Bring it," I growl, low and breathy, only for him to hear. "Or do you only think the hunt is fun when the prey can't fight back?"

With an animalistic snarl, he scrambles to his feet and catapults his body into mine.

He's slow.

And much shorter than me.

With way less muscle.

And even less coordination.

I could easily dodge his advance, but I still need this to look good. Just in case.

So I let him take the first swing.

I swivel my head at just the right moment, and his knuckles barely skim across my cheek. The only damage left from his punch is some ruffled facial hair.

My turn.

I push him away from me, just a smidge, giving myself room to work. I haul back and go for damn gold, striking a blow right across the apple of his cheek and busting his nose on the follow through. His head snaps to the side, and blood splatters from his mouth. A satisfying pain sears through my hand.

By now, a crowd has formed. From my periphery, I see Belly and Dottie. I expect to hear screams and shouts, a flurry of activity as people race to call 911. But I don't hear anything. Not even from his partner in crime.

The only person making a noise is Levi.

He cries out. He stumbles, wobbling to and fro, with his arms flailing beside him for balance. Once he has his bearings, he screeches and flings himself in my direction. He jumps in the air and tries to full-body attack me.

It reminds me of a cat jumping on a tree trunk and trying to climb. Under different circumstances it would be comical.

I shake him off, and he lands on his butt. He doesn't even have time to blink before I'm squatting over him and slamming his back to the ground. I grab the collar of his shirt and lift his head to protect it from busting open on the wooden floor slats. I mean, I'm looking to beat his ass, not bash his brains in. Despite this little episode, that's not who I am.

Clenching my jaw and tightening my fist, I land another blow, this time focusing on his nose and mouth. There's a distinctive crunch, and blood starts gushing from his nose like a waterfall. He howls and tries to curl into a fetal position, which he can't do because my thighs are blocking his legs.

I reposition my fingers, feeling the burn of my own splintered and cracked skin. I'm about to hit him again when a firm hand squeezes my shoulder.

"That's enough, Ridge."

Belly's voice is calm and collected. Soothing and hypnotic.

It tranquilizes my subconscious, taking with it my urge for physical violence.

Folding over his body, using my weight to shackle him, I position my lips next to his ear. "You stay the hell away from Orah. And Tabby. Understand? No phone calls. No secret messages. No bribes. Nothing. If you mess with them, I *will* come for you."

I crawl off Levi's bleeding and crumpled body. Taking a few steps back, I wipe the spittle from my mouth. I force gulping breaths of salt air into my lungs, and hold them for a beat of two before releasing them.

One. Two.

One. Two.

One. Two.

Finally, Colby, who's been superglued to his chair this whole time, shuffles to Levi's side and helps him up. As soon as he's back on his own two feet, he pushes his friend away, refusing to look weak after...well, after looking weak. "Get the hell off me." His command is gargled, like he's trying to talk while using mouthwash. He coughs and spits blood at Colby's feet. He wipes his hands across the front of his chest, spreading crimson fingertips across the fabric.

It instantly makes me think about Orah. And how she only wants to wear black now. So that the blood doesn't show.

He takes a step toward me, pointing a finger in my uninjured face. "You. Are. Dead." His pink and swollen left eye twitches. "You're gonna rot in prison for this."

"Really? You want everyone to know what we're fighting about? Make this public? That's the way you wanna play it? Air your dirty little secrets? Attorneys love this part of the discovery phase, if memory serves me."

"You have no idea who you're dealing with." He attempts to smile. "I'm gonna have so much fun fucking up your life."

I'm about to respond when someone else does it for me.

I could've anticipated Belly coming to my defense. Or Dottie. Hell, even Tim. But when Maude, one of the gin-rummy grannies, leaps in front of me, trying to block me from Levi's verbal assault, I can say I'm truly shocked.

Standing at four-foot eleven, and ninety-five pounds soaking wet, she's a force to be reckoned with. She cocks her red painted fingernails on her hips. "You attacked Ridge. All he did was defend himself." She tosses her hand to the crowd around us, wafting her perfume into the night air. "We all saw it. You're the one in trouble here, not him." She stomps forward. "You think we give two cents about your idle threats?" She shakes her head. "I know who your granddaddy is, boy. He's a crusty old fart who thinks his shit don't stink. He's been trying to ruin our town for years with his big-city ways and fancy-ass rentals. You think anyone here is gonna vouch for you? Over Ridge?" She sneers. "He's one of us. And you aren't."

"Ridge?" He works my name through his disgusting mouth, finally putting two and two together. "You're the firefighter."

"I think it's time for you to go," Belly interjects. "Before I call the law. I don't take too kindly to people assaulting my employees."

Levi casts his eyes between Belly and me. "Well, I don't take too kindly to people not knowing their place."

"You think reporters will take kindly to someone messing with the *teacher's pet*?" I snap, barking his own vulgar words back to him. "By the way, that *pet*? Her uncle's a judge."

That reality check finally sparks some life back into Colby, and he tugs on Levi's shoulder. "C'mon. Let's go. I don't need this." Levi jerks away from him, wincing in pain when the movement jiggles his head. Colby grabs his arm again, refusing to let go. "I'm not getting into trouble again because of you. C'mon."

I edge around Maude, cutting the distance between me and Levi. If he needs more incentive, by all means, I'm more than happy to give it to him.

He shuffles backward, nearly tripping over the toppled table. "Fine! We're leaving." And just because he's an asshole, he can't resist the urge to utter one last warning. "This isn't the end, firefighter."

Wanna bet.

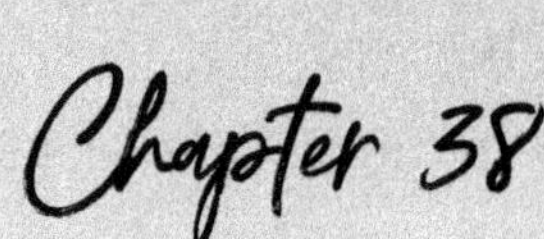

Chapter 38

Ridge

I lean back against the wall and take a few deep breaths, trying to calm myself for this afternoon.

The girls are using the restroom, and we're waiting for them right outside the door, refusing to venture too far away. Emmett's talking with one of the victim advocates, and John and Boaz are milling around in front of me. On the other side of the elevator, the door to the men's bathroom opens and Levi steps out, with his personal attorney nipping at his heels.

I straighten, standing to my full height.

His face is completely jacked up. Black and blue, red and swollen. His nose is covered with a large strip of medical tape, and his busted lip makes his formidable grimace look more like a lopsided smile.

Both John and Boaz take immediate notice of the little shitwad. Together, the three of us block the hallway. It's not like Levi would actually consider crossing the line of demarcation into the enemy zone, but there's no harm in playing it safe.

Someone leans out of a conference room at the very end of the hallway, near the stairs, and calls for Levi. He and his attorney scuttle in that direction and stand in a huddle with a guy in an expensive suit.

Boaz snickers and dramatically looks from my busted hand to Levi's face and back again. "Orah said you told her you hurt your hand at work."

I smack my lips together. "Technically, that's accurate."

John pushes his hands into his pockets and rocks back on his heels. "You know, Mrs. Levenson told us that he fell down the stairs at his beach rental. Apparently, his nose is broken. Said he's headed back to D.C., so some big-shot plastic surgeon can fix it."

"Huh. What a shame."

Boaz shares a glance with his dad, both of them giving a raised eyebrow to the other. Then, with a laugh, he claps me on the shoulder, "I can only imagine how good that felt. What I wouldn't give..."

I can't help the shit-eating grin that consumes my face. "I might've gotten a little carried away."

The other door opens, and the women quietly file out of the restroom—Orah and Tabby, Ann and Laurie. Orah doesn't even have to see Levi to sense his presence. Her shoulders tighten, and her back stiffens. She can feel his wickedness in the air.

Or, maybe she can just feel *me*, reacting to his wickedness.

By the time her eyes land on him, I'm already by her side. He chances a quick look at her, but then averts his stare. Fortunately, he's about to leave. Both he and Colby have already testified, so there's no reason for him to stick around.

I testified as well. After this small break, the session is closing so Tabby and Orah can testify with only the bare minimum of spectators present. Law enforcement has already sealed off this wing of the floor. That even includes the adjoined parking deck. I met them in the connecting breezeway so I could walk with them into the hearing room. Even though it's sealed, they could request the presence of certain family members, friends, or legal representatives. Both the Smith and Morrison families requested my presence.

This morning was hard on me...giving my accounting of events without Orah being here with me. But my session was open; I couldn't ask her to come to it. She would've been in the limelight. People would've seen her.

It doesn't matter that I referred to her and Tabby by their witness numbers, 127 and 128, people still know their names, know their faces. Especially Orah's face. After all, she's the social media star who's now become a recluse. For months, she's been internet fodder; and just when some of the hubbub was starting to fade, here comes the congressional inquiry, whipping everyone into a frenzy again.

She's the famous person who was wrecked by the infamous incident.

And that makes people giddy as hell.

His disheveled appearance takes her by surprise, and she instinctively reaches for my hand. When her fingertips graze over my bruised skin and cracked knuckles, a small little gasp escapes her lungs. She turns to me, wide-eyed and curious. She lifts my hand between our bodies. In slow motion, we both look down, studying my meager wounds.

Earlier in the breezeway, she noticed the damage right away. She flung herself into my arms, hugging me tightly. "What the heck happened to your hand?" she had whispered in my ear. That's when I told her that it was no big deal, that I had injured it at work.

With a tender touch, she traces one of the small cuts. "Work, huh?"

"It's nothing to worry about, Orah."

She gives a half-frown. "You sure about that?"

And then Tabby, ever the demure diplomat, inserts herself into the middle of our conversation, basically pushing her face so close to my hand it looks like she's about to lick my finger. "Daggum! Look at your hand!" She bounces on her toes, flopping her fiery hair over her shoulder. "Please, please, please, tell me you're the one who did *that*." She rolls her eyes to the back of her head, indicating Levi who's behind her, still hovering near the stairs.

"Tab..."

She whisper-squeals. "I knew it! Yes! That's so much more poetic than him falling down the stairs like some regular klutz."

Before I can say anything else, we're interrupted by Mrs. Levenson. She pushes open the swinging door of the main hearing room. A suited FBI agent is standing beside her. She glances around at our group. "It's time."

We're walking in silence down the hallway, making our way back to the breezeway that connects this building to the parking deck.

Nothing about that was easy. Some of the questions asked of Orah were not only invasive, but downright obscene.

The woman's a pillar of strength. I have no idea how she did what she did. But whenever someone would ask something—something that I was sure would send her over the edge and into a full-blown panic attack—she would pause, for a five-second count, and then glide her fingers over the bird charm of her necklace.

And she answered. Every single question.

Not only that, but she learned for the first time the things that she tried so hard to shield herself from by not watching the news or fully reading the inquiry prep packets.

How the perpetrators planned the attack for months. How they desired to target not only 'regular' civilians, but first responders as well. How they chained the doors and emergency exits to two of the auditoriums right before setting off the fire alarm, aka, right before shooting her and Tabby. How they planned to chain all three auditoriums but decided against it when one of the offenders realized his middle-school-aged little brother was watching the video game movie with a group of friends. How they shot first responders and patrons stuck in the corridors and common areas. How they detonated their rudimentary bombs. How they stood in the projection room and fired shots into the locked auditoriums, laughing and celebrating every single bullet that ripped through flesh. How they planned to release cyanide gas into the HVAC system as soon as first responders fully breached the building, hoping to wipe out anyone and everything that didn't die with the last round of explosives they were saving for those of us who just wanted to get into the building to help.

To render aid.

To do our job.

There's a crack of thunder in the distance. Through the tinted glass of the breezeway, I watch as storm clouds churn in the direction of home. If it's not currently raining in White Sky, it probably will be soon.

Fitting weather for my mood.

A state trooper is walking ahead of our ragtag group. Right behind him are Orah and Tabby, their arms looped together in solidarity. Tabby in her pink sundress, and Orah in her black slacks and black blouse. They both look so different from the girls I met in that storage room.

My Brave Girl has become My Brave Woman, right before my very eyes.

Every single day, she's fighting. She's clawing her way into a new life, into a new her. She's taking her meds, she's doing her therapy, she's facing those fuckwads at school. She's holding her head high and doing the impossible.

And I couldn't be prouder of her.

Or more devastated.

Because I'm never gonna get the gift of seeing her where I wish she could be.

In my life. In my arms. In my dreams.

As my very best friend.

As the other half of my heart.

As the mother to my children.

Ten years from now, we won't be buckling little kids into car seats and going to soccer games. We won't be hosting family game nights. I won't be dressing in a Santa costume and leaving flour footprints around the fireplace. And she won't be baking cookies for the neighborhood bake sale.

Because we won't even know each other.

Because I'm about to go my way, and she's about to go hers.

She just doesn't know it yet.

I'm so lost in my own thoughts that I'm completely caught off guard when John snags my arm, slowing my pace. His eyes shoot to everyone in front of us, and he takes a staggered step, making sure we fall back another couple of feet. "John?"

Releasing my arm, he taps the air, nonverbally telling me to lower my volume. Then, taking a deep breath, he guffaws, "You're breaking up with her, aren't you?"

What the hell? My heart stalls in my chest. "Wh—what? Breaking up?" I shake my head vehemently. "No, John. Orah and I aren't in a relationship. We're not dating."

He holds up a hand, trying to calm my flurry of denial. "I'm far from being a smart man, Ridge. If I've learned anything from these past five months, it's that." He clicks his tongue against his teeth. "But I know love when I see it. And I know heartbreak when I see that too."

I open my mouth. And then shut it. Because what the hell am I supposed to say.

"Wanna tell me what's going on?"

I flick my dress cap up my forehead, giving me room to scratch my face and tap my chin. There's no point in beating around the bush; he can obviously read me like an open book. "I have to cease all contact with her, or I'll lose my job. Not only that, but it'll follow me. They'll put a note in my file that I violated the Department Code of Conduct by forming an attachment to a patient." I swallow, and it makes a weird gurgling sound. "A patient who was underage when I treated her."

"Oh. I see."

"Being a firefighter, being a paramedic, it's my whole identity. It's the only thing I've ever wanted to be. If that gets taken away from me..." I trail off, unwilling to speak an alternative into existence.

"So they think what you and Orah have—what you feel—is wrong?"

"Yes, sir. They say it might not even be real. Maybe our emotions are clouded and false because of the intensity of the situation, the intensity of what happened in that room."

"Is that what you think? That what you feel is make-believe?"

My pained confession is so low I'm not even sure he can hear it. "I know it's real. But that doesn't make it right."

"So you agree with them? Your boss or whoever else? You think it's wrong?"

"I fell in love with your daughter the second I heard her voice that night. She was seventeen at the time. That alone makes it wrong, John."

"Have you told her that?"

Just talking about this has my stomach in knots. Drops of sweat run down my spine. "She's a smart girl. She knows that I think my feelings are unacceptable."

He sighs, taking a second to absorb my statement. "You're twenty-two, Ridge. Not forty-two. And she's eighteen now." He gives a lighthearted chuckle. "Eighteen and twenty-two. Damn, you're both still kids. Kids who have been through way too much in your short lives. If I could take the pain away from both of you, I would. In a heartbeat."

I'm fine with the pain. Because without the pain, I wouldn't have had her.

He knocks his shoulder against mine. "Did you know I'm six years older than Ann?" He wiggles his brow. "What about your parents?"

"Three-and-a-half years," I confirm.

His simplistic acknowledgment is laced with a boastful undertone. "I see." After a few seconds, he fiddles with his tie, loosening the knot around his neck. "And by the way, what I actually meant was...*have you told her that you're in love with her?*"

I'm fairly certain all the color drains from my face. I even trip over my own feet, catching a toe on the tile floor. "What?! Of course not. That..." I grunt in frustration, trying to find the right words. "That's my burden to bear."

He doesn't immediately respond. His eyes are trained ahead, watching Orah as she walks. Even from back here, I can feel her power, her resilience. "I hope you have girls one day, Ridge. A whole gaggle of daughters."

"What?!" My bewildered exclamation echoes between us once again. This time even louder than before, earning me a weird look from Emmett.

Instead of telling me what he means by that declaration, he dives head first into another line of haphazard chitchat. "Did you know my grandparents almost didn't get married?"

Uh, what?

How in the world would I know that? That's not really something we're talking about over the phone at two in the morning when Orah's crying and hyperventilating from a nightmare.

He accepts my silence as an invitation to continue. "My grandpa was in the service. He had been overseas for years during the war. When he finally got home, he wanted to surprise my grandmother. He didn't even tell her he had arrived back stateside. So the very night he gets home, he goes over to her house to surprise her with an engagement ring and...bam. She's standing on the front porch kissing another man."

Well, that's shitty luck. "What did he do?"

"He drove away."

Well, then what happened? "And then...?"

I mean, c'mon, I'm invested in the story now.

"She found out from a friend that he was home and that he had seen her on the porch. She went to the jewelry store, bought a man's wedding band, and showed up at Grandpa's house."

"She proposed to him?"

"Hell, yeah, she did. That woman was a spitfire. Of course, she explained the situation too. The guy was a friend of a friend who had gotten the wrong idea and kissed her. She said it only lasted for a second before she cut him off."

"So he said yes? And everyone lived happily ever after?"

"No. Grandpa said no."

Well, fuck a duck. If this story is somehow supposed to make me feel better, it's not.

"But then," he says, tilting his head back and forth, "things changed."

"What changed?"

"Destiny." We're nearing the end of the breezeway and about to enter the parking deck. "Destiny is made up of three things. Love, luck, and tenacity." He ticks the characteristics off on his fingers. "And sometimes those things travel at varying speeds. But when they synchronize? That's when your destiny finally becomes your reality."

And what if they never synchronize? Can a person still be happy if they never get to experience their destiny?

I'm about to ask him a question when an overwhelming sense of foreboding washes over me. It drowns all logical thought. It swamps my brain like a muddy bog, consuming all rational comprehension.

Orah can feel it too. Her step falters.

She turns to Tabby and whispers something.

A roll of thunder and a strike of lightning clash together in the sky, shaking the walls of the breezeway with electric violence.

The state trooper opens the door to the parking deck.

The girls cross the threshold behind him.

And then it happens.

I scream Orah's name.

Even before the cacophony of noise has a chance to hit my eardrums, I'm calling to her.

But it's useless.

I'm useless.

Because it takes less than one second for her and Tabby to be swallowed by the sea of reporters, cameras, and microphones.

I reckon for some of us love, luck, and tenacity will never be on our side.

And our destinies will always be right out of reach.

Chapter 39

Orah

It hurts.

Being in the middle of this mob actually hurts. Physically. Mentally. Emotionally.

I pinch my fingernails into Tabby's palm, doing my best to hold onto her. Trying my best not to lose her.

But that's difficult to do.

The crowd is pushing and pulling, undulating us from side to side, tossing us like driftwood in the ocean.

Someone knocks me in the ribs with a cell phone.

Another person hits the side of my head with a fuzzy, yet hard, finger microphone.

And yet another, stomps all over my feet.

People are breathing on me. Touching me. Snapping my picture.

All without my permission.

They're slicing my brain open. Filleting my heart. Ripping at the scabs on my healing soul. They're marring me, marking me with fresh trickles of blood.

I try to block my face with my free hand, not wanting them to see the intimate parts of me. But even that action is pointless. Because a girl just slaps my hand away with her own and takes a picture.

They're all yelling and screaming, pelting us—pelting *me*—with question after question.

How'd your testimony go?

Any new details you can give us?

Were you dating one of the perpetrators?

Is it true you're getting a ten-million-dollar endorsement deal after this?

Are you starting a modeling career?

People are saying one of the bombs had your fingerprints all over it?

My vision pinholes with adrenaline, casting the whole scene in a wavy, hazy glow. My heart races, pounding a punishing rhythm that pulsates in the thick scar tissue decorating my torso. My lungs have stopped expanding and contracting. I'm not even sure of the last time I took a breath.

The state trooper has gotten swept away from us. They've blocked him between a support beam and a truck. And people are even taking his picture now and asking him questions like he has some kind of inside scoop. He's trying to push his way back to us, but it's a losing battle. He's barking orders into his radio, no doubt requesting backup and additional officers for crowd control.

So much for the laws about the identities and pictures of minor-aged victims. These guys definitely aren't worried about the repercussions of that. Hell, the majority of these guys probably aren't even reporters. They're most likely social media stars or just 'regular joes' looking for a moment of excitement.

A tall lady in a baseball cap jostles into me, severing my connection with my best friend. With a high-pitched shriek, Tabby slips away.

I bounce on my toes, trying to catch a glimpse of my family.

With one bounce, I see Dad. Momma is folded against his chest, and he's holding the back of her hair. My eyes flicker around the crowd, and I think I see Mr. Emmett and Mrs. Laurie, but I can't be for sure.

"Bird!"

His voice rises above all others, echoing across the steel rafters and concrete beams. It's commanding. Demanding. All-encompassing. It's marked with equal parts of fear and courage, each emotion refusing to submit to the other.

He emerges from the middle of the crowd, like a phoenix rising from the ashes. He's erasing the distance between us like the people separating us are nothing more than a mere annoyance. He fights with his body, using every muscle and every inch of his six-foot-two frame to shoulder through the throngs of intrusive men and women. Pressing through the mob, he tosses the offending humans out of his way, scattering them left and right.

And Boaz is right behind him, keeping pace, refusing to back down.

Despite the chaos, I can feel a change in the atmosphere.

My head swivels back and forth, watching as handfuls of police and state troopers and federal agents swarm the area. Some burst through the breezeway door that we came from, and others run up from the far end of the parking deck.

When I turn back, looking for Ridge, he's no longer there. A fucking panic like I've never felt before devours me. It gulps me in one giant swallow, leaving no crumbs behind.

I squeeze my eyes closed, pinching my lids together so tightly that purple and black spots dance from one side to the next.

One. Two. Three. Four. Five.

One. Two. Three. Four. Five.

One. Two. Three. Four. Five.

Hot tears scald my skin, rolling down my cheeks in sweaty, sticky sheets of salt.

His lips brush against my earlobe. His words fly into my soul on a feathered exhale, engulfing me in warmth and comfort and protection. "I'm here, Little Bird."

And with that, he dips down, circling an arm under my knees and hauling me into his arms. I burrow my head in the crevice of his neck. "Tabby?"

I don't think he can hear me, but the vibration of the two-syllable name across his flesh is unmistakable. He slides his mouth back across my ear. "Boaz has her."

For the first few seconds, people are still assaulting us, ping-ponging against us in a wild pile of arms and legs. The police are shouting, feet are moving, car alarms are blaring. Ridge's grip on me is tight and unforgiving. I'll be surprised if I don't have bruises in the shapes of his fingertips tomorrow.

The crowd around us thins. Ridge takes longer strides, walking with purpose and determination. There are no longer hands touching me without permission. Taking a chance, I glance up. My face is flushed by the heat of my tears and the scorch of his skin. Sure enough, Tabby's right in front of us, cocooned in Boaz's arms. Her fingers tangle in his hair, pulling him closer. It's like she's trying to make him a part of her, trying to absorb him into herself. Her sobs are loud and uncontrolled, and they break my already-shattered heart. And then what pulverizes it even more is the gentle and loving way that my brother tries to soothe her. "Shhhh. It's okay, Tab. I'm here. It'll all be okay."

In front of Boaz and Tabby, our parents are jogging, trying to keep pace with several police officers who are heading in the direction of our parked cars. I peek behind Ridge's shoulder. There's a couple more law enforcement officers following us, and behind them is the mass of people, which has somehow grown even larger. A row of police, with arms outstretched, is blocking them from pursuing us.

We make it to the other end of the parking deck, where both of the family SUVs are parked next to one another. There's a bustle of activity as Dad and Mr. Emmett talk to the police. Momma and Mrs. Laurie are huddled together, sniffling and crying. Their faces are stained with smeared makeup.

I snuggle against Ridge's chest. Despite the sweat dotting my forehead, my body shivers like a winter's frost is in the air. My fingers wrap around one of the large gold buttons attached to his fancy jacket. I twist it back and forth like a doorknob.

One. Two. Three. Four. Five.

Boaz opens the back driver-side door to the Morrisons' car and gently deposits Tabby inside, taking time to buckle her seatbelt for her. When he tries to pull his hand away, she cries out and clutches the sleeve of his white dress shirt.

"We'll escort you out of the parking deck and through town," says a man wearing a black suit. When he slides his hands onto his hip, I can see a badge and a gun. "Are you heading back to the hotel? Hitting the interstate? What were your plans before this?"

"Interstate," Boaz snarls. "We're not staying another fucking minute in this town."

"But all of our stuff is still at the hotel," Mrs. Laurie mumbles.

"Fuck our stuff. We'll buy new stuff," Boaz growls.

"What if they follow us on the interstate?" Dad asks. "What if they're camped outside of the hotel?"

"They want Orah." Ever the professional, ever the Hero, Ridge is calm and stoic, but the comment itself immediately garners attention. Everyone turns to look at him. "They want Orah," he says again. "It's her they wanna interview; it's her they wanna photograph."

The black-suit guy studies me before conceding. "Yeah, appears that way." He gives a small, empathetic frown. "Governor said she was an internet star."

"They're anticipating that she would either go to a local hotel or go home. Either way, they'll expect her to be with her parents. What we need is a diversion." He nods to Mr. Emmett. "Let the Morrisons head home. Follow them on the interstate for as long as it takes to make sure they're safe. I'll take Orah with me. Back to White Sky. I'll have her lie down in the backseat so no one can see her. The Smiths can go back to the hotel and pack up everyone's stuff. That'll give you time to clear the hotel of anybody who may be watching them. Then they can come pick Orah up." He turns and speaks directly to Dad. "Head home from there, using only the backroads. Stop midway, though, and stay the night at a motel, just to play it safe."

All of the men in charge look around, rating the effectiveness of the plan with a series of grunts and grumbles. Dad nods, "Sounds like a good plan to me. Emmett?"

Mr. Emmett nods. "Yeah. Good with us."

Mom and Mrs. Laurie share a quick hug, and then Momma scurries over to me and Ridge. She peppers a line of kisses in my knotted hair. "My baby. It's all gonna be okay, honey. I promise."

"Where are you parked?" asks the federal agent.

Ridge bobs his head toward his feet. "One level down."

The guy uses some hand signals and orders two of the officers to escort us. "Just two. We don't want to draw unnecessary attention."

Dad pulls his car keys out of his pocket and opens the door for Mom. "C'mon, Ann. We need to do this quick." She gives me one last kiss and hurries to climb in. "Son?"

Boaz glances down at Tabby. "I'm going with the Morrisons. I'm staying with her."

Dad scrapes a hand across his face. "Yeah, that's a good idea."

Boaz leans in. Gently speaking to Tabby, she gives him a soft smile and takes a staggered breath before finally releasing his hand. He shuts her door and stalks over to us. He plants a quick peck on my temple and locks eyes with Ridge. "Take care of my sister."

"Always," Ridge answers without hesitation.

Dad gives Boaz a quick hug before turning to us.

I tap Ridge's chin with my forefinger. "You can put me down." My throat is scratchy and weak from choking back my own sobs.

He gently sets me on my feet.

Dad envelops me in his embrace. Sniffling, he pulls away, darting his eyes between the two of us. "You're brave enough to weather anything that may come. Both of you. Remember that."

And when he turns and walks away, Ridge slides his hand into mine, and I have to wonder if that was a declaration of our strength or a warning of what is to come.

Chapter 40

Orah

I'm glad the rain stopped.

For a while, it was falling so hard on the windshield it reminded me of the muffled sounds of gunfire and explosions. And that's the last memory that I needed floating around in my brain. I was basically catatonic for the first half of the drive to White Sky. But eventually, Ridge pulled me out of my paralyzing panic, and I crawled from the backseat and into the front passenger seat. The lull of the road pulled me into an exhausted slumber, and I slept. With his arm draped across the console and me using his bicep as a pillow. I just woke up about five minutes ago as we were driving through the streets of White Sky.

He pulls into the parking lot of an apartment complex. The weathered gray wood and white trim building fits in perfectly with the rest of the town. The front area is decorated with large, swaying palm trees. "Your apartment?"

He points to the second story. "That one. With the white Adirondack chairs out front."

I lean my head against the headrest and try to force a relaxing breath into my lungs. Of course, I fear there's not much relaxing in store for me tonight.

Because I have to tell Ridge the truth. The truth I've been hiding for the past several weeks.

And this little incident did nothing but cement my decision.

I know I'm doing the best thing for me, for my mental health, for my healing. I don't think anyone in their right mind would disagree with me after seeing that mob today.

All those people vying for the opportunity to get next to me.

To see how I've changed.

Actually, no. That's not right.

They didn't wanna see how I've changed; they wanted to see how I've broken.

Because if my life had taken a turn for something better instead of something worse, you can bet your bottom dollar that no one would be there to photograph it.

No one would be there to commemorate it. To memorialize it.

They wouldn't give two shits about it.

They only care about the ruined pieces of me. Not the restored pieces.

I glance at Ridge, taking in the rugged perfection of his profile. The sunburnt apples of his cheeks. The strong line of his nose. The firmness of his square jaw, playing hide and seek underneath his beard. Which happens to be trimmed a little shorter than it was when he came to see me for my birthday that wasn't my birthday. I can only assume, he styled it shorter for today's inquiry, for the way he had to dress in his Class A uniform.

And he looked so handsome in that outfit.

He lost his hat somewhere in the melee. And his fancy jacket was torn at the seam of his right shoulder. I toss a glance at the back-seat where the jacket is still crumpled. He had covered me with it when I was lying down, trying to escape the scrutiny of anyone who might've caught wind of our plan. I laid there toying with the strings from the rip, pretending it was my favorite blanket.

I tug down the visor and check my reflection in the small mirror. As suspected, I'm a frightful mess. My eyes are bloodshot and swol-len, decorated with black circles from my mascara. My cheeks are blotchy and tacky with dried tears. And my lips are swollen, probably from gnawing my teeth back and forth across the tender skin. "Oh my." I chuckle, trying to make light of the seriousness that resulted in this disheveled appearance.

"Here." Ridge leans over and pops the glove box that's in front of me. Reaching inside, he grabs a foil packet decorated in little pink flowers.

Makeup remover.

He tugs one of the moist towelettes from the top and holds it in front of me. "Ella left these in here."

"Ella. Your cousin?"

He gives me a nod. "Mmm-hmm."

I'm about to pluck it from his fingers when he yanks it away. "Just so you know, you're beautiful. On the outside. And the inside. Some messes don't need to be cleaned up. They're meant to be there." His Tiger Eyes dance across my stained face, creating a tactile intimacy so powerful that my knees start to shake.

Giving me a shy smile, he hands the towelette to me. With my heart in my throat, I turn back to the small mirror and do my best to clean myself. I'm righting the visor and looking for a place to put my used rag when his cell phone starts vibrating. He pulls it from his trouser pocket. "It's your parents." Instead of handing the phone to me, he answers. My cell phone is still in the back of my parents SUV; so it's not concerning that they're having to call Ridge to speak to us.

I listen to their one-sided conversation, and when he hangs up, he tells me that they've packed up the rooms and are on their way here. Fortunately, none of those scoundrels were staked out at the hotel. "They should be here in less than an hour."

One hour.

Sixty minutes.

Three-thousand-six-hundred seconds.

That's all the time I have with him until...

Until who knows when.

"Should we go inside?"

He glances up at his second-story apartment like it's some kind of house of horrors. "Ummm. The beach is just across the street. Feel like a walk?"

"Sure. A walk sounds nice." I smile, biting back a laugh because it's pretty clear to see that My Hero is still fighting the battle to be a gentleman.

Me. Him. Alone in his apartment together.

Oh, the scandal.

What would people think?

What would people say?

What if there were people watching us right now? People wanting to make sure that we don't talk to each other, don't hold hands, don't hug?

One day, Ridge will realize that no one cared. All of that drama was—and is—in his own head.

We both get out of the Jeep, and Ridge walks around to meet me. "Crosswalk is over here." We make our way across the parking lot, and he holds open a pedestrian gate for me. Taking my hand in his, he ushers us across the two-lane road and onto the wooden boardwalk. There's a small sandy parking lot on the right side that has a colorful sign announcing both the public beach and Belly's Beachside.

"I'll get to see Belly's?"

He's rolling the sleeves of his white dress shirt up to his elbows. The flex of his muscles is mesmerizing, calming. Each curl of his finger and twitch of his tendon sends a shot of tranquilizing serenity to the restless corners of my brain. "No, we don't serve food. So..." He leaves me to fill in the blanks.

"So I have to be twenty-one to enter."

"Yeah."

We pass over the rolling dunes and sea oats, and the ocean comes into view. The rain may be gone, but the dark gray storm clouds are still rumbling and churning. The wind is whipping, and the waves are cresting high and turbulent. The barely visible sun is set low on the horizon, quickly readying itself to bid goodnight.

On the left, down a small sidewalk that cuts off from the main boardwalk, is Belly's. It's vibrant and old, oozing old-school beach charm, with a large patio deck on the back side, facing the water. We continue down the boardwalk and when we get to the end, Ridge stops to take off his socks and shoes. He tucks them into a little wooden cubby. I slide my black flats into the hole next to his and start to walk around him when he grabs my ankle. He makes a tsking sound between his tongue and his teeth. Grabbing the hem of my tight, black ankle pants, he rolls them up just a couple of times so they come to the bottom of my calf. When his fingers graze my skin, tingles rush up the length of my legs and pool into my groin. He gives himself the same treatment. His trousers, of course, are looser than mine, and one leg comes completely unrolled the second we step onto the sand.

He looks down and frowns at the offending fabric.

It's quite possibly the cutest thing I've ever seen, and I'm unable to contain my giggles.

We trudge through the cloud-cooled sand, walking closer to the shoreline.

Every step brings with it a heaviness. The weight of a burden that I'm about to dump on his shoulders.

Because not only am I about to tell him that I love him. But I'm about to tell him that I'm gonna leave him.

Chapter 41

Ridge

This is quite possibly the most beautiful I've ever seen her.

She's staring out at the crashing ocean waves, a stunning vision dressed in black. Strands of her raven hair have escaped her bun, and they dance in the wind, wild and free. Her storm-cloud eyes widen in awe, watching as the sky and sea meet, forming a formidable wall of power and pain, dominion and violence. Gray and black and white, with only the smallest strips of pink and yellow and orange peeking at us from far in the distance. With her right hand, she traces the bird charm of her necklace, once again counting the small diamonds, row after row.

One. Two. Three. Four. Five.

One. Two. Three. Four. Five.

One. Two. Three. Four. Five.

I guess it's quite fitting that the day I'm gonna leave her is the day that gifts me with the most breathtaking image of her. It blesses me—and curses me—with the vision that's gonna play on repeat in my mind for all of eternity.

But is that what I want?

Do I want only a vision of her? And not her?

What would happen if I were to choose Orah over my job? Choose her over my passion? Choose her over the part of me that makes me 'me'?

If making that choice fundamentally changes who I am, would she still want me?

Does she even want me now?

"My turn," I say, breaking the comfortable silence.

A smile tugs at the corner of her mouth. "Your turn, huh?"

"What are you thinking about?"

Her smile fades just as quickly as it appeared. "I'm thinking about how I have to tell you the truth again."

What? The power of her statement has my heart skipping a beat. I wrap my hand around her forearm, forcing her to spin toward me. "What? The truth about what?"

Her red-rimmed eyes hold a sadness that wasn't there before. Everything that crowd did to her was superficial. The anguish powerful but temporary. This? This is something different. This exists beyond minutes and hours. This melancholy lives in a realm of forevers and nevers.

She takes a step closer to me. Her feet shuffle sand around mine. With a tender touch, she works her fingertips down my nose and over my lips. Her butterfly caress sends a heated sensation down the back of my throat and into my stomach. Landing on my chin, she taps it. I can't help but wonder if my freshly trimmed beard prickles her skin.

Her hand falls to her side. "I'm leaving."

Fuck me. Here she is, devastated by the idea of leaving me to go back home. All the while, she has no idea that I'm about to upend both of our lives.

Choose work?

Or choose her?

Choose what's right, but *feels* wrong?

Or choose what's wrong, but *feels* right?

Wait for destiny?

Or make our own?

And then it hits me. Like a thunderclap to my soul. Louder and brighter and with more fury than any emotion I think I've ever experienced before.

And I know without a doubt what to do...

"Orah, we should—"

"I'm going back to Alaska with Boaz."

Her interruption catches me by surprise, and it takes a moment for me to process her announcement. "Huh? You're going with Boaz? On vacation?" The wind blows a strand of hair in her mouth. Reaching out, I hook it around my finger and tuck it behind her ear.

"No. I'm moving to Alaska." She blinks, slow and lazy, like the syllables are cumbersome to speak. "Indefinitely."

Indefinitely.

She's moving to Alaska. Indefinitely.

I can't function.

I'm a chaotic jumble of questions and comments, worries and fears, relief and solace, heartache and torment.

What. The. Hell.

"Wh—what?" I mumble, not even sure where to begin.

"It's too hard being here." She flops a hand in the air, nonverbally indicating, basically, the entirety of all land masses between Florida and South Carolina. "Today was a prime example of that." She sighs. "The looks, the stares, the people talking behind my back. It never ends. It never stops." She presses her lips together in thought. "I can't heal, can't go forward, when I'm trapped in the dungeon of my past. Yes, I'm the one who built the walls to it. But Levi tossed me in. And then those boys locked the door and threw away the key." She gives a half-hearted shrug. "I know we said we were gonna save each other, but I need to rescue myself first."

I stumble backward, physically impacted by the honesty of her declaration.

She's absolutely right.

This whole time I've been acting like I'm the only one who can save her. The only one who can make her whole. The only one who can give her what she needs.

The truth of the matter is...I've been nothing but a hindrance, a roadblock in her road to recovery.

Chief Latner was right.

Dr. Evans was right.

My love for Orah may be real, but that doesn't mean it's the best thing for her.

If love alone could heal a person, she would've emerged from that supply room pristine and unscathed, without so much as a scratch. But my love didn't heal her. In fact, quite the opposite. She reached for me, cried out to me, wanted me. And then she nearly bled to death.

I pluck a random question from the muddled labyrinth of my mind. "What about school?"

"The school board approved me for remote learning. I'll finish the rest of the school year via web-based courses. In fact," she lowers her eyes and peeks up at me from beneath her thick, black eyelashes, "I haven't been to school in the past three weeks."

"Three weeks?! You...you already knew three weeks ago that you were gonna do this."

Her cheeks pink, and she gives me a barely perceptible nod.

"You'll live with Boaz? Doesn't he travel a lot? Between all of those remote towns and villages up there? Will it even be safe for you?"

"I'll be traveling too."

I stab my hand through my hair, grunting when my fingers catch in a knot. "What?"

"I'll be working for a bakery." Squaring her shoulders and lifting her chin, she stands a little straighter. There's an undeniable twinkle in her eyes, an excitement that's warring with the ever-present fear and sorrow. It immediately captures my attention. It's like I'm watching an emotional sword fight. "There's a bakery that's headquartered in Fairbanks. They have satellite bakeries in Coldfoot and Deadhorse. I'm gonna be baking, Ridge. Making all sorts of desserts. And once I learn more, Naja—she's the owner and friends with Boaz—she's gonna put me in charge of some of the spike rooms and all of the desserts and baked goods for them." I must make an unusual face because she jumps right into an explanation. "It's these rooms that the big companies provide to their workers and all of their visitors. It's like a mini grocery store, and everything in it is free. But most of the companies contract with her for the desserts and homemade bread and that kind of stuff. And not only that, but she's starting an event planning division too. All of those companies, and even the government people like Boaz, have important visitors and meetings and conferences. And they need help planning all of that."

And now, the sword fight is happening in my own body. I can't believe how proud I am of her. She's clearly happy about this, about the possibilities for her future. Which makes me happy. Fucking ecstatic, really.

But there's also a part of me that's devastated. Because she made the impossible and difficult decision for me. With one fell swoop, she solved the problem I've been wrestling with for months.

She's ending this.

She's leaving me.

"Wow. That...that sounds amazing, Little Bird. I'm really, really happy for you."

She gives a shy little shrug and wipes a rogue tear that falls from her eye when she blinks. "Thank you." She takes a steadying breath, and her hand skitters over her right side, fiddling with the underside of her breast area. A shock of panic whips through me, wondering if something is wrong with her healed wound. But her hand flutters away, and she sighs, the throaty sound getting caught in a whimper of giggles. "Oh my gosh. I was so scared to tell you."

She bounces closer and takes my hand in hers, absentmindedly tracing my calluses and rough spots, and of course, the cuts from my run-in with Levi. I wonder if she can feel the hatred I have for him seeping through the slits in my skin. "The cell service is terrible. It barely works. But the Internet is almost perfect. We can do video chats. Really, that's better because we'll be able to see one another. We can come up with a schedule that works." Her eyebrows lift. "You know...dates."

When I don't say anything, she chatters, filling the void. "And we'll be coming home for visits. And of course, you can come and visit me. Boaz won't mind; he would love to see you."

God help me.

This hurts.

"Little Bird." Her nickname strangles me, making me weak and vulnerable. "That won't work."

Her brow crinkles in confusion. "Vacation won't work? But I thought you get two weeks of vacation time? Have you already used it all? When does it start over?"

My heart turns to stone. It sits heavy and still in the cavern of my chest. It weighs me down, creating a pressure so strong it feels like my breastbone may snap in two. "Not that. I'm talking about everything. Staying in touch. Having video chats. Visiting. Us being...*us*."

The color washes from her face, leaving her pale and haunted. The light in her eyes dulls. She drops my hand. "Ridge?"

My name on her lips.

One simple syllable filled with equal parts of adoration and abhorrence.

"You're right, Orah. About being trapped in the dungeon of your past, in the prison of that night. And I'm a part of that. I'm a reminder of the bad in the world, of the evil that happened to you. I want you to find yourself, to find your happiness, to find your job. And you won't be able to do that with me."

Her jaw slacks open.

After a five-second delay, she closes her mouth. Her head wobbles back and forth in denial. "No. No. No. That's not right. I need you. I can't do this without you."

"You can't do this *with* me." I step even closer, wrapping my hand around the back of her neck, stopping her movement, forcing her wandering eyes to focus on me. And only me. My chest skims against hers. I close my eyes, crippled by the despair and anxiety permeating the air, like smoke from a fire. And when I open them, I acknowledge the truth that I refused to believe. "You never needed me to save you, Zipporah. You're the strongest person I know. You're resilient and brave and utterly remarkable. But if we keep clinging to each other, we're both gonna drown."

"That's a lie. We won't. We'll survive. That's the only way we can stay alive." She swallows, gagging on her trapped sob. "I was gonna ask you to wait for me. To stand by me. To be with me. To...to love me."

My body hums with anger, tight and tense and irrational.

Fuck destiny.

Fuck love and luck and tenacity.

I'm angry. I'm angry that the fates brought us together in such a cruel way, and they're ripping us apart in an even crueler way.

Because how can we love each other, build a life together, and be each other's everything if we're only fragments of ourselves.

She smacks me on the chest. Hard and unforgiving. "Did you hear me?" And then she growls, overcome with the rage that she's absorbed from my own body. Her palms slap against my torso, over and over. She shoves with all of her might, doing her best to push me backward. My hand falls from her neck, and I allow her to punish me. I move my body with her words, giving her the upper hand, giving her the control. I walk backward through the sand, making sure I stay close enough to catch her in case she stumbles.

"I." *Push.*

"Said." *Push.*

"Love." *Push.*

"Me." *Push.*

After one last thrust, she stops. Heaving dark and heavy breaths from her lungs, I can see her aching with a misery that's as old as time itself. She sniffles and swipes her fingers under her nose, wiping her snot and tears. "Tell me you love me."

"No." It's the single worst thing I've ever said. It takes all of my strength not to double over in excruciating pain.

She shakes her head again, this time slowly, deliberately. "Say it! I can feel what you feel, Ridge." She taps her heart. "I feel *you.* Every single time my heart beats."

"I can say the words, Orah. But my words won't make you whole."

She rears back, physically assaulted by my roundabout admission that I am, in fact, in love with her. And by the fact that the three-word, most powerful sentence in the English language, won't magically solve our problems.

If only she could see… what's shattered in her eyes is wholly perfect for me. But as long as she thinks she's broken, we'll never work. Because I'll keep trying to save her, and slowly, we'll both sink under the water.

Suffocating our careers.

Suffocating our spirits.

Suffocating ourselves.

And then suffocating each other.

"So, that's it? We're done? Our friendship? Our lives together?" She wiggles a finger between the two of us. "Whatever this may have been?"

All I can do is nod.

With short, choppy movements, she wipes the tears from her face. We both stand there, just staring at one another for who knows how long. I take my time, trying to memorize every last detail.

The one hair at the nape of her neck that curls, despite her having straight hair.

The freckle on the apple of her right cheekbone.

The contour of her hips.

The way her necklace nestles between the delicate V of her collarbone.

The way she's finally painted her nails and toes again. In black polish.

And she's doing the same. Her eyes travel the length of my body, blanketing me from head to toe in devoted attention.

"Kiss me goodbye, Ridge."

"What?"

She swivels her head, watching as the waves pound against the shore. The small strip of sunlight has slipped below the horizon, and the ominous rain clouds are turning the dusk into evening, without any permission from the moon. After a minute, she turns back to me and repeats her request. "I want you to kiss me. If this is our good-bye, I refuse to accept it, I refuse to acknowledge it, until your lips have been on mine."

Heat coils low in my stomach. My nerve-endings catch on fire. Refusing to drag my hand down my face and tap my chin, I shove my hands in my pockets, searching for a way to center myself. To ground myself. To regain control.

Because isn't that what I want?

To be in control...

"No, Zipporah. We can't."

Closing her eyes, she does her special count. I follow along with her as she speaks the numbers. Her lips purse around them, mouthing them into life. When finished, she slowly puts one foot in front of the other, erasing the distance between us. "I'll head back up and wait for my parents."

But then, when she shifts, making a move to walk right past me, I lose my fucking mind. My arm snatches around her waist, possessively tugging her in front of me. Her breath whooshes across my face. The scent of her shampoo and tears mingle with the salt and sea. On instinct, her arms fold around my neck. One hand slides into my hair. Her fingernails scrape against my scalp. Her other hand sweeps into the collar of my shirt, searching for the comfort of the jagged scar on my shoulder. And when she finds it, she sighs.

"Why?" My voice rips from the hollow abyss of my soul. It's a rumble of darkness, carved from the deepest caverns in the world.

Her eyelids grow heavy with want and longing. "Because. Was it even real? If you never taste the love that you poured into me, the life that you gave me...was it even real?"

My hands circle around her. My fingertips trail down her spine, charting a course to the alluring curve above her ass. She raises to her tiptoes. And when her back arches, pushing the length of her torso against mine, I snap.

My mouth crashes into hers, my tongue instantly sliding past her already-parted lips.

Oh. Holy. Fuck.

My heart detonates in my chest, sending scalding, fiery blood pumping through the desolate parts of my body. Parts that just moments ago were dying and disappearing, maimed by the horror of never seeing Orah again. White, sizzling passion consumes me, morphing my every fantasy into reality.

Her lips are soft and plump. Her tongue hot and wet.

She tastes of happiness and joy, sadness and regret.

She tastes like life.

She moans and mewls, instantly opening her mouth wider, pushing me deeper, giving me more.

And I take it.

I take every single inch she gives me.

I swirl my tongue around hers. I suck her bottom lip between my teeth. I bite and tease and lick.

And then, for full seconds at a time, I pause, just breathing her in. Just relishing in the fact that she has air in her lungs and a heartbeat in her chest. I inhale her panted breaths, refusing to exhale, wanting nothing more than to hold her lifeforce in my own lungs—until my world fades to black and I never have to worry about facing a day without her.

She claws at me, sinking her fingernails into the waxy skin of my left shoulder, determined to draw blood, determined to leave me with a visible wound.

A talisman. A reminder. A memory. Just something to match the invisible injuries that we'll both carry. For who knows how long.

And when I feel the skin break, and I hiss through a bite of pain, she swallows the sound with her kiss.

My body shudders. My brain feels feverish. My knees quake.

In fact, I'm not even sure I can hold us upright anymore.

And so, I don't.

Clutching her in an unforgiving grip, I lower us to our knees, never severing the connection of our bodies.

My hands slide up the small of her back and around to her hips. I map every bend. Every angle. Every curve. And when my thumb slides underneath the hem of her shirt, and I feel the burn of her bare abdomen, it's too much. I quickly pull my hand away and resettle it on top of the safety of her black blouse.

Her own hands shift to my face. Cradling my jaw, she tenderly caresses her fingertips over my beard. The loving touch is hypnotic, lulling me into those dreams I squashed—dreams of soccer games and Santa costumes and cookies before bed.

Her fingers slide up and down the sensitive arc of my jawline.

Up. Down.

Up. Down.

Up. Down.

She sways from our kiss, just barely, just enough for me to feel the vibration of her voice against my tongue. "Ridge."

Her plea is the most erotic thing I've ever heard in my entire twenty-two years on this earth.

I open my mouth, ready to do the same, ready to declare my love for her with a whisper, with a prayer, with an utterance.

With one simple name.

And then... she pulls away.

She stands up.

She dusts the sand from her black pants.

And she wipes the flood of tears that I didn't even realize were soaking us both. Now that she's away from me, separated from my embrace, I can feel the wetness drenching my facial hair, the moisture coating the skin of my neck.

"Goodbye." Her farewell guts me.

I can't even move. I can't even stand up. I can't even turn around.

Because if I do any of those things, I'll chase her.

And we both know that's not what we need.

So instead, I turn my head, barely catching her profile before she walks out of frame.

"Do you believe in destiny, Little Bird?"

"If we ever see each other again, you can ask me that question."

To be continued in...
Dancing on the Ashes: The Flames Duet Book Two
Available Now

Gratitude

Ridge and Orah...

Phew. This one took it out of me. The dynamic of their relationship (in both books of The Flames Duet) was a fine line. Like walking a tight rope over a den of rattlesnakes. I pray I did them justice. And I pray that you love them just as much as I do.

Because despite my never-ending love for Crutch and Holt, I gotta say...Ridge is one hot damn of a man.

A super big thank you, with hugs and kisses to the Original Halcie Dawn Permanent ARC Team. My OG Gals! Thank you for your friendship ideas and input. You are invaluable to me... Heather S.S., Jenney M., Ashley R., Erica A., Ali S., Amber W., Jennifer S., Jessica V., Jessica A., and Kandi S.

And on top of that, this year gifted me with a Street Team! Yeah, that's right. I'm that cool. LOL. I've been able to meet and connect with some amazing friends via Halcie's Honeys. I'm so grateful that you're in my life and taking a chance on little ol' me and The Hill Family Universe. Thank you, thank you, thank you... Mudge, Payton, Brittany, Jennifer S., Ali, Ashley G., Jenn G., Amber W., Amber T., Jenney, Dara, Filippa, Madison, Melanie, and Nicole.

Thank you so very much to Mudge with Kindles and Coffee Author Services. I'm so happy we connected. You are so kind, hardworking, beautiful, friendly, and just all-around awesome. Thank you for putting together the Halcie's Honeys Team, and thank you for helping me navigate the trenches of social media.

And of course, I can't thank Mudge without thanking the other team member of Kindles and Coffee Author Services, Payton (aka smut.n.sowers).

Together, Mudge and Payton have eased my burden. But I think what's most important is that both of these women are not only pillars of strength in their personal lives, but in the book community. They love and support their authors wholeheartedly. They're my Lucy and Ethel. And I'm blessed to have them in my corner.

Thank you so very much to Erica Anderson with Get Lit Author Services. You have been so kind and supportive. Your content creation is gorgeous, and I will be forever grateful that we had the opportunity to work with one another.

And a special thank you to some of my other social media and book conference/signing friends I met. I love y'all! Thank you so much for your kindness and support. Y'all made my first signing events so much fun! I'm proud to call you my friends, and I'm so glad we met in person... Jenna C. (and sister Sarah), Hannah M., Kim B., Sandy, Sarah A., Jessica P., Carrigan, Kennedy, Tina O., and Chrissy P. I know I met more, and I promise to keep better notes next time. LOL!

Thank you to Stacey Blake with Champagne Book Design for designing the most gorgeous covers ever. Like ever. You have brought all of my visions to life. And you hang in there with me when I change my mind. Which seems to happen frequently. LOL. You have given life to The Hill Family, and I can never repay you for that. I fall more in love with each new cover we do. I can't wait to see what the future brings for us.

Oh, my Sweetie Elaine.... a huge thank you to my dear friend, Elaine York with Allusion Publishing. Well, I was a little late on getting *Dancing on the Ashes* to you. Hehe. Like I said, my mind writes way faster than my hands do. But you hung in there with me, and you just rolled with the flow. Thank you so much for all of your hard work. Thank you for your friendship. I love when we talk; it feels like I'm talking to a member of my family. We go together like Chick

Fil-A French fries and Coke. You always seem to know when I need an encouraging word or laugh. You make me a better writer. And I promise to one day know when to place a comma after 'so' or 'but'. Above all, I hope I make you proud.

And a huge thank you to my book conference "assistants," Dandy and Aunt Karla. And Cindy too. Man, we had some fun. And I can't wait for more!

To Dandy and Big, aka the most amazing parents ever... I love you. The level of your support never ceases to amaze me. From doing my grocery shopping so I don't have to take a break from writing to watching your grandpup to cooking for us. I'm blessed beyond measure because the Lord didn't gift *me* to *you*; He gifted *you* to me.

To my Boo Boo Bear, my college student... I am so damn proud of you. You are the bright light in my day. I am so excited for all of the amazing adventures that you're going to experience in your life. You're intelligent, kind, handsome, compassionate, and still...a king of one-liners. I love you, son.

To Kuntry, my husband and my best friend... I can't believe how much I love you. Every day, you shower me with love, generosity, compliments, and encouragement. I feel like something has shifted in us these past few years. As we got older, and as I was forced to take a step back (albeit, an unplanned one) from my "day job" career, I can't help but sense a change in our relationship. And it's one for the better. Our love has deepened, our connection has grown, our passion has flourished, and our need to rely on one another has strengthened. I know I'm about to head back to the work drawing board, but I promise you, those things will not change. You are my home. And as Ridge would say, you are my destiny. I'm so glad our love, luck, and tenacity were in sync. You are my world.

To the Lord my God, my Almighty Savior Jesus Christ... Thank you. Your blessings pour over me. I am loved and worthy by Your Grace. You sustain me and keep me whole. All glory be to You.

<h1 style="text-align:center">About the Author</h1>

HALCIE DAWN is a happy and blessed wife and mother. She attended the University of Alabama where she graduated with a bachelor's degree in Business Management. A lifelong avid reader, her love affair with books started with the original *The Babysitter's Club* series when she was in the third grade and morphed into a love of all things romantic. After years of thought and countless dreams about the sexy men and strong women of the fictional Hill Family, she penned her first contemporary romance. *The Reality Duet—Escaping Our Reality* (Book One) and *Finding Our Reality* (Book Two) released in November 2024. *The Skeptic's Duet—The Skeptic's Playbook* (Book One) and *The Believer's Game* (Book Two) released in April 2025. When not writing or reading by the swimming pool, she can be found watching true crime documentaries or *Psych* (for the millionth time). Halcie lives in Alabama with her amazingly wonderful, funny, kind, and handsome husband and son. And she lives next door to her parents, whose antics often have her laughing so hard she pees her pants. But without a doubt, the star of the home is the family morkiepoo, Princess Doodle Fluffybutt.

Connect with Halcie:
Linktree: https://linktr.ee/halciedawnromance
Website: https://www.halciedawn.com/
Instagram: https://www.instagram.com/halciedawnromance/
Facebook: https://www.facebook.com/halciedawn/
Facebook Reader Group:
https://www.facebook.com/groups/halciedawndaydreamers
TikTok (Reels): https://www.tiktok.com/@halciedawnromance
TikTok (Static Posts): https://www.tiktok.com/@authorhalciedawn
Threads: https://www.threads.com/@halciedawnromance